Commedia della Morte

By Chelsea Quinn Yarbro from Tom Doherty Associates

COMMEDIA DELLA MORTE

A NOVEL OF THE COUNT SAINT-GERMAIN

Chelsea Quinn Yarbro

TOR®

A TOM DOHERTY ASSOCIATES BOOK

NEW YORK

COMMEDIA DELLA MORTE: A NOVEL OF THE COUNT SAINT-GERMAIN

Copyright © 2012 by Chelsea Quinn Yarbro

A Tor Book
Published by Tom Doherty Associates, LLC
175 Fifth Avenue
New York, NY 10010

www.tor-forge.com

Tor® is a registered trademark of Tom Doherty Associates, LLC.

Library of Congress Cataloging-in-Publication Data

Yarbro, Chelsea Quinn, 1942–
    Commedia della morte : a novel of the Count Saint-Germain / Chelsea
Quinn Yarbro.—1st ed.
        p. cm.
    "A Tom Doherty Associates book."
    ISBN 978-0-7653-3104-5
  1. Saint-Germain, comte de, d. 1784—Fiction.   2. Vampires—Fiction.
I. Title.
    PS3575.A7C656 2012
    813'.54—dc23

                                                        2011033201

First Edition: March 2012

Printed in the United States of America

0   9   8   7   6   5   4   3   2   1

This one is for

Marsha Quick

with thanks times two.

Author's Note

The latter part of the French Revolution is known as the Terror—roughly 1793–1795—and with good reason: carnage was at an all-time high during those hectic years, impacting almost everyone in the country. Denouncements with the flimsiest backup were often sufficient to doom an individual or a family to hasty death; shortly after the end of this story, a law was enacted which declared that accusation was the same as conviction, and the havoc was racheted up across the country. Many of the records of that period still remain, and they reveal a state of civic policy that was as capricious as it was lethal. Although the upper classes were the most consistently accused, they were also those who gained the most interest outside of France, so that much of what we know from that time is colored by showing more attention to those of high social standing than those of more modest rank, many of whom suffered as much as their social superiors did. Nonetheless it is certainly true that even before the infamous law was enacted, those with high social rank were often targeted for no greater crime than being well-born. Intellectuals were another group who frequently found themselves before the Revolutionary Courts for what they said or thought; merchants could be accused of gouging in their pricing, and end up in prison for their failure to support the work of the Revolution. But the Terror did not pop out of nowhere; it was the product of increasing social hysteria as well as vicious political infighting.

Not all the damage was done by revolutionaries themselves: many gangs and factions took advantage of the social upheaval to gouge out what advantage they could from it, and through the opportunities presented by the legal chaos, to gain wealth and influence for themselves. Then the efforts to hold on to that power became paramount, leading to political skullduggery and corruption of staggering proportions that spread well beyond Paris—which, as the capital of the country and center of Old Regime activities, garnered the most international attention—to the country in general. This was especially true in such cities as Marseilles, Lyon, Toulon, Bordeaux, Arras, and Nantes, where various Revolutionary Tribunals and Revolutionary Assemblies vied with one another, the National Assembly in Paris, and other groups in an attempt to wield as much power as possible, and to be rid of any and all rivals. The desire for revenge against the aristocrats was of long standing, and readily inflamed through rhetoric and bribes, as well as the promise of advancement. Political deals as much as patriotism marked the Terror, and contributed to the rampant depredations of the various mobs. As the number of available aristocrats lessened, these cities, like Paris, targeted intellectuals, clergy, foreigners, and rich men with revolutionary zeal, because they were most often the objects of resentment by the lower classes who were the most tenacious of the revolutionaries in these regionally important cities. Although many of these excesses are not as well documented as the events that took place in Paris, there are remaining records of the extremes embraced by many cities and towns at the height of the lunacy, as well as a vast number of scholarly studies on the reasons for and the results of those bloody years.

To handle all the various new regulations and laws, a massive new bureaucracy began to form, none more significant than the various Departments for Public Safety that sprang up in many cities, replacing what were viewed as hopelessly corrupt police forces. In time, these Departments became so powerful that by the time the Paris Committee for Public Safety was formed the power it had amassed was such that detention by its officers was sufficient to send those arrested to the guillotine without the nuisance of a trial, or the presentation of any evidence to support the arrest.

Calendar reform was under discussion but had not yet taken place, so dates at this time were generally consistent with the standard European calendar, although a few cities had developed reformed calendars of their own, and strove to put them into common use, but without any widespread success. For the sake of clarity, I've used the standard calendar even in cities where new municipal calendars were endorsed by Assemblies and Tribunals.

Dangerous as France was to many of its people, there were a few who managed to thrive in the turmoil without being part of the political systems: radical artists of all sorts were often welcomed by the Revolutionary Assemblies, not only to promote enthusiasm for the Revolution as a glorious event, but to provide some appearance of culture in the midst of pandemonium. Poets, novelists, painters, lyricists, singers, actors, and to a lesser extent journalists often enjoyed a hectic celebrity for as long as the public and the Revolutionary Assemblies and Tribunals endorsed the various principles the artists expressed, and so long as they were approved, they were the darlings of the public, lionized and revered by the men newly in power. Fame could then be a double-edged sword for the artist who fell from favor, for their very notoriety made escape and evasion unusually difficult. Those who managed to survive the Terror often became the leaders of the artistic movements of the early nineteenth century.

Travel at the time was precarious, and not simply for the usual reasons of poor roads and highway robbers—French border guards often imposed heavy customs payments on those entering France, and were known to seize the goods and livestock of those attempting to leave. Merchants from Italy, Spain, Holland, and Germany were regularly subjected to the threat of imprisonment if they refused to pay the outrageous sums demanded by the border guards. Peasants displaced from their lands often found themselves forced to give up their few possessions for the chance to leave the country alive. This kind of extortion was most prevalent in areas where the border guards were paid low wages or not paid at all, a circumstance tolerated by the Revolutionary Assemblies throughout the country as a means of demonstrating the advantage of cutting taxes; during the two years of the Terror these abuses increased until some of the guards themselves were condemned for betraying the Revolution and met with the same fate as the hapless aristocrats, clergy, and intellectuals did.

Neither Italy nor Germany at that time was united, which made response to the French Revolution a complicated matter, for each of the various duchies, kingdoms, bishoprics, states, palatinates, and other territories had their own dealings with France, or with regions of France, some of which were semi-autonomous. Most of the nobility of Europe were worried about the French Revolution, which they were justifiably afraid might spread beyond France. For that reason not all of the hodgepodge of countries were willing to receive refugees from the Terror, and most were wary about endorsing the Revolutionary Assemblies as legitimate governments, which lessened the number of escapees who sought out Italian and German havens. Great Britain took in a sizeable number of French refugees, as it had taken in French Protestants after the Saint-Bartholomew's Day Massacre; so did Holland and Sweden, and a fair number of French fled to North and South America, with the greatest number in North America going to Quebec rather than to French centers in the United States; New Orleans, which had been used as a destination for deported French criminals, was not viewed as a desirable destination by many of those leaving France. Various political and intellectual groups in Britain and Scandinavia supported the French Revolution, among them the Lunar Society in Birmingham, England, who occasionally sent observers to cover the events, whose reports show growing concerns for the increasing excesses they observed. South American countries were divided on policies regarding Revolutionary refugees, although some found safety on Caribbean islands. Being adamantly Catholic, Spain became a refuge for many of the priests, monks, and nuns who were not willing to be martyrs to the New Order in France.

Well into the nineteenth century, French had a great many regional dialects and naming traditions, both for people and places, as well as dialects related to class. Some of the usages in this novel reflect those regionalisms, and are of the places and periods of the story and its characters; at the time of this book, French had been regularized for the educated, but a great percentage of the country kept to old forms of speech and nomenclature, which are reflected in these pages. One linguistic development of the Revolution was the incentive for towns with names associated with religion to change them to something more in tune with the times. Many of the new names were changed back after the rise of Napoleon and the subsequent return of the monarchy, but a few caught on and remain fixed to this day.

Since many, but not all, of the most active revolutionaries came from the working class, once most of the nobility and intelligentsia were dead or gone from the country, there were increasing flare-ups with the bourgeois; at the height of the Terror there was a sharp upturn in accusations against shopkeepers, artisans, manufacturers, and lawyers, a sign of the depths of what would later be called class warfare. Even servants could be condemned for no greater crime than earning a living. Few of the accused middle class had the means to flee, or the inclination to abandon their homes and businesses. The small number who could afford to leave almost everything behind and start over often chose not to, unwilling to admit defeat or to give the appearance of consenting to the claims of their accusers. Any supporters of these bourgeois rarely came forward on their behalf, wanting to avoid the scrutiny of the Revolutionary Tribunals, or the city mobs.

Fashions reflected the social change, shifting with unusual abruptness from Old Regime to Revolutionary modes. The mid-eighteenth century had been a period of opulence in dress, with upper-class men and women in costly fabrics and elaborate garments, wigs, and accessories that were copied on a less grand scale by as many of the middle class as could afford such display. By the time of the Revolution, fashions had become far less flamboyant; the "natural" look was in, often with a nod to the styles of ancient Greece in women's clothes, when corsets were minimized and the waists of dresses moved up to just under the breasts, although that new line had not caught on in most circles at the time of this story. Wigs were rarely worn except on certain formal occasions, and knee-britches gave way to trousers. Simplicity in style was suddenly acceptable, and elaborate accessories and jewelry were replaced by far less conspicuous ornaments to dress, and restraint in jewelry. Cotton lawn and fine muslin replaced satin and silk; panniers and petticoats disappeared from formal women's wear, at least for a quarter century. Another shift in fashion came in the form of household decor: from 1750 onward, improvements in the technology made the making of mirrors considerably less costly than it had been, and brought mirrors out of the realm of luxury items available to the wealthy few, into affordability for middle-class and bourgeois households. Having mirrors in businesses and houses became a sign of having arrived, and they were to be found almost everywhere.

In the latter part of the eighteenth century the Commedia del'Arte troupes were declining, giving way to established public theaters, and resident companies of actors, but a few such troupes still remained, touring the towns and cities of Italy and France; it was Commedia del'Arte troupes that first put women on the stage, and over time, nearly 20 percent of those troupes were run by women. Traditional Commedia del'Arte plays rarely had written dialogue as such, but had set scenarios, which the actors performed by ad libbing within very specific parameters. The plays they offered were generally broad comedy, slapstick, and farce; by the time of this story, the remaining Commedia del'Arte troupes offered greater variety in their fare, and began to specialize in certain theatrical styles tailored to their audiences; the six stock characters of traditional Commedia del'Arte scenarios were giving way to new personages, larger companies, and a much wider range of dramatic subject matter. Traveling players of all kinds were turning into regional performers with wide repetoires and more complex theatrical effects, with the single exception of trained animal troupes: these were enlarging their regions, becoming the true precursors to the traveling circuses of the following century.

Although most of the events of the story are historically accurate, I have shifted some of them slightly in time for exigencies of plot and story length; I trust that this will not compromise the novel too much for any reader familiar with the chronology of the actual events.

There are, as always, a number of people to thank for their help in the preparation of this book: thanks to Bailey Adams for access to maps of the French roadways at the end of the eighteenth century; to Susan Duttle for summarizing the changes in various regional Revolutionary Tribunals and Assemblies, including the Girondais movement in Lyon and its conflict with the National Assembly in Paris; and to Leonard Schoen for disagreeing with her, thereby opening up possibilities for my story line to use; to Michael Ivory for information on regional and class dialects in eighteenth-century France; to Harry Jecks for information on the later history of the Commedia del'Arte; to Ed McEller for supplying translations of legal proceedings of the time; to Victoria Smith for information on the daily lives of Commedia del'Arte players; to Penelope Weiss for filling in gaps regarding border policies and the refugee issues during the French Revolution, and the regional differences that impacted national policies. Errors in historicity are, as always, mine, and should not be held against these good people.

Also on the list of thanks are Libba Campbell and Maureen Kelly, who read the manuscript for errors; to Jim Gates, Deena Love, and Howard Risser, who read it for clarity; to Bill, Suzon, Gaye, Megan, Charlie, Peggy, Steve, Marc, Lori, Brian, Jim, Shawn, Maureen, David, and Christine; to Sharon Russell, Stephanie Moss, and Elizabeth Miller, for their insight and support; thanks to Neil Gaiman for his generous quote for this series; to Paula Guran for webmastering ChelseaQuinnYarbro.net; to my agent, Irene Kraas, for persistence in the face of strong headwinds; to the incomparable Wiley Saichek for all the Internet promotion, including the blog tour; to all those at Tor for sticking with the series; to Robin Dubner,

Saint-Germain's (and my) attorney; to the good people at Dragon-Con for importing me yet again to talk vampires; and to the booksellers and readers who have hung in with this series, which is now twenty-five books long and, I hope, counting.

CHELSEA QUINN YARBRO
September 2010

PART I

PHOTINE THERESE D'AUVILLE

Text of a Notice of Detention issued by the Revolutionary Tribunal of Avignon for Madelaine de Montalia at her estate, Montalia, carried by Revolutionary courier and delivered five days after it was ratified by the Deputy Secretary for Public Safety in Avignon.

From the Revolutionary Tribunal of Avignon:

This is to inform the woman known as Madelaine de Montalia that she is to regard herself under house detention by the Revolutionary Tribunal of Avignon. Any attempt to flee or to resist this order will result in her immediate transportation to Avignon for public execution. She is required to house and feed the Revolutionary Guards who will shortly arrive to enforce this detention; all costs of such maintenance shall be borne entirely by the woman Madelaine de Montalia. Failure to conform to the orders contained in this Notice in any particular will result in imprisonment for the woman Madelaine de Montalia. No challenge to this Notice will be accepted by the Revolutionary Tribunal of Avignon, and any attempt to circumvent the conditions contained herein will be regarded as willful disobedience to this lawful Notice and will result in imprisonment.

We are informed that the woman Madelaine de Montalia has a long-term guest who lives with her, Theron Baptiste Heurer, formerly of Bourges, as well as a staff of nine for the chateau and ten for the cultivation and tilling of the fields and vineyards of the estate, all of whom will be allowed four days in which to decide whether to depart or remain with the woman Madelaine de Montalia, with the understanding that if they remain they may well share her eventual fate. Safe conducts for the members of her household and guest that will include up to four persons will be delivered by the Revolutionary Guards; these will be valid for twenty-one days, after which they will no longer secure any borders-crossing for anyone attempting to use them for that purpose.

The woman Madelaine de Montalia will be informed of any change in her detention, and will be required to hold herself in readiness to comply promptly with any and all orders from the Committee for Public Safety of the Revolutionary Tribunal of Avignon, or any Revolutionary Tribunal recognized by the Revolutionary Tribunal of Avignon. This Notice is to be given primary authority in regard to the woman Madelaine de Montalia and until such time as it is officially rescinded, to be adhered to in every detail.

This on the 22nd day of June, 1792.

Long live the Revolution!

Long live the People's Justice!

Georges Marie Forcier
Deputy Secretary for Public Safety
Revolutionary Tribunal of Avignon

1

"I need you to do this for me. If you don't leave in the morning, the opportunity will be lost, and neither of us will be secure here," Madelaine de Montalia said to Theron Heurer with growing emotion; she made herself speak softly in case one of the newly arrived Revolutionary Guards was listening outside the door. "Go while the safe conduct is valid. If you wait—"

"But I don't want to leave you—*because* those damned Revolutionary Guards are here. I don't like the look of them. Worse than gutter-scum. Those men are beasts!" Theron folded his arms and glared at Madelaine de Montalia to keep from revealing the level of dread he felt on her behalf.

"I've dealt with worse." Madelaine had a sharp, unpleasant memory of the cellars beneath Hotel Transylvania and Saint Sebastien's coven, half a century ago; she shook her head as much to banish the recollection as to dismiss his worries. "You have to go."

"But wouldn't you rather have me here?"

"Yes, if that were my only concern for my safety. But I'm only safe for as long as I can be sure of loyal friends. Whomelse can I trust with this errand but you? And what will the Revolutionary Courts demand of me next? This has to be done quickly or it may be too late." She paced the floor in the salon des fenetres, her soft-violet silken skirts clinging to her body as she moved, the golden summer light making the room glow; where it touched her coffee-colored hair, it added an aureate sheen. It was a bit too warm for comfort but not hot enough to be miserable. "I would feel less worried if I knew you were out of France."

"And I would feel worse, if I abandoned you, especially to the chaos of the Courts," Theron declared staunchly but not loudly. He was tall and well-built, with light-brown hair and a lively countenance. At twenty-four he thought of himself as both a poet and a man of the world, in a position to advise this young, lovely creature who had welcomed him into her elegant life and her bed.

"I have to get word to Saint-Germain somehow," she told him in a serene tone, but there was something in her violet eyes that was adamant.

"Send Bescart. He's Swiss. They'll let him cross the border." His face was flushed and his eyes shone as he regarded her.

"Bescart is planning to leave tomorrow, with his wife and children. Why should he do this for me?" She waited for him to answer, and when he did not, she tossed her head, making the little curls around her face dance. "He might say he will do as I ask, but I doubt he will actually do it."

"He's been loyal so far."

"Oh, yes. But things have changed, and his loyalty is with the Revolution now, or so he tells me. He says he bears me no ill-will, but that his cause must be with his people. He supports the Revolution, not the Old Order, though he says I have been good to him and his. Some of the others feel as he does, and who can blame them?" She sank down on the chaise in the bow of the windows that gave the room its name. "If you won't take a message to Saint-Germain for me, I don't know who will."

"Are you so certain that he'll help you?" He hesitated, then went on, "Do you know that he can do it?"

"Oh, yes, on both points," said Madelaine. "He and I are blood relatives. He will help me. He has done so in the past."

"Not during a revolution," Theron said, determined to make his point.

"That doesn't matter." She held out her hands to Theron. "And dear as you are, you can't achieve the results that he can. He has . . . skills that you and I lack in these matters. Not all my fortune and all your family's wealth could pay bribes enough to get me free now that the Revolutionary Tribunal has its hooks in me."

Theron held back from her. "But this Saint-Germain can?" He sounded incredulous.

"If it takes bribes, yes. He has a great deal of money. But he has other means at his disposal as well, and those are what I rely upon." She took his hands in hers.

"So have I, if it comes to that," said Theron.

"Not as he does." She drew him toward her, smiling at him in a most tantalizing way. "I'll order a horse, a remount, and a mule for you tomorrow morning, and I will have Gigot prepare a basket of food and drink for you. I know there is a tent you may take, and a bedroll. And a sack of oats for your animals."

"But I haven't said—"

"Stay at inns, not monasteries, while you travel. You know what they're doing to clerics." She frowned slightly. "Be careful of others on the road."

"If I agree to go, I'll bear all this in mind." He studied her face. "You're serious about this Saint-Germain, aren't you?"

"Deadly serious."

"You say this man is in Padova?" His expression had softened.

"He is presently connected to the Universita, and he has a business in Venezia. He goes by Conte da San-Germain in Padova." She knew that Saint-Germain had both a publishing and a trading company, but decided not to complicate her persuasion with unnecessary information. "I will provide you with directions."

"A professor of some sort, then, is he?" Theron regarded her with undisguised dubiety.

"Among other things, yes. He has been about the world a great deal."

"Then I take it he isn't a young man," said Theron with a look of ill-concealed hope lighting his face.

"No, he's not," she replied, coaxing him down beside her. "I think you will like him, once you cease to be jealous."

He stared at her, shocked. "Jealous? I? Of him?"

"It is certainly in accord with your demeanor," she said lightly, teasing him. "You may discover that he likes your poetry enough to publish it. You must take some of your best work to him. You can conceal my letter to him among your poems." Her smile faded. "He has a publishing company in Venezia, and he often receives manuscripts of all sorts; no one will think anything of you giving him your poems." The publishing company was, as she knew, one of several, but she kept that to herself.

"I haven't said I'd go yet," he reminded her.

"But you will, won't you? For me?"

"I will consider it," he conceded.

"Excellent." Her kiss was lingering and evocative, sweetly languorous; she wound her arms around him, feeling his arousal against her thigh. She leaned into him, guiding his hand to the swell of her breast. "I knew I could depend on you." She kissed him again, with more fervor than before.

After a long, delicious silence he pulled away. "If you insist, I suppose I can go."

Madelaine kept hold of him. "Thank you."

"Not just because you kissed me," he said flatly.

"Of course not," she said. "You have begun to realize that my request is sensible for the both of us."

"Perhaps," he said. "I don't like leaving you." He continued to caress her through the silk of her high bodice.

"Nor I you, but that is out of our hands now." She sighed, and let go of him. "Later. When we can be truly alone." With a regretful chuckle she got to her feet. "And speaking of matters out of my hands, I must see Gigot to arrange a meal for the Guards."

"Let Bescart handle it," Theron suggested.

"He's packing. Besides, he'd let Gigot feed them swill, and that would do me no good." Her smile was wan.

"Will feeding the Guards well help?" Theron asked.

"It might." She glanced toward the door. "And I must take care to do all that I can to treat them respectfully."

"Why?"

"Because, cher Theron, they can make my detention pleasant or difficult, and I would rather it be as pleasant as possible. Not slighting them should have a better result than treating them like barbarians, since they are as much spies as guards." She took a deep breath. "And to that end, when we dine tonight, we must argue. Nothing vile, but forceful, so that you may wash your hands of me. If you wish to express regret, do so, but make it clear that you and I have reached an impasse. That way, no one will wonder at your departure. Unless they see some disagreement, they will suspect a ruse, and that won't suit our purpose."

"I don't want to argue with you," said Theron anxiously.

"Still, it would be better that you do it. I don't want you to be detained."

"They won't detain me," he said with more bravado than conviction.

"No, they won't—not if you're in Padova." She went the length of the room, her face set in determined lines. "These Revolutionaries are hungry for blood, and they will not be easily sated. All through the country, the National Razor is busy shaving heads at the neck. I would prefer they spare me mine." Her irony was too strong for Theron, who did his best not to look shocked at her bitter humor.

"If I decide to do this for you, I would like a very wondrous farewell tonight," he said, reaching out for her again.

"That you shall have, no matter what you decide," she promised.

His voice dropped to a kind of purr. "I'll think of every way to please you, and you will use your sorcery on me."

She evaded his embrace. "Yes. Tonight. Not just now with the Guards outside the door."

He stepped back from her. "You kissed me," he reminded her.

"So I did. And I will do more. But not here. We want them to believe our argument, don't we?"

"I suppose so," he said, looking a bit sulky.

Madelaine reminded herself that he was only twenty-four. "You will be well-rewarded for waiting."

"I have no doubt of that." The purr was gone.

"Until then, keep in mind that we must remember that we are being watched. Tonight we will be private."

He let out an abrupt sigh. "What do you plan to do once I'm gone?" he asked more loudly as he shot a glance toward the door.

"Put this house in order as much as I can with a reduced staff. Gigot will stay on to run the kitchen, but only four will be left in the house, and six for the fields, and who knows? more may leave in the twenty-one days granted in the safe conduct. If Maxime will remain as well, the mansion may not fall into ruin. I have to assume that there will be a few more who prefer safety to good pay." She gave a little shake of her head. "If we shut up six of the rooms, the task of caring for the place shouldn't be too overwhelming."

"That sounds as if you intend to do some of the work yourself," said Theron, his disapproval obvious.

"Of course I shall." She shook her head. "Oh, Theron, Theron, I am not some hot-house flower, to be coddled and pampered. I know how to sweep a room and scrub floors, and dress a chicken, if it comes to that. I can mend clothes and lay a fire." She looked him steadily in the eyes. "You may not believe it, but I would be delighted to go on an antiquarian expedition to Egypt or India, or . . . oh, I don't know. Anywhere there are ruins of ancient cities."

Theron laughed as he reached out to stroke her cheek. "You want the adventure, the romance. But you don't know the dangers and hardships such expeditions face."

"Yes, I do, and I welcome them; I've told you before that I know what such expeditions are like, and I don't make light of the hard-ships they entail," she declared, then added quietly, "Say nothing more now; this would be a perfect argument for tonight."

"But—" He stopped himself, aware that in some way he could not understand he had overstepped himself. "I'll leave you to think about what you have said, I know it was only fancy that inspires you. I would not like to think that you would so demean yourself that you would set aside all propriety for the sake of exotic travel."

"So would I," said Madelaine bluntly. "I don't think travel is demeaning. When you consider some of the places I have gone—" She moved past him. "I'll be in the kitchen for the next hour. I'll see you when you dine this evening."

He could not stop himself from saying, "And you will not eat with me, will you?"

"No; you know I will not. When have I ever?"

His smile was charmingly reckless. "In bed."

Rather than laugh, Madelaine gave him a warning look. "That is between us," she whispered. "It is nothing to jest about."

His face fell. "I suppose you're right."

"In this I am." She raised her voice once more. "Are you considering the safe conduct, then?"

"I don't know," said Theron, taking his cue from her expression. "I may. At least I'll give it some thought."

"Of course," she responded with exaggerated courtesy while mitigating her sarcasm with a wink. "Well, if you must, you must."

"This is not the time to discuss this. As you say, you have things to do." He gave her an answering wink, then turned and stormed out of the salon, leaving the door open in his haste to be gone.

Madelaine watched him go, wondering how much of his indignation was performance and how much was genuine, thinking that Theron might yet bring them both to ruin. She smoothed the front of her dress, and went out the door, passing between two Revolutionary Guards as she did, and made for the kitchen, doing her utmost to keep her worries from being too apparent in her demeanor.

"Madame," said Gigot as Madelaine entered his hot, cavernous domain. "You are most welcome." He was large and loose-limbed, in his mid-thirties, of a comfortable size, and with a rumpled face that gave him the air of an affectionate hound.

"Thank you, Gigot." She looked around. "Your scullions are leaving?"

"Only Pierre. Dion is staying for now, and Maxime. Dion's out turning the cheese in the creamery." His attempt at a smile was wary. "I can't say if he might not change his mind and decide to leave."

"Well, if he does," said Madelaine in a rallying way, "I can turn cheeses, and bake bread if I must."

Gigot could not conceal his shock. "It wouldn't be right, Madame. Not even Maxime will turn cheeses."

"It isn't right that the Revolutionary Guards are here, but that can't be changed, so we must accommodate. Let us hope that the worst we will have to do is turn cheeses." She settled on the bench near the enclosed ovens. "Since they are here, we, perforce, will house and feed them." For a moment she paused, seeing increasing dismay in his eyes. "There are nine of them, aren't there?"

"Yes. With two couriers due tomorrow." Gigot sounded disapproving. "Eleven rough villains, with the manners of brigands."

"Then prepare them a good supper. Make them a meat pie with the last of the hung beef and the small pork sausages. We have vegetables enough to make the pie a sufficient meal in itself, don't we?"

Gigot shrugged. "If you require it."

Before he could become intractable, she held out a hand to him. "Oh, Gigot, think. If we anger them, or show them any contempt, it is not they who will suffer for it, is it? Treat them well, and we will stand in less danger from them than if we defy them. Don't you see that?"

He nodded slowly. "It upsets me to cater to such men as they are."

"They aren't my favorite house-guests, either, but that is out of our hands now."

Gigot reached for a celery-root and began to trim it. "This, cooked with the beef and sausages, some cabbage, and some turnips, should suffice. I will make the dough for the crust as soon as

I finish chopping this." He waved his wedge-knife as if it were a sword, then set it down with a bang. "I have onions and garlic. There's beef stock in the pantry, only a day old. Chervil, savory, thyme, a little pepper to liven it, and they will be satisfied." He paused. "I'll make something a bit better for the household, and your companion."

"Thank you, Gigot," said Madelaine, rising from the bench. "I think you and I should plan meals for at least two weeks, so that we can secure the things we need for the Guards." She saw him rankle, and went on, "We will need to be prepared. If we don't make plans now, who knows what they might decide to commandeer for their—"

"We should lock the pantry, and the wine-cellar. And the creamery," Gigot said emphatically.

"By all means lock whatever you wish."

"Do you think this will be over in two weeks?" Gigot asked.

"No, I don't. I think it will get worse," Madelaine said, her voice flat. "We have to be ready for whatever comes." She pressed her lips together. "Does Dion know how to butcher? With Olivier going to his brother in Autun, we'll be without a butcher here, and I don't trust any of the Guards to know how to slaughter a hog and dress it. I daren't think what they would do to a lamb."

"Saints save us! No." Gigot was shocked. "Better that I should do it, and I am only a cook."

"There is nothing *only* about your cooking," said Madelaine.

"How would you know? You never so much as taste it," Gigot responded, his manner lightly teasing.

"I can smell, and I know aroma from odor," she answered in the same manner.

"Madame is most kind," said Gigot with the suggestion of a bow.

"Oh, Gigot, don't play with me," said Madelaine.

He chuckled. "Very well. Tell me what you want me to serve your friend for his supper tonight."

"Nothing too fancy; perhaps ribs of lamb with sauteed cabbage;

the Guards will notice if you make one of your special dishes, and might not take it in good part that Theron has better fare than they. Be sure that the Guards have large helpings." She did her best to smile at him. "I am sorry you've been brought to this state, Gigot. If you decide you'd rather not remain, I would certainly understand."

Gigot gusted out a sigh. "Where would I go? Who would hire me in these times? I haven't the disposition to be an innkeeper, and there is no one now who can afford to maintain the kind of household I am accustomed to cooking for."

"True enough," said Madelaine. "Well, I am pleased to have you with me, whatever your reason for staying."

"If I had a wife or children it might be different, but since I don't . . ." He made another sweep with his knife to finish his thoughts.

Whatever Madelaine might have said was silenced as Bescart came into the kitchen. She regarded him steadily, but with a sinking sensation in her heart. "Good afternoon, Bescart. How are your preparations coming?"

"The carts are mostly loaded, and we have chosen two mules and a spare to pull them," he said gruffly, pulling at the lobe of his large ear. "I was coming to ask for some cheese and sausage and perhaps a smoked ham to take with us, for food. I don't know where we'll find farmers willing to sell us provisions, and half of the travelers' inns are keeping their doors closed." He stared at her with a mixture of defiance and shame in his stance. "If you'll permit it, of course," he added.

"Certainly you may have food; I told the household that this morning, and nothing has changed," said Madelaine. "All of you who have chosen to leave have been promised food for your journeys, and you shall have it."

Gigot scowled, but said, "I'll bring you two rounds of cheese—the large ones. I have a fennel-sausage made with veal—you know them; the ones that are as long as your forearm and big around as a large beetroot—you shall have three of them. They're in the pantry. I can fill a jar with pickled onions-and-cucumbers. If Madame will permit, I will give you three bottles of white wine."

"Yes. That should keep you and your family for a few days," said Madelaine.

"You are generous, Madame," Bescart conceded.

"I would not like it said that I haven't made reasonable settlement on you. I know you already have the funds I've provided." Madelaine took a step toward him. "Let us wish each other well and part friends, Bescart."

"Giving me a year's wages and a letter of introduction is a kindness, Madame, but you are a noble and I am not. There can be no friendship between us now." He turned away from her and spoke to Gigot as if Madelaine had vanished. "I will come for our food in an hour or so. And we will dine in our quarters tonight. My wife will do a baking before ten tonight; you will have bread for tomorrow. We will leave at first light, so that we will not have to travel much in the heat of the day, and can nap, like civilized persons do."

"I've sent for my nephew to do the baking," said Gigot, trying not to reveal the extent of his disapproval of Bescart's departure. "He should be here in two days. In the meantime, Remi and I can make loaves for the household."

"If your nephew answers your invitation, you mean. In these days, who knows if he will take the chance." Bescart gave Gigot a searching look. "You should come with us, Gigot. It isn't safe to stay here any longer."

"Montalia is my home, as it was my father's," Gigot said firmly. "I won't leave it just because some upstarts from the city have taken it into their heads to try to drive me away."

"As you wish," said Bescart, tugging at his earlobe again before he swung around on his heel and stomped off to the outside door.

"Well!" exclaimed Gigot when Bescart had closed the door behind him. "What do you make of that?"

"I suppose he's frightened." Madelaine shook her head. "And he may be right—those of us from the Old Order are now at the mercy of the New, and he wants to be on the winning side."

"Do not despair, Madame," Gigot said, his voice ragged.

Madelaine managed a kind of a smile. "I will do my best not to, Gigot."

Encouraged, the cook went on, "It will all come right. You'll see."

"Do you think so: perhaps." She started toward the corridor that led to the dining room, but paused in the doorway. "For to-night, do something remarkable for my guest. He will be departing tomorrow, and I want him to have a memorable meal tonight."

"Would lamb do, with rosemary and garlic? And a creamed-chicken soup with fine herbs?" Gigot's eyes shone at the prospect.

"It sounds delicious. I can almost taste it," said Madelaine, and added, "I will be in my study for an hour or so. I have a letter I must write." And saying that, she was gone.

Text of a letter from Madelaine de Montalia at Montalia to il Conte da San-Germain in Padova, written in Latin, and carried by Theron Baptiste Heurer, delivered twenty-two days after it was written.

> *To my most dear, most cherished San-Germain, the greetings of Madelaine de Montalia,*
>
> *This is being carried to you by Theron Heurer, who has been my companion for the last four months. He is a poet of some promise, but still too filled with the sense of his own genius to have done great work yet, though it may be in him. I have tasted his blood five times, but no more than that.*
>
> *He will tell you that I have been confined to Montalia on the order of the Revolutionary Tribunal of Avignon. There are nine Revolutionary Guards posted to my home, and a pair of couriers are supposed to arrive in a day or so, I assume to keep the Tribunal informed*

of all that happens here, and may yet carry a warrant for my arrest and imprisonment, which would take me away from here.

I know that you warned me of this when I left your house in Verona. You said that the Revolution might well deteriorate into squabbling, vindictive gangs, but I thought that a woman in my position would not come to the attention of any powerful Revolutionaries so that I could be left alone to preserve my estate and my dependants from Revolutionary excesses. You came for me at the beginning of the Revolution, and I was glad to go with you then. I know you disagreed with me when I returned to Montalia, saying that the worst was still yet to come, and that I would not be safe. You were right. I should have allowed you to persuade me to remain. Yet you, of all people, must understand the tie I feel to this place: it is my native earth, and though not of my blood, these are my people, or they were.

Half of my household has left, granted safe conducts for the period of a month. I suspect more may decide that it is wiser to be gone from here than to remain. I do not trust these men, and so have taken to sleeping with a poignard under my pillow, and when I go about on the estate, I keep a charged pistol with me. Some of the Guards laugh at me, thinking that I have no knowledge of firearms, but if they attempt to force themselves upon me, they will learn otherwise. I am doing my utmost to make this unpleasant arrangement as bearable as it can be, for I do not wish to be denounced to the Revolutionary Tribunal.

Which brings me to the purpose of this letter: dearest San-Germain, will you please come and get me before they chop off my head? I would attempt to get away through my own efforts, but if I am caught making such an attempt, the consequences would be immediate and severe; I would like to avoid the True Death for a while longer, and I am relying on you to help me to realize this goal.

I know I needn't ask, but be kind to Theron, for my sake. He is a bit vainglorious but his heart is good, and he truly cares for me.

I will look forward to your arrival in poor, belea- guered France, and until then, I hold you in my heart, as I have done from the first time we met, forty-nine years ago.

Your Madelaine
at Montalia, on the 5ᵗʰ day of July, 1792

2

Sunlight lay like warmed honey over Padova; it heated the piazze and mercati, gilded the buildings with its glorious shine, added its glow to the stark courtyard of the Universita, and sank into the cobbled streets so that the air shimmered above the stones like ripples in a stream. The people went along slowly, pacing them- selves in order not to take more of the sweltering air than was nec- essary, their faces shiny as they made their way to their homes and student rooms to wait out the most intense heat of the day. The air was redolent with odors from people, animals, plants, and the river, running green toward the lagoon of Venezia. Market-stalls were busy in the last hurried effort to get the day's sales done; around the Universita, cafes hastened to finish their serving so that everyone could get away to nap through the heat of the day, which today, everyone realized, would be greater than usual.

In the mansion Ragoczy Ferenz, Conte da San-Germain, had bought nearly a decade before, all the windows were open in the hope of catching a hint of breeze off the Adriatic Sea, a day's travel away. The building was on a rise—one of the few in the city—and offered views in almost all directions. The grounds, while not extensive, were handsomely laid out, showing the city and the countryside to equal advantage. Two guest-houses at the rear of the formal gardens were occupied at present by a troupe of Commedia del'Arte actors hoping to gain the Conte's official patronage. To that end, they had erected their stage between the guest-houses and were busy completing their first rehearsal of the day before they retired for the afternoon.

From his vantage-point at his third-storey window, da San-Germain watched the actors working; his laboratory occupied most of the top floor of the mansion, overlooking the gardens and a bit of the countryside beyond. He did not mind the heat, for it, like cold, had little effect on him; there was no trace of sweat on him, nor any other sign of discomfort. He wore a white cotton smock not to keep cool, but to save his silken shirt and black linen trousers from the spatters of azoth that made the secret of the Philosopher's Stone possible. He was preparing a batch of base metal to go into the athanor for transformation; by nightfall he would have another dozen ingots of gold. He turned away from the window and smiled to himself. There were many at the Universita who scoffed at him for his interest in the study of alchemy, at which da San-Germain would remind them that Isaac Newton had practiced the ancient art and declared that he had not learned all there was to know of it. Just before he placed the alembic in the alchemical oven, there was a knock at the door.

"My master?" came the voice of Roger, his long-time man-servant.

"What is it?" da San-Germain asked, keeping most of his attention on what he was doing.

"You have a visitor." Nothing in Roger's voice suggested that this was remarkable in any way.

"I need ten minutes," said da San-Germain, then asked, "Do you know him?"

"No. He says he's a poet. From France."

"Ah." Da San-Germain set the alembic in the retort vessel and carefully closed the steel-and-glass door, latching it securely. "Show him to the library and tell him I will join him shortly."

"Shall I have Giorgio make a tray for him?"

How many times, and in how many ways had da San-Germain offered this most basic hospitality? He had long since lost count. "Yes. If you would. He'll know what's best to serve on a day like this." He reached for his timing clock, and set it for five hours and forty-two minutes, then checked the athanor's bellows mechanism; satisfied, he straightened up and picked up the container for the azoth, which he returned to its well-insulated strongbox, which in turn was secreted in the bottom of a banded chest; in spite of the heat, his face and neck were dry. With his strongbox secured, he removed his smock and hung it over a peg on the wall, then left the room.

Roger, who was standing at the head of the stairs, said, "You'll need a neck-cloth and a jacket."

"I know. And I trust you, old friend, to recommend the appropriate ones for me before you attend to our poet from France. I need a little more time to put myself in order for—" He locked the door to his laboratory and slipped the key into his trouser pocket. "I will need a clean shirt—I trust there are a dozen or so in the armoire?"

"Of course." Roger started down the stairs, his expression showing signs of worry. "You'll want the black linen swallow-tail coat, and the embroidered waistcoat—the one of Egyptian cotton." Then suddenly he blurted out, "Do you suppose that Madelaine has met with some misfortune?"

"That was my first suspicion, though I hope—" da San-Germain answered with a touch of vexation in his manner. "I hope we're both wrong."

"Where are you going now?" Roger asked.

"I should do a little more in my forcing house. I would prefer the leaves of the plants not burn in this heat."

"Are you going to open the ceiling panels?"

"Yes," said da San-Germain. "Is Ugolino about?"

"I believe he's giving his attention to the fruit trees in the garden. Do you need him?"

Da San-Germain shook his head. "Not peremptorily. Let him finish with the fruit trees; if it continues hot through the week, he might not want to get back to them for a fortnight. There'll be time enough tomorrow to have him assist me. But those panels need to be raised now. Please offer my apologies to the French poet." He took the rear stairs, leaving Roger to go about his tasks.

In the kitchen, Giorgio Belcosa, his shirt open to his waist, was standing over a large vat of cold tomato soup, stirring it judiciously. He looked up as da San-Germain came through, on his way to the garden door. "Do not fret, Conte. I will have the mid-day meal ready for the players in less than ten minutes. I know they are hungry, but the day is hot, so I will not burden them with more than their stomachs will want. Nothing too heavy. In this weather, too much food is as bad as too little."

"True enough," said da San-Germain, who had not endured such discomfort for millennia. "What other than the soup?"

"A salad of lettuces and asparagus, red onion slices, and grated cheese, with lemon slices and olive oil to dress it. Very light, very tasty. This soup, which is robust without being heavy, will complement it." He smiled contentedly. "There's bread and new butter as well, and wine."

"It sounds an excellent repast," said da San-Germain.

Giorgio gave a single laugh, saying good-naturedly, "How would you know? You never eat."

"Not with company," da San-Germain agreed, not wanting to renew an old, genial dispute with his cook. "Has Roger told you about the guest?"

"That he has. I've set out some soup and slices of smoked ham on a tray for him, with bread and butter, quite sufficient for such a visitor. Also I provided him a very nice Trebbiano—not that you'd notice the quality."

"No. I do not drink wine," da San-Germain said. "But, thanks to you, I keep a good cellar, or so I've been told."

Giorgio laughed and put a large metal pot on the iron stove and filled it with water from the kitchen ewer. "Scalding chickens, for tonight," he explained. "I'll have Teobaldo pluck them, after his mid-day nap."

"A messy chore," da San-Germain remarked, who had many times in his long life done far worse than pluck and dress chickens. "Make sure he has two pails of water to wash himself in when he's done. You don't want feathers all over the kitchen."

"That is why I'm glad to have Teobaldo to do it." He winked and went into the pantry to retrieve the four newly killed chickens hanging on thongs from a hook. "Those players have healthy appetites."

Da San-Germain passed on into the kitchen garden, and from there into his forcing house, which was even warmer than the kitchen had been; it smelled of growing plants and loamy earth, and a faint suggestion of moisture clung to everything. He took a long rod with a tip of bent metal, raised it, and unlatched the first of six large glass panels that formed the roof. He pushed the panel upward until there was a loud click as the holding mechanism locked the panel open. He repeated this with the next five, then left the forcing house; he went directly to his own apartment, where he pulled off his shirt and wiped himself with a towel, to rid himself of any trace of detritus from his laboratory. After a brief consideration of the shirt, he tossed it aside and selected another one, with ruffled cuffs and a standing collar from the armoire, along with the black swallow-tail coat and cotton waistcoat that Roger had recommended.

He dressed quickly, being careful to align his buttons correctly; that was one hazard of dressing that occasionally frustrated him: his lack of reflection made such details easy to miss. Finally he pulled a silk neck-cloth from the drawer of his dresser and secured it in a casual knot. Last of all, he ran an ivory comb through his hair. Satisfied that he was ready, he left his apartments, descending the stairs quickly but without apparent haste; as he entered the corridor to the library, he almost ran into Roger, who was coming the other way.

"I've put him in the library, as you asked. Teobaldo brought the tray." Roger gave da San-Germain a rapid scrutiny, adjusted the neck-cloth. "No fobs and seals?"

Da San-Germain shook his head. "Only my signet ring. Anything more might look reactionary to him." He twisted the silver ring on the little finger of his right hand with the incised image of an heraldic eclipse—a disk with raised, displayed wings, enameled black. He nodded to Roger. "Am I satisfactory?"

"You are," said Roger. He stepped aside.

It was a short walk to the library; da San-Germain moved quickly along the corridor and through the large central hall, then opened the double doors to the library. He looked toward the handsome Turkish couch fronted by a low butler's table, which held a tray of light foods, a carafe of wine, and a short-stemmed glass. Da San-Germain had been expecting to find his guest there, enjoying his soup and smoked ham; when he realized that the Frenchman was not there, he glanced down the long, shelved wall, and saw the young man at the far end of the room, standing on a footstool, reaching for a worn leather volume of Medieval verses. "Good day to you," da San-Germain said in slightly old-fashioned French. "And welcome."

Theron turned toward da San-Germain, his face flushing from more than the heat. "Good day," he replied as he put the book back and stepped down from the stool. "I hope you don't mind—you have such a wonderful collection, I couldn't help myself. I didn't mean—"

"Not at all," da San-Germain replied. "They are here to be read." He crossed the room to where Theron stood; he could see his visitor taking stock of him, and felt a twinge of amusement at the young man's perusal. "Let me welcome you to my house. I am Ragoczy

Ferenz, Conte da San-Germain, at your service." He smiled at
Theron and nodded a polite half-bow, his expression one of genial
curiosity. "And who are you . . . ?"

"Theron Baptiste Heurer. Madelaine de Montalia sent me. I
have a message from her for you." He looked his host over carefully
as he returned the bow, and then, in the spirit of the new times,
offered his hand. "I have just this morning arrived in Padova. I came
as soon as I was settled in my room."

Da San-Germain shook it, his small hand proving to have a
firm grip. "I gather from my houseman that your errand is urgent?"

"It is." He gave a tentative cough, then began what was certainly a rehearsed recitation. "I regret to inform you that she—
Madelaine de Montalia—has been detained by the Revolutionary
Tribunal." He reached into the inner pocket of his fawn-colored
hammer-claw coat and brought out a sealed letter; San-Germain
noticed that his neck-cloth, though artistically tied, had wilted,
losing its fashionable shape. "She asked me to bring this to you."

"When was this given to you?" da San-Germain asked as he
took the letter.

"July fifth," Theron answered promptly. "It took me fourteen
days to get here. I was held up at the French border for a day, while
they made sure my safe conduct was genuine, and my second horse
went lame three days ago."

"You came alone?" He did his best not to open the letter with
unseemly haste.

"I had two mules and two horses—Madelaine's doing, of course;
she even provided me with food and a tent—and I kept to the village
roads, as she recommended I do." He gave a self-effacing smile.
"They aren't as fast, but there are fewer soldiers, and fewer high-
waymen, on them."

"A sensible decision." He nodded in the direction of the couch.
"Won't you sit down and have something to eat? I'll need a little
time to read this."

"Certainly," said Theron, and hastened to the couch. Curious as he was, he did not allow himself the luxury of watching his host for fear of appearing to intrude on him while he read.

Da San-Germain walked some short distance down the library, toward the large, empty fireplace. He broke the seal impatiently and unfolded the heavy paper, smoothing away the wrinkles as he read Madelaine's missive, worry building in him with every succeeding word. Telling himself it could be worse, and almost believing it, he refolded the letter and slipped it into his sleeve before he turned and went back to the couch. He pulled up an elegant upholstered chair and sat down, his face revealing nothing of his thoughts. "I gather you were with Madelaine when she was detained."

"I was," said Theron, then paused to swallow before going on. "I wanted to stay with her—the Revolutionary Guards were little better than street-fighters, and all of them are eager to be in charge of everything as if they had more authority than they have been granted—but she persuaded me to come to you. She told me she could manage for herself so long as she remained at Montalia."

"Very wise of her, to send you," said da San-Germain. "And for you to come to me so promptly."

"I sought you out as soon as I took a room at the hotel near the river. The one with the yellow front."

"The Hotel Franchesi," said da San-Germain. "I understand it is comfortable. But if you like, you may command a room here at any time."

"That's most hospitable of you, Conte." Theron filled his glass with wine and said, "To Madelaine."

"Indeed," da San-Germain agreed. "Do you know how much of her staff was still with her when you left?"

"Her cook was staying. But about half of them left, or were planning to leave after I did." He frowned. "I couldn't convince her to come with me."

San-Germain repeated, "Very wise."

"How do you mean?"

"If she had attempted to flee, you may be sure she would

have been apprehended and held as an enemy of the people, and it would be far more difficult to rescue her."

This time Theron wondered what da San-Germain meant when he said difficult, but he could not summon up the courage to ask; for all his cordiality, Theron found his host imposing, carrying an air of authority that could not be banished by good manners and generosity. "Yes. Well, she plans to remain there until she can be sure of departing safely. She will not try to free herself, and the reasons you state are part of her concerns. She relies on you to accomplish what she cannot."

"I will do my utmost to accommodate her," said da San-Germain, with more force than he had intended.

Theron looked up from his tray, something like alarm in his eyes. "Conte? You mean you will—"

"In her letter, Madelaine asks me to come to France to help her. She is of my blood, so, of course, I will do it."

"Do you plan to go shortly?" Theron took another large sip of his wine, his eyes revealing excitement mixed with alarm.

"As soon as I may, once I have more confirmation from a few remaining contacts in France." He was already deciding which of his various associates he should approach for help. "I should be away within two weeks. It is important, I think, to be fully prepared before arriving in Avignon than to try to improvise afterward."

"Oh, yes," Theron agreed, wanting to gain the good opinion of this self-possessed foreigner. "A better idea, and safer, too."

"Just so," da San-Germain concurred. He studied Theron for a time, keeping in mind what Madelaine had told him in her letter. Finally, as Theron was beginning to squirm under this scrutiny, he said, "It was good of you to do this for her—brave as well."

This tidbit of praise produced a self-satisfied smile. "That's kind of you to say, Conte."

"If you like to think so." He watched Theron refill his glass. "Tell me: how did the Revolutionary Guards seem to you?"

"Like sweepings from the gutter," said Theron, and drank.

"Yes, I understand. That is always the way with such forces. But what was their demeanor toward Madelaine?"

"What do you mean?" He forked a slice of the smoked ham onto a slice of buttered bread.

"Were they angry? Spiteful? Uneasy? Lascivious?"

Theron took a bite and chewed energetically. "Oh. I see what you mean. Let me think." He took another mouthful of wine to wash down the smoked ham and bread. After a brief pause, he said, "They certainly looked at her in a carnalistic manner, and one was more of a bully than the others. But they also seemed a little intimidated by her. It's hard to describe."

Although da San-Germain knew precisely what Theron was struggling to identify, he said, "Which do you think was the stronger?"

"When I left," Theron said, "they were slightly more intimidated than lustful, but that may have changed since I've been gone. I have little faith in the few of her servants who have pledged to remain with her; I feel certain they will all leave, in time." His last words came out in an unhappy rush.

"So long as some of her staff remains—which seems likely, at least for a while, as you say—I doubt the guards will overstep themselves," said da San-Germain in such a way that Theron was hard-pressed to conceal his shock. "Unless she is moved."

"The Revolutionary Guards are bullies," said Theron with an expression of revulsion clouding his handsome features.

"All bullies are at heart cowards, Monsieur Heurer," said da San-Germain. "Pray, do not abandon your meal because of me."

"Then you won't join me?" Theron asked, plainly uncertain how to proceed.

"I have dined already," said da San-Germain.

"The way Madelaine dines?" The instant he said it, Theron wished he had not. "Not," he went on his hasty apology, "that it is any of my concern."

"You're right," said da San-Germain, not elaborating on what he meant; nonplussed, Theron had another sip of wine and struggled to gather his thoughts. "Aside from being under detention, is there any indication that Madelaine is in immediate danger? Has she been accounted a traitor? Are there accusations laid against her?"

"I would have thought detention was danger enough," said Theron as sharply as he dared. "I know of no accusations, but it would not surprise me if some discontented peasants came forward to denounce her."

"Perhaps I should say it another way: what are the chances of Madelaine being imprisoned?" da San-Germain asked smoothly.

"I don't know. It depends on the Revolutionary Tribunal in Avignon." He took a handkerchief from his pocket and wiped his face. "At present they appear to be satisfied to keep her at Montalia."

"But they could change their minds, could they not?"

"Or they could shift her to another jurisdiction," said Theron. "That is the more likely, from what little I've learned."

"So I gathered," said San-Germain, and waited for Theron to explain.

"Avignon isn't as bad as Paris, or some other places," said Theron as soon as he recognized that da San-Germain wanted more information. "At least not yet," he added. "But if Avignon shifts her to another Revolutionary Court, there could be real trouble."

"So where she is held could change, and change quickly, couldn't it?" asked da San-Germain.

"I think so," said Theron, not wanting to be too alarming. "And the courts are already unreliable."

"Then we shall have to plan for the worst, and make all efforts to reach her sooner rather than later." He looked toward the shuttered windows. "If you would like to take your afternoon's repose here, there's a withdrawing room through that door. You would be most welcome to stay."

"Don't you want to know anything more?"

"Not at present, no," said da San-Germain. "I have much to

consider before we speak again. Enjoy my library while you're here. You may tell my staff what they may do for you—food, drink, a place to rest, a turn in the garden, whatever you would like." He offered Theron a slight bow, and went toward the door.

"Conte," Theron called after him. "What do you plan to do?"

"I don't know yet," said da San-Germain. "But it must be done speedily, whatever it may be. Otherwise we risk losing her to the Guillotine."

Theron shuddered. "I couldn't bear that." He glanced covertly at da San-Germain, and caught a look of anguish that vanished so quickly that he was unsure he had seen or only imagined it.

"I'll send out couriers today," da San-Germain said with calm determination. "I'll have to leave you for an hour or so while I attend to putting these missions in motion." He gestured to the well-laden shelves around him. "I hope you won't hesitate to explore what this room has to offer, today or any other day."

"That is most kind of you, Conte," said Theron, resuming his meal; then, sensing he had not said quite enough, added, "All your offers are gracious ones."

Da San-Germain gave a courtly nod, and stepped out into the corridor, closing the door at once, not wanting Theron to see the distress he felt. He leaned against the polished panel, the image of Madelaine shining in his mind: Madelaine as he had first seen her, in the autumn of 1743, before she came to his life the following year; Madelaine in Vienna in 1752, when he had been going from Praha to Athens and she had been a guest of Herzog von Brunn; in 1780 during a brief sojourn in Roma; and six years later in Trieste. "France is on fire, and it may be that Madelaine will be in danger of burning with the rest." Forcing such thoughts from his mind, he lengthened his stride once he was away from the library, he called for Roger, beckoning him to join him in his study. "And bring a fresh jar of ink. I'll need Giuliano to carry a message to Venezia for me."

"How soon?" Roger inquired.

"Immediately, or as soon as can be managed," da San-Germain

said as he shut the door and went to his desk. "He's to go to the Eclipse Trading Company and speak directly with Oddysio Lisson." He sat down, pulling three sheets of paper from the drawer; all bore his eclipse device in the upper center of the page. He selected a quill, trimmed it, and held his hand out for the bottle of fresh ink. As soon as he had opened it, he dipped in the nib and began to write, saying to Roger as he worked, speaking the language of the Byzantines, "I must find out how things stand for Eclipse Trading in France, and whom, among my factors, I may trust."

"This has to do with Madelaine?" Roger asked in the same tongue.

"It does."

"She is in danger?"

"Yes, and it will not lessen. I must find her and bring her out of the country." He signed and blotted the first sheet, then set to work on the second. "I want Giuliano to impress upon Lisson the urgency of this mission."

"I'll explain it to him," said Roger. "Unless you would prefer to do it yourself?"

"I rely upon you, old friend," said da San-Germain with a quick, one-sided smile.

Roger took the first letter and slipped it into his inner breast pocket. "Will you want the couriers to carry back replies?"

"Yes. I'll explain it all to Lisson as soon as this second note is done." He continued to write, his small, precise hand quite legible in spite of the haste in which he worked. "Give Giuliano money enough to spend a pleasant evening in Venezia, including sufficient funds for a good hotel, and enough to stable his horse in Mestre. I shall expect him back by tomorrow evening." After scratching his signature, he blotted the second sheet and began on the third; Roger took the note and folded it before putting in with the first. "If there are any problems, I want a full account of them from Lisson, and from Giuliano."

"Of course," said Roger.

"I'd like you to send Vittorio to Genova in the morning. I want to put the factor there on alert, in case Madelaine should need to leave from that port, though I doubt we will risk making for the south coast. I prefer the Swiss border, or the Italian one, if it can be arranged." Da San-Germain concentrated on his writing for more than a minute, then reached for a heavy envelope on which he wrote *Oddysio Lisson,* and said to Roger, "Giuliano knows where to find Eclipse Trading, doesn't he?"

"He does," Roger said, keeping his tone carefully neutral. "Are you worried about getting Madelaine out of France?"

"I am." He tucked the letter into the envelope, lit a candle, and brought out his sealing wax, working it in the candle's flame until it dropped a gobbet of red on the candle, making it sputter. The next splatter of wax sealed the envelope, and da San-Germain pressed his signet ring into it, leaving an impression of his eclipse behind. "Give it a moment, and then call for Giuliano."

"Which horse do you want him to use?" Roger showed no change of emotion, but there was a subtle shift in his stance, as if to hurry the message.

"The light bay. She has Barb blood and will not be as bothered by the heat as some of the others would be. He can remount coming back if he goes to Nino Baldalucci's stable." He tested the seal with his finger, then, satisfied it had cooled and set, he handed it to Roger. "There." He stood, glancing toward the window. "I know the day is hot, and it is hard time to take to the road, but it must be done. See that Giuliano has extra coins in his purse. When he returns, I'll give him an extra payment for his trouble."

"Should I tell him that?"

Da San-Germain shrugged. "If it will speed him on his way." He went to the door. "I need a little time to myself."

Roger nodded. "Where will you be?"

"I will go back to the laboratory for a short while, and then I'll rejoin Monsieur Theron in the library."

"You're troubled," Roger said.

"For good reason, I fear," da San-Germain answered as he turned and went off down the hall toward the stairs.

Text of a letter from Oddysio Lisson in Venezia to Ragoczy Ferenz, Conte da San-Germain, in Padova, carried by da San-Germain's courier and delivered thirty-nine hours after it was written.

> *To the esteemed Ragoczy Ferenz, Conte da San-Germain and owner of the Eclipse Trading Company, the faithful greetings of Oddysio Lisson, factor and manager of Eclipse Trading Company in Venezia, on this, the twenty-first day of July, 1792,*
>
> *My dear Conte,*
>
> *Yesterday evening, your messenger delivered your letter to me, and I will hasten to respond so that your courier may bear this back to you with all dispatch.*
>
> *By noon I will dispatch Salvatore Campo and Gabriello Donat to France, one to Avignon, and one to Lyon, according to your instructions. Both will carry the instructions entrusted to me by your courier, and both will obey them to the letter. If you should wish it, I can also send Aroldo San-Marino to Le Havre on the Silver Dawn, which sails for Barcelona, Lisbon, Le Havre, and Amsterdam in two days. It will take him some time to arrive, but he will be able to help secure you and your companions passage from that port if you require it, once he has dropped anchor there. I will also, as per your instructions, send you all reports I can gather on the situation in France, particularly in regard to the actions of the Revolutionary Courts and Tribunals, with special emphasis on the major cities, where the Revolution is being most keenly prosecuted.*
>
> *There are a few reports included with this letter, all*

obtained within the last week, one from Marseilles, one from Nantes, and one from the Swiss border where, I have been told, the Revolutionary Guard has reinforced their presence with a plan to stop those fleeing the country from crossing the frontier and getting beyond the reach of the Revolutionary Courts. If it should prove helpful, I can also send out paid agents to test the level of effectiveness these most recent reinforcements have achieved; there are three clerks in this office who would be delighted to have an adventure without sacrificing making a living. Although all of them long for excitement, none of the three has shown any sign of recklessness, which is to our advantage in this instance. You have but to tell me that you want them to undertake such a mission and I will have them away within a day of receiving your authorization.

Gian-Franco Montador, who handles all dispatches from this office, has vowed to devote himself to your endeavor; he has had an aunt in Holy Orders executed in Nice, and he has become adamantly opposed to the Revolution in France. You may repose complete confidence in his commitment to your enterprise.

On more ordinary concerns: the Curlew *has completed refitting and will be ready to take on cargo in five days. Marcantonio Giustin will be her capitan; he has signed his shares-agreement already and is putting together a crew. The* Stella Marina *is overdue, but being on so long a voyage as she is, the tardy arrival may mean nothing; other capitans have mentioned more severe storms than usual off the southeast coast of Africa; returning from China, Batavia, and India, as the* Stella Marina *is doing, could mean a month in port to avoid battling those storms. Capitan Ferran is a prudent man, not given to taking chances, so I do not feel any anxiety*

about his current absence. The Boreas *has returned
from South American ports; she will need some repairs,
but nothing significant. I will plan to have her away
again in three weeks, God willing and Capitan Deme-
trio d'Inccina recovered from his fever.*

    It is an honor to serve you, Conte,

Your most obedient
Oddysio Lisson
Factor and manager
Eclipse Trading Company in Venezia

3

"Would you really allow us to perform *Phaedre?* Racine's *Phaedre?*" Photine d'Auville stared at da San-Germain, her lovely pansy-
brown eyes theatrically wide, the beginning of a smile quivering
on her rose-bud lips; she shivered with expectancy. "Truly?" She
had just emerged from her mid-day meal in the dining room of the
guest-house, the first of her troupe to leave the table and return to
their platform in the garden; statuesque and luxuriously propor-
tioned, she was stunning. Even now, when in preparation for a brief
afternoon rehearsal, she had pulled her hair into a tawny knot on
her head, leaving her neck bare, she was enchanting, and she knew
it. The corsage of her violet Mosul-cotton dress sported a modified
standing ruff instead of a fichu, which showed her neck and shoulders to advantage, and offered a glimpse of the swell of her breasts.
The modified drape of her skirt was in the currently fashionable
Piedmontese silhouette, and moved with the occasional soft breath
of the warm summer wind that carried the scent of the fields and
vineyards beyond the walls of Padova. "Properly? In French? Not
commedia style?"

"Well, you are a tragedienne, aren't you? You know the courtly style—you were trained in it."

She beamed at him, her smile like a fanfare. "I've missed the classics. To get to do proper acting again . . . I can't begin to tell you."

His dark eyes brightened, relishing her delight. "The Universita would welcome the chance to see the play, and you have actors enough to do it." He came to the edge of the rehearsal-platform, leaning against it, his black swallow-tail coat showing no signs of padding, nor a trace of binding beneath the white linen of his shirt. His stocky, trim figure was at once handsomely turned out, yet without any signs of vanity in his bearing. "Could you do it in a week, or perhaps a little more, if you had the assurance of a proper theater and an audience? The Universita would like to have it done—"

"That would be difficult," Photine said, as quickly downcast as she had been elated.

"Why?" His question was not a challenge.

"We need sets and costumes as well as rehearsal, and all these things take time."

He nodded. "If you had seamstresses and carpenters and painters working for you, do you think you could do it? Could your troupe be ready?"

"If we have the opportunity to rehearse in the theater where we are to perform, yes," she said, then cocked her head. "Are you serious?"

A desultory breeze played with the cotton curtains framing the platform, heralding the arrival of afternoon. Da San-Germain offered her a suggestion of a bow. "I am. So are the Doni of the Universita."

There was a silence between them. "I'll have to ask my actors," Photine said, revealing her determination in the way she held herself. "May we have ten days to rehearse? A little more time would be helpful."

"If that is what you require." He was unperturbed at these requests; he gave her an appreciative smile. "Is there anything else?"

"I won't know until I speak with the troupe. Perhaps."

"Tell me what you decide, and I'll do my poor best to accommodate you," da San-Germain said urbanely, taking a step back from the platform. "I will inform the Doni when you have determined what you want to do."

She studied him, measuring his candor through narrowed eyes. "What would *you* like me to do?"

"Whatever serves you best," he said before he started through the garden toward the mansion. "Just bear in mind that the Universita would like it sooner rather than later."

"Da San-Germain!" Photine projected her voice, stopping him. "We'll do it! In ten days!"

Da San-Germain concealed a smile as he turned around to face her. "Thank you. I'll send word to the Universita." Then he resumed his stroll back to the terrace, knowing that by dusk, Photine would come to his withdrawing room for a private hour with him. Once on the terrace, he lingered, selecting a chair in the shade where he sat down to pass the afternoon riposino watching the sky as it slowly faded toward the hush just before sunset. It was a luxury, he thought, to have time to set his thoughts running back over all the centuries he had lived: there were thirty-nine of them, or very nearly. The first five of those centuries still had the capacity to make him wince at how he had lived then. Nineveh and Babylon were horrors—as had been many other periods in his extended life—but what happened after his centuries at the Temple of Imhotep at least had been the work of the living, and not of his doing. In the back of his mind was the image of Madelaine and the plea in her letter; his concern for her had become an undercurrent in his thoughts since Theron had brought the missive to him. He reviewed everything he had learned about the increasing violence in France, and knew he would soon have to have some viable plan in order to bring her safely out. As he considered the coming performance of *Phaedre*, the first framework of a plan began to take shape; he gave his thoughts free rein as the afternoon settled in over Padova. The stillness that marked the time of day was soothing, and da San-Germain felt a gentle pang that he was not able to enjoy the afternoon riposino as most of the residents of Padova did: napping was one of the many pleasures lost to him when his breathing life ended.

Finally, when the city had been bustling again for more than an hour, he rose and went into the ballroom, moving quickly through the mansion to his study, where he sat and wrote a note to Professore Don Gustavo Moroponte, informing him that Photine d'Auville and her company of players would need to rehearse in the theater where they were to perform. As he signed his current name, he briefly recalled all the others he had had. For almost a minute he was very still; then he folded the letter, sealed it with wax, and rang for one of his servants.

"This is to go to Professore Moroponte. His rooms are—"

"I know where they are," said Stagio, who had lived in Padova all his seventeen years, and whose father ran a tavern catering to students. "Do I wait for an answer or return at once?"

"If you would wait, it would be most useful, and would spare him having to send one of his students here later." Da San-Germain smiled briefly, holding out the letter to Stagio, along with a small silver coin.

"Certainly," said Stagio, taking the letter and the coin in hand and bowing slightly to da San-Germain before he strode purposefully from the room.

Da San-Germain got up from his writing table; there was a clamor of bells summoning the faithful to Vespers. Markets that had been opened since the end of the afternoon repose were now being closed for the night; the sounds from the streets and piazze changed, and the rhythm shifted to a more celebratory tempo, heralding a festive night. Standing by the window, da San-Germain listened to the din that was too chaotic for music, but too cadenced to be noise. When the sounds lessened, he closed the shutters on the windows and left the room, going to his withdrawing room, anticipating Photine's arrival.

His withdrawing room was elegant and comfortable at once,

with a low table of inlaid woods flanked by two sofas upholstered in heavy Chinese silk the color of pomegranates. Tall chandeliers holding over a dozen candles each stood on tables that flanked the fireplace—screened and empty at this time of year—and four sconces held more candles next to Venezian deeply beveled mirrors that enhanced the glow of the flames da San-Germain had ignited with a lucifer, its sulfurous odor dissipating rapidly; he took care not to look into the mirrors, which would not reveal his reflection, no matter how brightly the candles shone; even after more than three millennia, like crossing running water, the absence of his image in the glass left him with a sense of vertigo. When the sconce-candles were ablaze, he returned to the center of the room, trying to decide if the chandeliers ought also to be set alight as well, or if half-darkness would be more welcome. Finally, reminding himself that Photine was an actress, and used to the glare of footlights, he ignited the candles on the chandeliers, deciding that their brightness would be appreciated on this warm evening.

Stagio found him there a short while later and handed over Professore Moroponte's reply.

"He will show your players where they are to rehearse tomorrow morning," he informed da San-Germain.

"I will see they are there," da San-Germain said, and motioned the young man away, then glanced at the clock on the mantel: ten minutes past eight.

"He will meet them in the courtyard of the Universita, at nine of the clock," said Stagio from the doorway.

"Grazie," said da San-Germain, going to the clavichord in the corner and touching the keys abstractedly, his thoughts wandering.

Some fifteen minutes later Photine arrived, dressed more elegantly than she had been earlier that day. Her blue-and-white-striped taffeta skirts rustled as she burst into the room. "I apologize for being late, but it couldn't be helped." She sighed in exasperation. "I was handing out parts for *Phaedre* to my troupe, and there was some . . . some minor difficulty with the role assignments."

"Has it been settled?" da San-Germain asked, no trouble in his voice.

"At least for now, it has," she said, shaking her head. "Constance still wants a more important part, but . . . she isn't young enough for Aricia—Sibelle will play that part—but Constance doesn't like the role of Oenone; she says it isn't challenging enough for her, that it limits her, though she knows she's the only one of us suited to the role . . ." She let the words drift away, showing it was out of her hands for now.

"Constance is the one who takes care of your costumes, isn't she? A woman around forty?" He pictured the middle-aged woman with the long face and rangy body.

"The same. She usually takes the Mother, the Innkeeper's Wife, and Wise Woman roles. I've told her that Oenone is just such a role, but she doesn't agree. At least she's willing to let her daughter play Ismene, which makes matters a bit easier; she has great ambitions for Olympe, and Ismene is a good role for her, though at nineteen, she may find the subtlety of the role beyond her. I was able to convince Tereson to agree to play Panope, though she prefers to dance and mime than speak. She has stagefright, and often stammers." She came to his side, standing behind him while he continued to play, this time with more attention to his music than his musing. "What tune is that?"

"It's by Handel." He continued with the little minuet.

"I like it. It's a bit old-fashioned, but I like it." She leaned against his back, her breasts pressed to his head.

"So do I," he admitted, and said nothing more until the end of the piece.

She waited a moment after he had finished the air, then said, "You do play very well."

"Thank you. Music has been my solace for most of my life." He cast his mind back to the days in Egypt when he had first begun to learn to play. Then he had been taught by priests on the Egyptian harp, a skill he had maintained for more than eight centuries. Over the millennia he had mastered other instruments, and had taken to collecting them during the last several centuries of his life.

"It can be that," Photine agreed. "But it can stir other emotions as well."

"Of course," said da San-Germain, swinging around on the bench and wrapping his arms around her waist. "Of which were you thinking?"

She bent artfully and kissed his forehead, lingering just long enough to ensure his excitement. "You will have to discover that for yourself."

He eased her down onto his knee, holding her effortlessly. "Don't you think you might help me?"

"Certainly," she said to him, and kissed his mouth with determination and skill that gradually warmed to awakening passion. When she pulled back from him, she was breathing a little faster.

Da San-Germain traced the line of her cheek with one gentle finger. "What would you like me to explore first?"

She laughed softly but with eager anticipation. "Perhaps it might be best to get me out of my stays first? I don't want your fingers getting pinched." Reaching over her shoulders to the laces tied at the top of her bodice, she tugged the bow-knot undone and tugged at the laces to loosen them. "The corset—"

"I can deal with it," he assured her, pulling the lacing loose and then lifting the bodice over her head and tossing it onto the chair beside the clavichord. Deftly he worked at the heavier laces of her corset, using that activity to stroke her shoulders and back while he worked at separating the ends of the undergarment from neck to waist.

"It is sweet of you to do this," said Photine, playing with his silk neck-cloth; she hesitated to undo its knot. "Bayard thought it beneath him to—" As soon as she mentioned her former patron's last name, she went silent, hoping she had not made a dreadful gaffe; few men, she knew, liked to be reminded of their predecessors.

"If Bayard took no pleasure in removing your clothes, then he is a fool," said da San-Germain, feeling the laces release another notch lower; he continued to pull on them, making steady progress. "If you'll hold still, I'll have it off in a minute or two."

"You may do as you like, Conte." Feeling relief surge through her, to be replaced by a frisson of anticipation; pleasure-prickles rose along her arms and shoulders. Photine leaned down to kiss him again, holding his lips with her own until her breasts swung free of her corset's stays, revealing nipples and areolas slightly brightened with rouge. "There," she said, dragging the corset over her head, claiming the undergarment for herself so as to keep his attention on her body, not the clothing that covered it. "I can manage the skirt. At least I have no panniers to wrestle with." She deftly unhooked the skirt's waist-cords, and loosened the petticoats beneath, letting them drop, then stepping over them, now wearing gartered silk stockings and walking slippers of soft Florentine kid dyed dark-rose, with two leather flowers framing each tongue.

"The couch?" she suggested, bending to gather up her skirts, and moving around him to put them on the chair with her bodice.

"If that would please you," he said, getting to his feet and going to the couches. "Which would you prefer?"

She kicked off her slippers and came over to him, taking advantage of the light to make the most of her nudity; her breasts were opulent and high, her body showing her thirty-four years but trim enough to allow her to play ingenues some of the time. There was no self-consciousness about her, for she was used to being looked at, and she delighted in the effect her body had on men, especially men of quality who had not become corrupted by the lures of perversity. She glanced quickly at da San-Germain, trying to read his preference in his manner, but could discern nothing from him. After regarding the two couches, she shrugged. "They are the same."

He nodded to the one nearer the door. "The back of this one can be lowered. You might find it more comfor—"

Her eyes brightened. "What a good idea. You must have thought of it yourself." She reclined on the couch, making sure she displayed her body seductively while he operated a hidden lever that dropped the back, making the couch open on two sides. With a tantalizing smile she reached up to him, every subtlety of her gesture voluptuous and tantalizingly languid. "I don't suppose you're going to disrobe?"

"I'll remove my coat, if you like," he offered, and unfastened the buttons, then shrugged out of it, revealing that he wore no waistcoat.

Photine rolled slightly to make herself more comfortable and to display the curve of her waist to advantage. "I know you prefer to keep your clothes on, but I still don't see how you can satisfy yourself so . . . encumbered." There was a hint of inquiry in her observation, and she watched him with sharpened interest.

"You know how I do that: I find my satisfaction—all my satisfaction—in yours." He flicked the corner of her mouth with a gentle finger. "What gratification you achieve, I too, experience, no more and no less." He hung his coat over the arm of the other couch, then came around the table to sit beside her.

"I know that's what you told me," she said archly, holding out her arms to him. "But I have never known a man who made such a claim and then did not assert the right of penetration as his due."

"So you don't entirely believe me." He drew her up close to him, and again felt her ardor flare. "You think that I may yet demand—"

"Possession?" she ventured.

"I have no desire to master you, Photine: I want you to be free of all restraints and completely gratified when we're done. Don't you grasp that yet?"

"No; not entirely, though the two times we have met this way before, you have done nothing more than what you said you would do, and that is most remarkable. It is an unexpected benefit of your affections. And since you have been veracious with me, I will do what I have promised to do." She pressed her open mouth to his while she seized one of his hands and ran it over her flank and then between them so he could cup her breast. As she broke their embrace, she added, "I'm content as long as you are." There was a note of dubiety in her words that she could not entirely conceal.

"I'm content," he said before kissing the line of her brows and the lids of her eyes. "For now." He went across the bridge of her nose and along her cheekbone to the top of her jaw, bestowing swift kisses all the way.

"You are . . . very good at this," she whispered, stretching so that the whole of her torso pressed against his. She was warming to his touch in earnest now, and her flesh seemed more pliant under his small, expert hands.

He continued to kiss her, now her brow, now the corner of her mouth, now the place where ear and jaw created a sensuous hollow. His lips were light, as teasing as a feather; he was unhurried in his ministrations, matching his stimulation to hers, aware of every refinement of response she provided, and adding to her increasing ardor by evoking more pleasure with every exploration he made of her. Gradually she leaned back from their entangled arms, but only to give him greater access to her body. There was a slight flush on her face and neck, and it was spreading down to her breasts, obscuring the color already applied there. She laughed a little, with unstrained joy at what she knew was coming. "You know what pleasures me."

"I have some notion, but I believe that there is more within you that has not yet been touched." He fingered her nipple, turning the stiffening flesh gently, blowing softly on it while he rolled it between his thumb and first finger, taking care to give her only excitement, without any hint of pain.

"That's . . . delectable," she sighed, surprised that such little titillation could awaken so much desire.

"Then I'll do the same to the other," he said, and began on the other nipple, taking his time to be sure that she derived maximum pleasure from him.

"How . . . did you . . ." She inhaled sharply as she felt her entire body become more sensitive; now his touch radiated this stimulation through her so that when the tip of his tongue lightly brushed her nipple, it rippled along the pathways of excitement from her head to her toes, then began to gather in the cleft between her legs.

While he flicked at her breasts with his tongue, intensifying her fervor as well as the blush which now spread almost to her waist, he began to stroke her hips with long, languid motions that reached her knees. "You have exquisite physicality, Photine," he murmured as he caressed her thighs.

"You . . ." Whatever she was going to say was lost as a preliminary spasm trembled within her, and her body tightened in anticipation of her release.

"You needn't hold back on my account," he whispered.

"But you—"

"There's time for more," he pledged, and tenderly took her nipple in his mouth.

Her culmination shook, pulsing deep within her; she was unaware of the soft cries she made while he continued to fondle her. Gradually the rapture passed and she stared up at him. "How did you do that?"

"I did very little—this is your fulfillment." He took her hand and kissed her fingers, then turned it over and kissed her palm. "You were kind enough to share it with me."

"You took nothing for yourself, as you did on the previous occasions," she chided him with a lazy smile.

"Not yet. I told you there is more time." He leaned down and nuzzled her breasts, and heard her heart speed up again.

She closed her eyes and lay back, her body seeming to hum expectantly. "I'm willing to spend it any way you like." Through half-closed eyes she watched him, wondering what he would do next.

With gossamer caresses he began again to resume the honing of her passion, his lips following his hands along the contours of her body, never hurrying, never demanding, bringing forth the whole scope of her hedonism. She had never before felt as comprehensive a rousing as what she experienced now. At last he explored the soft folds between her legs, his ministrations kindling an abandon that would have surprised her had she not been consumed in the ecstasy that overwhelmed her as he enfolded her in his arms, his lips on her neck, his esurience finally luxuriating as the culmination of her own desires was accomplished.

Some little time later, Photine stretched, managed not to yawn, and looked up at da San-Germain, who was still sitting on the side of the couch. "I don't know how you did that, but I'm thrilled that you did."

"I did only what you enjoy," he told her as he tweaked a curling tendril of her tawny hair back into place.

"That you did," she said with deep satisfaction. "And nothing I dislike—except that you did not—" She made a gesture that mimed the act she meant. "I feel that I have deprived you of your release."

"You know that can't happen," he reminded her. "I lost that capacity many, many years ago. I have what you have, nothing more and nothing less."

She propped herself on her elbow. "But I'm afraid I'm cheating you." Before he could speak, she waved him to silence. "I know—you have what I have."

"Then I won't have to explain again," he said lightly.

"But you must understand that your . . . situation is very . . . unusual. I've never known any man who . . ."

He offered her a sad smile. "Remember, Photine; I am not quite a man."

"And you're not quite alive, either, or so you say," she countered, daunted by the sorrow in his enigmatic eyes. "But I find that hard to believe. Not a man!"

"No, I'm not." He slid a little nearer to her. "I hope this doesn't frighten you."

"Frighten me?" Her laughter was brittle, and she made herself stop. "I've faced audiences that would terrify an angel; you hold no dread for me. I am surprised that you should have to ask."

"Have you forgot what I told you?" His voice was soft, as if to spare her any dismay.

"I remember everything you've said." She caught his hand in hers. "You said that if we lie together more than five or six times I may become like you when I die, and would have to learn to live as you live. I have tried to believe you, but it isn't the sort of thing I expect to hear from a lover. It sounds . . . unreasonable."

"That's an interesting choice of words," he said, moving so that she could snuggle up against him, content as a kitten.

For a short while she seemed to doze, though her breathing made it apparent she was not asleep. Then she stretched languidly, opened her eyes, and said, "It must be wonderful to be an exile."

Startled, he asked, "Why do you say that?"

"Oh, just that you are not allied to anyone—not a lord, not a cleric, not a—"

"Patron?" he suggested.

She slapped his hand in playful remonstrance. "Or anyone else. No one has a call upon you, and you have no obligations beyond those of your own making. You can choose your own way, and be beholden to no one. You can go anywhere without care, you can be anyone you want to." She gazed wistfully at the distant window. "It must be lovely to be so free. I can't imagine the adventures you have had."

"Adventures," he echoed as he felt memories well in him, but said only, "It is easier to be free if one is rich, which, fortunately, at present, I am."

"A good thing for me, and my troupe, as well," she said, sounding a little disappointed for reasons he could not fathom. "And my troupe and I have work to do."

Realizing that she wanted to leave, he lifted her hand and kissed it before he rose. "Come. I'll help you dress."

"More a lady's maid than anyone in my troupe," she said. "I'm grateful. Trying to dress properly without any help is an ordeal."

"How do you mean?" he asked.

"Just tightening the laces requires tying oneself into a knot," she said, demonstrating the acrobatic posture needed for her to be able to tighten the laces of her corset. "The women trade off assisting one another to adjust their stays."

"Is that a satisfactory arrangement?" he asked, taking care not to sound too curious.

"We manage well enough most of the time," Photine said, being deliberately vague.

Da San-Germain came up behind her and took the undergarment in hand. "Let me do this for you; there's no need for you to tangle yourself so uncomfortably when I am here." With a few twitches, he settled the corset in place around her and began to pull the laces. "How tight do you want these?"

"Tight enough. I'll let you know." She stood straight to help him work. "That is tight at the waist, but not too tight. The same tension will do all the way up the laces."

"Very good," he said, continuing at his self-appointed task.

A minute or so later, she said, "You do this very well."

"Fashion makes demands: one learns to accommodate them." He thought of the extravagant body cosmetics of the Athenian youths in Socrates' day; of the elaborate wrappings of a formal toga in Imperial Rome; of the embroidered paragaudions of Byzantine fashions; of the stiffened silk caps of the professors at Lo-Yang, before Jenghiz Khan began his campaigns; of the complicated head-dresses of the Bohemians, five centuries ago; of the elaborate cart-wheel ruffs and jeweled cod-pieces of the Elizabethan court, two hundred years past; of the grand court clothing in the mud and mire of Sankt Piterburkh not quite a century ago . . . He tied the laces at the top of the corset and tucked the ends inside the undergarment. "There." He bent and kissed the nape of her neck. "Will that do you?"

"You accommodate more than I would have expected," she said archly as she bent awkwardly to gather up her petticoats and skirt, dragging the ties up to her waist and securing them quickly.

"What would you like me to do now?" he asked, regarding her with interest.

"That's very nice, but I would like you to lace my bodice, if you don't mind?" She found herself marveling at his accommodation; his response was all she wanted, appreciative and gallant.

He picked up her bodice and slipped it over her head. "Will this do?" He tugged on the laces to get her approval of his adjustment.

"A little tighter," she suggested, and stood still, feeling the bodice-back close over the laces of her corset.

"As you wish," he said, and complied.

When she felt him tuck in the bodice-laces, she swung around to face him, her thoughts no longer on the transports they had shared such a short while ago, but on the coming preparations for Racine's great tragedy. "So, Conte. Tomorrow we begin to prepare the *Phaedre*. Will you want to watch us rehearse? The first few days are not likely to be very interesting—more stage movements and working out the placements of the properties and scenery, but you're welcome to join us."

"I may," he said. "Unless you would prefer that I wait a day or two, when you are more familiar with how you will play it."

She leaned toward him to kiss his cheek. "I don't know how a man of your rank can be so understanding of our needs, but I thank you for it."

"You forget I'm an exile; you and I have more in common than you realize." He stepped back from her. "That, and your son is jealous of my attentions to you, I think."

She sighed. "Enee is young, but trying to be my protector and guardian. Don't think ill of him."

"I'll try not to, but I had best let you have some time with him; I don't want to encourage his rancor. As you say, he is young, and he has an exaggerated sense of his maturity." He took her hand and kissed it. "Best go out by the terrace door and through the garden. Your troupe will be wanting to see you."

"So they will," she said with a small, artistic sigh. "This has been a most astonishing hour."

"That it has," he told her with warmth in his dark eyes.

"I'm thankful to you for all you've done for me." She made a little curtsy. "Shall you want an account of our first rehearsal, since you won't attend?"

"Only if there's something you need me to address with the Universita," he replied, and reached for his coat, pulling it on as he walked beside her to the door of the withdrawing room.

"I trust your knowledge, and your good sense. You need not give me constant details of what transpires." He adjusted his neckcloth and collar, then opened the door for her. "I look forward to seeing you perform, Photine; you and all your troupe."

She gave him her most melting smile. "It will be a joy to play a classic again."

"Then I am delighted to have helped bring this about." He gave her a long, steady look. "You must tell me if the site is not to your liking."

"I will, but I have no doubt that all will be—" She stopped herself. "Time enough tomorrow for such talk. Now, I must hie myself back to my players so that we may read through our parts again before we have supper. You have a most generous cook, you know." Glancing at the sconces, she said, "A pity the mirrors are so small and deeply beveled. I can't see enough of my reflection to be certain my hair is in order."

"It isn't, quite," said da San-Germain, opening the door for her. "But there is a breeze that can account for it."

"Ha! If you believe that, you don't know how actors think," she said, and with a roguish wink, she was gone.

Da San-Germain bowed his head, listening to her departing footsteps and trying to discern how much of what they had shared was intimacy and how much was superb performance.

Text of a memorandum from Vivien Zacharie Charlot, Deputy Secretary of Public Safety of Lyon, to Jean-Claude Sauvier, Deputy for Public Safety of Dijon, carried by Revolutionary Guard couriers and delivered three days after it was written.

To Jean-Claude Sauvier, Deputy Secretary for Public Safety of Dijon, the fraternal greetings of Deputy Secretary for Public Safety of Lyon, Vivien Zacharie Charlot, on this, the 2ⁿᵈ day of August, 1792,

All hail the glorious Revolution!

My dear Deputy Secretary Sauvier,

It has come to the attention of our Revolutionary Court here in Lyon that many of the regional Revolutionary Courts have become overwhelmed with carrying out the people's business and can no longer mete out justice in a timely way. I am writing to you and to several other regional Revolutionary Courts to inform you that we at Lyon have the capacity to handle many more cases of suspicions that there may be those holding reactionary opinions, or protecting members of the nobility who deserve to be brought before the people to answer for their crimes, or those who have taken in the clergy in the misguided belief that these superstitious frauds will gain them access to heaven. We have thus far uncovered four groups who have harbored aristocrats, claiming that these enemies of the people were not exploiters and criminals, but sound landlords, worthy of respect and protection. They have paid the price for their stubbornness and folly.

If you have in your custody any who might fall within these categories, or who have demonstrated other criminal inclinations, and would want to have them dealt with with dispatch, I ask that you consider the offer of the Revolutionary Court of Lyon and send the accused, under appropriate guard, to us. You may rest assured that they will receive our full attention, and that their wrongs will be fully and quickly addressed in the name of the people.

We of Lyon are seeking to ease the burdens of those regional Revolutionary Courts that are unable to deal with these cases with vigor and speed, or who have not the facilities to hold the reactionary elements of the region, so that the aristocrats or religious may not, through the passage of months, come to be regarded as sympathetic figures, who could then be permitted to leave France without answering for the many abuses they have wrought upon their people. Here you may be sure we are intent on swift justice, and will not be swayed by sentiment, misguided piety, or inappropriate nostalgia.

This offer has been extended not only to you, but to the Revolutionary Courts of Grenoble, St-Etienne, Avignon, Clermont, Nevers, and Limoges; it is the hope of our tribunal that you will consider our offer and inform us of what you would want from us in this regard, and thus enable the work of the Revolutionary Courts to go forward. It is our duty to the people of France, who have for so long borne the weight of the aristocrats' feet upon their necks to see that the wrongs they have suffered for so long are redressed through the most effective prosecutions our Revolutionary Courts can provide, as well as the full satisfaction of the law, and to that end, we of Lyon seek to answer these demands. I most sincerely entreat you to allow us to augment your work for the glory of our Revolution.

Long live France.

Long live the Revolution.

Yours in justice,
Vivien Zacharie Charlot
Deputy Secretary of the Department of Public Safety
Lyon

4

Theron paused in his pacing down the library to regard da San-Germain with a mixture of worry and frustration. Finally he halted and burst out in French, "But how on earth do you think you can get into France? The borders are watched. There are agents of the Revolutionary Courts everywhere, and others, who want to gain the good opinion of the Revolutionary Courts. If they should discover you, you would be a danger to Madelaine, not a help. Then, both of you would pay the price for your high-handed audacity." He was dressed for the theater in clothes worthy of a diplomatic reception: his coat and knee-length britches were heavy black silk, his waistcoat, neck-cloth, and stockings were perfect white. Although there would be no ball that evening, he had donned dancing pumps, and carried an ebony walking-stick. His hair, newly cut, was combed into artless waves, giving him the currently fashionable wind-tossed look.

"Then I will have to take care not to be discovered for what I am, will I not? To that end, I have been speaking with men who were dispatched to France. Two of them have returned, and you may hear—after the play—what they have observed. They will bathe and dine while we attend the performance, and be ready to give us their thoughts when we return. If anything they say distresses you, you must say so, and I will take your reservations into account." Da San-Germain was as elegantly clothed as Theron, but his presence lent his appearance a quality of understated authority that commanded the attention of others. He had worn ruby instead of mother-of-pearl studs and cufflinks, and this small addition set him off as much as his manner did. "I know you will have questions for them, but I ask you to withhold them until we have their preliminary account of their travels." His French was almost flawless, if a trifle old-fashioned, and tinged by an accent that Theron had been unable to place.

"All very well and good," said Theron impatiently. "But what will you do with what they tell you?"

"Why, learn from it, and plan. We will need more than one way to get Madelaine safely out of France, in case the circumstances of her detention change, and we cannot wait until the hazards are upon us to decide what our options are, not if we are to succeed." He motioned to the tray of wine, cheese, pickled relish, and bread set out on the central table. "Have something to sustain you. This is going to be a long evening. You will want to have something to eat now, I think, rather than wait until supper after the play."

"Thinking about food and the theater! How can you care about such things when you know that Madelaine is in danger, and waiting for you to come?" His exasperation gave his words a sharpness that went beyond what was acceptable in polite company, but da San-Germain took no umbrage at his outburst.

"Whether or not you have something to eat, or you and I see *Phaedre,* will make no difference in Madelaine's situation this evening. If denying yourself the pleasures of life while you can savor them gives you some kind of satisfaction, then it seems to me that you've misunderstood much about Madelaine. Take what enjoyment you can while you may. You're not likely to have the chance to do so once we're on the road." He made an infinitesimal pause, then added, "That is, if you're still determined to come?"

"Of course I'll come. What kind of poltroon do you take me for?—not come!" His scorn was almost palpable, and he underscored it with an abrupt bow that bordered on contempt. "Grand merci."

"What I propose may not be to your liking," da San-Germain warned. "The risks are very real, and once begun, we will not have many opportunities for insouciance."

Theron rounded on him. "Then you *do* have something in mind."

"I trust I do, at least the beginning of an idea," said da

San-Germain. "I will know more once I speak with the men who were in France at my request. All I have from them at present is a cursory report. After I hear from them in greater detail, I'll put my full attention on the possible ways that we—"

"I want to hear what they have to say!"

"You may join us, of course, and listen to their reports," said da San-Germain, speaking as calmly as he could, attempting to rein in Theron's impulsivity. "But again, I implore you to let me ask the questions when we meet with these couriers." He chose his next words carefully. "You're an impetuous young man, and in your fervor to learn as much as possible, you may keep them from providing information that we can use. In your efforts to urge them to—"

"I'm not such a fool as that," said Theron, flushing.

Da San-Germain raised his fine brows; he said nothing but "May I pour you a glass of this excellent Lachrymae Christi?" He began filling a glass before Theron responded.

"You're a most perplexing fellow, Conte. I don't know what to make of you." He came to the low table and took the glass of wine da San-Germain held out to him.

Da San-Germain inclined his head. "As you say."

"Why does the Universita want a performance of *Phaedre* anyway?" He took the glass and tasted it. "Yes. Very good."

"A number of the professors are championing French culture, since so much of the populace in France appear to be bent on destroying it. Racine is as much out of favor as Molière and Corneille, and it is likely that it will be some time before the French rediscover them. So the Universita is seeking to preserve what they see as admirable in French achievements, and this is one of the ways in which they intend to do it." Da San-Germain indicated the tray. "Do help yourself, Heurer. My cook will be offended if you don't eat what he provides."

"And it wouldn't do for Giorgio to be offended, would it?" Theron finished the wine in his glass and reached for a wedge of cheese.

"Certainly not," said da San-Germain. He held out the wine

bottle and refilled Theron's glass. "Have you done any more work on your narrative poem?"

Theron realized that he could not ask anything more about Madelaine for the time being, and so he took a judicious sip and said, "Nothing that I like. It all comes out stilted."

"I see," said da San-Germain, to keep the young man talking.

"I've tried various ways to approach the work, but so far, it hasn't . . . been cohesive enough." He took a bite of the cheese, saying around it, "This is really excellent."

"I should hope so," said da San-Germain, watching Theron start to pace again.

Theron finished his wedge of cheese and tossed off the rest of the wine in his glass. "I keep wondering what's happened to her. She's been in the hands of the Revolutionary Guard for longer than I want to think about."

"She's a very capable woman. Don't underestimate her," da San-Germain said quietly.

"Capable she may be, but most of these men are monsters, without conscience and without honor," Theron declared. "What can she do against such men?"

"A great deal, if it should come to that," said da San-Germain, moving to claim the wine-glass. "If you have a little more food, you won't feel the wine so much."

"I'm not a green boy," Theron protested.

"Perhaps not," said da San-Germain, knowing that one of the reasons that Theron was so insistent was that he was afraid that a green boy was precisely what he was. "But you will be more comfortable for a bit more food. The carriage will be ready in twenty minutes, to take us to the theater; I need to have a word with Roger before we go."

"All right," said Theron, picking up a slice of bread and smearing it with pickled relish. "This should help stave off hunger-pangs."

"It should," said da San-Germain, setting down the glass again and motioning to the settee. "I'll return in a moment. Have another wedge of cheese, why don't you?" Without waiting for an

answer, he slipped out the door and went up the stairs to his laboratory, where he found Roger sorting out a number of jewels into
piles.

"Are you leaving for the theater?" Roger asked in Imperial Latin,
looking up from his task.

"Shortly. Heurer is chastising himself for planning an evening
of entertainment. He thinks that if Madelaine is in danger, we mustn't
indulge ourselves." He spoke in the same tongue, but with the hint
of a foreign accent that marked all his speech.

"Because of Madelaine? As if his self-denial will spare her?"
Roger ventured.

"What else?" Da San-Germain went to the window and stared
out at the dusk. "A clear night ahead."

"There are clouds in the west," Roger said, returning to his sorting. "The wind is picking up, as well."

"And we could have a storm late tonight. I know."

"Are you still planning to leave in three or four days?"

Da San-Germain pressed his lips together before answering.
"Unless I learn something from the couriers that would change the
situation, yes, that's my plan. So far, the players seem to be our most
prudent approach."

"Have you discussed it with Photine?"

"Not specifically, no; I plan to do so tomorrow, after she has
garnered well-deserved praise for *Phaedre,* and will be looking for
another project for her troupe. Until then, I will not have her full
attention," he admitted, then shook his head. "I don't know if she'll
agree to the plan when she learns what I have in mind. But the
couriers said that players are still welcome, at least those who do
Commedia del'Arte material and can set up in market-squares for
the people's entertainment."

"I think she might be eager to undertake something so daring,
and her troupe has done Commedia del'Arte," said Roger, a suggestion of amusement in his austere features. "It's as exciting as
anything that happens in the dramas she most admires."

"Perhaps. But the actors don't really die, even in the tragedies, and they might, if they come with me." He looked down the room at the athanor. "How much longer until the gold is ready?"

"Not quite an hour," said Roger, his steady answer concealing his increasing concern for da San-Germain. "If Photine, or her troupe, refuses to go, will you—"

"—still go myself? Of course, old friend." His smile came and went quickly. "You needn't have asked."

"Will you allow me to go with you?" Roger studied the jewels in his hand.

"I'd welcome you," da San-Germain assured him.

"And you will leave Dudone in charge here?"

The mention of the aging steward, Dudone Sassi, gave da San-Germain several seconds' consideration. "If he is willing; he may not be, not any longer. If he isn't, I suppose Abramo will have to run the household."

"Abramo," said Roger, doubt apparent in all his demeanor.

"You aren't sure about him," da San-Germain observed.

"No, I'm not. I don't know that Abramo will want to have so much responsibility, not with both of us gone from the house." There was only a flicker in Roger's faded-blue eyes, but it was enough to alert da San-Germain to the full range of his reservations about young, inexperienced Abramo Legno.

"Yes, he is a bit lazy, which may be because of his youth rather than a lacking in his character; he isn't completely feckless. He may find that he likes being in charge, and be willing to undertake the responsibilities of steward." He pulled a small box from his waistcoat pocket, removed a lucifer, and struck it, lighting a branch of candles near the door. "While I'm at the performance, if you'll think about how to deal with the steward and understeward, you and I will discuss it further, after Heurer and I have spoken with the couriers. Will that satisfy you?" He asked the last in Italian.

"Yes, my master, it will," said Roger. "I trust you'll enjoy the evening. From what I have heard, they will put on a fine performance."

"Thank you; I intend to." He opened the door. "You can still change your mind and come to the play."

Roger shook his head and cocked it toward the windows that overlooked the garden and the rehearsal platform. "I know it by heart already."

"Then I won't coax you," said da San-Germain, and went out of his laboratory, returning to the library, where he found Theron sitting on the couch, pouring himself another glass of wine; most of the cheese was gone. "We should be departing in a few minutes, Heurer. Do you have your cloak?"

"The night is so warm, it seems a pity to wear one," Theron said, putting the nearly empty wine-bottle back on the tray and picking up his lion-headed cane.

"There will be a breeze later, and perhaps rain; you'll want one then. Better to prepare for rain than to be completely off-guard." Da San-Germain expected no reply and got none; he went to the door and called out to Petronio, the night footman, "Will you fetch Signore Heurer's cloak, and mine, if you please?"

"At once, Signor' Conte," Petronio answered, and hurried off to the vestibule, pausing only to light the lamps of the entry hall.

Da San-Germain waited until Theron had finished his wine, then said, "Our cloaks are waiting, and the coach will be at the door in a few minutes."

"All right," said Theron, and got carefully to his feet, making an effort to show that he was not the least bit tipsy. "Lead the way, Conte." He followed da San-Germain out into the corridor, and along to the entry hall, where Petronio stood, two black-silk cloaks over his arm. One was lined in deep-red peau-de-soie, the other in pale-blue satin; Petronio fitted the red-lined cloak over da San-Germain's shoulders and handed the blue-lined one to Theron. Making a face, Theron swung his cloak around himself. "I'm ready."

"Then let us step outside, so we may not delay the coachman," said da San-Germain, and opened the door for them both.

Feo Guistino, the burly coachman, drew up the four gray Kladrubers as the two men came down the broad steps to the roadway. "Good evening, Conte, good evening Signore Heurer," he said as he signaled to the footman riding on the rear of the carriage. "Remo, the door for the gentlemen."

The footman was already opening the modified Berlin's door and letting down the steps. He ducked his head respectfully, and held the door open; as soon as da San-Germain and Theron were in the carriage, he put up the steps, secured the door, and climbed onto the back once again; Feo set the vehicle in motion, turning down the hill toward the bridge, the lanterns set at either side of the driving-box illuminating the street.

Ten minutes later, Feo drew in near the front of the Hall of the Muses, joining a line of carriages letting off playgoers. The piazza was busy with all manner of people—professors, lecturers, students, merchants and their wives, travelers, even a few priests— coming to see the great French version of a classic Greek drama; the piazza was crowded. More carriages came up behind da San-Germain's, jostling for a favorable place in the line and slowing progress to almost nothing.

"Feo," da San-Germain called out the window, "let us down here. You can turn around more easily here than at the entrance to the hall."

"We're nearly there," Feo shouted, then whistled to the team through his teeth.

"Which will be a short walk for us, and bring us there in two minutes, without you having to jostle in line," said da San-Germain. He reached to the door, opening the latch and letting down the stairs. "Come, Heurer."

"Right behind you, Conte," Theron declared, preparing to alight.

Belatedly Remo appeared at the door just as da San-Germain

stepped onto the paving stones. "I am here, Conte," he said as if to apologize for not tending to the door himself. He offered a half-bow, and held the door for Theron, closing up the coach so abruptly that the on-side wheeler tossed his head in disapproval.

"Return for us in two and a half hours," said da San-Germain to Feo. "Stay under the arcade if it's raining." He nodded once and strode toward the Hall of the Muses, Theron hurrying along beside him, for although da San-Germain was almost a head shorter than Theron, he moved more quickly.

"You've taken a box," said Theron, panting a little.

"Of course. It would offend Photine if I did not," da San-Germain said, a suggestion of amusement in his eyes.

"It will be a joy to hear French again," Theron confessed.

"And superb French, at that," said da San-Germain, reciting from memory.

> *"Pourquoi, trop jeune encor, ne putes-vous alors*
> *Entrer dans le vaisseau qui le mit sur nos bords?*
> *Par vous aurait peri le monstre de la Crete,*
> *Malgre tous les detours de sa vaste retraite."*

"Act two, scene five, I believe," said Theron, stepping into the loggia of the Hall of the Muses, where a group of musicians were playing, and more than fifty people were milling about, looking for friends, and discussing the play they were to hear.

Da San-Germain presented his tickets to the footman at the central door. "The central box, as you see."

"Will you want wine and—"

"No, thank you. My friend will want a cognac at the end of the second act." He handed the footman three silver coins. "For your good service."

The footman bowed and stepped out of the way so they could pass on to the marble staircase that would lead them to their reserved box.

"Kind of you, Conte, to order cognac for me."

Da San-Germain smiled at Theron. "Think nothing of it."

A lackey handed them a playbill, announcing the progression of acts and scenes, as well as the players and their roles.

Theseus: King of Athens . . . Crepin Sillondroit

Phaedre: Wife of Theseus . . . Photine d'Auville

Hyppolytus: Son of Theseus and his first wife, Antiope . . .
   Pascal Aube

Aricia: Princess of Athens . . . Sibelle Joyau

Oenone: Phaedre's personal body-servant . . . Constance
   Lacet

Theramenes: Hyppolytus' tutor . . . Valence Oiegris

Ismene: Aricia's friend . . . Olympe Lacet

Panope: Phaedre's waiting-woman . . . Tereson Fosse-
   grande

Guards . . . Hariot Cotesud, Lothaire Malfaire, Enee
   d'Auville

The summary of the action of the five acts of the play followed, both in French and Italian, with a short article by Professore Don Gustavo Moroponte on the history of Jean Racine and his work, with emphasis on *Phaedre*.

"Not bad, as far as it goes," said Theron as they entered the box, removed their cloaks, and took their seats next to the rail at the front of the box; beyond them the Hall of the Muses was brilliantly lit by numerous candles in three vast chandeliers and twenty sconces along the wall, each one blazing with a dozen lit tapers.

"Did you read it already?"

"I skimmed it," said Theron. "My Italian isn't advanced enough to give his work my full appreciation, and his French is too academic for my taste." He put down the playbill and adjusted himself near the front so that he could rest his elbows on the upholstered rail. "No curtains," he observed.

"The Church disapproves of curtains on theater boxes," said da San-Germain. "They claim it encourages licentious acts if curtains can be closed."

Theron shook his head. "What hypocrites." He glanced at da San-Germain. "Do we expect anyone to join us?"

"No," said da San-Germain.

"Then I can make myself comfortable," said Theron, stretching out his legs along the edge of the box.

The crowd in the theater grew larger and more boisterous as the playgoers made for their seats and boxes. It was slightly more than fifteen minutes later that the play began; as the audience hushed, the curtain rose, revealing Hyppolytus and Theramenes in a Greek colonnade, discussing the missing Theseus.

By the time the cognac was delivered to Theron at the end of the second act, the lackeys had replaced most of the tapers in the sconces and there were splashes of wax all through the theater; a few of the candles in the massive chandeliers had guttered, but not enough to darken the hall.

"What do you think of it so far?" da San-Germain asked Theron when the footman had left the box.

"It's better than I thought it would be," Theron said, unaware of the shock he had caused his host. "It's actually quite good."

Da San-Germain studied Theron's countenance, asking quietly, "Why did you expect something less . . . satisfactory?"

"Oh, you know . . . commedia players attempting Racine." He sipped at the cognac. "This is really fine. I wonder how they came by it?"

"Most gracious," said da San-Germain, a hint of irony in his words.

"Well, in these days, I know there may be problems with getting genuine cognac out of France—along with many other things, of course." He stared out at the curtain that concealed the activity on the stage, but the sound of hammers revealed the work going on. "They rehearsed thirteen days?"

"Yes."

"Then this is more impressive. Madame d'Auville is to be commended for what she has accomplished."

"I hope you will tell her that," said da San-Germain; chimes sounded for the third act.

"Three more acts to go," said Theron with satisfaction, his words underscored by a soft grumble of thunder.

At the end of the play, the audience applauded enthusiastically; each actor was greeted with hurled bouquets as well as cries for the last act to be repeated, accompanied by the first purr of rain.

Photine was beaming as she stepped to the edge of the stage to address the people who had seen the performance; speaking in Italian, she began, "You are too kind, all of you, and we are grateful to you for your attention." Her beautiful voice silenced the audience. "My players and I are thrilled to know that you have enjoyed this magnificent work of Racine's, which is dear to our hearts for its own sake, as well as a crown of the French theatre. Perhaps in future we will be invited to perform for you again?" This brought a loud cheer of support that blended with the increasing din of the breaking storm. "For now, we must leave the stage and return to our lives, as you must leave the hall and return to yours. We thank you for your generous reception, and we look forward to another evening with you in this splendid hall." She curtsied deeply and stepped back to join her troupe.

"Nicely done," Theron approved as the actors moved upstage and the curtains closed for the last time, accompanied by a low, thunderous growl from the waxing storm.

Da San-Germain said nothing as he donned his cloak and went out of the box to join the rest of the audience making for the exits; his face was thoughtful as he struck out for the loggia, looking for his modified Berlin in the crush of carriages clustered around the main entrance.

Feo, covered in a heavy coat of boiled wool, was waiting near the head of the line of carriages; Remo came off the rear of the Berlin, his hat dripping, to open the door and let down the steps as da San-Germain and Theron hurried up to them; Theron had pulled one side of his cloak up over his head; da San-Germain had not bothered.

"Take us back to the mansion," da San-Germain called out to the coachman as he settled onto the leather squabs, taking comfort in his native earth that lined both the floor and the upholstery of the vehicle, lessening the discomfort from the thrashing rain.

Theron sat back as the coach moved forward, their way brightened by the reflection of the lantern-lights on the pelting rain. "Quite a downpour," he observed; as thunder rattled the clouds, the team faltered, then resumed the slow trot through the streets. "I'm glad you didn't decide that we should walk to your mansion."

"I'll have to send Feo back to the hall, to bring the troupe home," said da San-Germain, more to himself than to Theron.

"They're actors. They must be used to enduring the weather," said Theron dismissively.

"It doesn't follow they should have to when relief is available." He glanced at Theron. "It will not interfere with our discussion with the couriers."

"I didn't mean that," said Theron, though it was obvious that was precisely what he meant; the rain increased, drumming on the sides of the coach so that it sounded as if the vehicle were a drum.

"Do not think unkindly of Photine's troupe, Theron. They may be the only way that Madelaine can leave France."

"And you'd trust them?" Theron was scandalized. "They're actors! They cannot be depended upon."

Da San-Germain regarded Theron for a long, silent moment, then said, "I will do you the courtesy of forgetting you said anything so uncharitable."

"Uncharitable?"

"If Photine and her troupe are willing to risk their lives for Madelaine's deliverance, then surely they deserve more esteem than you begrudge them." He spoke levelly, but there was a disquieting light in his enigmatic gaze.

Theron shifted on his seat and looked away from the Conte.

"You are placing too much trust in them, if you think they will do such a thing."

"I'm willing to rely on you, and you are a poet," da San-Germain pointed out.

"That's different. I love Madelaine." He straightened up, pulling his cloak more firmly about him.

"And you suppose that because the players don't know her, they will see no sense in trying to get her out of the country? You know they love drama, and what greater drama could there be than such a rescue?" He managed a self-deprecatory cough. "At least, that is the argument I intend to use with them when I address them tomorrow morning."

The coach swayed as it rounded a corner, and a small rivulet ran in at the edge of the door, spreading out between their feet.

"You believe they will accept your offer?" Theron moved enough to keep his feet from getting any wetter.

"I hope they will," said da San-Germain.

"Ha! You have reservations about them, as well!"

"Hardly reservations," said da San-Germain, and went on to explain, "I want those who would rather not join us to stay here in Padova. Our undertaking will be dangerous. No one will be forced to accompany us."

Theron thought this over. "If you're so certain that some of them will take this chance, then I look forward to you putting it to the test." He folded his arms and leaned away from the small trickle of water, retreating into silence until they arrived at da San-Germain's mansion and left the carriage for the snug warmth of the main hall.

"Do you want to wait on supper, and see the couriers first?" da San-Germain asked as they gave their cloaks to Petronio.

"If it is agreeable to you," said Theron, worried that he had offended his host.

"I have said that it is," da San-Germain reminded him with an urbane half-smile. "I'll ask Giorgio to keep your supper warm for you." He signaled to Petronio, and repeated his request. "Tell Giorgio Signore Heurer will dine with the players when they return." He ignored Theron's indignant exclamation as he went down the corridor toward the withdrawing room where the couriers waited.

Text of a letter of agreement between Ragoczy Ferenz, il Conte da San-Germain, and Photine Therese d'Auville, recorded in Padova on the 17th day of August, 1792.

> *On this day in the Palazzo Comunale di Padova, it is agreed between Ragoczy Ferenz, il Conte da San-Germain, a foreigner resident of Padova, and Photine Therese d'Auville, theatrical manager, French subject, to wit:*
>
> *That il Conte da San-Germain will pay the theater manager d'Auville the amount of two hundred louis d'or in order that theater manager d'Auville may prepare her troupe for a Commedia del'Arte tour of French cities, performing such works as il Conte da San-Germain should require of her company. That amount is a separate payment from the individual fees paid to the actors and other members of the company and is payable on the signing of this agreement, and which is counted and the full amount verified by the Treasurer of the Palazzo Comunale di Padova as a condition of this signing.*
>
> *That the tour specified herein shall commence no later than three days after this agreement is signed and registered; should the tour not commence in that time, Photine d'Auville will forfeit half her payment in gold, and will be denied patronage by il Conte da San-Germain.*
>
> *That il Conte da San-Germain shall accompany the tour, with his manservant, Roger, and the French poet, Theron Baptiste Heurer, who, along with il Conte*

da San-Germain, shall prepare texts and scenarios for the troupe to perform, and shall assist in such performances in any capacity designated appropriate by the theater manager and manager of the troupe, Photine Therese d'Auville.

That all charges and provisioning for il Conte da San-Germain, his manservant, and Theron Baptiste Heurer shall be borne by il Conte da San-Germain, as will any legal fees, taxes, duties, or other charges levied against any of these three.

That il Conte da San-Germain shall cover all expenses of the actual venture, including costumes, sets, properties, food for all the company, and such lodging as travel may require. He will also provide wagons, horses, feed, and a farrier for the tour, and for any legal fees, taxes, or tolls incurred on the tour.

That il Conte da San-Germain will provide a patronage to the troupe, on the completion of the tour, for five years that will include housing, meals, reasonable amounts for clothing, a stipend for usual expenses to all members of the company, rehearsal space, and such transportation as the troupe may require.

That the terms of this agreement may be redefined or canceled upon one week's notice by either party, at anytime of the tour, and that negotiation of modified terms at such time is mandatory. As long as the tour commences within the time designated herein above, the sum of two hundred louis d'or will not be diminished if this agreement is renegotiated in any way, but shall remain wholly the treasure of Photine Therese d'Auville; all other charges and expenses are subject to adjustment, modification, or cancellation upon mutual accord of the parties who are signatory to the agreement.

That this is the whole understanding of this agreement, that it does not violate the laws of the city or the

*Church, and is registered in the Palazzo Comunale as
such on this, the 17th day of August, 1792.*

*Enrico Euginio Albergese
Recording Clerk
Palazzo Comunale
Padova
(the official seal of the Recording Clerk)*

*Ragoczy Ferenz, il Conte da San-Germain
Photine Therese d'Auville
(his sigil, the eclipse)*

5

"It would probably be wisest to go into France from Switzerland,"
Gabriello Donat said to da San-Germain and Photine as they poured
over the unrolled map of western Europe on the trestle table in da
San-Germain's laboratory. "It's the long way around, I realize, for
where you want to go, but it's not as chanceful as the southern roads
are. Everyone I spoke to said the southern routes are the more dangerous, and slower. You'll be lucky to do more than seven leagues a
day, with the wagons and carts, and hardly more than ten riding with
remounts and without vehicles. Those entering France from any
Italian state are likely to be detained." He rubbed his eyes with his
thumb and forefinger, then sniffed noisily. "There is still great fear
among the Revolutionary Courts that the Church will send in spies
and priests to subvert the Revolution." He straightened up, blinking.

"Which supposition, I suspect, is well-founded," said da San-
Germain.

"It seems so; everyone's looking for priests, to inform on them
or to hide them, or both," said Donat, sighing; the afternoon was
turning hot, and he was still tired from his journey into France.

"From what I saw in Lyon, many strangers from Italy and Spain were hauled before the Revolutionary Court and accused of plotting with the Church against the Revolution. There's more of that kind of thing in the north than in the south. Marseilles simply disposes of anyone they don't like the look of, or so I was told; they imprison or kill them. Lyon goes through a sham of a trial before they kill you, unless you're an aristo or a religious, and all they do is a denouncement and a sentence." Because he was ruddy-haired and fair-skinned, as many from Venezia were, he had not been subjected to the kind of indignities that could lead to execution. "My German is convincing enough that I escaped notice."

"You were fortunate, if half the rumors are true," said Photine, her finger following the road from Verona into Switzerland. "If we go north and enter France from Switzerland, how hard would the journey be? How long might it take? This road looks like it could be difficult to traverse. Is it steep, or narrow?"

"In places it is both, but it is well enough traveled to demand maintenance, and should not be too arduous a journey." Donat rubbed his eyes again. "Your pardon, but they itch."

Da San-Germain gave him a quick scrutiny. "I have an ointment that should relieve you, if you will permit me to give it to you."

"Grazie," said Donat, with a flourish of his hand.

"The inns and monasteries along the way—are they still taking in travelers, or must we make other plans?" Photine asked.

"They are, at least until you cross into France; then you will be best served by finding a farmer or a village if you need a place to stay. Some of the smaller villages have inns still open, but you may prefer something less exposed. For you, your wagons should be shelter enough for you, and safer than the towns and cities."

"That seems ominous," said Photine, her face going pale.

"You're French, so you and your people shouldn't be in too much danger. And players are still very welcome in France, even in the cities, so long as the people like the performances and there are no official complaints." He sneezed suddenly, and pulled his handkerchief from his pocket to wipe his face and blow his nose.

"Campo said much the same thing the other night," da San-Germain remarked. "When you tendered your first reports, he said that many of the people don't look upon the executions as entertainment, though some do, but that many attend the killings so that they will be seen to support the actions of the Revolutionary Court. They're eager to be amused in other ways."

"That's what I saw, as well. Lyon is a bloody place these days—don't go there unless you must. The Revolutionary Court there is being vengeful, and those loyal to Paris are at odds with the Girondais. There are rumors that other Courts will be using Lyon's services to speed along the work of the Revolution, which is likely to mean more slaughter." Donat pointed to the road up the Rhone Valley. "There are places to stay along here, but there are many spies in the region, and some of the towns are said to be controlled by gangs, not true revolutionaries. I'd keep to the south, but not so far as Marseilles."

"We're bound for Provence," said Photine, studying the map. "I thought we would go from Padova to Verona, to Milano, to Torino, and from there, cross the French frontier on one of the three roads leading to Avignon. That is much closer to Montalia, isn't it, than going over the mountains into Switzerland, and then back south into Provence?"

"It is a short distance beyond Saint-Jacques-sur-Crete, which is east of Avignon," da San-Germain said as he pointed to the location on the map.

"There—you see? It is closer." Photine studied the map, her lower lip caught in her teeth as she thought. "It might also be faster still to go from Milano to Genova and along the coast, enter France at Nice, and take the road to Saint-Andre-les-Alpes. That could bring us quite near to Saint-Jacques-sur-Crete. It looks possible to me."

Donat shrugged. "Then you'd best talk to Campo. He went to Avignon; I was sent farther north." Donat wiped his eyes again.

"Wait a moment," said da San-Germain, and went down the room to an old red-lacquer chest. He took out a small jar and brought it back to Donat. "Put some of this on your eyelids. The itching should stop."

Donat took the jar, opened it, and smelled the ointment, then took a little of the substance onto his finger, closed his eyes, and smeared it on. "It feels . . . cool." He handed the jar back to da San-Germain, who screwed the lid back in place.

"It should do," said da San-Germain. "If you want more, you have only to ask."

"You're most . . . most considerate, Conte." He turned his attention to the map. "I went through Grenoble on my way to Lyon, and the place was in turmoil. There were many travelers seeking to leave France, and trying to reach Switzerland, or Italy, for that matter, and the officials in Grenoble are charged with the task of making sure no enemies of the French Revolution are allowed to escape. In France the people may be filled with Revolutionary zeal, but there are many who are afraid of what may become of them now that the Revolutionary Courts are meting out justice as they see fit. Everyone says that all that's needed is an envious neighbor to inform the Committees for Public Safety, and it's as good as a death sentence."

"Tell me, would it be safer to go through Switzerland and turn south, or enter France through Italy, and travel west? I have more remounts stabled on the northern road than the western one." Da San-Germain indicated the long road through the Maritime Alps. "Or should I ask Campo?"

Donat shifted uncomfortably, finally saying, "Yes. Ask Campo. He'll know better than I. All I have to offer is rumors for the south." He clicked his tongue. "Having your own horses along the way may speed your travel—it did mine." Then he blinked twice. "My eyes are improving. The itch is nearly gone. What did you give me, Conte?"

"The ointment is an anodyne mixture." It was one he had learned in China, more than twelve hundred years ago; he looked over at Photine. "So, what is your preference?"

She continued to stare at the map, saying as she did, "Well, if this Montalia estate is your goal, I think going to Torino and west toward Avignon would get us where you want to be more quickly than using the Swiss roads, although they're better, and probably safer. But there are hazards everywhere, aren't there? Would Savoie or Piedmont make a better point of entry, do you think?" Her face brightened. "If we come down from the north, we'll have more chances to perform, of course. There are more towns along the Rhone than in the mountains. It would mean inns and market-towns, which gives us more opportunities than camping in open fields."

"True enough," said da San-Germain. "And it is still my hope that we can leave tomorrow. What do you say?"

"The day after would be better. I realize now that we'll have to carry more than I thought we would. We may even need a fourth wagon." She beamed at him. "That's provided for in our agreement, isn't it?"

"It is," he said.

"Splendid," she declared. "A fourth wagon, with the necessary horses, driver, feed, and anything else that I can determine we may need."

Da San-Germain nodded, saying, "But we will have to leave early on that day. You understand that, don't you?"

She stood a little more stiffly. "I do grasp the terms of our agreement, Conte, and I know what I must do. Never doubt it, and never doubt that I will fulfill my obligations. But it would be injudicious of me not to take into account the conditions we will encounter, at least so far as we can determine them, and prepare accordingly."

"An excellent point," said da San-Germain. "Very well, you may have your fourth wagon and one extra day."

"Merci bien," said Photine with a slight curtsy.

Donat sneezed again. "Do you need me any longer, Conte, or may I—?" He gestured toward the door.

"You may go. And, if you would, ask Campo to come up." He watched Donat leave the laboratory, then said to Photine, "Are you willing to take the road to Avignon?"

"I believe we must," she said, still contemplating the map. "If time is pressing, we would do better to take the straighter course. I can see the advantage of going as far as Grenoble, to make ourselves known as entertainers and lessen any reservations about the company, but it would mean we wouldn't reach Provence until the autumn was upon us. For the sake of our mission, we should keep to the south. Unless," she went on in a more speculative manner, "what we learn from Campo informs us that that would be too dangerous."

"On that we are in accord," he said, moving to the other side of the table. How many times he had crossed from Italy to France, and France to Italy! How many different names had been used on borders that rarely remained the same for more than half a century! With a little shake of his head, he banished his memories, intent on choosing the most expedient road for them to travel, he put his attention on the map. "How are your preparations coming?"

She stepped back from the table. "Giorgio has been most helpful in our planning. He has provided us with cheese and sausage and pickles enough to feed us for a month, I think, and has given me a list of items to purchase as we travel."

"How practical of him. For you may yet tire of cheese and sausage and pickles, you know, and want a chicken or lamb," said da San-Germain, doing his best to decide what she expected him to say about their plans.

"Oh, we certainly will. And when that happens, you will purchase meals for us, or a goose or two for our cooking pots." She offered him a kind of smirk. "Do you intend for most of us to sleep in or under the wagons?"

"That will depend upon the weather. There are four drop-beds in three wagons, and we can bolt another two or three into the fourth wagon." He paused. "I can provide tents for up to eight, if that's necessary. In hot weather, the tents are more comfortable than the enclosed wagons are."

"That's so." She might have said more, but Salvatore Campo knocked on the door.

"Enter," da San-Germain called out.

Salvatore Campo came in promptly; he was brown-haired and blocky of build, with a large nose, big hands, and heavy brows that would one day be shaggy; he moved with a steadiness of purpose that gave him the same demeanor as many military men possessed. He nodded to da San-Germain, saying, "You wanted to see me, Conte?"

"I do. Madame d'Auville and I are trying to decide which way her commedia troupe should go into France; there are a great many options, and we must choose one by tomorrow. We will leave the day after." Da San-Germain saw Campo nod, and Photine offer a grateful smile. "We want as little fuss as possible, so we would like to know what you encountered on your trip to Avignon, what problems you observed, and what caught your attention." He put his hand on the map. "Anything you tell us will be most useful."

"Well," Campo said as he came over to the table to examine the map. "The coast road is dangerous—robbers and pirates and smugglers and who-knows-what in every bay and inlet. I spoke to three merchants who had been robbed on that road in the last two months. If you go that way, go well-armed."

"We're going here," said da San-Germain, putting his finger near the spot that marked Saint-Jacques-sur-Crete.

"Then, were it me who was making the trip, I'd go from Milano to Cuneo and take the road west from there, the one that goes through Barcelonnette. There's been some trouble in the region—peasant uprisings, for the most part—but that area of the mountains is so remote that there shouldn't be much to contend with, except the occasional robber, and you ought to be able to deal with such fellows. The people in the region are weary of fighting and might be glad of seeing a commedia troupe." He stood in thoughtful silence. "Two nights ago—I mentioned that the killing is increasing in Marseilles, didn't I? I'd stay away from there."

"You did, in your preliminary report," said da San-Germain.

"Thought so; I wasn't tired enough to forget that," Campo said. "The border will be the most risky place in your tour. The men at those posts have strict orders to stop all those who might be against the Revolution." He addressed Photine. "You will want something very captivating and new to perform, or they'll be likely to forbid you permission to enter France. It can be outrageous, maybe shocking, so long as it's new. Anything old-fashioned, no matter how trivial, or how grand, for that matter, is considered dangerous, or reactionary."

"My players aren't trivial," Photine announced.

"I didn't say they were." Campo pulled at his short beard. "But to many of the Revolutionary Guards, a clown could be seen as a subversive if he was too classical in his style: the same thing for actors playing courtly dramas." He coughed delicately. "I saw a juggler—an African—chased from the border-crossing by dogs. They said he was a spy because it was said that he'd performed for the Duc d'Orleans."

Da San-Germain was not surprised to hear this, but Photine was appalled. "How do you mean, chased by dogs?"

"You know: guard dogs, big ones. The Revolutionary Guards let them savage the juggler before calling them to order. The juggler lost a hand and an eye, they say." Campo shook his head. "Have something new to show the guards at the border or be prepared to be turned back. They will probably require you to perform without charge—you should expect many such demands. The Revolutionary Guards are not the only ones who expect favors from travelers."

"Would it be wiser to choose a smaller town for crossing than a big one?" da San-Germain inquired as if the answer were not especially significant.

"It depends," Campo answered after taking several seconds to frame his answer. "There are fewer guards at small crossings than larger ones, but they can be more peremptory than guards at more active stations."

"So tell me," Photine began archly, "if you were going to Saint-Jacques-sur-Crete, which way would you choose?"

"I would probably take one of the roads that goes from Cuneo to Avignon, and hope that the guards at the border are reasonable men. Or that you can bribe them handsomely. You will need to have money for that, or favors of other sorts." His grin was mirthless, his smoke-colored eyes cynical.

"Do you think that we would be able to get there in good time? Some of the mountain roads are in poor repair," da San-Germain observed.

"So they are," said Campo. "The same can be said for the main roads in these days." He rubbed the back of his neck as if easing strain. "Getting out might be more difficult than getting in. You'll want to use a different route out than the one you came in by."

"Why is that?" da San-Germain asked.

"The guards will be suspicious of a troupe of actors keeping to only one road coming and going, and that could mean being detained and questioned." He shook his head twice. "Find a different road out."

"Very well," said da San-Germain, and added to Photine, "You may get to perform in more places than you thought you would."

She curtsied, her face revealing only that she had heard. "Which way would you leave, Signore Campo?"

"I would depart by going to Digne, then following the Durance north until it reaches the Torino Road. There is a small garrison at Briançon, where you should have no trouble leaving the country. From there, it is simply a matter of following the road to Torino." He paused a moment. "You should be able to cover eight leagues a day, if all goes well, and the weather is with you. Otherwise, you will need to find a place to wait out storms and landslides."

"But Briançon is in the heart of the mountains," Photine exclaimed.

"My point, Madame," said Campo. "Most of those trying to escape France want to avoid the mountains, making instead for easy crossings and safe harbors, which is where the spies gather to find them, and where the Revolutionary Courts are most arbitrary." He put his hand on the map. "The mountain towns are isolated, and will be glad of your troupe coming to play for them; you should not encounter too many questions."

"Should not?" she echoed.

"There is always the chance that the mood of the people will change once more, and then, well, who can say?"

"Who, indeed," da San-Germain said quietly. He stared down at the map. "I can see the wisdom of your advice, Campo. I thank you for what you've said."

"And I thank you, as well," said Photine.

Campo ducked his head. "Pleased to be of service," he said automatically. "You've paid me very well."

This candid admission made Photine smile. "Truly," she said.

"If you will remain here in Padova until tomorrow, I'll increase your payment: we may need to consult you again," da San-Germain said to Campo. "For now, Donat may return to Venezia, if he wishes. Unless you'd rather travel together?"

"I'll stay until tomorrow," said Campo. "So will Donat, I'd guess."

"As you like. For now, leave us to determine our actions." Da San-Germain indicated the door. "Take your riposino; and when you waken this evening there will be a feast for you and the players."

"Grazie," said Campo, turning and leaving the room without any further comment.

The laboratory was silent for a few minutes while Photine studied the map, her brows drawn down in concentration. At last she raised her head and looked at da San-Germain. "Very well; we can agree on a plan, and an alternative." She touched the map. "It seems to me that going north would only serve to slow us down in reaching Montalia, so traveling to Cuneo and learning which road west is the one that is likely to be the least trouble is probably going to bring us to the place more quickly." She smiled in anticipation. "Would you agree?"

"I would," he said.

"Are you planning to take one of the couriers with us?" Photine asked. "In case we should need to get messages back to Padova or Venezia?"

"I hadn't thought of it, but it is a good notion," he said. "If either is willing to go."

"And what about the weather? Snow comes early in the mountains. Do you think we should prepare for snow as well as robbers and Revolutionary Guards?"

"If all goes well, we should be in Padova again before October is very old."

"Ah, but if all does not go well, Conte—what then?" She tapped the mountains on the map. "I wouldn't want the company to be stranded for the winter."

"Nor would I," da San-Germain agreed.

"So the southern route will be our choice, and if we are delayed, we will have to select another road for our return." She thought as the clock on the end of the trestle table chimed one. "Oh, dear. I'll be late for dinner, and Giorgio will be annoyed."

"You needn't linger on my account. Go eat. We can resume our planning when the riposino is over." He took her hand and kissed it. "You are being most diligent in your readying for travel."

"We've toured enough, my troupe and I, to know that preparations are necessary, and without having plans in place, there is much that can become—"

"Difficult?" he suggested. "Dangerous?"

"True hardships," she said, and moved away from the table. "Before I lie down for the afternoon, I'll speak to Feo about a fourth wagon, and all that must go with it, including a driver." She took a few seconds to show that she was considering possibilities. "Do you think you could spare Feo himself? He is a better coachman than Gualtiero."

Da San-Germain recognized this ploy as a performance, but he gave her an old-fashioned bow and said, "If it would ease your mind, then surely you must ask Feo if he is willing to come with us."

"I will," she said, and left the room in an admirable flurry of skirts and smiles.

Left to himself, da San-Germain went to the window, looking

out over the city with an expression of utter blankness; his thoughts were far away, following his memories of the roads they were deciding to travel. After ten minutes, he shook himself out of his recollections and went down the room to the banded chest under the window that looked south. He removed a key from an inset in the nearest and unlocked the chest, reached in, and drew out four sturdy leather bags with markings on them; although the bags were heavy, da San-Germain handled them as if they contained nothing more than chaff. As he gathered them together, they clinked as the gold coins inside shifted against one another. Once again he locked the chest, returned the key to its place, and closed all but two of the shutters to keep out the heat of the day. He could smell the rich aroma of Giorgio's household dinner, and for an instant regretted that he no longer had the capacity to consume such food. Stepping outside the laboratory, he locked the door and went quickly down the stairs to the ground floor, then out the study door and along to the stable, confident that all the household was at table, and the horses were all grazing in the field at the side of the garden.

The wide center aisle of the stable was just now filled with four wagons and two carts; new wheels leaned against all six vehicles, with leather straps around them to allow them to be secured to the cart or wagon for which they were made. The wagons were paneled and covered, each providing bunks inside for four or five people as well as cabinets and shelves to carry possessions and provisions. The larger cart was enclosed—and its floor lined in his native earth—the smaller one open, and it was to the larger cart that da San-Germain went. He climbed onto the driver's box, slipped back a slat in the footboard, and set the four sacks in the small space revealed; they fit with little room to spare. Satisfied, da San-Germain moved the slat back into place, got down from the box, and started back to the side-door he had used only a few minutes ago.

As he opened the latch, he heard a voice from inside exclaim, "If you come through, I have a pistol."

Da San-Germain stopped. "Dudone?"

The old steward gave a soft yelp. "Signor' Conte! What are you doing outside?" He flung the door open and stepped back, his pistol trembling in his hand.

"I have had a last look at the wagons and carts." He smiled sardonically.

"Oh. No, Conte," he said in sudden abashed confusion. "You have no need to explain to me. No need at all. Of course you do not. This is your mansion. I am your steward." He bowed in the old-fashioned manner. "Come inside. Prego."

"Grazie," said da San-Germain, closing the door behind him. "Put your pistol away and go along to your dinner."

"Si. Si." He bowed again. "A thousand apologies, Conte."

"None are necessary. It is a relief to know how diligent you are in protecting this place." He meant this as far as it went, but even saying such words brought him qualms: what would have happened if Dudone had fired?

"Il Conte is most generous, most forgiving." Dudone turned away, his face blank from chagrin.

"Think nothing of it." He moved away from the old man, wondering again if Dudone was still prepared to run the household in his absence. He cursed quietly, knowing that his visit to the stable would be common knowledge among his household by the time dinner was over, and that now he would have to keep watch in the stable through the night. He secured the outer door and went toward the front of the house, all the while musing on how Dudone came to be keeping guard in his study rather than sitting down to dinner with the rest of the household. He kept mulling over his concerns until he came to the library, where he found Theron taking his dinner on a tray while he read a three-hundred-fifty-year-old book of erotic lyrics written by a French bishop, his attention so rapt that he visibly jumped as da San-Germain came into the room.

"Comte," he exclaimed in French. "I thought you were upstairs." He closed the book and set it on the couch beside him.

"I was. Now I am here." He spoke in the same tongue as he looked around at the shelves. "I have been trying to make up my mind which books to take with me, so I'll have something to read."

"You've packed some books already," Theron said, reaching for his glass of Nebbiolo, and drinking most of it in two gulps.

"Those were of dramas, so we will have something to work with for the troupe," said da San-Germain. "Now I want something I can read for recreation, something to distract me. What would you recommend?"

"This is your library, Comte," said Theron.

"I gather I would do better with something not in French, something fairly new, and definitely not political." He strolled down the room, looking at the titles on the shelves. "Something in English?"

"Too many aristos are escaping to England," Theron said.

"So they are. Not English, then." He walked a little farther. "I have a book of Russian stories. Does anyone escape to Russia, do you know?"

"No one I've heard of," said Theron.

"Then Russian it shall be." He pulled the step-ladder near and climbed up, reaching for the top shelf, and taking down a pair of books in green-leather binding, their titles embossed in bold Cyrillic letters: *Tales of the East,* and *Tales of the West.* "These were printed in Sankt Piterburkh in 1724, among the first books to come out of the new publishing houses there."

"Then they're too valuable to take on such a journey as we're making," Theron said at once. "A pity."

Da San-Germain kept the books in his hand. "The value of books is in the reading, Heurer. As leather and paper and ink, they mean little unless they are read. That is their purpose." He thought of the thousands of books he had lost over the centuries, and of his own publishing houses, in Amsterdam, in Venezia, and in Copenhagen. "These will do very well," he declared. "Who knows? they may even inspire a play or two."

Theron shook his head and poured himself more wine.

* * *

Text of a letter from the Revolutionary Tribunal of Avignon and the Revolutionary Court of Avignon to Madelaine de Montalia at Montalia, delivered by Revolutionary Guard courier, five days after it was written.

> *To the woman known as Madelaine de Montalia, the summons of the Revolutionary Tribunal of Avignon: on this, the 21ˢᵗ day of August, 1792:*
>
> *Madame,*
>
> *It is the order of the Revolutionary Tribunal and the Revolutionary Court that you are now under arrest and must proceed at once, under armed Revolutionary Guard, to Avignon to stand before the Revolutionary Court to answer for your crimes. Any members of your household still remaining at Montalia are to be given pensions, livestock, and property before you leave, with copies of all grants witnessed by officers of the Revolutionary Guard and one person of known integrity living within three leagues of Montalia.*
>
> *You will be allowed to bring three changes of clothes, as well as such garments as cloaks and other outer wear as may be necessary for the journey. Also five sets of underclothes and two corsets in order that you may present a proper appearance before the Revolutionary Tribunal. One nightrail and one simple robe-des-chambre will be acceptable as well, so that no immodesty will result during your confinement. Two pair of shoes and two hats may also be brought. Such items for personal use as brushes and combs may be carried as well, but no patches or other cosmetics, no jewelry, and no scent will be allowed either for this journey or for any appearances before the Revolutionary Tribunal or the Revolutionary Court.*
>
> *Your failure to comply with any requirement listed*

*will be regarded as an act against the Revolution, and
result in an increasingly severe standard of detention.*

*Be aware, woman, that your crimes and the crimes
of your ancestors will be judged by the Revolutionary
Court and your punishment determined by testimony
of such witnesses as may appear before the Revolutionary Tribunal and the Revolutionary Court in Avignon.
Your trial may take up to fourteen months to com-
mence, so you will be granted time to send requests to
those you want to appear on your behalf to attend upon
our sessions. The testimony of your fellow-criminals
will not be accepted: any defense you offer must come
from those you have oppressed, and those you have
had in your household. All others will be turned away.*

Long live France!
Long live the Revolution!

Georges Marie Forcier
Senior Deputy Secretary for Public Safety in Avignon
Revolutionary Tribunal of Avignon

6

"How many houses do you own, Conte?" Photine marveled as their
train of wagons and carts pulled into a courtyard of a C-shaped
house not far from the old Roman amphitheater in Verona; she had
spent the last hour beside him on the driver's box of the larger cart,
her face sheltered from the sun by a wide-brimmed straw hat; as
they entered the city, she used it to wave at the guards, grinning in
admiration at the piazze and churches as they made their way
through the streets. Now she looked around in astonishment at the
vast old house that stood behind strong wooden gates which had

swung open on their approach and were now closing behind them. The afternoon light gave the stones a warm glow that made the house more inviting than forbidding, although she suspected that the place could be quite formidable under less sunny skies. She did her best not to appear overly impressed.

"A fair number," said da San-Germain as he pulled in the mules drawing the cart and raised his hand to Roger, who came hurrying across the courtyard to welcome him. "We made good time."

"You did. When I left this morning to come ahead, I thought I wouldn't see you until sunset. If then. Yet here you are, more than two hours before nightfall. Did you go on through the afternoon without a riposino?" Without waiting for an answer, he pointed to the archway leading to the back of the house. "The stable's that way. There are nine stalls, and two small paddocks for the remuda horses. The rest will have to be kept in line-stalls for the night, which should be mild, so they can cool off."

"Eighteen horses and six mules," Feo called down from the box of the largest wagon. "Are there grooms here, or must we attend to them ourselves?"

"Two grooms, one of them hired for our stay," Roger answered, and waved the company on through to the rear. "Those who aren't needed for unhitching and tending, come with me into the house."

"Should I go in?" Photine asked da San-Germain. "And the rest of the actors? Or do you need our help."

"Go in, if you would. Have your actors bring inside only the things they'll need for tonight and tomorrow; that will get us on our way in good time come morning."

"We're a commedia troupe," Photine said with a bit of sharpness in her voice. "We know how to manage touring. We'll sleep in haystacks, if we must, and be on the road before the farmers are awake."

"Of course," da San-Germain assured her. "My maladroit—"

"And mine," she countered quickly. "It has been a long day and we're both tired. I'll remind my troupe to treat this as if it were any stop for the night. Will that do?"

He gave her a quick smile. "So long as you tell them that there are comfortable beds for them, and a bath-house for later tonight. Go with Roger. I'll be in as soon as the cart is stowed and the mules are cared for." He held out his hand to help her down, and kissed her cheek as she set foot on the ground. "There are seven guest-rooms in the house. Some of the company will have to double up for the night."

"After the wagons, it will be luxury itself, sleeping in a proper bed, no matter if there are one or two of us in them," she said as she reached the cobbled courtyard. "I suppose there'll be food shortly?" She looked around and saw eight of her troupe getting out of their wagons, bags in their hands, moving slowly while they accustomed themselves to walking again. "We'll need a rehearsal this evening. I trust there is room for it."

"Yes; a meal is being readied now, and once you've dined, there will be time for rehearsal. Roger will show you the house. You may choose where you would like to practice; you can arrange with Roger who is to sleep where, and when you can bathe."

"We'll have a genial evening, by the sound of it; will you watch the rehearsal?" It was an impulsive offer, and she was startled to hear herself make it. "We're just starting out on Monsieur Heurer's scenario."

"I'd be delighted. I want to thank your players who drive for you for all they did today. They've done well."

"We will be pleased," said Photine.

"And perhaps your son will finally speak to me." He softened his remark with a smile.

She looked around, not comfortable speaking about her fifteen-year-old son. "Enee is a sulky boy just now, showing disrespect and very little courtesy to anyone. I try to give him his head when it's not too . . . He rarely likes men who like me; the more gentle-manly my admirers are, the more Enee resents them, so he sees you as very bad. Why, he's even jealous of Theron. I know I don't

have to ask you to be kind to him; you have been patience itself
with him."

"I have been, have I not?" he asked kindly, and was not surprised when she paid no attention.

"I know he's been . . . surly since we started traveling," Photine
admitted. "It's his way of telling me he's no longer a child." She gave
an eloquent shrug. "But he'll be more courteous once we begin to
do plays."

"So you've said."

"He keeps to himself most of the time, and I don't like to interfere. He no longer wants to delight his mother, for that would be a
concession he would not want to make. I want him to work out his
life for himself." She moved back, no longer wanting to talk about
Enee. "I'll go get my night-case and tell the others to do the same."

"Thank you. I'll join you directly." He lifted the reins and whistled to the pair of mules pulling the cart, guiding them toward the
archway; behind the cart came the spare mule, pulling on his lead
as if reluctant to go one step more. The wagons and the second cart
began to move off toward the arch as well. The passage echoed with
the sounds of hoofbeats and the creak of wagon wheels.

The rear courtyard was cobbled, taking up much of the space
between the back of the house and the stable. Two long drinking
troughs flanked the stable door, and to one side of the stable were
two fenced paddocks, with a solitary mare grazing in the nearer
one. The four household grooms were busy getting ready to sort
out the teams of horses and mules. Bits of straw littered the cobbles,
a visible testament to newly bedded stalls waiting inside.

Two grooms came running out of the stable to meet the wagons
and carts, calling out to the various drivers to enter the stable
through the door and line up for unhitching.

"Pascal! Hariot! Urbain!" Feo shouted out to his fellow wagon-
drivers as he caught the end of his whip and stowed it in its sheath.
"Follow me! Wagons first! Michau, you follow il Conte! Andiam'!"

A ragged line was formed; the wagons filled the center aisle
while the grooms and the drivers set about freeing their teams

from the wagons, and leading away the spare horses hitched to the rears of the wagons. A system of hanging hooks accommodated the harnesses and bridles. As soon as the horses were haltered their leads were tied to heavy iron rings in the pillars that lined the central aisle. Once the horses were ready to be groomed, the wagons were moved up, so that there was now room for the carts.

"A good stable, small as it is," Feo approved as he came down from his box and swaggered up to da San-Germain's cart. "The tack-room's that way?" he guessed, pointing to the door off to the right of the aisle.

"Thank you; and yes, that's the tack-room. Grain barrels are in the compartment beyond," said da San-Germain as he climbed down and went to lead the spare mule to the nearest pillar, where he secured the lead rope. "Would you hand me the stiff brush?"

Feo reached in the back of the cart and pulled out the small box of grooming supplies. "Here you are, Conte."

"Best get used to calling me Ragoczy; the title will be a problem in France," said da San-Germain.

"So it will," Feo said. "Better remind the troupe." He considered the name. "Ragoczy. Hungarian?"

"In a manner of speaking," said da San-Germain.

"I wondered where you were from." Feo moved aside so the pair of mules that pulled da San-Germain's cart could be taken in hand by the grooms.

"The eastern Carpathian Mountains," said da San-Germain, not mentioning that his people had left that land almost four thousand years ago.

"You're a long way from home, Ragoczy," said Feo.

"That is not uncommon for exiles; it tends to be part of the . . . the process," said da San-Germain as he began to brush the spare mule; five hundred years ago, he would have added something more ironic to his observation, but he no longer bothered to. By the time he was finished with the three mules associated with his cart, sunset was staining the western sky orange and pink, fading to lavender and tarnished silver. As he stepped out of the stable, he paused to look at the display, making note of the unusual intensity of the red band of light.

"Could mean wind tomorrow," said Feo as he came up to da San-Germain, joining him in the contemplation of the sky.

"It could," da San-Germain agreed.

"It will be what—three, four days to Milano?"

"Very likely, unless the troupe finds a place to perform." He glanced at Feo. "How likely do you think that will be?"

"Who knows? Ask Hariot, or Aloys, or Urbain—they're part of the troupe, they know what Photine is likely to do. The troupe is eager to perform, but it will delay us. Are you willing to change your plans?"

"If necessary."

"The troupe could become restive without a performance to test the new scenario," Feo said after a moment's consideration. "Ask Madame—"

"I realize that they want to perform. I was hoping for an outside opinion on what it could do to change our travel."

Feo sniffed, uncertain if this were a compliment or a slight; he glanced at da San-Germain from the tail of his eye and decided to answer. "They've got two plays ready, and the new one Heurer is writing for them, so they may decide it's time to test the audiences. There're Brescia, Villa Sole, San-Pellegrino, and Bergamo to pass through before we reach Milano, and it may please Madame to have her troupe practice in one of those places—or all of them." He chuckled. "Valence is expecting it will be all; he doesn't want to turn down any audience."

"I'd wager Milano is certain for a performance," said da San-Germain.

"Do you have a house in Milano, or will you put us up at an inn?"

"It will have to be an inn, I'm afraid," said da San-Germain.

"Then you'd better choose one near a piazza where the troupe can set up their stage, otherwise we'll have them traipsing through the streets in full mufti," said Feo, and strode past da San-Germain toward the rear door of the house. He paused before he went in. "Urbain and Pascal would like to be allowed to carry pistols. They're afraid of robbers."

"I'll consider it," said da San-Germain.

"Does that mean no or perhaps?" Feo asked, and ducked into the house.

Da San-Germain lingered a little longer, then followed Feo inside. He had turned down the corridor toward the main staircase when he heard Photine behind him. "Is anything wrong?" he asked as she bustled up to him.

"No. Not really. But something has occurred to me," she said, coming and taking him by the arm. "Where can we talk privately?"

"There is a withdrawing room a short distance down this corridor." He could sense only enthusiasm in her, with a small quiver of discomfort. "Has anything gone wrong?"

"Wrong? No, no, nothing like that. But there is something I must discuss with you before I broach the matter to the troupe." She went through the door he opened for her, and after a swift look around the withdrawing room, she came up to him, her eyes bright. "You recall what Campo told us? That the Revolutionary Guards are looking for the new, and the possibly outrageous?"

"Yes," he said neutrally.

"Well," she declared, "I've been thinking about that, and I believe I've hit upon an idea that could make a difference for us." She turned away from him, took three steps, and turned back. "I've hit upon a name for the troupe."

"A name?"

"Yes. Commedia del'Arte may sound much too old-fashioned to gain the approval of the border guard, but what if we were Commedia della Morte? It sounds not only like a troupe of actors, but one that has taken a new approach to playing. They won't look for Harlequin and Columbine in a troupe with such a name." Her smile was dazzling. "What do you think? It's outrageous, it's new, and it still identifies what we are."

Da San-Germain let the name roll around in his mind; finally he nodded to her. "It does have an outre charm."

"That's what I thought." She almost bounced with exuberance as she came up to him again. "Do you like it? Do you think the border guards will approve of us, with such a name?" She was speaking French now, and almost laughing.

"They may, at that," he told her. "But you will need material that justifies such a name, or it may work to your disadvantage."

"That's why I came to you first. Do you think you can work out scenarios for us that reflect the name? Nothing too grim, of course. The people of France have enough grim in their lives without our adding to it. But ironic, humorous scenarios would be effective, don't you see? Something that has figures in winding-sheets with skull faces for a kind of Greek chorus to scenes of the Old Regime's excesses. The Old Regime can be broad comedy, but the figures in winding-sheets should not be. Perhaps they shouldn't even speak."

He cocked his head. "I think I understand your intention here." He kissed her forehead. "And I think you may well be inspired, ma belle."

Her blush caught her unaware, and she strove to conceal her confusion. "Well, if the troupe endorses it, Commedia della Morte we will be, and to the devil with those who dislike it." She gave him an impulsive hug. "Thank you, thank you, Comt . . . Ragoczy. I'll leave you now, and I'll have a word with my troupe." She paused dramatically. "Oh, Urbain told me he doesn't want to go into France after all. Will you try to reason with him? Or persuade one of the others to take up his duties?"

"Very well," he said, and opened the door for her.

He left the room and continued on to the main staircase, climbing it swiftly but without obvious effort. The gallery along the western wall was fairly narrow but nothing too confining, and he was soon at the door of his private apartments, where, once inside, he took off his light-weight driving-coat and draped it over the back of a chair before opening the armoire to see what selection might be there.

Only three suits hung on the pegs inside: a black silken suit for formal occasions with a jewel-embroidered waistcoat and a white silk shirt; a woolen suit for winter, and a linen one for summer. He removed the linen suit and considered it. The coat was hammer-tailed, of a dark-burgundy shade, the unmentionables were black, the minimal waistcoat was ivory, and the shirt was white. He decided it would do for the next leg of their journey, so laid it out on the chest-of-drawers while he considered his undergarments. He had just chosen short underdrawers when Roger knocked at the door.

"Enter," said da San-Germain.

Roger did that. "The bath-house is heated, if you would like to bathe while the troupe dines."

Da San-Germain nodded. "You think of everything, old friend," he said.

"After so long, I should hope so," Roger responded with only a slight glint in his eyes revealing that he was partly jesting. "Do you want the driving-coat washed tonight?"

"If you would, please, and pack what I have in this"—he pointed to the armoire—"to add to the rest. I think I may need more clothes than we assumed when we set out," said da San-Germain, beginning to undress. "Is my robe in the bedroom?"

"I'll get it for you," said Roger, and went past da San-Germain into the ascetical bedroom that had a narrow bed atop a heavy chest that was filled with da San-Germain's native earth, a night-stand with a branch of three candles on it and a small pile of books, a pair of pegs for clothes where a heavy cotton robe hung, and a clothes-press. He took the robe and went back into the parlor. "Here it is."

"Thank you," said da San-Germain as he took off his shirt and added to the pile of coat and waistcoat on the chair. "Will you need another chest for the clothes?"

"I'll find one if I do," Roger assured him.

"Thank you," da San-Germain said, then asked, "Did Photine decide where they will rehearse?"

"In the great hall, of course. They've moved back the chairs and the carpets and marked out a space in chalk for their playing area; it's about the same size as their wagon-platform, so they can set up their actions without worrying about adjusting them later." Roger picked up the clothes da San-Germain had removed. "I'll have the lot washed tonight; there are ample clean in the wardrobe."

"Thank you. We'll have few enough chances to clean clothes between here and Montalia." He turned away from Roger as he stepped out of his unmentionables and underdrawers, then accepted the robe, pulled it on and belted it, then turned back to Roger. "I think we should invite the troupe and the drivers to bathe when they've eaten, don't you? They're as grimy from travel as we are."

"It seems a good notion," said Roger. "As you say, they're all dusty from the road." He pointed to the suit on the chest-of-drawers. "Would you like me to lay that out properly while you have your bath?"

"If you haven't other matters that need your attention," said da San-Germain, and started toward the door. "Oh, and will you see if we can spare a dozen white sheets?"

"What for?"

"For Photine's troupe, of course." He paused. "I'll explain later."

"Very well. I'll find out about the sheets," Roger promised da San-Germain as they left the parlor, Roger to go to the study to consult the house inventories, da San-Germain to go to the bath-house to spend half an hour soaking in warm, rosemary-scented water, his deep tub set in a restorative bed of his native earth.

By the time he had dried himself off and dressed once again, da San-Germain felt much restored; he went down to the great hall where the troupe was gathered, rehearsing a new scenario, one that had to do with a foolish master with a clever servant. Pascal Aube, in the role of the clever servant, Berrmont, was standing near the center of the room with his arms folded, his sides clutched in his right hand, glaring at Photine.

"It won't work. Not the way the scene is written. It doesn't play, not convincingly, and nothing I can do will change it. The words are wrong." He glanced at Theron. "Servants don't quote poetry, not that kind of poetry, not in this kind of play."

"But it shows how extraordinary he is," Theron said, rising from his chair at the end of the room. "He isn't the usual kind of servant. He *does* quote high-minded verse."

"But he's supposed to outwit his master, not out-quote him," Pascal insisted.

"He can do both," said Theron, defending his script.

Constance, who was repairing the seam on one of the knee-britches that would be needed for this play, looked up from her needlework and said, "Pascal's right. If he does any poetry, it better be scurrilous, or bawdy."

"But he's the hero!" Theron protested. "He should have nobility in his character."

"Oh, for Saint Jude!" Pascal burst out, and rounded on Crepin, who was playing his master. "What do you think? Does it make sense for me to wax lyrical when I'm trying to deceive you?"

Crepin thrust out his lower lip, then said, "Not in this context, no, it doesn't." He addressed Photine. "I think the poetry should be changed or eliminated." He sounded as solemn as a judge, and looked as dignified.

"Aha," Pascal said.

Theron came to the edge of the playing space now. "But that makes Berrmont a corrupting figure, not an instructive one, and then Chambertain becomes a dolt."

"Chambertain *is* a dolt!" Crepin said, throwing down his sides to make the point more forcefully.

"That he is," Pascal seconded.

"But he doesn't play that way," Crepin insisted, flinging one arm out. "He comes off as malevolent, manipulative."

"He's *blind,* that's the *point* of the scene," Theron said. "He's unaware of the greater world around him. That's the basis for the whole first act—his insensitivity to anything but his own desires! Can't you see?"

"Gentlemen." Photine held up her hands. "Enough. We won't settle this by posturing or explaining." She stepped into the playing area and picked up Crepin's sides, handing them back to him as she addressed the three men. "Obviously there is still work to do on this scene. Pascal, I want you to discuss the matter of the poetry with Monsieur Heurer. For now, we'll rehearse the scene with Sibelle and Enee." She clapped her hands. "Two chairs, and something for the arbor in which they meet."

Da San-Germain stepped up to help Hariot and Lothaire move the furniture. "I'm going to need to make myself useful," he said to Photine as she gave him a startled stare.

"But . . . a stagehand? We have Aloys for that."

"What else would you recommend?" he asked, putting the chair he carried down where Lothaire pointed. "You told me you wanted me to do more than drive the cart for you."

"I have another idea for you, one I think you'll enjoy," she said, looking at him seductively.

He was interested, but said cautiously, "I need to know what you have in mind."

She made a show of musing on an answer, then said, "You play several musical instruments, don't you? Could you play the lute or the fiddle, or something louder, between the scenes? I know you said you prefer not to appear on the stage, but I know music would help."

Da San-Germain nodded. "I can bring along three or four instruments that I keep in this house and you may choose which you wish me to play, and when." He pointed to a narrow ladder leaning up against the side of the fireplace. "Would that do for the arbor?"

"I should think it might," said Photine, "if it can stand alone."

"It has a support leg," said da San-Germain, going to get the ladder.

It was almost nine o'clock when Photine called a halt to their rehearsing. "We must leave early tomorrow. Those of you who want a bath, go now. The rest of you, take your sides and work on your lines. We must be ready to play in two days."

There was a general groan, although no one was surprised at this reminder. Constance stuffed her sewing materials back in the hamper next to her chair, and announced, "Women first to the bath. You men will have to let us use the water first."

Valence, who was the oldest member of the troupe, said, "Have mercy on my old bones," and pretended to hobble toward the door.

There was a ripple of laughter from the others, except for Enee, who sighed heavily and rolled his eyes upward.

"The water is heated, and will not go cold for two or three hours," said da San-Germain, not wanting to explain the Roman hypocaust he had had built into the floor of the bath-house a century before.

"The night is warm enough," said Crepin. "Very well, we defer to the women." He bowed extravagantly in the old style.

"Good," said Constance. "Olympe, girl. Come with me."

"Yes, Mother," she said with deceptive docility.

"There are towels for you all in the dressing room next to the bath," said da San-Germain. "Use them as wraps and wear them to your rooms when you are done. There are baskets for your clothing."

"My, you are thorough," said Photine archly.

Sibelle and Tereson joined the other women, glad their evening's work was at an end. The five women looked to da San-Germain for directions.

"Go down that corridor to the third door on your left; it is painted blue. It has a stout latch on it, not just the usual kind. Go through it and along the covered walkway to the bath-house. It isn't far, just to the end of the garden." He motioned to the actors. "You men can wait three-quarters of an hour to bathe, can't you? I'll have my staff open a couple bottles of wine for you while you wait."

"In that case, certainly, we will be glad to let the women go first," said Valence for them all.

"Then come, ladies," said Photine, leading the women toward the corridor that led to the bath-house.

"So what do you think of the play I've written? Does it strike the right note?" Theron asked da San-Germain once the women were gone and the men were moving the carpet and furniture back into place. "Are you as bewildered as the rest are, or do you understand what I am attempting to do in the scenes?"

"I only heard a little of it," said da San-Germain.

"But you have read some of the pages already," he persisted. "What do you think of Aube's objections to his lines?"

"I'd have to see the whole of the scene acted in order to have any useful opinion," da San-Germain said in the same level tone.

Theron shook his head. "It won't do. You can't dodge the issue forever. You're the patron of this troupe—surely you have some say in what they perform?"

"I have made suggestions, but no demands," he responded quietly. "It isn't my place to tell them what to do, or how they are to do it. It is for me to make their performances possible."

"But it is for you to say what they are to play. It *is*. You're paying for them, you're supplying their wants. That gives you the right to require certain things of them." He glowered at the men of the troupe who had taken advantage of the moment to sit down together and go through lines, all of them speaking in undervoices.

"But, Theron, think. These men and women have worked together for six years. They know their strengths and weaknesses, and they have a responsibility to one another to support their work. They also know what their audiences prefer, and how to perform for them. I know very little of these matters." He saw the mulish disappointment in Theron's face. "Given their long experience together, you might want to take some time to consider what they recommend. It may be that what you have written isn't right for them, as they know themselves as players. Another troupe might view the work differently, but for now, at least weigh their comments before you refuse to change anything. I think you will find it will be worth your while." He moved away from Theron, privately doubting that he would willingly alter so much as a preposition.

Roger found him a short while later in the withdrawing room. "The women have left the bath. Should I prepare a withdrawing room for you and Madame, my master?"

"No," said da San-Germain. "She said she has much to do to-night. So I'll go along to the Inn of the Two Swans in an hour or so. The landlord's widow will have a pleasant dream, and I will be nourished for a time."

"And when will you return?"

"Before dawn. We will want to be moving by sunrise," da San-Germain said. "If you'll set out my driving-coat—assuming it's dry by then—I would appreciate it."

"As you wish. What would you like to wear?" He regarded da San-Germain for several seconds. "I assume you'll want something less grand for the road?"

"You're right. I'd like my canvas britches and riding boots, a cotton shirt, and a skirted coat. I believe there is one packed in my traveling case."

"You may depend upon me," said Roger.

"I know, old friend; and for that I cannot thank you sufficiently." For an instant there was a loneliness in his face that was shattering; then the look was gone, replaced by an urbane half-smile and a slight nod.

Roger concealed a sigh. "Which gate do you plan to use?"

"To visit the widow in her sleep? The side-gate: it attracts much less attention than the front." He caught the quick frown that flickered over Roger's features. "Don't fret over me; we both know that this is a sensible decision."

With more sharpness than he usually displayed, Roger said, "Which decision? spending the night with the widow, or going into France to bring out Madelaine?"

Da San-Germain offered him a gentle smile. "Why, both, old friend; both."

Text of a letter from Menaleo Podesta, Administrator of Markets for Cuneo, granting Photine d'Auville and her troupe the right to perform in the central piazza of the town.

To the leader of the Commedia del'Arte troupe, Madame Photine d'Auville, on this, the 29th day of August, 1792,

   My dear Madame d'Auville,

   For a consideration of two ounces of gold, your troupe is granted the permission of the Console della Citta and the Console del'Artei as well as the Console del Mercati to offer three performances of Commedia del'Arte plays to be performed in the Piazza San Giovanni Maggiore on the 31st day of August and the 1st day of September, 1792. You will have from two of the clock until four of the clock in the afternoon to complete your performance. All profit from such performances to be shared with the Console del Mercati at the rate of 40% for the Console, 60% for the troupe. Failure to comply with these terms will result in confiscation of all vehicles and dray animals of the troupe and a fine of five ounces of gold.

Menaleo Podesta
Administrator of Markets
Cuneo
(the civic seal of Cuneo)

7

"We will reach the frontier tomorrow, barring accidents or mishaps," said Roger as he rode into the camp the troupe had made for the night in a narrow valley just off the road; the mountains around them loomed black in the purple of twilight. Nearby a stream gurgled, and in the distance there was the sound of chanting coming from the convent of Sainte-Leatrice-des-les-Etoiles, where nuns spoke only to pray or sing the Hours.

"Then three days to Montalia," said da San-Germain, coming

away from the tethered horses and mules, now munching on hay, most with pails of water next to the food he had given them. "If we encounter no delays."

Photine, who had for the last hour been supervising the preparation of dinner over the fire, abandoned the four spitted ducks and the kettle of squashes, onions, and kale, and came to his side. "We've all been talking, my troupe and I, and I have a question I have to put to you: this relative of yours we're going to take into our troupe—I probably should have asked these things before, but there were so many other things to consider that . . ." She shrugged. "Can she do anything useful to us once we have her with us? She'll be more readily concealed if she can perform. Does she sing? Can she recite? Does she dance? I've been thinking about it, and I've decided that the more she can be like us, the easier she'll be to get out of the country. But that depends on her having some kind of talent."

"You'll have to ask Madelaine what she can do that might suit you. I know she can dance, and she plays the harpsichord reasonably well," said da San-Germain, careful not to praise Madelaine too much to Photine, who was already showing signs of having second thoughts about their mission. "You will know better than I what use she can be to you and your troupe."

"Um," said Photine, imbuing that sound with complex meaning, most of it expressing doubts and reservations.

From the cooking-fire came a sudden burst of laughter, and Pascal called out, "Tomorrow we buy ham from a farmer, or I'll—"

"Hunt rabbits," said Constance, unimpressed.

"Then we'll *all* hunt for rabbits," said Sibelle with a broad wink at Pascal.

Photine paid no attention to the badinage among her troupe as she continued to speak earnestly to da San-Germain. "I've already asked Heurer about her, and he tells me she is a paragon, which she may be, but that's not important to us if it doesn't include skills we need." She gave da San-Germain a challenging look.

"She does know a great deal about ancient peoples," Roger

remarked as if praising a niece or a prize pupil. "She can advise Heurer on writing scenarios based on vanished civilizations. She and the poet are already . . . close."

"Um-m," said Photine, giving this itterance a more dramatic reading than her simple *um* had received. She had wrapped a shawl around her shoulders and now she knotted it in place, for although the days were harvest-hot, the nights were cooler now, and here in the mountains, there was a sharp wind that picked up after nightfall.

"On a more practical level, she can sew, and make lace," said da San-Germain. "She can follow maps. She can drive a wagon. With Urbain leaving soon, and perhaps Michau as well, you may find her skill in handling a team useful. Lothaire will be glad of having an extra driver when his shoulder pains him."

"You can follow maps," Photine pointed out. "And you drive a cart; no doubt you can drive a wagon as well."

"So I do; but it might help to have two of us with the ability to use maps, in case there is something that separates some of our numbers from the rest. We should agree on places we can meet later if such a thing should happen." He looked steadily at Photine; she was almost as tall as he, and she knew how to use her height with most men; she realized that da San-Germain was not impressed by her efforts, and was about to make a new attempt at demonstrating her command, when he went on with unruffled calm, "You have nothing to fear from her, Photine."

"No, of course not. Only that she could get us all killed if she's discovered," said Photine with a disapproving sniff to restore her dignity as she laid her hand on da San-Germain's arm in a conciliatory gesture, her demeanor a careful blend of affronted pride and apology. "But never mind that now. We'll deal with that if we have to."

Enee came over to his mother, and without looking directly at her, asked, "Heurer and Crepin want to know if we're going to rehearse after supper?"

"It would be fitting, I suppose; better to do it here than where we have Revolutionary Guards watching us," said Photine, a last, critical glance directed at da San-Germain before she went back to the fire and cooking.

"She may yet be a problem," said Roger in Russian, watching Photine.

"She may," da San-Germain agreed in the same tongue.

"It's jealousy," said Roger. "The same as Heurer has. And Enee."

"I am cognizant of it," said da San-Germain, sounding world-weary. "Which is one of the reasons I'll spend part of tomorrow night with Photine. Her anxiety isn't for herself alone, old friend: she is afraid that once we have Madelaine safely across the frontier, I'll abandon the troupe, and her, though I have assured her that I won't. Photine is worried for all her company, thinking that Madelaine will leave us all exposed to official retribution, and she's not without grounds for such anxiety. But I have more immediate matters occupying my mind in her regard: what troubles me is that tomorrow night will be her fifth time with me, and I need to make sure she understands the risk she runs if we continue to a sixth time."

"Or a seventh, or eighth," said Roger.

"Yes, or more."

"I thought you'd explained the hazards before we left Padova," said Roger, unable to conceal his surprise.

"I did. But I don't know whether or not she believed me; she has told me she understands what she can become, and that it's of little consequence to her, which may mean that the thought of becoming a vampire has no dread for her, or that she doesn't believe that it can happen. She may think that my cautions are an eccentricity of mine, a kind illusion in which I indulge, or a way to account for my impotence. Ordinarily I can sense the difference with those I love, but not with her—she is often so caught up in the dramatic that I can't determine if she is giving me a true response or a fine performance." He stood still, watching Photine turning the spit while the ducks' skin crackled and spat hot fat into the fire, noticing how every gesture was practiced and skilled. "She may understand what I've told her, but she may not, or she may believe it as she believes she is Phaedre when she is performing Racine. Her performance would make it seem she is Phaedre, but she knows she is speaking memorized words and is recreating a tale that is many centuries old."

"Do you imagine you can convince her that the risk she runs is genuine?" Roger frowned slightly, trying to conceal his concern.

"I would like to think so," said da San-Germain, and added in French, "It is for her benefit that she understands me, and knows what will become of her after her life is over if she changes to one of my blood."

Roger nodded, and shook his head as Lothaire burst into song, recounting the story of what the widow found in the bird's nest that pleased her so much; the others laughed and applauded as he carried on. "Shall I broach another half-barrel of wine? We have enough to spare a cask of the Tuscan red."

"You might as well. They'll be glad of it, and, as you say, so far, we have ample," said da San-Germain.

Roger nodded and went to the rear of the larger cart to pull out the cask, shouting as he did, "To make supper heartier."

This was greeted with a ragged cheer and whoops of approval as the troupers scrambled to find their cups. Aloys brought out a pair of small hurdles and set them up so that the cask could stand upon the plank he laid between them.

"You can have as much as your leader allows you," Roger announced as he set the cask on the hurdle. "Just remember, we travel early in the morning, and you will need to be alert."

"We can appear alert," called out Pascal. "We've all done it before." He added a ripe chuckle.

"You'll be driving in the morning," Photine reminded him sharply. "You will have to be clear-headed."

Pascal threw up his hands in a gesture of surrender. "Very well. Two cups and I'll go to my bunk."

Roger knocked the wax seal off the spigot on the barrel. "Line up with your cups."

Enee shoved himself to the front, glaring at Roger as if to dare him to refuse to pour him a cup. "The Conte is a generous master."

"Ragoczy," Feo corrected him. "No titles in France."

"Remember, tomorrow night, we sleep in France, and we'll all be equals, free from oppression," Constance exclaimed as Enee took his wine and moved away; she beamed as she had her cup filled with wine. "To the glorious Revolution. May none of us die because of it." She gave a little curtsy as her toast met with hollars of approval.

"So you must tell me," said Feo, stepping up as Constance went back to her place at the side of the wagon where a lowered side served as a dinner table, "have you and Madame settled on a route out of France yet?"

"Not fixedly, no. We will have to see how things stand once we reach Montalia," said Roger.

"A wise precaution," Feo remarked with a slow smile. "We don't know yet what we'll find, do we?"

Roger motioned him on, and began to fill Crepin's cup.

By the time the troupe had all got wine, Enee had come back for more, while the rest of the company took up their bowls for the vegetable stew and slices of duck, to be accompanied by wedges of firm white cheese that Tereson was cutting out of the substantial wheel.

Theron was sitting on the step on the rear of the smaller cart, apart from the actors, his dinner-bowl in his hands, his cup of wine balanced next to him within reach on the step. His eyes were distant and he dawdled over his food, putting his attention on the revised scenarios he had been working on for the last five days; occasionally he nodded to himself, or frowned. He was clearly fatigued, his shoulders drooping, his clothing still in disorder from their long hours on the road. He half-rose as da San-Germain came up to him, then sagged back onto the step. "I haven't managed to work out the first transition yet, or even the best way to present it, if that's what's on your mind," he said.

"It isn't, but tell me why the First Corpse's appearance is so difficult; there must be a change you could make to . . . to ease it. Your other transitions seem to go well enough." Da San-Germain leaned against the cart, hoping to make the young man feel more comfortable than he seemed to be.

"I haven't thought of why the First Corpse should appear at all: what brings him forth? Why is it evoked, and by whom? The later ones are easy—they are the dead from the previous scenes, but the first one: where does it come from? Who is it? What is its purpose in coming? Does it seek to warn, or does it symbolize death itself? I can't work it out." He shook his head and spooned out a chunk of squash, blew on it, and began to eat.

"Perhaps the First Corpse is allegorical?" da San-Germain suggested.

"It's possible, but an allegory for what?" Theron asked, frustration in every lineament of his body.

"A figure representing the Old Regime?"

"That is one hypothesis," said Theron dully. "The stew's not bad."

"Tell Photine," da San-Germain recommended.

He shook his head. "She'll claim I'm trying to flatter her."

"Tell her anyway," da San-Germain said.

Theron cast him a scathing glance. "And have her mock my good manners? no thank you."

"Are you certain she will mock you?"

"Very certain," he said heavily. He ate more, scowling. When he had finished the wine in his cup, he said, "That First Corpse. It will haunt me until I can determine what its purpose is in the scenario. And Madame wants the scene ready tonight."

"So that is why you're wrestling with the meaning of the First Corpse," said da San-Germain.

"In part," Theron responded, going on reluctantly, "The First Corpse has bothered me from the first, though I know it has to be there to start the parade of them that develops in the scenario. But I need to have some way to explain what it is."

"Do you suppose that the figure might open the whole? Be a kind of prelude?"

Theron shrugged. "I'll think about it."

"For Commedia della Morte, the figure could be a representation of the troupe itself, a personification of the play and the players, the nature of the plays performed, a symbol for the difference between the moribund and the transition Revolution has brought about." Da San-Germain took a few steps back from Theron, knowing that the poet would need time to mull the possibilities over before arriving at any new decisions.

After the meal was over, Photine ordered the troupe to assemble around the fire, which she built up again so that it blazed, warm and brilliant in the vastness of the mountain night. "We will go through the progression of the scenes. Those of you who becomes Corpses will need to work on your stiff-legged walk in your winding-sheets, so that you can do it in unison without tripping. Remember you will be wearing masks, as well, so your speech will have to be very clear or no one will hear your lines." She asked Lothaire and Aloys to mark out a playing area, ordered Valence and Hariot to make torches for the standing spiral supports that would provide them light for their rehearsal. "Since we haven't a final script yet"—she flicked a disapproving glance in Theron's direction—"we must improvise our lines for a few more days, in the old commedia tradition."

"If we have to perform for the border guards?" Constance asked. "We won't be able to do the whole piece."

"We can do the two scenes we do have finished, with the lines set. That should be sufficient for half a dozen bored guards, especially if we ask them for their opinion so that we can improve our performance—every audience likes to make suggestions, and none more than men who are bored," said Photine, nodding in agreement with the sprinkle of laughter that greeted her observation. "So let us begin. Have your sides in hand, Pascal, Sibelle; take your places as soon as Aloys and Ragoczy have set up the chairs and the bower for you." She held up her hand to demand the attention of her actors. "Remember, not too sweet; this only *looks* like a romance. We don't want to create too much sympathy for Cleante and Desiree or their ending will be too sad."

Da San-Germain pulled a rehearsal chair out of the larger cart and carried it to where Aloys was waiting. "Do you know where we're to put these down?"

"One next to those three pebbles," Aloys said, pointing. "I'll put this one in its place." He seemed amused to have the troupe's patron serving as a stagehand; his blood-hound face lit up in a sarcastic smile.

As soon as the stage was ready, Photine took the script in hand, then summoned Pascal and Sibelle to take their places and begin. "Remember, not too sweet, perhaps just a little touch of foppishness, Pascal, and a flightiness, Sibelle." She leaned against the wagon, giving the actors her complete attention.

> *Cleante: Oh, my rapturous Desiree, what can we do to resolve the enmity that exists between our fathers, so that you and I may wed?*
>
> *Desiree: (sighing) I have tried every means of persuasion I can to soften my father's heart to your family, but he cannot be made to see that my only happiness lies with you.*
>
> *Cleante: Then we must consider an elopement. We must leave this place and find a haven where we can be together without fear.*
>
> *Desiree: Without money?*
>
> *Cleante: Each of us can bring our jewels and such possessions as will let us live as people of quality require. I have an inheritance from my grandmother that would buy us a house and land in America.*
>
> *Desiree: But your father would disown you—*

"Heurer!" Photine called out. "You should be here with us." She motioned to Sibelle. "Continue."

> *Desiree: But your father would disown you, and mine would order me to a convent if we were to do anything so reprehensible. Any hope of a life together would end, my most dear one.*
>
> *Cleante: No, that would happen only if we were caught. There are new laws that would prevent your father from sending you to a convent.*
>
> *Desiree: He could kill me, my beloved. The law still permits that.*
>
> *Cleante: I would die with you, if he did. (They kiss.) How could he bear to kill anything so lovely as you?*

Photine stepped forward to stop the scene. "I know we're supposed to be making fun of the aristocrats, but this is either too stilted, or not stilted enough, and that makes for confusion." She swung around to face Theron as he emerged from the shadows, a box of paper in one hand, a half-eaten apple in the other; he took a last bite and tossed the core away. "You must lighten this, Heurer. As it is, there isn't enough humor in it, or satire, or anything else that we can—"

"But these lovers don't see themselves as funny," said Theron. "They fear they may be tragic."

"Most characters in a good comedy *don't* see themselves as funny—that's what makes them amusing," Photine reminded him. "As to Cleante and Desiree, we need them to be just as absorbed in their problems as the characters in high drama are, but the tone has to be less . . . earnest." She pointed to Pascal. "What do you think?"

"I agree," said the handsome young actor, folding his arms and staring into the distance. "It has to be lighter or broader if we want to amuse the audience. As it stands, it won't make anyone laugh."

"There. You see?" Photine demanded of Theron.

Theron bristled, his brow darkening. "You don't understand what is happening in the scene."

"Well, if *we* can't understand it, how will the audience?" Photine challenged. "I admit I am baffled."

"Isn't it your craft to understand it?" Theron countered. "Aren't you supposed to find the elements that make for humor?"

"They have to be there to be found," said Pascal, his face impish. He looked over at Photine.

"Yes, that's our task," said Photine, surprising Theron. "But bear in mind, anyone may have an experience and not understand it, but to act an experience, the actor must understand what it is, what its meaning is. I'm pleased you grasp that." She assumed her most patient demeanor. "Your words may be amusing when read on the page, but the stage isn't the same thing as a book: what we play must be understandable and consistent in its presentation, which this is not. We want an abrupt contrast between this interlude and the appearance of the Corpses." She held out the pages to him. "You wrote this scene and we have done our best to play it, but, as you see, we don't know what the intent is. You must make it clearer."

Theron scowled. "You want more changes?"

"I fear we must have them, and have them by morning, or we won't have time enough to have the lines memorized before we reach the border-crossing; we will need to be ready by then," said Photine, softening her words with a winsome smile. "If you like, Sibelle, Pascal, and I will help you. We can read the words aloud and try to find a better way of making your purpose more apparent."

Valence stepped up to Photine. "If you don't need me, I'd like to have a wash and go to bed."

"Of course. All of you but Pascal, Sibelle, and Heurer may follow your example," Photine announced to the troupe at large. "This will take some time; make the most of your chance to sleep. The night-watch will begin shortly. Tonight it is Aloys and Urbain, then Feo and Ragoczy. Once the clean-up from supper is done, the rest of you may retire."

While most of the troupe moved off in the direction of the various wagons, Lothaire and Tereson poured the last of the stew into a large bowl, Sibelle glanced at Theron. "I think Desiree needs to be more of a coquette, feather-brained without being silly. When Cleante speaks of America, she could reveal her ignorance by saying something about the place that everyone knows is wrong."

"So this is more than the changing of a few sentences," said Theron, his face blank.

"If you cannot provide what we need, then we will have to improvise this scene, which wouldn't be a good decision dramatically," said Photine.

Standing off to the side with Aloys, da San-Germain said softly, "Best break out the lanthorns. They're going to need light for some hours yet."

"And be sulky as spring bears in the morning," Aloys agreed before raising his voice. "Madame, do you want the chairs and the rest put away?"

"No. Leave them. We may yet have to rehearse new lines tonight." She turned to Theron. "It is for you to write, but we must memorize and set action to your words."

"So you tell me," said Theron, covering his eyes with one hand. "Well. We had better get to it."

Photine beamed at him. "Very good, poet. I begin to hope there is promise in your plays."

"I don't need your sarcasm," Theron told her bluntly.

"I'm not being sarcastic—quite the opposite. For the first time I can see you may have the makings of a real playwright within your verses. You're showing a glimmer of comprehension of how a play is made." She took him by the arm and all but dragged him to the table where they had dinner. "Come. Sit down. Aloys, fetch us a lanthorn and paper."

"I have paper; I need pens," Theron added as he sat on the bench, setting the box in front of him; Sibelle took the place on his right, Pascal on his left.

"The rest of you," Photine called to the troupe. "If you can sleep, I suggest that you do so. We have much to do tomorrow."

Enee glowered at his mother. "Do you want me to stay with you?"

"Get some rest," she said to her son, and sat down beside Theron, unaware of the furious glance Enee gave her. "Shall we start our work? Pascal, what do you think would work in this scene?"

"A grandiose speech at the beginning, extolling Desiree and their love in such exaggerated terms that there is no feeling that it reveals genuine emotions; all over-blown and filled with aggrandizement," Pascal said, extending his arms dramatically. "And Desiree should respond with something equally elaborate."

Sibelle managed to curtsy while remaining seated. "Yes. That would be good."

Theron shook his head twice. "That would border on the burlesque."

"Exactly!" Photine rounded on him. "Yes. That's what's needed in this scene—a serious situation pushed to the extreme so that it becomes absurd. Remember the Commedia del'Arte traditions."

"You mean farce?" Theron asked, dreading her answer.

"Perhaps not as much a caricature as farce, but much nearer it than the play is now," Photine said with unexpected sympathy. "This is to be humorous, because that is expected, but you must underlie the humor with irony."

"And in all the other scenes, as well?" Theron asked, his face a mask of misery. "Is there no way to accommodate the profound?"

"You may let the First Corpse do that, if you like, in an epilogue; you may be as eloquent as you like then, so long as what is said isn't so morbid that it leaves a bad taste with the audience," said Photine. "If we try to convey too much depth, we're likely to be hauled into jail for presenting plays sympathetic to the Old Regime."

"So you keep saying," Theron muttered.

"And I think the Corpses should appear while Cleante and Desiree are kissing," Photine said. "That will provide a greater shock."

"But—" Theron began, then was silent.

"It is this contrast that makes the play daring, the absurd and the inexorable, which is what we want," said Photine with exaggerated patience. "We want the audience to stop laughing with a gasp, not a yawn."

"How can you ask this, after playing Racine?" Theron's caustic remark was intended to sting.

"For the same reason I do not wear the same clothes every day—acting is kept fresh through variety, as is life." Photine sat down at the end of the drop-table. "If one does the same thing always, it becomes stale."

Aloys, with two lanthorns in his hands, approached the table. "The oil should last four hours, Madame."

"Very good; thank you, Aloys; if you will take the first watch on the camp? Ragoczy can relieve you at midnight. We'll need the fire built up before dawn," she said, and placed the lanthorns so that they provided the largest pool of light on the table. "Now, let us start at the beginning of the scene and see what can be done."

Theron did his best not to sigh; he picked up a goose-feather, checked it to see the nib was properly trimmed, then looked about. "Where's the ink?"

Da San-Germain came up to him, holding out a standish of ink and a firkin of sand. "This should be sufficient for tonight."

"Thank you, Cont—Ragoczy," he said without a trace of gratitude. "I will do my best not to run out."

"Oh, don't despair," Photine advised Theron. "You will yet have the opportunity to write your tragic drama, but it won't be for us, not on this tour."

Theron stared at her in astonishment. "I saw you do Phaedre. You were magnificent, and noble. How can you . . . Variety. You don't have to tell me again." He took a sheet of paper from the box and smoothed it. "Eh bien," he said to Pascal, "what kind of excess did you have in mind?"

As if unaware of Theron's mockery, Pascal rose from the bench. "I believe Cleante would compare his passion to the effulgence of the sun, and Desiree to the radiant moon, that he might speak of Heloise and Abelard as paltry in their love, that he would extol his devotion as the equal to any lover in myth or history: Helen and Paris are mere playmates, Antony and Cleopatra are only political opportunists." He paused as if expecting applause; when none was forthcoming, he sat down again.

Tereson took the ewer of hot water off its stand next to the fire and used half its contents to wash out the stew-kettle, all the while whistling an aimless melody; Lothaire added three cut logs to the fire, then built up the low rim of earth around it. Olympe emerged from the wagon she shared with her mother and Sibelle, a basin in her hands for warm washing water. None of them paid attention to Theron, Photine, Sibelle, and Pascal.

Roger came up to da San-Germain, saying in Byzantine Greek, "Do you need me any longer tonight, my master?"

"I don't think so," said da San-Germain.

"Then I'll go and find something to eat." He held up his skinning knife. "I'll have my meal away from the camp; no one will mind that the meat is raw."

"Prudent as always, old friend," said da San-Germain, and went off to the larger cart, where he took up a seat on the rear of the vehicle and spent the next two hours watching Photine and Theron wrangle over the particulars of the play.

Text of a report from the Revolutionary Tribunal of Avignon to the Revolutionary Assembly of Avignon, delivered the day it was signed, carried by a Captain of the Revolutionary Guard.

> *To the learned Deputies of the Revolutionary Assembly of Avignon on this, the ninth day of September, 1792, a report from Evraud Marais, Maitre de Prison, the Revolutionary Tribunal of Avignon,*
>
> *Esteemed Deputies of the Revolutionary Assembly,*
> *In accordance with your instructions, I have prepared, and now submit to you, a report on the state of our prison:*

We now house 739 male prisoners, most of them enemies of the Revolution, but in that number are 114 criminals, 14 of them children under the age of nine. These two groups, the common criminals and the enemies of the Revolution, are kept apart from one another, and have separate squads of Revolutionary Guards to keep watch upon them. As you are aware, the prison has 120 individual cells and 20 general cells, all of which are overcrowded, which is contributing to the increasing incidents of disease and violence among the inmates. In addition, there are three general cells set aside for women prisoners which now number 83, of which 27 are nuns, 34 are prostitutes, and the remainder are enemies of the Revolution. The three general cells are each designed to hold twelve.

It is the opinion of the Revolutionary Tribunal that these numbers must be reduced for the safety of the public, and as we have not yet scheduled trials for most of the inmates, the situation is likely to get much worse before it is improved through the execution of sentences upon these prisoners. There is an offer from the Revolutionary Tribunal in Lyon to take on enemies of the Revolution for trial there, which I believe is an offer we must now seriously consider. If we sent only those accused of being enemies of the Revolution to Lyon, we would seriously reduce the crowding we experience and it would allow you to try those prisoners who are ordinary criminals before having to make decisions about the many additional enemies of the Revolution who are even now being rounded up by the Revolutionary Guards.

It is my belief that we will better serve France by consigning the enemies of the Revolution to the Revolutionary Tribunal of Lyon for their judgment, for not only is that city willing to aid us in this matter, the *place is far enough away that traditional loyalties will not be an issue as they are likely to be here, and the verdicts given will then better reflect the goals of the Revolution instead of the dedications of those who still harbor sympathy for the Old Regime. We have Guardsmen to escort them, and funds enough to pay for the journey.*

If you were to authorize the transfer of these prisoners, you could commandeer barges to transport the prisoners north, lessening the chances of escape as well as avoiding the dangers that may be encountered on the roads. We could have the prisoners ready to travel in two days' time if you will agree to my recommendation. The Revolutionary Guards currently sweeping the countryside are due to return in six days, and if we have not alleviated the crowding in the prison, it will be impossible for us to maintain order or even effective surveillance upon those we are charged with keeping within our control.

Sixteen men of the Revolutionary Garrison of Avignon are already on record as being willing to be part of the escort for these prisoners. Another 100 Revolutionary Guards should be an adequate number to ensure that the prisoners reach Lyon without serious incident. I ask that you take this under advisement as soon as possible, before we have a wholesale revolt in the prison and risk having our Guards killed by these enemies of the Revolution.

All glory to the Revolution,

Evraud Marais
Maitre de Prison
Revolutionary Tribunal of Avignon

8

"There are only two of us house-servants left here; there are four grooms and a shepherd as well, for what good they are. It would be wrong to admit so many unknown . . ." The man on the other side of the gate at Montalia faltered, trying to choose a word to describe the troupe of players gathered at the entrance; he was broad-shouldered, between thirty and thirty-five, with shaggy hair, two days of stubble on his cheeks, and looked to have recently lost flesh; the apron he wore proclaimed him the cook. "I haven't the authority to allow you to enter." He stared at the troupe as if hoping they would vanish, unwilling to let them in. "I don't know how I could be responsible for any mischief that might occur."

"Players don't always mean mischief," said Pascal with a winning smile; he and Photine had used the guest-bell to summon a warden and had almost given up waiting for anyone to answer the clang and permit them inside the walls. "Not often, in any case." He chuckled to conceal his relief that someone had answered their ringing, for it was mid-afternoon and he knew if they were not taken in here they would have only a few hours to find an inn or a place to make camp for the night. "Certainly not here."

"That is no reassurance for me," said the cook warily, his gaze directed at some point beyond the players. "How would those of us still here stop you if you decided to steal, or to vandalize the estate? Or set the mansion itself on fire? You have superior numbers. Two house-servants cannot contain you."

"We will give you our pledge that we will do nothing obstreperous, nothing unlawful, nothing against the expectations of hospitality," said Pascal at his most persuasive. "All of us, on the Cross, if you like, or the tricoleur, if you prefer."

"For pity's sake, don't badger him," Photine whispered to

Pascal as she cast an uneasy glance on the man inside the fence, trying to think of what she might say to persuade him. She moved a little nearer to the gate, prepared to extend her hand to the man if he presented her such an opportunity.

"Gigot, it's Heurer," Theron called out, descending from the second wagon and holding out his hand in a familiar way he had never before demonstrated to a servant. "What are you saying? Don't refuse us."

"Monsieur Heurer?" Gigot exclaimed in surprise, shading his eyes with one massive hand. "What are you doing with—"

Theron cut him short, stepping up to the gate to face him. "You say there are only two of you here. Who's left with you? Isn't Remi still here? I thought he was staying on. Where has everyone else gone? Where is Madelaine de Montalia? When did she leave?"

"A courier came and the Revolutionary Guards took Madame away; that was just over a week ago. The few servants who had remained here left, all but Maxime and I; we were charged with care of Montalia. The grooms have been charged with keeping the horses ready for the Revolutionary Guard; they stay in the stable. We're supposed to maintain this place, all of it, orchards, gardens, house, stable, livestock, and fowl, the two of us. Two." He reached for the lock on the chain that held the gate closed. "If you are with these . . . folk, I believe it may be all right to admit you." He pulled an iron key from the pocket of his apron, an air of resignation about him like a cloak. "You understand that you can't stay?"

"You're most kind," said Photine with a smile calculated to melt the iciest heart.

From his place on the driving-box of the larger cart, da San-Germain frowned at the cook, his eyes becoming keener as he listened for what Gigot would say, his concentration much greater than it appeared to be.

"We don't want to be here more than two days at most, to rest and to make plans, since we are looking for Madame de Montalia," Theron explained. "If you can tell us where Madelaine has been taken—?"

"They told us she was going to be held at Avignon," said Gigot as he worked the key in the lock.

"Why?" Theron demanded.

"Who can say?" Gigot pulled the lock open and removed it from the chain, then started to unwrap it from the gate. "The men who are in charge now, they do as they like, when they like, to whom they like—as bad as those they replaced, if you ask me." He stepped back, pulling the complaining gate open, and standing aside to permit the wagons to move through; his expression was dour. "No one is safe, no one." He looked directly at Theron. "That includes you, Monsieur Heurer."

"I'll remember that," said Theron.

Gigot nodded. "Lead these people up to the mansion; take your vehicles around to the stable. I'll warn Maxime to be ready for you, with beds and blankets, then I'll try to put a supper together for you, though there's not much in the larder and no one wants to hunt. Replace the lock when you're all inside. We want no more guests today, particularly no more unexpected ones." With that graceless remark, he trudged away up the curving drive, not bothering to check on the troupe to see if they followed him.

"What on earth has happened?" Photine asked da San-Germain as his cart rolled through the gate. "Why is your kinswoman not here?"

"It would appear she has been arrested," said da San-Germain in a very neutral tone; he pulled in his mules and moved enough to allow her to join him on the driver's box.

"That much is obvious. I wondered if you knew the reason why," she said as she clambered up beside him.

"How could I?" He set his pair in motion again. "I've had only the one letter from her, and I gathered from it that she was confined to her estate. If she wrote to me about her arrest, I haven't received the letter."

"But that changes everything, doesn't it?" Photine adjusted her skirts and laid her hand on his arm. "What do you want to do about it?"

"Go to Avignon," he said grimly.

"I didn't think you'd do anything else," she said.

"If you think it too dangerous, you may return to Padova," he offered. "You've risked enough coming this far. Feo can escort you back, if you like."

"What good would that do?" She expected no answer and got none. "Well, we should be able to perform in Avignon, that's something," she said, doing her best to make light of the fear that clutched her.

"That will get us into the city, and may . . ." His words trailed off as he became lost in unwelcome thought: Madelaine in prison. The very notion was appalling. He fought off a welling of memories of prisons he had occupied, from the oubliette where he received offerings of young women sacrificed to his appetite, to the cell under the Flavian Circus, to the tower in Damascus, to the— He stifled the recollections, then turned to Photine. "We must prepare how we're going to introduce ourselves to the Revolutionary Assembly there."

"So we stay here tonight and tomorrow night? Heurer seems to think we will." Photine raised her voice enough to be heard by most of the troupe.

"The horses and mules could do with a rest," said da San-Germain distantly. "And so could your company."

Photine considered this. "How far are we from Avignon?"

"In leagues or in travel days?" da San-Germain countered, then softened his response. "We may have delays in our travel, so an estimate could be unreliable."

"Then how many days would you estimate it will take us to reach Avignon from here, if there are no delays and we aren't detained??" She clearly expected an answer.

"Four, perhaps five days, if the roads are open," said da San-Germain, "and if we travel through the day, no riposino."

"That's hard on the animals," said Photine.

"It is. If you would rather make the journey in six or seven days, the teams will be more rested, and so will we. But it may mean avoiding inns and markets while we go; the way things are at the moment, it will be risky to stay in remote settlements. There is so much coseismal opinion about in these times that doing any kind of performing could bring us trouble, and that could lead to consequences none of us would want."

"But won't we offend villagers if we don't perform for them? Surely they're eager for a little entertainment, to relieve the stress of the time?" Photine asked, nearly pleading. "Wouldn't our presence be an insult unless we performed?"

"Only if we try to lodge there." He gave her a quick, mercurial smile. "We'll be safer in cities than in towns. There are more opinions in them than there are in small villages, and that affords us protection." They had been moving up the curve of the drive through an avenue of cypress, and now emerged to see an elegant chateau ahead of them. It was in the style of the early fifteenth century, three storeys in height, made of reddish stone, with an addition on the northwest side that was less than a hundred years old, done in the fashion of the Sun King, including a large salon des fenetres that opened onto a terrace and overlooked a neglected rose-garden and a half-empty, brackish ornamental water framed by unkempt cat-tails.

"How unfortunate," Photine said as she took in the sad state of the place. "It must have been quite grand once."

"And will be again," said da San-Germain.

"Do you think so?"

"I know it would be Madelaine's intention," he said, obliquely.

"Slanting your bets," Photine approved. "Just as well, given what the world has become." She leaned against his shoulder to express comfort. "You're a good man, Conte; better than most of your kind. I pray that your loyalty is richly rewarded."

"I'm not seeking rewards—I want to see that Madelaine is safe."

Photine patted his leg affectionately. "You're too literal. There are many kinds of rewards; I wasn't talking of money."

"I didn't think you were," he answered, kindness returning to his dark eyes.

After that they went in silence until they reached the stable-yard, when Photine got down from the driving-box; before she took her troupe in hand, she looked at da San-Germain and said, "If ever I needed help from a kinsman, I would hope that he would be such another man as you are. I hope your Madelaine realizes how fortunate she is." With that, she turned away and shouted to Aloys, "Unhitch the teams out here, and line up the wagons against the far wall before you stall the animals. We'll need to set a guard to-night."

Da San-Germain watched her go, once again wondering how much of what she said was a performance and how much was sincere, and if, for her, there was any real difference between one and the other. Realizing he couldn't answer that question any more now than he had been able to since their first meeting, he set the cart's simple brake and climbed down from the driving-box, only to find Roger approaching him from the smaller cart. "Are your mules unhitched?"

"Hariot is attending to unhitching; he'll deal with yours in a few minutes. Urbain and Lothaire are handling the horses—Urbain will leave tomorrow. Feo's seeing to the vehicles," said Roger, and went on in the language of China, "What is this? Is Madelaine truly missing?"

"Apparently she is under arrest in Avignon," said da San-Germain quietly in the same tongue. "Not a good sign, I'm afraid."

"Certainly not," Roger said. He nodded toward the mansion behind them. "Do you think it wise to stay here? Could we be in danger?"

"For two days? How could we be? Who knows we're here." Da San-Germain began to disengage the harness from the cart. "Even if the servants send word to Avignon about our arrival, they won't be able to reach the city before we've left."

"True enough," said Roger, signaling to Hariot, who was leading the mules toward the stable, speaking in French, "They'll need their hooves cleaned carefully."

"And water and hay," said Hariot over his shoulder.

"The same for my team," da San-Germain called after him; Hariot nodded and kept on walking.

"I'll make sure all the animals are watered and fed," Roger said, once again in the Chinese of the northern capital. "You and Madame Photine can work out the housing arrangements with Maxime and arrange meals with the cook. If I have the opportunity, I'll try to find your chests of native earth, as well."

"Very prudent of you, as always, old friend; I needn't have any qualms while you're about," said da San-Germain, an ironic lift to his fine brows as he glanced toward the stable. "Let us hope I won't need the chests."

Roger ducked his head. "Best to be prepared."

"And in that same spirit, I'll arrange for your food with the cook," da San-Germain said. "I'd like to think that we can have an easy stay here."

"But you're uncertain," said Roger. "And not simply because you're worried about Madelaine."

"Not entirely, no; I see that the two house-servants left are exhausted, and there is more work to be done than we can supply."

"You want to put the mansion in order for her, don't you?"

"How well you know me," said da San-Germain, his expression turning sardonic. "And of course, I would like to believe that our arrival will not increase Madelaine's danger, but it may, if it is reported in Avignon."

"Why should it be?" Roger asked. "What danger does a group of players cause her?"

"I have no idea—and that perplexes me more than the knowledge that she is in the hands of the Revolutionary Assembly." He moved away from the cart so that Hariot, who was returning across the stable-yard toward them, could lead his team away to the barn. "If I can find the opportunity, I'll want to sound out the cook."

"And give him cause to remember you?" Roger warned.

"If he is still here, he must have some loyalty to Madelaine remaining in him. He might be able to provide more information—"

"Let me do it," Roger said with more genuine emotion than he usually permitted himself to reveal. "Servants gossip, and any questions I ask will mean little to the cook. If you ask them, they will become noteworthy, and that—"

"An excellent notion, and one I might observe," said da San-Germain. "I'll await your report tonight."

Roger very nearly smiled, his faded-blue eyes brightening. "Thank you, my master."

Da San-Germain looked at him, bemused. "If I have done anything to deserve your thanks, then I am pleased."

Roger gave a nod that was more of a bow, and stepped away. "Will you be alone tonight?"

"I believe so," said da San-Germain, speaking in French once again. "Enee has been complaining about me again, and Photine wants to reassure him."

"Indulge him, you mean, which only serves to encourage him further," said Roger, still in Chinese, then raised his voice to speak to Aloys in French. "Do you need another hand to bed stalls?"

"If you're willing," Aloys said.

"Another pair of hands makes shorter work," said Roger, quoting the old saw from his long-ago childhood; he turned away from da San-Germain to take the remuda line to lead the reserve horses into the stable.

Da San-Germain watched him go, thinking as he often did, that restoring his manservant to life in the Year of the Four Caesars was one of the most providential actions he had ever taken; Roger was steadfast, loyal, and resourceful, unswerving in his devotion, able to deal with da San-Germain through all manner of perils. A number of all the things they had gone through together flickered in images through his mind: Spain, Italy, China, India, the Americas; he had a quick, agonizing memory of being taken down from a cross in Mexico, and his sense of obligation intensified.

"Ragoczy?" a voice said at his elbow, a bit more loudly than seemed necessary.

Da San-Germain turned to see Crepin Sillondroit standing slightly behind him, an expectant smile firmly fixed. "Yes?"

"You've been here before? They say you have." He pointed toward the mansion as if it were an illusion. "Is it true?"

"Twice; I have been here twice before," said Ragoczy, recalling attending Madelaine's funeral and the evening that followed when she wakened to his life; then the more recent visit, when he had persuaded her to come to Verona with him.

"It is the property of your kinswoman? That's what everyone is saying." Crepin did his best expectant look. "Ragoczy?"

He considered the actor. "Is there something you want to know?"

Crepin shrugged with elaborate casualness. "I was only wondering how safe you think the estate is."

"Safe? In what way?"

"Oh, you know—in terms of . . . locals." He pressed his hands together, his eyes moving nervously. "That village? Saint-Jacques-sur-Crete? Do you think there might be spies there? Or thieves?"

"Probably some of both," said da San-Germain with a gesture of unconcern. "But I doubt they pay much attention to what happens up here. We're more than three leagues away, and they have the last of the harvest to deal with."

Crepin nodded several times, his glance still jittery. "As you say. As you say. But there could be Revolutionary Guards in the village, couldn't there?"

"It's possible, but I don't think it likely. The village is on a minor road in mountainous territory. Now that Madame de Montalia has been arrested, I would guess that there are few landholders left in the region; we know the hostels are empty, and the monasteries. The Revolutionary Guard has better things to do than occupy villages like Saint-Jacques."

"Yes. Yes. I understand your meaning." Crepin said. "But it is still . . ." He abandoned his train of thought and tried something new. "Are we putting ourselves in danger by staying here? considering the owner is in the hands of the Revolutionary Tribunal?"

"Not that I am aware of, no," said da San-Germain. He moved toward the kitchen door, not wanting to contribute to Crepin's unease any more than he had already.

Crepin came after him. "But we could be—in danger, I mean?"

"Anyone in France could be in danger at present," da San-Germain said, more sharply than he had intended; he continued in a more conciliating tone, "So far, from what I have learned, which is little more than what all of you know already, players are welcome in France, so long as they don't keep to the old plays, but perform new ones. The scenario you're rehearsing now, with the Corpses, is nothing like any commedia troupe has done before, so it's likely that the play will be a success. You're probably going to be hailed as artists of the Revolution."

"I hope so," said Crepin, still doubtful.

Da San-Germain pulled open the door and stepped into the corridor next to the pantry. "Come ahead. The kitchen is on the left."

"My nose tells me that," Crepin said, and peered into its brick-walled depths, a wishful smile on his handsome features, the very image of happy anticipation.

The aromas burgeoning in the kitchen promised a tasty meal of roast pork stuffed with apples and sweet onions, a casserole of vegetables and cheese, and loaves of fresh bread. In counterpoint to the chop of his knife on cabbage, Gigot was singing one of the old songs of the region, about a lost lamb and a wolf.

"Your meal should be ready within the hour," da San-Germain remarked, and turned toward the front of the mansion.

"Does Photine know what you've told me?" Crepin asked, unwilling to give up his questions.

"I should think so," said da San-Germain, and continued walking. "We've discussed it often enough."

"Tell me if you decide anything has changed," Crepin called after him, then stepped into the kitchen, and asked Gigot if he needed any help.

As da San-Germain crossed the great hall, he heard Photine raise her voice. "No, Enee, I won't have it. You've been allowed too much license already." The sound came from the salon des fenetres.

"I don't have to obey you," her son challenged her. "You have no authority over me now that I'm fifteen."

"If you want a place to sleep and something to eat, I do. All the troupe recognizes it, including Valence, and he's forty-one." She was clearly agitated and doing her best to keep her impulse to rail at him under control. "This continuing defiance is most . . . distressing."

Listening, da San-Germain wondered what she had been going to say that she changed to *distressing*. He approached the salon des fenetres, feeling slightly uncomfortable at his eavesdropping; he was about to make himself known when Enee's next words held him to the spot.

"You won't let me take a few bottles of wine from this cellar, but you'll let your noble lover nibble your throat." He laughed, deliberately harsh. "You think I don't see what you hide beneath your collar?"

"Enee!"

"Don't look so shocked, Madame," Enee responded with elaborate scorn.

"Many men have their . . . their tastes," said Photine with studied indifference. "Not that it's any of your business."

"A man bites my mother, and I'm supposed to pretend it means nothing?" Enee demanded. "What kind of a son would that make me?"

"An obedient one," said Photine bluntly. "If I am not displeased with da San-Germain, why should you be?"

"He is using you, and you won't see it!" Enee yelled. "You do what he wants without a second to consider what it means. You were going to have four carts and now you have two. Because it's convenient for him!"

"Lower your voice," she snapped at him. "It's bad enough you spend your time sulking. I won't have you declaiming to the whole troupe."

"You're being used," Enee said again, in a quieter tone.

"And I am using him. What of it? Each of us is receiving what we want, so why shouldn't we continue as we are?" Photine paused. "If you are so determined to defy me, you will have to decide what profession other than acting you wish to pursue. I can't have you disrupting the troupe. You'll need to find a master who'll have you as an apprentice."

"You'd do that to me? Because of *him*?"

"Not because of him—because of me. You seek to undermine my authority and to make the rest of the troupe doubt my leadership. You behave like a wayward bear-cub. I can't have that, particularly from my son."

There was the sound of a hand slapped down on wood. "You're my mother, and you speak to me this way?"

"Whoelse will do it?" she countered. "I think you had better go to the room Maxime assigned you. Spend the evening reading, or doing something useful. Consider your situation. Do not indulge in wine or steal any more cognac. You have to decide what you want to do, and you'll need a clear head for that."

"You aren't serious, are you?" Enee asked in disbelief.

"I am."

"Get of a poxy whore," he muttered.

Photine's voice changed, turning imperious and cold. "What did you call me?"

"What you are," Enee blustered, and an instant later flung out of the salon des fenetres, hurrying away toward the rear of the mansion, paying no heed to the cry of protest from Photine as he left.

Da San-Germain remained in the shadow of the alcove for a few minutes while Photine gathered herself together. When he was fairly sure she had gathered herself well enough, he came to the door of the salon des fenetres. "I just saw Enee rushing through the great hall. Is anything the matter?"

"He's being a truculent child," said Photine, as much worry as disgust in her voice.

"He's jealous," said da San-Germain without any annoyance in his tone. "He's afraid you'll favor me more than you favor him."

"He may have reason for such fear, the wretch," said Photine darkly, staring at the door as if she thought he might reappear. "What does he expect?—that I'll turn away from a generous lover and patron because he's having a fit of the sullens?"

"Probably," said da San-Germain, and saw Photine give a single, resigned nod. "He wants to be sure that he's the light of your life."

"At the moment," said Photine briskly, "he isn't." She came to his side and leaned against him. "What am I to do with him?"

"That depends upon what you want of him," said da San-Germain, taking her into his arms.

"I want him to be a reasonable young man; at fifteen he should be able to do that," Photine sighed, easing her body more closely to his. "But for him, it may not be possible."

"It may not," he agreed, and met her lips with his own in a long, soft kiss.

"Do you think he should be apprenticed to some worthy trades-man, or an apothecary, or, I don't know what?"

If he felt that ending a kiss with a plea for her bothersome son was unusual, he made no comment on it; it was strange enough to embrace her in Madelaine's mansion. "I doubt Enee knows what would best suit him. It could be a factor in his jealousy—he's afraid of being adrift in a dangerous time."

"All times are dangerous," said Photine, moving half a step back in his arms.

"That they are," da San-Germain agreed. "But the danger is more apparent now than is often the case."

"And he is caught up in the excitement as much as any of them," said Photine on another, longer sigh. "I can't hold that against him."

"He wants to know what you expect of him," said da San-Germain. "Not that he'll comply with your wishes, but he won't feel so rudderless."

She looked at him, dawning surprise in her face. "He claims he wants to be the one to decide for himself."

"And he does, but not because he has had to grasp for it." He stroked her tawny hair. "You are a woman of . . . character," he said after a short silence. "He's used to you guiding him, and little as he wants to acknowledge it, he is comfortable with your direction; that comfort causes him to doubt himself, and so he turns on you, wanting to rule you in order to convince himself that he is capable of being his own master."

She blinked at him. "Not unlike Orestes," she said slowly.

Da San-Germain shook his head, offering her a half-smile. "Nothing so extreme. We are not living a Greek tragedy."

"I should hope not," she said in a rallying tone. "Well, I can see Enee will take some—"

"If you can, let him flounder for now. He'll be the better for it when he finally makes up his mind." He drew her to him once more. "If he gets into serious trouble, you can come to his aid, but be prepared to have him resent you for it."

"You speak as a man who has dealt with difficult sons," she said, her head cocked speculatively.

"I have no children: I told you that," he said gently. "But in my travels I've had much opportunity to observe."

"And closely, if this is any example of what you've seen," said Photine. "Perhaps you should be doing our scenarios for us, and not Heurer."

"You need a Frenchman to write for you. It's safer to have a French playwright."

"Unless he is accused of upholding the Old Regime," she said.

"Nothing in his work suggests that," da San-Germain reminded her. "He will seem more revolutionary because he's French than any outsider would be."

She kissed him lightly, then smoothly broke away from him. "We'll rehearse in this room after supper. I'd like you to come and watch."

"As I usually do," he told her, puzzled by her invitation.

"Exactly. I rely on you to see how the script may be improved, and to find a way to keep Heurer from penning long, extravagant speeches that only confuse the point of the play. He loves the sounds of his own words, and needs to think more of the sense of them." She took a step back, blew him a kiss, and made a graceful exit.

For a short time, da San-Germain stood alone in the salon des fenetres, his eyes fixed on the middle distance, and a half-century ago, when he had encountered Madelaine for the first time, when he had been able to bring her out of danger and into his life. He shook himself mentally, aware that this time he would be risking much more for them both, and jeopardizing Photine's commedia company as well. "Do I have the right to ask this of Photine? Should I send the troupe back to Italy?" he murmured to the tall windows, and had to be satisfied with silence for an answer.

Text of a report from the Revolutionary Tribunal of Valence to the Revolutionary Assembly of Avignon, carried by Revolutionary Guard courier and delivered three days after it was written.

To the Revolutionary Assembly of Avignon, the greetings of the Revolutionary Tribunal of Valence on this, the 16th day of September, 1792.

Most Esteemed members of the Revolutionary Assembly of Avignon;

This is to inform you that the barge bearing prisoners of your Revolutionary Tribunal has arrived here, and that the prisoners are in good condition, all but one, who, on the advice of the physician August Benizance, has been removed from the barge and allowed to travel in a light carriage with another female prisoner for a chaperone; the younger woman has a profound antipathy to the movement of water and was suffering so extremely that she was causing a disruption on the barge and it was decided that Benizance was right, and she should be removed from the barge for the rest of the journey. Both this young woman and her chaperone come from aristocratic families, and both are to answer for their crimes against the People of France at Lyon.

The barge is being restocked with water and food, and will lay over here for three days so that the tow-horses may rest, and the escorts have time to refresh themselves. For the three days, the prisoners will be confined in the Couvent des les Sacres Magi, which has stood empty for two years now, the Redemptionist nuns who lived here now gone to their reward through the good offices of the guillotine. Revolutionary Guards have been posted to watch the prisoners, and there is a squad of militiamen with muskets stationed in the adjoining hostelry, in case any misguided sympathizers should attempt to free the prisoners.

The prisoners will be allowed to have their clothes washed, and to bathe, but they will not be permitted to write letters or to indulge in religious practices. Since there are none to wait upon them, they will be given needles and thread to repair their garments if needed, and combs and scissors for their hair. Benizance has recommended that the prisoners be provided salves for those with sunburn, and camphor to reduce the presence of vermin in their clothing, but the Revolutionary Tribunal has yet to allow such indulgence, for since peasants have endured such torments as these prisoners do, it is fitting that they receive no succor. Benizance has issued a warning about fevers, but the Revolutionary Tribunal has yet to change its finding.

When the barge is safely away, another courier will bring you word of it, and you will be notified of any changes in the prisoners, their escort, or the time they are expected to reach Lyon.

    Long live the People of France!

    Long live the Glorious Revolution!

Durand Alphonse Odon
Clerk of the Revolutionary Tribunal of Valence

PART II

Ragoczy Ferenz, Conte da San-Germain

Text of a letter from Oddysio Lisson in Venezia to Ragoczy Ferenz, Conte da San-Germain and owner of the Eclipse Trading Company, to his house in Padova, carried by Eclipse Trading Company courier and delivered thirty-two hours after it was written, when it was dispatched by a second courier to Avignon, and never reached its recipient.

To the esteemed Ragoczy Ferenz, Conte da San-Germain, and distinguished owner of the Eclipse Trading Company, the dedicated greetings of Oddysio Lisson factor and manager of the Eclipse Trading Company in Venezia, on this, the 21st day of September, 1792,

My dear Conte,

Both Salvatore Campo and Gabriello Donat have returned to Venezia; they stand ready to come into France to be at your service, should it be necessary. It is unfortunate that neither of the men accompanied you when you departed with the performing troupe, but I understand that there were difficulties between them and a few of the actors, and it was decided that they should return here and hold themselves prepared to answer your summons. I must tell you that this arrangement troubles me, yet I will do as you instruct me. Thus: to increase our preparedness to respond to your orders, I have put two barquentines, the Sand-Darter *and the* New Moon, *on alert to set sail for Genova, should you require a departure by sea. Your factor in Genova has been notified that quick action may be needed from him, and to keep at least one ship in the harbor to bear you and any companions who may accompany you to Venezia. I fear that your factor in Marseilles has been taken by the Revolutionary Tribunal, and business suspended for that office, and therefore Genova is the nearest safe port to Avignon.*

I say again, I cannot be sanguine about your circumstances, and therefore wish to inform you that there are three couriers in Avignon who may be of use to you: they work from the Golden Cockerel on the Place des Bergers; I have used their services before and they have proved to be most reliable. Their names are: Giraud le Eperon, Jean Maigre, and Octave Jardin. They will recognize my name if you use it, should you decide to hire them. All three men have sworn support to the Revolution, and all three have been allowed to continue in their occupation, at least as far as I have been able to discover. If their position in the world has been compromised, I have no other recommendation to give to you but that you might want to arrange with one of your troupe to serve as your messenger, for it might prove too dangerous for any recognized courier to undertake such an assignment as what you may require. In ventures like this, plans must be fluid, since they may have to change quickly, upon occasion, more than once. I know you will bear that in mind when you travel.

In the eventuality that you leave France through the Swiss or German frontiers, I ask that you send word to me as soon as possible so that I may make suitable

*arrangements for you to travel in relative safety. I real-
ize you have offices of Eclipse Trading in many ports,
and that each should be able to serve you; still, I cannot
believe that all will be as secure as we may be in Venezia. The fires of revolution have been lit, and there are
many states in Europe that seek to warm themselves at
that hearth. Amsterdam may be fairly safe, in spite of
the hostilities with France, but even there trouble could
arise that would be as dangerous as any city in France
is today. I recommend that should you not be able to
return directly to Italy that you make for London or
any English port, for the English have taken in many
French, and would certainly extend their hospitality to
you. Your London office is smaller than some other
Eclipse Trading offices, but at present it can provide a
degree of protection many of your larger offices cannot.
Aroldo San-Marino seconds my suggestion in this
regard.*

The Eye of Heaven *has returned from the New
World with a cargo of cotton, tobacco, mahogany, tur-
quoise, silver, jade, and fur. The ship has suffered damage that will require extensive repairs, which I have
ordered. The* Stella Marina *has been seen at Tunis,
where she was flying the banner of the Algerians; it
would appear she has been taken by pirates, or com-
mandeered by the Algerians, and sold to the highest
bidder. I know nothing of what has become of Captain
Ferran and his crew, but I will make every effort to
discover their fates and report them to you. The* An-
dromeda *is ready to return to her home port; she's laden
with Antioch silks, Egyptian grain, Batavian spices,
Indian brasses, and Venezian glass, all of which should
sell most profitably in Stockholm. She is scheduled
to call at Messina, at Barcelona, at Cadiz, at Lisboa, at
Plymouth, and at Hamburg. Gian-Franco Montador has*

*provided copies of his dispatches for your review; they
are enclosed with this letter. I trust I have not erred in
sending this now, while you are in France.*

With prayers for your safe return,

Yours most sincerely,
Oddysio Lisson
factor and manager
Eclipse Trading Company
Venezian office

1

Growls and barking served as all the welcome the troupe was granted as they drew in at the Avignon gate in the turbid light shortly after dawn; six large brindled dogs held on chains lunged at the wagons, their noise alerting the ten Revolutionary Guards who manned the eastern gate, most of whom had gathered in the small guardhouse to avoid the chilly morning mists that clung to the ground like exhausted specters creeping back to their graves.

"No market today," bellowed a blocky man in a dirty uniform as he appeared in the gateway. To punctuate his remark, he belched.

"That's excellent. We need time to prepare and to apply for permission to perform," Photine called out in her most tantalizing voice from her place on the driving-box of the larger cart, where she huddled in a long cloak next to da San-Germain.

The Guard stopped still, caught by the rich promise in her voice. "Who are you?"

"We're a company of actors, French actors," Photine announced. "La Commedia della Morte."

"Della Morte? Not del'Arte?" The Guard laughed exuberantly at his own wit, and ambled up to the lead wagon, the dogs cringing around him, their guttural warnings muted for the moment. "I thought all you Commedia folk were del'Arte."

"In these times," said Photine in a manner filled with seduction and portent, "we must laugh at death if we're to laugh at anything. Our style is new, and our tale is, as well."

The Guard whooped and slapped his thigh, almost releasing the chain leash of the largest dog in his mirth. "You lot just might do for Avignon," he declared when his laughter ceased. "How is it you arrive so early in the morning? Half the city is still asleep."

"We left Saint-Vitre three hours ago," said Photine. "They're ending harvest there, and most of the village rose well before daylight, to get ahead of the rain they say is coming in the afternoon. The innkeeper asked us to be on our way so that his servants could work the fields."

"Have they made a good harvest? Half of it's likely to be confiscated before the rains start in earnest." The Guard did not bother to sound genuinely interested; he went on at once, "Eh, bien. Enter the city. If you know where you're going, go there directly. If you don't know, keep to the main streets and if there's any question about how you arrived, tell them Sergeant Poteau admitted you. That should be sufficient for you to avoid trouble." He waved, shaking his head and chuckling, as the wagons and carts rolled through the gate, the spare horses and mules bringing up the rear.

In the milky light of early morning, the city looked ill-used; garbage and offal stood unattended in the gutters; a gaggle of geese wandered through the alleys and lanes, pecking at the litter; crude posters announcing the names of those to be executed this morning were displayed in shop windows and on notice boards, and graffiti were scrawled in red paint on many walls. Shops were just beginning to open, so the crowd in the streets was still fairly thin. Those women out for early morning shopping went hurriedly about their business, often in groups of three or four. The men were more at ease; all of them displayed a tricoleur cockade on their hats or jackets. Many soldiers strutted their way in the middle of the lanes and avenues, forcing others to make way for them, enjoying the awe and dread they inspired. A few officials on foot or in chairs bustled importantly toward the center of the city.

"Nom de nom. I don't like it," Photine said quietly to da San-Germain. "Perhaps we should have remained at the Boeuf et Ange in Saint-Vitre."

"It was a wretched place," said da San-Germain. "They needed every hand for the harvest."

"It was wretched, but I don't think Avignon is much better," Photine said, her whole demeanor disheartened. "This was such a grand town, ten years ago. I cannot believe that it has fallen so far in so little time."

"Nor can I, but we must make the best of it."

"What do you suppose is going on?" She looked down one of the broader streets where a crowd was gathering.

"Executions," he replied tonelessly, nodding toward a poster.

Photine looked appalled. "Executions?"

"There are fourteen names on the newest posters," he said.

"Do you really think—"

"If the landlord at the Boeuf et Ange may be believed, they publish the names of the victims the day before, so that the people will be able to decide whom they wish to watch die," said da San-Germain. He studied the growing crowd, his face revealing nothing of his thoughts, which were filled with executions, including three of his own.

They were nearing the center of the city when Photine said, "A pity you don't have a house here in Avignon."

He had a quick memory of the days of the Black Plague, when the Pope still lived in Avignon, and the streets were lined with the dead. "I've had no reason to buy one, and this is not the time to try."

"No, it's not."

They rode in silence through the streets, trundling behind the wagons and followed by the smaller cart until they reached what had been the Place des Papes, but was now the Place du Rhone, where Photine called a halt to their vehicles. "That inn over there," she declared, pointing to a three-storey building with a sign-board showing a silver horse in mid-leap. "It looks a good size, and this square will be suitable for performing." She turned to da San-Germain. "Who will deal with the landlord?"

"I will do it, if you would like me to," he offered.

Photine considered his offer while thinking aloud. "We want to pay a fair price for our rooms and meals, and the care of our vehicles and animals, but no more than that; and we will want to have rooms so that we need not sleep more than two to a room, which this inn is large enough to supply without difficulty, by the look of it." She turned to him, including him in her ruminations. "The location is fine for our purposes; the square is large and the district isn't too shabby, or too grand." She pulled her cloak more closely around her shoulders. "If I have no man to speak for me, they will do their utmost to cheat me on the price." Her raised eyebrow was eloquent; this had clearly happened before. "Do you agree that we must stay here?"

He did not answer directly. "Then send Roger—it will look more established if you have a representative do your bargaining, someone who has the right mix of canniness and deference; the innkeeper will recognize a superior manservant at once. I'll do it if you like, but Roger will make the better bargain."

She considered his advice. "If you think it best. Have your man make our arrangements, provided he makes the best arrangement he can."

"He has long experience in such matters; leave it to him to make the most satisfactory terms for the troupe," da San-Germain said, casting his mind back to the many, many times Roger had done this for him in the past; he secured the brake and the reins of the two mules before he climbed down from the driving-box and came around the rear of the cart to help her to descend.

"I want him also to discover where we apply for a permit to perform, and what restrictions they have placed on performances. I need to be prepared before I speak with the authorities." She spoke quietly, making an effort to keep the rest from overhearing.

"As you wish," said da San-Germain, turning toward Roger and the smaller cart at the end of the troupe's train. "If you will, inquire what they will charge to house and keep us, two to a room, with a separate room for Photine, and what the costs for the animals and wagons are."

He nodded. "Shall I take the purse?"

"You'd better," said da San-Germain. "We're players. They'll want their money before they provide us so much as a cup of wine. And then ask where we apply for a license to perform."

"To convince the innkeeper of our legitimacy, my master?" Roger asked in Byzantine Greek, allowing himself a faint laugh, and went into the Cheval d'Argent, whistling to alert the landlord that customers had arrived.

"That, and that we wish to comply with the new regulations governing performers," da San-Germain called after him. "We don't want any complaints made against us."

"Will we have to compete with executions for an audience?" Constance grumbled as she climbed out of the front wagon.

Feo chuckled. "It will be a hard choice for some of them in this city. Well, it will be a test for the new play—blood or satire. We have novelty on our side, and that should spur interest. If they like it here, it will do well elsewhere." He yawned and stretched, then turned to offer a steadying hand to Olympe. Behind them on the next wagon, Aloys slumped over the reins, almost too worn out to move.

"Let us hope so," said Constance.

"Get down, get down," Photine urged, and was confronted by Enee, who had emerged from the third wagon.

"The Devil take it. That poet! He kept me awake with his scribbling!" Squinting into the morning gloom, he raised his voice. "Is there anything to eat that's hot? I swear I have chilblains, and it's only the beginning of October." He glared at Photine. "Did your foreign gentleman keep you warm, Mother?"

"That's between him and me," she replied, the words clipped.

"Did you please him?"

"Enough, Enee!" she ordered. "Help get the horses and mules into the stable, and brush them down. There'll be breakfast in a little while."

"Yes, Madame," Enee said, with an insultingly low bow, after which he answered the whistled summons from Feo.

Gradually all the company got out of the wagons, most of them groggy, all of them hungry; one or two of them were stiff from travel.

"Wretched weather, but it's always thus when rain is coming," Valence declared. "The mist should be gone in an hour or so."

"How did you sleep?" Crepin asked everyone in general, pulling on a cloak as he left his wagon.

"Well enough, I suppose," said Pascal, descending from the third wagon. "Mornings like this remind me of home—and why I left it."

"If a bunk in a wagon is preferable to home, then it must have been extremely dreary," Valence observed.

"It was," said Pascal in a tone that did not encourage more questions.

"The off-side mare has a loose shoe," Hariot told Feo as he got off the driving-box of the third wagon. "Her shoes should be pulled and her hooves trimmed, and she should go barefoot for a day or two. She's close to lame, and must be given a chance to rest. Let Aloys know when he wakes up, will you?" He scratched at the two-day stubble on his jaw. "I'm famished. When do we eat?"

"Shortly," said Photine, who had come up to him. "We're ordering food now. It will be ready in a little while."

"Good," said Hariot. "Where's the necessary house? I'm damned if I'll use a chamber-pot in an inn-yard."

"How should I know?" Pascal asked.

Da San-Germain pointed in the direction of the midden. "That way would be my guess," he said. "If not there, on the other side of the taproom."

Both Hariot and Pascal went off in search of it; a few minutes later, Constance followed them.

Roger emerged from the inn and nodded to da San-Germain. "I've paid for a week's rooms, board, and stabling for the animals as well as the right to put the wagons and carts in the coach-house, with a little extra for service. Wine and beer are not included in the price for food. The rates are high because the innkeeper does not know the troupe, but not outrageous. He's pleased, and so am I.

Permission to perform is granted by the Revolutionary Tribunal, where the costs are determined by a board of three members of the Tribunal." He spoke loudly enough for almost all the troupe to hear. "There will be breakfast in half an hour. They're working in the kitchen now, and they've sent a kitchen maid to the baker."

"Is there anything hot to drink now?" Feo called out to Roger. "Do they have coffee in this place?"

"If you ask the cook, he may have something for you," Roger responded. "You'll find him in the kitchen at the rear of the tap-room."

"I'll go ask," said Feo, signaling to one of the inn's grooms to tend to his team. "Give them a good brushing."

"You will supervise the stabling, Signor' Feo," Photine told him, her demeanor showing great purpose. "There will be breakfast when that's done."

Feo shrugged and changed directions toward the stable.

"Make sure my son helps," she called after him.

Unconcerned with the usual morning arrangements, Da San-Germain led his mules toward the stable; he had nearly reached the door when Theron, looking as if he had spent the night outside in a storm, hurried up to him. "When do you make inquiry about Madelaine? I want to go with you when you do."

"It would be fruitless to approach anyone in authority at this hour," said da San-Germain, noticing the febrile shine in the younger man's eyes. "And it wouldn't be wise to draw attention to our errand."

Theron shook his head slowly. "We'll have to get word to her somehow that we're here, and we'll soon have her released. She must be desolate with worry."

"It may not be that easy," da San-Germain warned him.

"Oh, there are probably bribes to pay, and certain expected sophistries to observe, but surely we can have her out in a few days." He shot a suspicious look at da San-Germain. "Or do you have other plans for her?"

"I have no plans until I discover what her circumstances are," said da San-Germain with deliberate calm. "It would be prudent of you to do the same. We don't know enough to make plans, let alone assume we know what will be required to gain her liberty."

Shaking his head, Theron swore quietly, then walked away without saying anything loud enough to be heard; da San-Germain continued on into the stable, where he haltered the mules and secured the leads to a stout pillar; he gave all three of the mules a bit of apple from the pouch on his belt under his driving-coat, and proceeded to remove their harnesses, and hung them on hooks on the wall, then gathered the combs and brushes from his grooming-box. By the time he led the three mules into a box-stall, he could hear the inn's porters removing the actors' cases from the wagons.

"I don't suppose you're going to go in to eat?" Feo inquired. "Everyone but your man, Hariot, and Enee have sat down."

"Not just now," said da San-Germain as he began to brush the largest of the three mules.

"Enee has left to watch the executions. He said he wants a good place so he will miss nothing." Feo gave a snort of laughter, and turned to leave, but hesitated. "You haven't seen Tereson, have you?"

"Not in here; I believe she went in to breakfast with Sibelle."

Grinning, Feo slapped the door. "Merci, Ragoczy. I'll find her."

Da San-Germain watched him go, then went on with the mules, using a pick to clean their hooves. As he straightened up, he noticed that Hariot was tending to the horses with the help of two of the inn's grooms; da San-Germain raised his voice. "If you want to break your fast, Hariot, I'll take over your work for now."

"No need," Hariot replied, panting a little from the speed of his efforts. "I'll finish up shortly."

"As you like." For the next hour, he worked on the animals while out in the stable-yard Roger supervised the porters carrying the troupe's chests and cases to their assigned rooms. By the time he emerged from the stable, the mists were lifting and the glare of sunlight promised a clear afternoon.

Roger was waiting in the short entry hall that led to the tap-room on the left and the stairs to the guest-rooms on the right; he spoke in the Latin of his living years. "Most of the players are in the taproom, finishing their meal. Lothaire has gone off for the morning, ostensibly to get the lay of the city. Madame has ordered baths for all who want them."

"Very practical," said da San-Germain, smiling a little.

"She's planning to go to the Tribunal shortly after mid-day, before the riposino." He paused. "I thought you might want to go with her. There is a great deal of information to be had from the Tribunal."

"You mean I can learn what they've done with Madelaine," said da San-Germain, his voice low even with the precaution of speaking Imperial Latin.

"It did seem likely." Roger saw Crepin coming their way, and said the last in French. "If there is any other service you require of me?"

"Not just now, thank you, Roger," said da San-Germain, nodding to Crepin as he passed them in the little antechamber.

"You have the room on the end of the north corridor on the floor above us; it faces the coach-house. The room has a valet's closet and I'll make my bed in there. There's a clothes-press in the closet, and a cot." Roger went on when Crepin was out of hearing range. "Feo and Hariot will be in the room next to us, and Photine will have the room opposite for herself." He held out an iron key to da San-Germain. "I've put Theron in the other wing, along with Enee and Aloys. And I removed the mirror from the end of the corridor and put it in Madame's room."

"Astute as always, old friend." Da San-Germain slipped the key into the outside pocket of his caped driving-coat, then went on, "I think I had better put on something more respectable than what I'm wearing now when I go the Tribunal with Photine. Driving clothes will not impress the delegates to the Tribunal."

Roger nodded. "The black swallow-tail coat and the burgundy unmentionables? And a linen shirt, I think, not a silk one; I will set them out for you." He paused, waiting for da San-Germain to indicate if this would serve his purpose.

Da San-Germain gestured his approval. "That should strike the right note—not too formal but formal enough to be seen as serious," he said.

"The players would be proud of you, choosing so appropriate an ensemble for your task, " said Roger, and moved away toward the taproom door. "I'll tell Madame of your intention to accompany her."

"Thank you." He was about to turn away, but inquired, "Is the large chest of my native earth in the room at the end of the north hall?"

"It is. And made up for you behind a screen."

"I need not have asked," he said by way of apology. "Then I think I may rest for two or three hours; it is likely to be a long day today, and a longer one tomorrow."

"I'll tell the chambermaids to leave you alone."

Da San-Germain ducked his head. "If you'll let Photine know that I'll be with her shortly before noon?"

"Certainly, my master," said Roger, and opened the taproom door; the buzz of conversation and the aroma of ham, fish, cheese, and fresh bread welled around the two. "And I'll speak to the cook about obtaining a duck or a goose, fresh killed. I haven't had a decent meal in four days—too many eyes on me."

"Enjoy it," da San-Germain said. "But don't forget there are more eyes here than the troupe's."

"I'll bear it in mind, and be careful of this damned proliferation of mirrors."

"It's hard to avoid them," da San-Germain said in a lowered voice. "But it's necessary."

"I won't forget," Roger said, and closed the door between them.

Da San-Germain turned away and took the stairs to the floor above, going to the room at the end of the north corridor. The key was stiff in the lock, but the door opened readily enough once the wards aligned.

Being on the end of the wing, the room had two sets of windows, one pair facing north, the other pair facing east, all still shuttered against the night; underneath these stood his two chests of clothes. A curtained bed was against the south wall, and the screen was on the far side of it; a small round table with two chairs and a small chest-of-drawers with a mirror completed the furniture in the room. Da San-Germain shut the door and tugged off his driving-coat, tossing it onto the curtained bed before unbuttoning his woolen jacket and putting it with the driving-coat. When he had set his jacket aside, he found the ewer and basin in the valet's closet. Turning the mirror to the wall, he washed his face and hands, used his shirt for a towel, and flung that, too, onto the cur-tained bed. His unmentionables followed the shirt; he quickly stripped all the way down to his underclothes, then went behind the screen and found his dressing-gown on the narrow bed that lay atop a chest of his native earth. This he pulled on, then climbed onto the thin mattress, stretched out supine, and settled himself into the stupor which, for those of his blood, served as sleep.

An inharmonious chorus of bells wakened him at mid-day, and as he stirred, Roger came around the end of the screen, a plate of raw slices of duck in his hand, an expression of dismay in his faded-blue eyes. "The day's executions are about to begin. They're making quite an occasion of it." As if to confirm this, a roar went up from a crowd some few streets away, accompanied by a pair of tuneless bugles.

"That would explain the noise," said da San-Germain, sitting up and blinking, feeling slightly dazed as he often did after resting.

"Most of the members of the Revolutionary Tribunal are at-tending the beheadings," Roger added, no sign of emotion in his voice. "So is the innkeeper, for that matter. The whole city seems to have come to a halt for the executions."

"Then it will be a while before Photine and I can call upon the clerks of the Tribunal." He got out of his bed and looked toward the shuttered windows. "I gather the day has brightened."

"And warmed." Roger indicated the table. "If you don't object—"

"By all means, finish your meal," said da San-Germain.

"I don't want anyone to notice my preference for raw meat," Roger said as he sat down at the little table, and picked up his knife again.

"Very wise," said da San-Germain, getting to his feet, untying the sash on his dressing-gown, and preparing to remove it. "Which of the linen shirts did you choose? the white one or one of the ivory?"

"Ivory," said Roger, his voice muffled by chewing. "I will have it for you in a moment."

"Do I need a shave yet?" He rubbed his chin and felt the beginning of stubble there.

"If you want one, I'll get the basin and the razor," Roger offered.

"Best not," said da San-Germain. "I shouldn't appear too well-groomed. The members of the Tribunal will be suspicious if I present too fastidious an aspect. Tomorrow will be time enough."

"Have you decided upon what you will tell the Tribunal clerks when you inquire about Madelaine?" Roger continued his meal while a second cheer with bugle accompaniment went up.

"I have. I will say I am a distant relative exiled from Hungary; the family is worried about her, and have asked me, since I am with the players, to find out what I can of her fate." He had taken off his dressing-gown and now stood in his undervest and drawers, trying to make up his mind if he should choose boots or shoes for the afternoon.

"It's a bit risky," Roger warned.

"I know, but I trust that this will make my explanation more convincing." He waited, and when Roger said nothing more, he went on, "As an exile, I'm not one of the aristos the Revolution condemns, and it would make sense that a well-born family in another country would send the black sheep to get information."

"I hope it will succeed," said Roger.

"So do I," said da San-Germain with more feeling than before. "If I'm not persuasive, I endanger more than myself, and you."

"That thought did occur to me," said Roger, taking another bite, then, after the greater part of a minute, asked, "Do you think you and Madame will . . . want privacy this evening?"

"If we do, it will be in her room," said da San-Germain, selecting shoes for his errand. "But she hasn't asked me yet."

"Do you think you might go out if she has other plans for to-night?" He asked it off-handedly enough, but there was an unmistakable seriousness in his faded-blue eyes.

"It's not unlikely," said da San-Germain, wishing he were at the villa in Lecco where he could avail himself of the Roman bath lined with his native earth. "She has much to do, and although she enjoys our dalliance, she is far more committed to the troupe than to the pleasure she has with me."

Roger was almost finished with his raw duck. "Then you should consider finding other nourishment. You will need your strength and your wits, my master. Hunger will not serve you well just now."

"No, it will not," da San-Germain agreed, coming out from behind the screen. "Where are the—"

"The shirt is on the peg on the far side of the bed, and the swallow-tail coat and unmentionables are in the clothes-press. I'll get them for you, if you're ready." He set his plate aside, and rose.

"My thanks, old friend." Da San-Germain went to get the shirt, donning it quickly. "This should have a neck-cloth, I think. And I'll need some kind of ribbon-knot."

"Red, blue, and white. I know." Roger had stepped into the valet's closet and was opening the clothes-press. "I took the liberty of getting a lapel-fan for you while you were sleeping. It's on the chest-of-drawers."

"Ah. Yes, I see it." He took the unmentionables that Roger handed to him, and stepped into them with care, tucking the shirt in as he buttoned the front flap. "No waistcoat."

"Too grand," Roger told him. "You're with players, not the regional magistrate."

Da San-Germain nodded. "An excellent point." He found a belt hanging on the peg next to the one that had held the shirt. "No suspenders either, I suppose?"

"The belt is what the players wear."

"That's so," da San-Germain agreed, and threaded the belt

through the buttonhole loops along the waist of the unmentionables.

"Photine asked me to mention the music to you an hour ago; she's fretting about it," Roger added as he took the swallow-tail coat from the clothes-press. "I trust this is neat enough. A few wrinkles are to be expected."

Another shout, this one louder than the previous ones, arose from the streets along with the clamor of bugles and the enthusiastic tattoo of a drum.

"As always, you are meticulous." He held the garment, examining it, then said, "What about the music?"

"Photine would like to know if you have something in mind to accompany the Corpses. She says you discussed it."

"We did. I haven't given it much thought." He looked about almost as if he expected the answer to appear in the air. "But I imagine I ought to, if we are to perform in the next few days." His expression darkened an instant, then returned to what it had been. "If you would, find the cimbalom for me while Photine and I are at the Tribunal. It should be under the seat in the larger cart, with two sets of hammers."

Roger gave him a startled look. "The cimbalom? Are you sure? I doubt anyone in Avignon has ever heard one."

"Exactly," said da San-Germain. "But they know hammered dulcimers, so the cimbalom won't be that foreign—just foreign enough, something to set the troupe apart from other players they may have seen. And the sound is a bit eerie." He reached for the swallow-tail coat. "A pity we couldn't bring the utugardon from Padova."

"It's too big to transport easily," Roger pointed out, handing over the coat.

"It's more drum-like in sound, for all it looks a bit like a 'cello." He donned the coat and turned to face Roger. "Which neck-cloth?"

"Something simple, perhaps the sprigged cotton," said da San-Germain. "It creates a more foreign appearance."

"So it does," said Roger, going to the smaller of the two traveling chests. "Black or white?"

"Black, I think."

"Very good." He sorted through the small closed boxes, then drew out a black neck-cloth of sprigged cotton, which he handed to da San-Germain. "Photine will appreciate your attention to details."

"I trust the clerks at the Tribunal will do the same," he said as he wound the cloth around his neck. "No starched collar."

"Certainly not," said Roger in mock horror. "Just let me tie the ends for you."

Da San-Germain gave a single, rueful laugh. "Oh, to have a reflection."

"Do you miss yours?" Roger asked as he busied himself with the neck-cloth.

"At times like these, I do," said da San-Germain, and changed the subject. "I'll need the small purse, and two dozen louis d'or. The Tribunal may not like aristocrats, but I don't doubt they'll accept their coins."

"Especially because you are a foreigner," Roger seconded. "Do you anticipate needing a bribe?"

"No, but I would be very surprised if there were not fees to be paid," said da San-Germain in a world-weary tone.

"Of course," said Roger. "There are always fees."

"What will come of all this killing?" Da San-Germain asked as the next cheer echoed through the streets, made louder by the bugles' chaotic fanfares.

"More graves," said Roger.

Nodding slowly, da San-Germain strove to shut out the sudden image of Madelaine on the scaffold that filled his mind. "Hope that there is good news at the Tribunal, and that they'll provide answers to us, whatever the case. I need to plan our next step, but I can't do it until I know what has become of her."

"Of course," said Roger, aware of the anguish that had overtaken da San-Germain. He stepped back. "There. Finished."

Another whoop from the crowd watching the Guillotine do its work rang through the city, with the ragged fanfare lasting longer than before.

With despair in his dark eyes, da San-Germain murmured, "Listen to them: they're mad for blood."

Unable to summon up any encouraging sentiments, Roger said, "I'll get your purse. You said you want two dozen louis d'or." Without waiting for an answer, he went into the valet's closet to count out the money from the small banded and locked box that lay in a hidden compartment in da San-Germain's smallest chest.

Text of two reports—one to Photine d'Auville, one to Ragoczy Ferenz—sent by messenger to the Cheval d'Argent by the clerks of the Revolutionary Tribunal of Avignon.

> *To the leader of the acting troupe Commedia della Morte, presently in residence at the Cheval d'Argent, Place du Rhone, from the Revolutionary Tribunal of Avignon, on this, the 6th day of October, 1792.*
>
> *Madame d'Auville:*
>
> *After due consideration, the Committee for Public Affairs has agreed to grant you a permit for three performances of the play which scenario you presented to the Tribunal two days ago, said performances to take place on Tuesday, Thursday, and Saturday next, to conclude before noon, in the Place du Rhone, subject to the review of your script by our Office of Public Morals. Should any portion of your play be deemed inimically against the Revolution, your performances will be canceled and the performance fee retained by the Committee for Public Affairs in recompense for your breach of contract.*
>
> *The fee for such performances has already been received by this office, and only a twenty-percent contribution of your earnings from the performances will be required of you at the conclusion of your three performances. At that time you may apply for an exten-*

sion of this permit, and if there has been no complaint lodged against the play or any of your company, another three performances will be licensed.

Vive la Revolution!

Jean-Simone Chastal
Clerk of the Committee for Public Affairs
The Revolutionary Tribunal of Avignon

To the Hungarian exile, Ferenz Ragoczy, presently resident at the Cheval d'Argent, Place du Rhone, a member of the acting troupe Commedia della Morte, from the Revolutionary Tribunal of Avignon on this, the 6ᵗʰ day of October, 1792.

Monsieur,

The records of the Committee for Public Safety inform me that the woman you seek is no longer in the care of that Committee in Avignon, but is, with other enemies of France, being transported to Lyon, where she, and those others with whom she travels, will face the full might of the law for her many offenses against the People of France. You may inform her Hungarian kinsmen that justice will be done upon her, as it will be done on all those who abused the People of France. Any attempt to interfere with that justice will bring the attention of the Revolutionary Courts upon you and whatever members of your family remain within the borders of France; the Revolution has a long arm, and a longer memory.

Vive la Revolution!
Vive la France!

Beniguet Francois Dassin
Clerk of the Committee for Public Safety
Revolutionary Tribunal of Avignon

2

Da San-Germain finished adjusting the tuning-pegs on his cimbalom, then reached for the skull-mask that would complete his costume, which consisted of a winding-sheet wrapped around him, covering the black unmentionables and shirt of ecru silk he wore. Seated as he was at the side of the two wagons that with lowered side-panels provided the stage for the troupe's performance, he could watch the Place du Rhone gradually fill with citizens; in traditional Commedia costumes, Valence, Crepin, Olympe, and Tereson made their way through the burgeoning audience, entertaining the people with mime with the intent of enticing them to remain for the play. The banner above the stage bore the name of the company and their play: Commedia della Morte.

"We start as soon as the clock strikes the hour of ten," said Photine, coming around the end of the wagon toward him with an anxious glance at the clock-tower at the far end of the square; she was in her costume for the play but had not yet added her wig, crown, and out-sized rings to complete the appearance of her character. "Our license requires us—"

"That will allow two hours for the performance, which is ample. Even if the audience is deeply enthusiastic, at our last rehearsal the play lasted only an hour and a half, which gives us more than enough time to finish by noon," da San-Germain reminded her in a calming tone. "The Tribunal will have no complaints on the play's length."

Valence and Olympe improvised a little dance, and attracted another dozen or so people to approach the curtained platform. They bowed extravagantly and looked about for more townsfolk to lure to the platform.

"If they do, they'll stop us, finished or not." She shook her head as if she were certain this would happen.

"I don't see why they would bother," da San-Germain said, keeping his tone carefully neutral. "There are no executions scheduled today."

"Just as well for us, I think," she said, her eyes on the gathering in front of the wagons.

"Very likely," he said, to let her know he was listening.

"I'm sorry, Ragoczy." She fussed with the lavish fall of lace on her corsage. "You know I'm always nervous before we start." With a sigh, she sat down on the rear steps of the wagon. "I don't suppose you've seen Enee?"

"Not for more than an hour." He laid his hand on her shoulder. "Do you want me to send Roger to look for him?"

"No; I've put Roger to work keeping track of our masks; this isn't the time to mix them up, as we did rehearsing," she said hollowly. "I told Enee at breakfast that he would have to be here by thirty minutes until ten. If he isn't . . ." Her words faded into another sigh.

"He isn't crucial to the performance," da San-Germain said gently. "If he doesn't return in time, it won't ruin the play. We can manage with one fewer Corpse and Lackey."

"Yes, we can manage," she admitted, dejection in every line of her drooping figure. "He is so feckless. He doesn't understand."

"Why should he understand? He does this to upset you," da San-Germain said. "The more distressed you appear, the more he counts himself successful."

"I know, I know, and I am almost out of patience with him for these petulant tricks of his; he's fifteen and no longer a child, to be coddled and indulged," she said, a bit more brusquely, trying to convince herself as well as da San-Germain. "But he is not nearly as experienced, as knowledgeable as he fancies himself. He could get into, oh, all manner of trouble, and this is not the time or the place for such folly."

"He could, and you're right—this would not be a good place to catch the attention of the officials. The repercussions could be more difficult than he imagines." He tied on his mask, and his voice became muffled. "But your telling him that will not persuade him. He might listen to Hariot, or Feo, if you would like me to have a word with them after the play."

"Oh, would you?" She gave him her most tremulous smile. "He *might* listen to one of them." Then she reached for his hand. "I would hate to have to get him out of trouble while we're going after your kinswoman. It could prevent us from pursing her." Her expression shifted. "Are you sure that she will be in Lyon?"

"Not completely certain, but from what I've learned since the clerk sent the note to me, I have confirmed with two Revolutionary Guards that a barge was taken north with a number of prisoners on it, almost all of them aristos or religious. I have to suppose, since she's not on the list of official prisoners here, that she is among those on the barge, bound for Lyon." He felt a shudder of sympathy for Madelaine, constrained to travel over running water, which for those of his blood caused vertigo and seasickness. Being a prisoner was bad enough, but the enervation that the river would cause would double her misery.

"And you're determined that we should pursue her?"

"Yes, Photine, I am, and I will do so." He saw her dismay before she could conceal it. "You needn't come with me if you would prefer not to."

She stared at him, her whole attention on his dark, compelling eyes in the papier-mâché skull-mask. "I've said I would help you find her, and I will."

From the far side of the stage, they heard the jangling sound of a tambourine, a signal to the mimes to return to the wagons to prepare for the performance.

"I'll have to finish dressing in a few minutes," said Photine.

Da San-Germain smiled his encouragement, but realized she could not see it. "You will do well, Photine. Your actors are all rehearsed in their parts. You will succeed."

She gave a nervous shrug and got to her feet. "Start playing five minutes before the play begins. Remember, no merry songs."

"I'll keep to the dirges and laments," he promised. "I know the ones you prefer."

She was about to walk away, but stopped. "Have you seen our poet today?"

"Not since early this morning," he answered. "He seemed to be preoccupied."

"About what?" It was impossible to tell what she was seeking in that simple question.

"I have no idea. He said nothing to me." He did not add that Theron seemed to be annoyed with him, though he wondered if he should mention it.

"Well, I trust he'll be here for the play. It is his work, for the most part, and we will need to discuss the audience reaction when the performance is over; there are changes that we must have." She waved to him once, then went off toward her wagon, her step dragging as if she carried a great weight on her shoulders. She paused to make a quick perusal of the people at the front of the wagons, then went on, a bit more energetically.

Da San-Germain watched her go, wishing he could think of some way to cheer her, but he had seen her perform many times and realized that her current state of anxiety was part of her means of making ready. He gave his attention to his cimbalom once more, testing the strings with the tips of his fingers to make sure they were holding their pitch. Out of the corner of his eye, he saw Aloys close the heavy, fringed curtains across the front of the platform and begin setting up the hard stage bed with its garlands of paper flowers, and the small table for the first scene of their play.

Feo came around behind the wagon, saying, "I'm looking for Enee—have you—"

"—seen him? Not recently," da San-Germain told him. "Nor have I seen Theron in the last two hours. Other than that, everything seems ready."

"Well, that's one fewer Corpse for the final march, and one less

Lackey for Photine in her scene. The poet, though, he ought to be here, so he can see how the play is received, but I guess it isn't entirely necessary." He shook his head. "That boy, he's another matter altogether—he is determined to get into trouble. He is intent on putting his mother in a difficult position, and to test whether she will stand by him."

"That he is," da San-Germain agreed, surprised at the acuity of Feo's understanding. "And she is aware of it," he added, then selected the harder hammers for the cimbalom; they were made of wood and looked like long-handled shallow spoons. "It's almost time to start the music. What do you think of the crowd?"

"I don't know. It looks a little small to me, but I'm new to all this," said Feo, a rascally smile brightening his face, "and this is the first real performance I'm seeing, so I have no way to judge." He ducked his head. "That mask is . . . unnerving."

"You've seen it before," said da San-Germain, surprised by the observation.

"I know. It must be the occasion. This isn't practice anymore, is it?" He stepped away from da San-Germain, taking up his place on the platform beside the curtain-pull for this side of the stage.

Da San-Germain shook his head. "No. No more practice," he said, and began to play on the cimbalom, hammering the strings lightly at first, drawing out a plaintive folksong from the instrument. At first few of the people gathered in front of the two wagons paid any attention, but as the sound grew louder, more of the audience listened, caught by the haunting tune. They became quiet, and moved closer to the stage, and da San-Germain began another song, this one from his homeland, a somber kind of march that prepared the audience for something disturbing.

Suddenly Lothaire, in his Corpse costume, stepped through the curtains and bowed to the assembled spectators; da San-Germain's instrument went silent.

First Corpse: How often have we had to see
Death displayed as liberty?

Heads offered up as proof of right
Or proof of law, or proof of spite:
The living find cause for this display
Though fear it may reach them one day.
How often have we had to mourn
For those whose fault was being born?
Yet soon or late, the end must come
And all of life be then the sum
Of days, and be they few or many,
Laden with years, or hardly any,
Welcome or dreaded, all the same,
In obscurity or fame:
Thus these scenes will surely show
That in triumph or in woe
None may stay the fatal hour,
Nor withstand its mortal power.
No king, no beggar, no cadet
Can change the time once it is set.
For soon or late, Death comes for all,
And all that lives is in its thrall.
So take what solace that you may
From what we show to you today.

He bowed again, and stepped back as the curtains were pulled open; the curtain on the right side of the stage concealed his exit even as it revealed the boudoir of a courtesan of the old school, in the person of Olympe Lacet, wearing a sacque-backed negligee, a white wig, and elaborate make-up with patches by the corner of her mouth and above her right eyebrow; she was surrounded by paste jewels and paper flowers. She sat on the end of the bed, reading a note from an admirer. The first scene of the play had begun.

Tereson, in the character of Olympe's maid, came in with a lavish bouquet of white roses made of paper, and presented this to Olympe with a flourish, announcing that a caller was waiting, offering an elaborate description of the man and what he could provide, emphasizing her comments with exuberant gestures, her lithe movements more like dance than mime. Olympe appeared to listen with an air of satisfaction while she admired her bracelets and rings, and when Tereson had finished her catalogue of the new client, asked that he be sent up. Tereson bowed and departed to the right; Olympe picked up a hand-mirror and primped. In a short while, Hariot entered, resplendent in garments twenty years out of fashion, holding on to a tall cane. His face was aged with paint and there were marks on his cheeks and nose that suggested the client suffered from carnal diseases. He bowed and kissed Olympe's hands, exclaiming on her beauty all the while. She heard him out with an air of boredom, then patted the bed beside her.

The audience chuckled, anticipating what would happen next.

Da San-Germain began to strike a single string, softly but steadily.

Tereson staggered onto the stage, announcing another visitor, but with a demeanor of horror, and before she could conclude her description, she fell as Lothaire entered and pulled her into the fold of his winding-sheet.

The audience gasped, and a murmur passed through the crowd, and then a few of their number moved a little nearer to the stage, aware that they were seeing something unfamiliar. The easy excitement that had possessed the audience changed to attentive curiosity. A pair of older women left the gathering, shaking their heads in shock and disapproval.

On the bed, Hariot and Olympe went still, and then, as the First Corpse approached them, they rose and began to follow Lothaire and Tereson, marching across the stage like a procession of automatons to the grim notes from the cimbalom. A moment later, the curtains closed and Olympe reached for her skull half-mask, and tied it on as she stepped out through the opening in the curtains.

> *Second Corpse: I, who lived for gaiety and vice,*
> *Am now but food for worms and cold as ice.*

She went on while behind the curtain the scene was changed as quickly as possible, to the garden for Cleante's and Desiree's dialogue where Pascal and Sibelle would argue the merits of eloping.

Photine slipped in beside da San-Germain, now fully dressed and made up for her scene that was the next-to-the-last in the play. "I wish we didn't need these speeches to cover the change of scene, but it can't be helped." She laid her hand on his arm. "How are they taking it?" she whispered while Olympe continued to recite her couplets.

"They seem to be interested," da San-Germain said softly, continuing his steady beat on the single note.

"Have you seen anyone from the Tribunal watching?"

"Not that I've recognized, but that doesn't mean that some of the audience isn't from the Tribunal."

Sibelle hurried onto the stage, her costume rustling. Pascal was behind her, putting on his tricorn hat. "How much more time?" he mouthed to Photine.

She held up four fingers, meaning two couplets to go. "I'll leave you," she breathed into da San-Germain's ear before she slipped away.

Feo went to pull open his side of the curtain.

The play progressed steadily, the scenes moving along, some of them touching but most of them amusing enough to evoke laughter from the audience. Da San-Germain continued to play music and to sound the single note—moving up the scale by half a step with the end of each scene. By the time Photine appeared as the Queen in the final scene, the audience was beginning to relish the appearance of the Corpses, and to find their abrupt intrusions mordantly funny; the shock the First Corpse had occasioned at the beginning had given way to ironic anticipation.

The Queen ordered her Favorite to undertake a voyage to the New World, to claim lands not already gobbled up by England and Spain, and carve out for her a simple, earthly paradise. She rhapsodized on the magnificence and tranquillity that she would find there, and the happiness that had so long eluded her. The Favorite offered lavish promises and the vow that he would rather die than fail in his appointed task—a pronouncement that drew a cynical giggle from some of the spectators—and departed with a flourish. The Queen, left alone, debated with herself about her responsibilities and the power she would not be able to keep in the idyll she sought, and wondered which was more acceptable for her. Her Minister of State arrived to tell her of enemies massing on her borders and the need to send the army into the field to stop them. She told the Minister of State to summon her Generals, and when two had arrived, the Corpses came, too, now increased in number to five.

At this, the audience applauded, and a few tossed coins onto the stage. The last round of couplets roused more enthusiasm, and as the curtains closed and the troupe readied themselves for their curtain-call, two of the Corpses went out into the audience to collect more coins. Da San-Germain played a morose little march while the actors acknowledged the clapping and cheers of the crowd, and by the time the Corpses returned with their boxes of coins, the people were beginning to drift away from the wagons.

"Keep the curtains closed for ten minutes," Photine ordered Aloys and Feo. "We won't take this down until the audience is gone."

"As you like," said Aloys. "I'll have a cup of wine while I wait, if it suits you." His manner indicated that he cared little for what she thought.

"Just don't go far," Photine told him as she came up to da San-Germain, who had removed his mask. "You did very well."

"Thank you," he said as he finished unwinding his shroud. "I gather you're pleased with the way the performance went? The people were pleased, I thought, once they realized it was not usual commedia." He put the cimbalom hammers back in their case.

"Overall, I believe we succeeded. But I need to talk to Heurer about some of those couplets—they sound so labored. We need more ease in phrasing." She looked about as if expecting to find Theron waiting nearby.

"I haven't seen him," said da San-Germain. "Like Enee, he has not made an appearance."

"That's most . . . inconvenient," said Photine. "I will have to have a talk with him about the between-scene couplets—they're too much like doggerel. We need something more inspired, less heavy-handed, more in keeping with the rest of the play." She caught sight of Valence and signaled to him, saying over her shoulder to da San-Germain, "We'll meet later. I do want to spend a time with you privately. Tonight, perhaps, if that will suit you. Just now I have others to attend to."

Da San-Germain watched her go, then put his cimbalom back in its case, placed it in the driving-well of the nearer wagon, and donned a short pelisse of light-weight wool. He handed his mask to Roger as he made for the door of the Cheval d'Argent. "Has the take been counted yet?"

"No, not yet," said Roger, hanging the mask on a peg with the initials *S-G* written in chalk above it. "I saw Theron return during the last scene of the play. He's probably in his quarters or the taproom."

"I'll try the taproom first," said da San-Germain, and nodded to Roger before he moved toward the door to the inn.

"He seemed surly when he went in," Roger called after him in Byzantine Greek.

Da San-Germain gestured an acknowledgment. He was surprised to realize that he was feeling a bit tired, for he did not think he had exerted himself a great deal playing, but he had done little else to account for his fatigue. He took a minute to consider this development, and decided that he, like the actors, had been caught up in the demands of the performance, investing his music with the added stimulation the audience provided. For a second he recalled Giorgianna singing Scarlatti's music, a century ago, and the vigor that marked her performance, and the weariness that set in when the opera was done. He paused on the threshold of the taproom, which seemed dim after the brightness of the square; light was harder on his eyes than darkness, and in a moment, he could make out the entire room without difficulty.

Theron was in the far corner of the room, a large glass of red wine sitting on the table in front of him; an empty glass stood next to it. Looking haggard, he stared off into the distance, deliberately unaware of his surroundings. Even when da San-Germain approached, Theron seemed not to notice.

"The play went well," da San-Germain said as he reached Theron's table.

Theron said nothing.

"I believe Photine would like to talk to you about some changes." Without waiting for an invitation, he pulled up a chair and sat down opposite the poet. "I was surprised you weren't here for the performance."

"I know the lines," said Theron heavily, and picked up his second glass, drinking down half of it.

"But that isn't the same as seeing how an audience takes to it," da San-Germain observed, keeping his manner affable.

Theron shrugged and finished the wine, and signaled the man behind the bar for another; he cocked an eyebrow at da San-Germain.

"Thank you, no; as you may recall, I do not drink wine."

"Right. Right," said Theron, and indicated he wanted two glasses.

"Is something the matter?" da San-Germain asked, not wanting to challenge Theron when he was so determined to get drunk.

"Not that you would care," said Theron, glowering.

"Ah. What have I done to offend you?" he asked.

Theron laughed, a bit too loudly. "Done? It is what you have *not* done that troubles me," he said.

"And what might that be?"

"You haven't pursued Madelaine's case with the Revolutionary Tribunal," he said, making it an accusation.

"I was informed that she is no longer in their jurisdiction, so pursuit here would glean little beyond what I already know. I will have to go to Lyon to determine what is to be done next. The clerks here aren't willing to provide much information beyond what they sent three days ago." He did his best to sound reasonable, but was aware that this would not be acceptable to Theron, who was taking the two full glasses of wine from the barkeeper's tray.

"And you think that sufficient?" Theron asked belligerently. "She is in grave danger; you should do more to secure her release."

"She is on a barge bound for Lyon: what do you suggest I do." He regarded Theron steadily.

"You could do *something*." His face flushed darker. "There must be someone at the Tribunal who could give you more information. Why haven't you sought someone out who could tell you—"

"Since I had hoped not to alert the clerks to the depth of my interest in Madelaine, I think what I have done was all I could do. I gather that you have made a point of bringing her to official attention." He contemplated Theron's demeanor as he reached for the nearer glass of wine. "I wish you had discussed your plan with me before you spoke to the clerks of the Tribunal."

Theron's words were beginning to slur when he responded. "I suppose you would have advised me to do nothing—as you have done."

It was tempting to inform Theron of the damage he had caused, but da San-Germain knew the poet was in no fit condition to listen to any argument sensibly, so he only said, "I thought coming to France was a good start to aiding her, but I gather you deem it—"

"Devil take you, Comte!" Theron burst out, his face reddened with wine and choler. "You know the kind of danger she is in, and yet, you hold back."

"And what would you do, if it were your decision to make?" He managed to give his question a touch of amusement; he could see that the barkeeper was paying more attention to them, his vulpine face sharpened by interest.

"I would find her at once, and wrest her from her captors." He took another drink.

"And how do you propose to accomplish that? Do you think

those guarding her would permit you to simply take her without any resistance?" He gave a low chuckle. "No, Theron. Your scenario is most heroic, but far from convincing. And the role you imagine for me seems more villainous than what you originally put forth in your little drama."

Theron gave him a look of puzzlement, and shook his head, baffled, but the barkeeper nodded once and grew less attentive.

Da San-Germain leaned forward, his head only inches from Theron's, and said in a low, penetrating voice, "If you want to help Madelaine, you would do well to keep your plans to yourself. You have postured enough. The barkeeper has been listening to us, and will undoubtedly report what he hears. Speak to me about a play, not about your plans to deliver Madelaine to safety."

Theron stared at da San-Germain, affronted. "How dare you address me in—"

"I will address you as I see fit," da San-Germain said more softly, yet with such icy intent that Theron coughed in shock. "You are increasing her danger with your bravado, and I will not permit you to do so. Your impulsive actions will put her in peril beyond what she endures already. Think! You may take pride in your diligence, but you are exposing Madelaine to closer scrutiny, which will make our work harder when we find her." He gave Theron a long moment to react; as soon as the young man blinked, da San-Germain went on in the same quiet, relentless tone. "So. You will guard your tongue, and you will not venture to the Revolutionary Tribunal again. You will tell me about your new play, and your desire to act the main role, but you will say nothing more about Madelaine. Do you understand me?"

"I understand," Theron muttered, cowed, and pushed back from da San-Germain. He downed the last of the wine in the third glass and rubbed at his face. "I know I haven't the experience the others in the company do," he said more loudly, "but I'm the poet, and I know how the lines are to be spoken."

"That's as may be," said da San-Germain, his voice now placating instead of threatening. "But I think Madame may be right, and one of the company should do the role. And perhaps someone else should play the Comte. Crepin perhaps. He has the way of it."

Struggling to master his disordered thoughts, Theron picked up the last glass of wine. "I will consider what you say."

"That's all I ask," said da San-Germain, getting up from the chair.

Theron blinked at him as he took a gulp of the wine. "Tell Madame I'm . . . I hope the play went well."

"Why not tell her yourself, later?" da San-Germain slightly inclined his head and left Theron to his bibulous indulgence.

"Ragoczy," Feo said as he passed da San-Germain; he was coming in as da San-Germain was going out.

"Feo."

"Photine has asked me to go look for her son. Do you have any suggestions where I might try?"

"No, I don't, any more than others in the troupe might know," said da San-Germain. "But when you find him, you might try to impress upon him that he is putting himself in danger to no purpose."

Feo laughed once. "He'd take that as praise."

"Then you will know how to express your warnings so that he won't make that mistake," said da San-Germain. "This company needs to avoid anything that could redound to its discredit."

"On that, I agree," said Feo, turning back toward the door. "Do you think he would want to seek out Revolutionary Guards?"

"It's possible," said da San-Germain. "Foolish, but possible."

"There's a gaming den near the Pont d'Avignon. I'll try there. That boy is likely to think he's clever with dice because he won a little money from Lothaire."

"It would be a good place to begin; but don't be too obvious in your search; we don't want him to go to ground." Da San-Germain started up the stairs, intending to go to his room for a little quiet while the troupe had their dinner; he was startled to hear Roger call him from the door that led into the kitchen. Coming back down the stairs, he asked, "What is it?"

"A man from the Revolutionary Tribunal is asking for Madame. She isn't at the wagons."

"I gather the matter is urgent?"

Roger shook his head. "I imagine so, knowing the Tribunal, but he told me nothing more than he wishes to speak with her."

"Let me talk to the fellow while you see if you can find her."

"Where would you advise me to begin?" Roger inquired, his voice entirely neutral.

"You might seek for her at Valence's wagon," said da San-Germain with a slight, sardonic smile. "Knock first and give them a little time. They have often . . . gratified each other at the conclusion of performances."

If this surprised Roger, he concealed it. "I'll attend to this at once."

"Where is this official of the Tribunal?" da San-Germain asked before Roger could slip out through the kitchen.

"He was with Aloys when I came in. Aloys is taking down the curtains and stowing the stage furniture." With that, he was gone.

Da San-Germain went out to the side of the platform, and saw a man of about thirty in pale unmentionables and a hammer-tailed coat with broad lapels and a standing collar attempting to engage Aloys in conversation; the older man paid the younger one no heed, but worked steadily, folding the curtains and putting them into their large chests. As he approached the stranger, da San-Germain said, "I understand you would like to talk to Madame d'Auville, who is occupied at present. Will I be an acceptable deputy for her? I am Ragoczy Ferenz, the musician for the troupe."

"Good of you to offer," said the newcomer, an exasperated cast to his countenance. "Where is Madame d'Auville?"

"She is with some of her troupe. There is a great deal to do before the actors will be ready to go in to dinner." He smiled affably. "I wear only cerements and a mask; I have almost no costume to care for, and no paint to remove. Let me answer what questions you may have to the limit of my knowledge until Madame d'Auville can join us."

"That's a handsome offer," said the man from the Tribunal. "Very well. Is there somewhere we can get out of the sun?"

"There is the taproom, but the poet who provided the scenario and lines for our play is there, and has been imbibing rather freely."

"Need we sit near him?" He gave a kind of smirk, and held out his hand. "I am Evre Durandelle, secretary to the Revolutionary Tribunal."

"An honor," said da San-Germain, and began to walk toward the inn once more. "Can you give me some idea what your purpose is?"

"Well, the matter is a bit delicate. A few of the members of the Revolutionary Tribunal were hoping to arrange some private entertainments with Madame d'Auville and a few of her troupe." He pursed his lips. "Something unusual and very discreet."

Da San-Germain hesitated for no longer than a breath, then said, "Then I will probably be unable to help you. Such matters are beyond my place in the company. You will have to make your inquiries directly to Madame d'Auville."

"Of course," said Durandelle smoothly. "Then I shall have to wait for her to finish whatever she is doing?"

"I'm afraid so," said da San-Germain, with a hint of a bow. "Is there any other way I might be of service to you?"

"Not just at present," said Durandelle. "You may go about your business." He waved da San-Germain away, and continued on into the taproom.

Text of a broadsheet distributed throughout Avignon by a group known as the Revolutionary Artists and Writers.

Citizens of Avignon
You have a grand opportunity to see something innova-
tive and truly revolutionary in dramatic performance!
The Commedia della Morte is presenting a play of

the same name that successfully brings home the true significance of our Revolution, and with daring wit that makes what would be beyond the limits of artistic taste into an incisive and occasionally poignant demonstration of the need for revolution beyond the simple political turbulence that has accompanied our casting off our ancient chains for the vigor of freedom.

We are informed that the company will offer their play three more times, unless the Revolutionary Tribunal extends their license to perform. We urge all people in the city who have any interest in the significance of these times to attend the play and to encourage others to attend the play, so that there may be useful discussion growing out of the experience these accomplished actors bring to their challenging scenarios. We must be thankful for the talents of our modern playwrights and actors who can so clearly show the character of the Old Regime and the purpose of our Revolution. Consider the work of Jean-Marie Collot d'Herbois, and all he has done for our national cause, and give respect to the Commedia della Morte for their artistry and their zeal in the aims of our Revolution. It is through such talent that we will fulfill the promise we have struggled and sacrificed to achieve.

It is the goal of the Revolutionary Artists and Writers to reveal the entirety of revolution in all our work; the Commedia della Morte sets a superb example that we may all strive to emulate and through that emulation, to excel in our arts to the limits of genius and liberty.

3

"Tomorrow we arrive at Lyon; your journey's end," the Revolutionary Guardsman announced with a sly grin to the gathering of men and women standing on the low wharf where a barge was tied up; his breath smoked in front of his face and he pulled on his gloves as he looked over his prisoners. He was a Corporal, and as such, although not the oldest, was the senior-most Guardsman present. He raised the collar of his greatcoat with deliberation, showing his prisoners that, unlike them, he had the means to protect himself from the weather. The first drizzle of rain was falling around them, dank and chill.

"Will we have anything more than bread this morning?" asked an old woman in a soiled gown of damask and lace.

"Why would you?" the Guardsman asked; during their northward journey from Avignon, he had grown to despise these highborn cowards, who allowed him to bully them, and cringed when he shouted at them. Where was the dignity and power they had brandished in the face of the poor for so many generations? he asked himself as he swaggered along the edge of the wharf.

"Because we're cold," she answered, her tone blunt until she began to cough; she bent double, her face showing red splotches.

"Everyone is cold," the Corporal said dismissively, taking obvious satisfaction in the prisoners' misery. "You're no different now than the people you abused and starved to suit your whims. Be glad that we give you so much—you withheld food and fire to your servants and your peasants, and now you're paying the price for your neglect." He gestured to the old town walls behind him. "The people of Sainte-Sophie would probably provide you slops, if you ask them—same as their swine."

"You had hot pastry to eat!" the old woman protested, her complaint broken by her eruptive coughing.

Around her a few of the other prisoners mumbled agreement, less vigorously than she had spoken, but more troublesome for being sullen; resentment had been simmering among them and today was high, and this miserable day only served to sharpen their rancor. A few voices were loud enough for the Guardsmen to hear a smattering of derogatory words, words that alarmed the Guardsmen. Two of them drew their pistols.

The Corporal shook his head and spat in their direction. "What grandeur you have now, you pathetic creatures. Go on; huddle together. You're wretched as beggars."

From her place behind the Guardsmen, Madelaine raised her voice. "If you don't feed them something warm, they will become ill, and that would not redound to your credit. Three have died since we left Avignon; more might bring you—"

Wheeling around, the Corporal raised his hand, ready to strike out at her. "Another word, and you'll ride on the barge again! Then we'll see who's ill."

Madelaine went silent but there was no mistaking her anger, or her disgust.

The old woman struggled unsuccessfully to stop coughing; she clung to the arm of the middle-aged man next to her, looking deeply embarrassed by her helplessness. The man patted her shoulder and took a step back from her, wiping his hands with a torn handkerchief. The old woman continued to cough; she was visibly trembling. A handsome woman in her thirties wearing a badly soiled satin dress handed her a fur-trimmed cloak, and glared defiantly at the Guardsmen, daring them to take the cloak away.

"You have charity for your own kind," the Corporal sneered. "How compassionate you are."

Someone among the prisoners screamed a curse.

The Corporal drew his pistol and fired into the crowd of prisoners; it was impossible to say if he had taken deliberate aim or not. An instant later, a cry went up from the old woman, who sank down onto her knees, blood pumping from a wound in her neck; she was coughing still, but sounding more as if she were drowning than ill. "That is what happens to you if you speak against the Revolution. One of you dies."

Exclamations of dismay went up around the old woman as rain and blood mixed on the garments of those near her, and soaked the damask of her dress. Another of the prisoners, a man in the ruins of clerical garb, pushed forward and began to recite Extreme Unction for her, though it was apparent that she was almost dead, for the blood running from her wound had slowed and no longer pulsed.

"Vain, greedy, and superstitious—so completely useless," scoffed the Corporal before he strode toward the groups of six other Guardsmen who waited with their horses and the mule-drawn wagon to begin the trek northward once more. He made a fastidious motion with his hands as if to rid himself of the taint of death. "Where is the tow-horse? Has anyone seen the barge-master?"

"You're a fool, Niege," said one of his comrades. "You'll have to explain that shooting when we get to Lyon. They're sticky about abuse of prisoners."

"Because they want the kill for themselves," said another.

"Do you think any of them will care? If they bother to ask, I'll tell the Court that the old woman showed me disrespect and encouraged the same in her companions, and it will suffice. You're a sentimentalist, Bonfils. Genevere's right. What's one old Comtesse, more or less? She'd have probably died of her cough in a week or so, in any case, and spared the executioner the trouble." He grabbed Madelaine by the elbow. "Which mount is hers, today?"

"The one with the side-saddle," said Genevere, taking his pipe from between his teeth. "Or were you planning to ride that one?"

The laughter that greeted this question was harsh; the grins were ferocious. One of the Guardsmen made a suggestive gesture with his hand at his groin.

Madelaine pulled her arm free of his grip. "I can manage myself, Corporal," she said with as much dignity as she could muster.

"Naturally you can. You've demonstrated you can keep up with the best of us," he rejoined as he shoved her toward the blue-speckled white gelding that stood patiently at the end of the line of horses. "But we don't want it said that you were not treated as the enemy of the people that you are. You are in custody, and must obey us or suffer the consequences." He reached for her, preparing to lift her into the saddle.

"I will manage," she repeated, not wanting him to touch her.

He made a point of showing disinterest, speaking in a flat voice with an air of boredom. "Anything you like, Madame. You have only to name it." He offered her an insulting bow and turned away as she tested the girth, tightened its billets, then fitted her foot into the stirrup and pulled herself up, using the leg-support to do it. She settled into place, adjusted her skirts, and gathered up the reins.

Genevere swung aboard a seal-brown Spanish mare with a single white foot and an elegant curve to her neck, letting her caper a bit before pulling her head down and steadying her; he was chuckling at her antics as she half-reared before coming to order. Madelaine watched him with approval, as she had during all their journey north, impressed by his skill in the saddle as well as his kindness to his mount. The Guardsman, unlike some of the company, was fully at ease with riding and seemed to like horses.

"What do we do with the body?" The cry came from one of the prisoners, and was seconded at once by another. "Or do you intend it to lie here on the wharf?"

"You can't take it to Lyon. Wrap it in the cloak. Throw it in the river," said Corporal Niege, sounding offended. "If anyone finds it downstream, they can bury it, if they like." He approached a broad-chested red roan, patted the mare's rump, then vaulted into the saddle. As he adjusted his stirrup-leathers, he called out, "Faille, ride down the river road and find the barge-master. Tell him to hurry. We need to be under way shortly, and that means having the tow-horse to pull the barge."

Another one of the Guardsmen mounted up and headed south,

his head turned away from the cluster of horrified captives; the prisoners were struggling with the dead woman, trying to move the body to where they could shove it into the Rhone, while the priest recited the *Requiem* for the repose of her soul.

Watching Faille as he spurred his horse to a canter, Madelaine shook her head at the poor seat he had, and she wondered, as she had several times before now, how he had come to be assigned to a mounted company, and was required to spend long hours in the saddle. She felt pity for the fellow's horse, to have so clumsy a rider; nevertheless, she was grateful for the diversion he provided her. Keeping her attention on Faille's amateurish horsemanship stopped her from protesting in outrage the off-handed killing of Auralie, Comtesse de Saint-Sorrai, and the insolence of Corporal Niege.

"So, Madame Montalia," said the Corporal with mocking courtesy, "are you prepared for a hard ride today?"

"I'm prepared for a wet one. That will be hard enough," she answered.

"This is the first real rain of the autumn," the Corporal observed. "At least there isn't much wind."

Bonfils shook his head. "Not yet."

"It may come up later," Madelaine agreed, and looked at the other Guardsmen as they prepared to mount their horses; it was an effort to speak of such trivial matters when she wanted to scream. "And there will be mud."

"Good thing then that we have only the one wagon," said the Corporal. "If there is too much mud, we can put it on the barge."

"And lead the mules," said Bonfils, signaling to the Guardsman who drove the wagon. "Up you go, Claudin."

"I'm ready when the tow-horse arrives," he said as he got into the driving-box, where he gathered his greatcoat around him, then took his place. "But I don't like to keep the team standing in weather like this."

"Possibly you should walk them up the tow-path a way," said Corporal Niege. "Try to avoid the mud."

"Mud makes hard-going for the tow-horse as well as for mules,"

Madelaine said; hearing a splash from next to the wharf, she winced.

"You're a fool to be so maudlin," said the Corporal, noticing her reaction. "A body is nothing more than meat and bone."

Madelaine almost added *and blood,* but the thought made her more aware of her hunger; she kept the words to herself, as if to stave off the pangs. She had taken no nourishment in more than a week and she was depleted of energy to a degree that distressed her. A dreary finger of wind bent the rain and she felt a cold trickle down her neck; she reached to pull her hood more closely around her face.

"So tell me," Corporal Niege began as he nudged his roan next to Madelaine's spotted gelding, "what do you think the Revolutionary Court will do with you?"

"Take off my head, as you well know," she said calmly. "It is what you demand so that there can be no going back to the old ways." She felt a pang of regret that her life could end so soon—not even half a century of vampire existence!—if Saint-Germain could not contrive some way to reach her before her sentence was imposed and carried out. She realized she had been slumping and straightened up in the saddle.

"A pity to sacrifice one so young, Madame," the Corporal said, mocking her.

"I no longer feel young." She knew he could not guess the meaning of her answer and took some satisfaction in the realization that she had been able to maintain her true nature in secrecy; as imprudent as it was, she wanted to challenge him, to make him admit his satisfaction in the increasing slaughter the Revolution had spawned, to acknowledge that so much death did not serve justice but revenge, yet she said nothing more.

Disappointed by the lack of response Madelaine offered him, Corporal Niege swung his mare around and shouted, "You prisoners! Get aboard the barge! Stay in the cabin! We will leave as soon as the tow-horse is here. Be ready!" He added under his breath,

"We're already two days behind our schedule. We won't make up much time today."

The prisoners started along the wharf toward the barge, all of them moving slowly, all of them shivering and sodden. They reached the boarding-plank and went aboard single file, clutching the flimsy hand-rail as they went as the plank bent and swung. One of the men tripped and nearly went into the river, but was spared that as two other of the men seized his arms and pulled him back onto the unsteady boarding-plank. Last to step onto the barge was the woman who had given the Comtesse her cloak; she paused and looked back at Corporal Niege with such utter contempt that he swore at her.

Claudin started his team off along the tow-path, whistling encouragement to the four disgruntled mules; the team responded by tugging unequally in their harness. He pulled his hat down low to keep the rain out of his eyes, then reached for his driving-whip, swinging it experimentally, flicking the water off it before he caught the end of the lash and returned it to its bracket. The mules settled down to a slow jog, all four of them finally working together.

"Don't go far!" Corporal Niege yelled at Claudin. "The tow-horse should be here shortly."

"You hope," Claudin answered.

Bonfils laughed cynically, shaking his head.

"It's the weather," said the Corporal to his men. "The barge-master is late because of the rain."

"Very likely, and hardly surprising," said Bonfils, who had mounted a ewe-necked bay. "But if we aren't under way soon, we won't reach Lyon today; we'll have to stay on the road another night. More delay! The Revolutionary Court at Lyon may not be pleased that we have taken so long to get to them."

Corporal Niege scowled. "We can commandeer a place at Cours la Pleine. The garrison there has room enough for us and our animals."

"That place is more a ruin than a fortress; it's been there since

Charlemagne; the rafters are home to bats and the cellars are filled with rats," Bonfils objected, but shrugged. "Still, we'd be out of the wet."

"Better than a tent," Genevere remarked, and turned to the sixth member of the escort, a taciturn Gascon named Troisbec. "Do you think we'll reach Lyon?"

"No," said Troisbec. "Not tonight with the rain."

"If the rain doesn't last? What if the afternoon clears and we have a dry evening?" the Corporal asked, determined to get the answer he sought. "One of the farmers at the inn said it wouldn't last past mid-day."

"I doubt that," said Troisbec.

"If we leave within thirty minutes?" Corporal Niege pursued, glowering as he saw Troisbec shake his head.

"It takes twenty minutes to harness the tow-horse," Genevere said. "Since the horse isn't here yet—"

"A pox on Faille and the barge-master!" Corporal Niege burst out. When the others remained silent, he added, "They'll regret their delay."

"You won't report either of them to the Revolutionary Court, Niege, and you won't complain of us, for your sake as well as ours," said Bonfils, his manner somber, his gaze hard. "It's a dangerous precedent, to start denouncing our deputies and blaming Guardsmen. Who knows where it would end?"

Troisbec offered a sneering laugh.

"Listen to him, Corporal," Madelaine advised. "Think of how your Revolution began and what it has become." It was dangerous to point this change out to him, but she could not refrain from speaking up. "Aristos and clergy first, then intellectuals and lawyers. Now they're killing shopkeepers and servants. Eventually they may get around to Guardsmen."

Corporal Niege muttered an obscenity, but offered no argument. He clapped his heels to his mare's sides and sent her into a sudden canter; he reined in just as the horse was about to go onto the wharf.

"Better to use the tow-path," Bonfils recommended sardonically.

"Be quiet," the Corporal told him.

Madelaine turned the spotted gelding toward the tow-path, hoping that she might be allowed to ride a short way along the river; she had sat this horse twice before and found him a comfortable ride, with a gentle trot and a collected canter and enough stamina to carry her for miles without flagging. She reached down and patted his neck; she was sorry she had no bits of apple or grapes to give to him as she would have done for her mount before she was taken prisoner.

Another gust of wind sent the rain spattering, and two of the horses shying, while the barge rocked more energetically.

"May they all perish from boils!" Corporal Niege shouted.

Madelaine, who had been looking south along the tow-road, suddenly narrowed her eyes. "I think Faille is returning."

"And the barge-master?" Corporal Niege demanded, swinging his roan around to get a better view of the road.

"I don't see him," she said. "And no tow-horse, either."

Corporal Niege forgot himself enough to swear "By the Virgin's Tits!"

It was apparent that Faille was alone as he rocked cumbrously on his horse's ungraceful canter, his elbows flapping like useless wings. As he drew near, he shouted, "The tow-horse threw a shoe. The farrier is with him. As soon as he's reshod, the barge-master will bring him and we can be under way."

"But that could take up to an hour!" Corporal Niege complained. "Did you impress upon him the urgency of our mission?"

Faille slowed his horse to an uneven trot. "I did: the barge-master said he wouldn't risk the tow-horse going lame on the tow-path. He said that if he did, it could slow us down by more than a day, having a lame tow-horse." He came up to Corporal Niege. "The farrier is already working on the tow-horse, Corporal. What else could I do? I thought you should know as soon as possible."

Corporal Niege mumbled something; when Genevere asked

him to repeat himself, the Corporal said, "Cursed reactionary. He probably supports the Royalists."

"The horse cast a shoe," said Bonfils to Claudin, who had brought his team back to the small paved area in front of the wharf. "That has nothing to do with politics."

"Hah! How did he come to cast the shoe?—tell me that," said the Corporal. He sat back in his saddle. "Well, we might as well go into the town and get some cheese and a cup of wine. Bonfils, you stay here and guard our prisoners and the horses. I'll bring you something to eat when we return."

Bonfils sighed. "And the mules?"

Before Corporal Niege could answer, Madelaine said, "I'll help you walk them, since I'll have to walk my horse."

"And do what to them?" Corporal Niege inquired with the air of one prepared to criticize.

"See that they don't . . ." She let the words fade. "I'm concerned about the animals, not your mission. I have no reason to harm any of these animals, nor would I; my argument is not with them. But think the worst if it suits you."

"Why would you aid us?" Claudin asked, suspicion apparent in his tone and posture.

"I thought that was obvious. It's not *you* I want to help, it's the animals. Why should they suffer on your account?" She squinted up at the sky. "I think the rain is lessening—not much, but a little. In an hour, you may have drier skies and a tow-horse. Until then, these creatures need to be treated well, or they won't be able to carry us as far as Cours la Pleine, let alone Lyon. That is where you are planning to stop for the night, isn't it?" She looked directly at Corporal Niege. "Cours la Pleine?"

"I suppose it must be." He gave a weary sigh, then motioned toward the gates of Sainte-Sophie. "Let's go. Claudin, turn your mules over to Bonfils." He pointed to Madelaine. "And you, Madame, will dismount and stay on the wharf. Don't try to get off it. Bonfils will tend to the horses and the mules. You can keep to the planks of the wharf." He leveled his finger at her as if it were capable of firing a ball.

"You're being careless with your animals," Madelaine said as she dismounted and held out the reins to Bonfils.

"Do you think so? I wonder why," said Corporal Niege as he gestured to the rest of the Guardsmen to follow him, calling over his shoulder to Bonfils. "Watch Madame as well. She'll probably try to slip away, as she did in Temps d'Ete." The unfamiliar new name of the ancient monastery town came ineptly to his lips. "Don't be afraid to shoot her, in the leg if you must, but be sure you stop her, even if you have to kill her to do it." The grin he wore was vulpine, and he put his hand on the handle of his pistol.

Madelaine wanted to give the Corporal a sharp answer, but was sensible to the risk she would be taking, and, having watched Corporal Niege kill the Comtesse Saint-Sorrai hardly more than half an hour ago, was certain that he would not be adverse to adding another victim to his roster, so instead she turned to Bonfils. "I won't try to run. Where could I go that you could not catch me—or shoot me?"

"She has a point," said Genevere, who was bringing up the rear of the Guardsmen. "Walk the horses but keep her in sight. The nearest stand of trees is a long way off, and the fields are open and flat." He whistled, the derisory sound echoing off the village walls.

For the next half-hour, Madelaine stood on the wharf, as close to the land as she could without going beyond the limits that Corporal Niege had set for her. She felt overwhelmed—she missed Theron and she longed for Saint-Germain. For a while she paced up and down its confines, hoping that movement of her own would off-set the enervating impact of the water moving beneath the heavy planks; she soon grew tired, so sat on the edge of the small loading platform and cast her thoughts back over all she had hoped to do in the next century, but that soon disheartened her, so she abandoned it for a more consoling line of thought: her time with Saint-Germain at Lecco and Padova. She had to admit that his warnings were correct, and she had been unwise to return to Montalia.

Better to have remained with him, she told herself. It had been only a summer, but she had treasured every moment of it. They could no longer be lovers, but that, much as she missed the singular passion they had shared, was a small price to pay for his company. Of all the things she despaired of that came with the True Death was the loss of him. There had been so little time to take advantage of her undead life! Had she not lost her tears when she changed, she would have wept with vexation. She had made many plans for travel to ancient places in order to explore the vanished peoples who had lived at those sites. The certainty that that could no longer happen brought a new rush of despondency, and she focused her thoughts on Theron, hoping that would assuage her increasing sorrow. She began to pace again. Finally, as the rain was turning to mizzle, she saw the barge-master approaching, leading a large sorrel draught horse; this was not the horse that had pulled the barge since their journey began, and Madelaine became curious.

So had Bonfils. He stopped the animals in his charge and shaded his eyes to stare at the unfamiliar horse on the barge-master's lead-rope. The horse had his collar and surcingle already buckled on, and moved energetically in spite of the gelid morning. "What happened to Forte?" he asked, meaning the missing tow-horse.

"The farrier says he's developing ring-bone and is unsound." the barge-master answered, raising his voice.

"What misfortune." Bonfils studied the new tow-horse. "Belgian?"

"And Percheron, so the breeder assures me—not so big but just as sturdy. He's taken Forte in trade for a stud. He says for so large a horse to be fourteen and only now getting ring-bone should be a good mix for his horses. Big horses, like big dogs, don't last as long as the smaller ones do." The barge-master came up to the wharf. "This fellow is six. He's got at least another six good years in him, God willing." He crossed himself, though such a pious act had been forbidden by the Revolutionary Assembly of Paris, then pretended he had not made this illegal gesture. "He will reach Lyon without difficulty, and bring the barge back to Avignon without difficulty."

"Then hitch him up," said Bonfils brusquely. "I'll go into Sainte-Sophie and get the others; let's hope they're not too drunk to ride." He rounded on Madelaine. "You. Hold these reins until I return." He turned back to the barge-master. "Keep an eye on her; she's a prisoner and must not escape."

"I will stay with the horses." She looked about and shook her head. "There's no place around this town I could run that you wouldn't find me. The land's too open."

"See you remember that," said Bonfils as he thrust the reins into her hands. "I won't be long."

The barge-master gave Madelaine an appraising glance. "You're the one who gets sick on the water, aren't you?"

"Sadly, yes," said Madelaine.

"Fine folk have delicate senses, I'm told." He had led the horse onto the wharf and positioned him for harnessing him to the barge.

Madelaine could think of nothing to say in response; she watched the barge-master finish his task, keeping all other thoughts from her mind.

Ten minutes later Bonfils came back, Corporal Niege and Claudin with him. They strode up to the barge-master and inspected the new tow-horse. "More problems?" Bonfils asked.

"Only adjusting the harness. Forte had more heart-room than this fellow does." He patted the flank of the sorrel. "But he's sturdy enough for the work, never fear."

Corporal Niege shook his head. "And if he gives out on the road, what then?"

"He won't," said the barge-master. "He can move against the current all day and take no harm from it." He gave the Corporal a skeptical look. "How do you come to know about horses so suddenly?"

"My father kept a posting inn. I've seen horses aplenty." There was more bluster than information in his words.

The barge-master harrumphed and went back to work on the harness.

"The horses are ready?" Corporal Niege asked.

"I have the reins," Madelaine said from her place at the edge of the wharf. "The piebald chestnut is restive."

"Aren't we all," said Claudin, taking the reins for the wagon's mule-team from her. "A good thing they didn't try to bolt. You couldn't have held them."

Madelaine said nothing; although she knew that she was stronger than the breathing men around her, in her depleted state she had to admit that Claudin might be right. She gave the reins of the other horses, save her spotted gelding, to Bonfils. "Where are the others?" she ventured to ask.

"They're having a basket of food made up, so if we have to eat on the road, it will be better fare than what we have eaten these last three days. So we'll have a good meal come noon, just as we had a good breakfast. And those at the inn are enjoying a last cup of hot wine." Bonfils hesitated, then added, "Not that it means anything to you."

"Meaning you won't feed any of it to the prisoners," said Madelaine, trying not to sound too acrimonious.

"Meaning that even if we did, you wouldn't eat it." With that, he swung around on his heel and led the horses away.

Watching him go, Madelaine had the uneasy sensation that she had been careless, letting the Guardsmen see that she did not take food with the rest of the prisoners. She got back on her horse and brought him around to the tow-path just as the rest of the Guardsmen came pelting through the gate of Sainte-Sophie, both Troisbec and Genevere carrying large baskets.

"There's cold tongue-and-mustard and new bread in this," Genevere crowed, holding up his basket. "The cook was generous with us."

"Vive la Revolution!" yelled Bonfils, and was echoed by the other Guardsmen.

Madelaine watched them, her expression unreadable, as she prepared for another day on the banks of the Rhone, with the Revolutionary Court and the Guillotine of Lyon waiting for her, a day and a half away.

* * *

Text of a report filed by Vivien Zacharie Charlot, Deputy Secretary for Public Safety of the Revolutionary Tribunal of Lyon, and presented to the Committee for Public Safety on the 7th of October, 1792.

To the Members of the Committee for Public Safety, the Deputy Secretary for Public Safety presents this report for their review:

Most worthy Members of the Committee,

As you are doubtless aware, there is great unrest and dissension in the city due to the conflicts arising from arguments between those citizens who support the policies of the National Convention and those who support the policies of the Girondais, who continue to oppose the execution of Louis XVI. There have been violent confrontations in the streets that have left men injured or dead, and for now, the Revolutionary Guard has been unable, or unwilling, to call these groups of antagonists to order, claiming that they are not concerned with such issues.

I have made a list of those citizens who are known to be active on both sides of these issues and I urge you to consider imposing fines or jail sentences for inciting their comrades to these extreme measures, for it is my belief and the belief of many of the staff of the Department of Public Safety that these disputes are going to become more frequent and more violent unless steps are taken to contain them.

Whatever disagreements these factions have may be taken up by the Revolutionary Tribunal and the Revolutionary Assembly in order to establish the means to resolve any bones of contention that exist. It may be necessary to detain those who are the most vociferous members of the opposing groups in order to allow more reasonable men to arrive at terms that both sides can endorse and uphold. I am convinced that if you fail to act, more slaughter will result, either from these citizens, or from the authorities in Paris who are committed to uphold and champion the Revolution at any cost.

The more ferocity we display now, the longer it will be until we can restore Lyon to the market-city it is, and begin to rebuild our fortunes. Bad fortune breeds bitterness as surely as it contributes to crime and poverty; the Revolution can still bring favorable business to our citizens if we do not allow this degree of enmity to continue unabated. There are men of good-will on both sides of the arguments, and it is through their efforts, not the extreme posturing of the most avid of their leaders, that we shall find a way to restore unity to our government and remain true to the principles that brought about the Revolution. As men sworn to defend France and the Revolution, surely you can do no less than bring about a restoration of order among our citizens.

We have established our Courts as centers for justice: it behooves us to show that we extend that concept to those among us who are unwilling to observe the conduct appropriate to citizens of a great city and an olympian country.

Vive la Revolution!
Vive la France!

> *Submitted most respectfully,*
> *Vivien Zacharie Charlot*
> *Deputy Secretary for Public Safety*
> *Lyon*

4

"But we've been licensed for two more performances," Photine protested in French-accented Italian; she was sitting in the private parlor of the Cheval d'Argent, the remains of a roasted chicken and sauteed greens on her plate before her; she had a glass of wine in her hand that glowed like rubies in the candle-lit dusk. She was fashionably dressed, her embroidered peach satin corsage edged with knots of lace that matched the lace at her wrists; a broad, deep-red sash slightly above her waist emphasized her figure, and her satin skirts shone glossily. "How can we reject such a handsome opportunity?"

Da San-Germain kept his voice level, speaking in the same language. "It is most flattering, I know, but we have to leave for Lyon tomorrow. We have already been here longer than either of us supposed we would be. The Revolutionary Tribunal in Lyon is calling for trials in ten days from today, if the courier who arrived here this afternoon is to be believed." His fine brows snapped into a frown that vanished almost at once. "If you want to do one more performance before we go, I won't prohibit it, but we must not linger. We'll have to move quickly if we're to be in Lyon before the trials begin—which we must do. There's too much at stake." He was in black: swallow-tail coat, unmentionables, waistcoat, and silk shirt, making him part of the shadows where he stood at the side of the hearth, out of range of the mirror above the mantel.

"But you—" She stopped herself and offered a conciliatory smile. "All right, yes: I did agree that we would help you to find your . . . your relative, and bring her out of France. You've done everything you pledged to do, and I will not abrogate my side of the bargain because it's turned out to be less favorable than we could have anticipated. We are to help Madame de Montalia to leave France, and will have the opportunity to perform a new play, all of which you will pay for. Those were the terms. We're only here because of you, and without your patronage, we would be in a difficult predicament."

"I wasn't going to bring that up," he said, and bent to set a spark to the kindling and wood laid in the fireplace. "It is my honor to sponsor your performances, both here and in Padova, no matter what the circumstances. But performing is not the only purpose of this trip. I cannot lose sight of the reason we came here." He stepped back into the shadows once more, deploring the ubiquity of mirrors in his thoughts; it had only been in the last fifty years that mirrors had become a common decoration in taverns and bourgeois households, and he found their proliferation an intrusion.

"Which means that we must respect your demands," she countered, making this concession gracefully. "And, as our patron, you are the one to decide how we are to conduct our tour."

"But neither of us anticipated your success," he admitted. "It would be easier to leave had your play not been so much approved by the Revolutionary Tribunal."

She made a gesture that acknowledged his observation. "We're actors. We seek applause. Even Heurer is flushed with pride now."

Da San-Germain came toward her. "I have promised you that you will have every opportunity to perform as we travel, and I will hold to that promise. You deserve the fruits of your art. Were Madelaine's situation less precarious, I wouldn't object to your troupe remaining here for another week, but under the circumstances—"

"Life and death. You made that very clear." She gave a little sigh. "It's hard to argue with that. You deserve an answer, and you are entitled to my cooperation. You shall have both, to the extent that they are in my power. " Lifting her glass, she offered him an ironic toast, then said in a more cordial tone, "You know, you have a beautiful voice. Not the way actors have beautiful voices; yours is more musical, its expression more private."

He would not be put off by her unexpected praise; he met her gaze, his dark eyes compelling, his demeanor almost tranquil in his conviction. "I don't require you to like this change in our plans, and if you are determined to remain here—which you may decide is better for your troupe than traveling to Lyon, though you may be equally popular there—Roger and I will go on alone. We haven't much time to reach Madelaine before she is brought to trial; after that, we'll have three days at most to remove her from prison and find a safe route out of the country, or lose her to the True Death."

"That would be very dangerous," she said, shocked by his imperturbability. "You could be taken prisoner, and then you would die with her."

"There is always that risk," he said; the first twists of flame appeared among the paper and twigs. "Being with your troupe would give us some protection; our chances for a successful escape improve if we are with you."

She blinked, trying to decide if he were serious or merely trying to coerce her into acquiescing to his demands. "The troupe will not be pleased—both with the delay and with having a fugitive with us."

"They knew they would be sheltering an aristocrat during our return to Padova," said da San-Germain, a bit puzzled. "Why does that bother them now? Are they afraid that their fame might make them more vulnerable?"

She regarded him, perplexed but not quite annoyed. "They knew they were performing a rescue, and that was a great adventure, something worthy of Sophocles or Racine; they assumed that they would be taking her out of Avignon, not Lyon, and that it would be before she was to appear in the Revolutionary Court. But once she is tried and is convicted, then the adventure becomes dangerous for the troupe as well as for your relative, and they do not want to put themselves at risk of imprisonment or execution." She reached out and brushed his hand with hers. "Surely you can understand their feelings? Would you blame them for not wanting to risk their lives?"

"Probably not; I expect no such sacrifice," da San-Germain agreed.

"But you cannot promise that there is no possibility of trouble, can you?" She tapped her fingers together as her only indication of annoyance.

He met her eyes. "No, I cannot."

"Then you will have to accept their dissatisfaction with the change in our arrangement, when they learn about it." Her smile was understanding and heartening, but it did not touch her eyes.

"How much will they have to know? Can we keep anything from—"

Photine laughed, a knowing, guileful sound. "No one keeps secrets in theatrical companies—no one. They will all know, no matter what you tell them, or withhold from them. That's why I haven't spent more time alone with you: my players could find out too much and then none of us would be safe."

"But they knew you shared my bed from time to time," he said.

"Yes, in Padova where you housed and kept us all. It was expected. Even Enee, no matter how badly he's behaved, understood that you were going to be my lover, since that is the way things are done. They knew little about the . . . manner of our passion, which is in our best interests. But living so closely together, they could easily find out more than either of us would want them to learn, and who can tell what they might do then." She drank again, leaving a small amount in the glass.

Da San-Germain wondered if her concern for the gossip of her troupe were the only reason for her avoiding him, but he did not want to be distracted. "Tell your troupe that there will be performing opportunities in Lyon to more than match those here, and a larger population to see them. The city is in foment, if the rumors are to be believed, and the play is likely to be a reflection of the citizens' current understanding, and therefore will be approved. It should command a large audience, and more attention."

That possibility had not struck her before. "Foment can work against us, too," she said cautiously.

"It can, of course."

For the greater part of a minute she was silent. To cover her ruminations, she drank the last of her wine and made no objection when he refilled her glass. The fire was beginning to take hold, shining more brightly than the candles now. "Ordinarily, I would ask the troupe to decide."

"Ordinarily, a laudable policy," he said, sitting down across the table from her; he leaned slightly forward yet did not reach out to touch her.

"But they would debate and cavil until our license here runs out and we have to leave; actors enjoy such contention, it hones the skills to argue," she admitted, a touch of amusement in her words. "You say that would be an intolerable delay—which I do not doubt. The reports from Lyon are distressing. Everyone knows that the Revolutionary Court has taken prisoners from more places than Avignon, and the city is willing to kill anyone who acts against the Girondais, as well as those deemed enemies of the Revolution."

"That's true," he said. "The Girondais have the upper hand now, but they may not be able to sustain their hold. Their disputes with Paris are becoming more rancorous by the day, if the reports are accurate."

"Knowing that, you're still set on going there?"

"I am."

She drank a bit more wine. "Would you take Roger and go? Really?"

"Yes."

She could not question his determination; she set the wine-glass down. "Very well. If that's the way of it, we must honor our agreement. We will leave after tomorrow's performance. We should be able to cover three leagues by nightfall."

"Unless it rains again," he said, apprehension revealing the depth of his anxiety for the first time since he had entered the parlor.

"So you're worried about the weather as well as the distance," she exclaimed.

He responded indirectly. "Even if we can manage more than eight leagues a day in clear weather, which may not be possible, rain could stop us. Then we would be fortunate to cover three leagues in a day."

"We can't perform in the rain, either," said Photine. "We must hope we reach Lyon before the autumn closes in."

"We must also hope that rain doesn't slow our return to Padova. We'll need to move fast once we have Madelaine." He motioned toward the door at the sound of a soft tap. "Are you expecting anyone?"

She shook her head, her mood transformed from genial to anxious. "No. And I thought the troupe was getting our cases packed. Why? Did you hear something?"

"A knock, or so it seemed. Of course, it could be just someone passing the door."

"Listening at the door, more likely," said Photine. "Open it, if you think there's someone there." She held up her hand and ticked off possibilities. "Why would anyone be disturbing our conversation? Might there be trouble of some kind? Perhaps one of the horses or mules is ailing."

"I doubt that." He had inspected the wagons and carts two days before, and had summoned the farrier to check the shoes on their horses and mules yesterday. Feo and Aloys had busied themselves in doing the necessary minor repairs to the tack and harness, so that did not seem a likely concern. "Which of your actors would interrupt your supper?"

The second soft knock on the door was startling, though both of them expected it.

"It's Feo," said the quiet voice. "There's trouble."

Da San-Germain went to open the door, regarding the coachman with keen eyes. "Has something happened?" he asked, standing aside to admit Feo into the parlor; Feo gave Photine a half-bow.

"What is this about?" Photine asked him, her demeanor imperious, showing him that she did not like having her conversation interrupted by a coachman.

"If it weren't urgent—" Feo hesitated, then launched into an explanation. "There is no easy way to tell you, Madame, so I'll just say it: your son has been accused of cheating at cards. The Guards have taken him into custody and are claiming that he must be tried for his crime."

"Crime? He can't . . . Enee is too—" She was about to say *young* but stopped herself, and listened.

"When did this happen?" da San-Germain asked.

"A little more than an hour ago," Feo said. "In the tavern at the river's edge, at the old bridgehead, the Pont Roman; rivermen go there, and smugglers from the south." He gave an apologetic sigh. "I would have come sooner, but I followed the Guards to see what they would do with him."

"Do they brand the hands of card-cheats here?" Photine asked, going pale as she waited to hear what she would say; in her distress, she had gone from Italian to French.

"Who knows?" Feo answered, but would not be put off his point. "It is a risk it would be unwise to take. The Revolutionary Tribunal is strict in enforcing the law. Better not to get into the toils of the Revolutionary Tribunal in the first place."

"Where is he?" da San-Germain asked in French.

"At the moment he's in the Revolutionary Tribunal's jail, awaiting official charges," said Feo in Italian. "If his fine is paid, and something given to the bailiff to grease the locks, as they say, he could be out tonight." He paused, his expression becoming speculative and guileful. "If he is brought before the Tribunal, then matters get much more difficult."

Photine took all her wine in a single gulp. "You must take me to him, Comte." She started to rise.

"No, Madame," da San-Germain objected, putting his hand gently on her shoulder. "This is not your duty, though he is your son. Let me do what I may to secure his release. I think you will do more good by remaining here with your troupe. If you are with us, you could be questioned, and that might cause more trouble."

"I could say it must be a misunderstanding, that my boy is new to gaming, and at most he has made a mistake, not committed a crime." She had returned to Italian for Feo's benefit.

"As every mother would claim," said da San-Germain quietly. "No. Have it seem that you do not believe the accusation, and think it beneath your attention."

After giving da San-Germain an inquisitive look, Feo nodded. "He's right. If you run to him, they will be sure he is guilty."

"Enee," she whispered, and began to weep. "Spare him, Conte," she implored, her hands clasped and her face shining with tears.

"I will do what I can," he answered, then looked at Feo. "Have you seen my manservant?"

"Roger?" Feo snapped his fingers. "The last I saw he was in the stable, loading one of your chests into the larger cart."

"Excellent. We will seek him while we saddle our horses," said da San-Germain energetically. "Madame, go to your actors and rehearse. It will steady your thoughts and give the appearance that you are not worried on Enee's behalf."

She clutched her linen serviette and wiped her eyes, struggling to regain her composure. "If you think it best . . ."

"You will agree if you only consider your boy's predicament," said da San-Germain, refilling her glass with the rest of the wine in the bottle. "For the sake of your son, think of this as a performance, and you must succeed." He signaled to Feo; the coachman gave a suggestion of a salute. "We should be back within two hours. If we're not, we will need to think of some other means of freeing Enee."

Photine pressed her lips together, refusing to cry again; finally she said, "Bon chance," and waved him out of the room, Feo half a step behind him.

As they hastened down the corridor to the entrance to the inn, da San-Germain lowered his voice, saying, "How strong is the case against Enee?"

Feo turned up his hands to show he had no idea. "One of the men playing at his table accused him. I'm told he was drunk and belligerent."

"The accuser?"

"Yes. Which is something in Enee's favor." Feo glanced into

the taproom, where most of the troupe was assembled. "Should we tell the Guards about the rehearsal?"

"No," said da San-Germain. "If we tell them, there will be speculation that would distress Madame. They may assume that the rehearsal is a ruse—which it is—and order her to appear before the Revolutionary Tribunal to explain her lack of supervision of her son." He paused, his countenance thoughtful. "For all the Guards like our play, they think actresses are trollops, and would be apt to treat her disrespectfully."

"She can be eloquent," Feo remarked.

"That, too, might seem deceptive to the Guards," said da San-Germain, lengthening his stride. "Any appeal she makes herself could bring about precisely what she seeks to avoid—a cancellation of her license to perform, and a fine. If she tells them too much, they'll be certain she is lying, and that will be held against Enee as well as the troupe."

"And in that event, our departure could be delayed by several days," said Feo cannily.

"That it could," said da San-Germain without any sign of emotion.

The evening air was cool, with a skittery wind that nipped at them like a hungry chicken. They crossed the inn-yard to the stable, where they found Roger strapping one of da San-Germain's chests into place in the bed of the larger cart.

"The players will need our help loading up after their performance tomorrow; I thought it best if most of our cases and chests were stowed tonight." He rubbed the front of his dove-gray coat. "What do you want, my master?"

"You know me too well, old friend; I can hide nothing from you," he said with a hint of a smile. "I want the square wallet in the old chest," he said, his description deliberately vague.

"He's going to get Enee out of jail," Feo explained.

"It is likely to be expensive," Roger said.

"Keep that in mind when you bring the wallet," da San-Germain recommended.

"I'll be back in ten minutes," said Roger, and left the stable without asking any questions.

"You're planning to pay for his release, then?" Feo asked. "The little weasel hates you."

"I won't be doing it for him," said da San-Germain drily.

"Nor entirely for his mother," Feo said with a knowing look.

"No, not entirely." Da San-Germain started toward one of the box-stalls where two of the troupe's horses were standing. "The saddles are in the tack-room. Mine is—"

"—black with silver fittings; yes. I'll find it." He strode off toward the tack-room, signaling to one of the grooms to assist him while da San-Germain picked up a brush from the grooming-box next to the stall and let himself in with the two horses, haltered both animals and gave them a perfunctory brushing. Feo brought da San-Germain's saddle, saddle-pad, and bridle from the tack-room and set them on the stand outside the door. "I'll get the Italian saddle, the one with the extension behind the cantle, for the boy to ride on."

Da San-Germain haltered the gray gelding and prepared to lead him out of the stall. "A good choice." As he secured the gray's lead-rope to a ring in the pillar next to the stall, da San-Germain called out to Feo, "Have you seen Theron this evening?"

Feo's voice was a bit muffled, but he replied, "Not this evening. I saw him this afternoon in the Plume et Papier, where the writers meet. They were feting him in grand style: wine and pastries and grilled meats—wine most particularly."

"Let us trust the style is not too grand—we don't want to have to deal with the Guards and the Revolutionary Tribunal more than once tonight." Da San-Germain took the hoof-pick, bent over, and lifted the gray's front on-side hoof. He worked quickly and silently, making his way around the horse, then put the pick back in the grooming-box and reached for the saddle-pad.

"My master," said Roger as he came up to him; da San-Germain had finished saddling and bridling the gray, and he gave his full attention to Roger. "I have put in some of the stones from the alabaster casket, in case they will be useful." He nodded to Feo, who was finishing tightening the girths on the mouse-colored mare.

"Many thanks," said da San-Germain as he took the thick leather wallet from Roger; he knew they had no alabaster casket with them, but that the one in Padova contained a great many jewels da San-Germain had made in his athanor. "You always anticipate what I'll need." He buckled the wallet onto the rings on the pommel of the saddle, then mounted up. "We should be back within two hours."

"With Enee."

"Precisely." He watched while Feo adjusted the head-stall on the mare's bridle; the mare stopped fussing with her bit and stood quietly as Feo buckled her throatlatch, lifted the reins over her head and vaulted into the saddle. "Ready?"

"That I am," said Feo, gathering the reins to his hands.

Before he left the stable, da San-Germain said to Roger, "If you can, go find Heurer. He may still be at the Plume et Papier. Bring him back here, whatever his condition may be, and see that he watches the rehearsal. We want no more questions asked about anyone associated with the Commedia della Morte. If you have to bring him back on one of the mules, do it."

Roger nodded twice. "I will."

"Try not to let him make a scene," da San-Germain added.

"I will," Roger repeated, and stepped back as da San-Germain and Feo rode out into the dark street, going toward the light that marked the Place de Ville, and the Revolutionary Tribunal in the Hotel de Ville. They went at a walk, avoiding gathering-places in the narrow streets, and arrived at the Place de Ville in a little more than ten minutes.

"I'll mind the horses, Ragoczy," said Feo as he dismounted in the crowded square in front of the Hotel de Ville.

"Thank you," said da San-Germain, and made for the doors of the Hotel de Ville, which were well-lit and stood open, Guards flanking the entrance. He stepped into the foyer and found himself surrounded by men assembled in clusters, all talking in lowered voices that made the chamber echo with their various discussions; undeterred by the clamor, da San-Germain looked about for the sign pointing the way to the holding cells; he finally found it at the top of a flight of lamp-lit stairs, which he descended without undue haste, using the time to take stock of the setting so that he could deal with any abrupt changes he might encounter. At a door with a sign saying CLERK OF THE COMMITTEE FOR PUBLIC SAFETY, he paused, and after a moment of consideration, knocked.

"Enter," said the person within.

Da San-Germain had not worn a hat, so he could not remove it as a sign of respect. With his head slightly lowered deferentially, he entered the room. "Good evening, Citizen," he said in the approved manner.

"Good evening, foreigner," said the man behind the desk; he was of medium height and looked to be between thirty-five and forty, a fussy fellow in a blue serge coat and dun-colored unmentionables; his fingers were ink-stained, as were his cuffs, and he gave da San-Germain a swift scrutiny as he half-rose from his chair. There was a tricoleur knot of ribbons on his lapel, which he touched as he looked up at the newcomer. "What is your purpose here."

Da San-Germain recognized the man from his previous visit to the Revolutionary Tribunal; he concealed his distaste of the man with an urbane smile. "I am Ferenz Ragoczy, Citizen Dassin; I am with the Commedia della Morte."

"I know who you are. I remember your first visit—the Hungarian exile looking for a French relation," said Beniguet Francois Dassin, the Clerk of the Committee for Public Safety. "What do you want? I have no more information on your relative."

"That does not surprise me. But no, that is not why I am here." He gave the clerk a slight nod. "You have in one of your temporary cells the son of the owner of the Commedia della Morte, of which company I am honored to be a member. I am here to secure his release, if that may be arranged."

"And who is this person? We have several men in our cells."

Dassin folded his arms and stared past da San-Germain toward a second, smaller door.

"He is a youth, only fifteen, and recently has become a bit wild, as such youngsters will do. His mother was told that he had got into trouble at a tavern, and asked me to settle whatever money may be needed for his misbehavior, and bring him back to her." He once again offered a little bow.

"What kind of misbehavior?" The clerk was scowling.

"From what his mother told me, he had been involved in a dispute about a card game."

"Oho! *That* youth. The dispute was more of a brawl," the clerk declared.

"Truly?" Da San-Germain offered an expression of incredulity. "I wouldn't have thought he would be so reckless."

"You said yourself that the young man was becoming wild. You must know that wildness can lead to trouble." Dassin leaned forward, resting his crossed arms on his desk. "What he is accused of doing is more than a little wantonness, it is criminal. Cheating at cards is a fraud."

"If he did it, he must have done it badly, since he was caught," said da San-Germain, his gaze steadily on the clerk.

Dassin shook his head. "On the contrary. He was quite clever."

"According to whom?" Although da San-Germain remained unfailingly polite, he made his question pointed enough to require more than a simple answer.

"Jean-Marcel Painsec, the man he tried to cheat. He, too, has been detained until he is sober enough to make an official complaint."

"Ah. Then the matter is not yet settled," said da San-Germain, more relieved than he was willing to let Dassin know.

"Not until Painsec files a complaint or withdraws it." Dassin disengaged his arms and laid his hands flat upon his desk. "There is a fine, of course, no matter what Painsec does; the young man caused an uproar in a public place. That cannot be allowed to go unredressed."

"No doubt he did," said da San-Germain with perfect neutrality. "I suppose he had been drinking."

"Not nearly as much as Painsec had, or he might have passed out and avoided all this disorder," said Dassin with a hint of scolding. "The lad has claimed that it was Painsec who cheated, but what would you expect?" He looked at da San-Germain inquisitively, waiting for his next move.

"Suppose I could guarantee that the youngster will be gone from this city by tomorrow afternoon? Might that make your decision whether or not to release him to me easier?"

Dassin looked at da San-Germain. "How can you offer such a guarantee?"

"The troupe will be departing tomorrow after their noon performance. We want to travel while the weather remains good." He made a gesture that took in the entire countryside. "You know how the roads are once the rains start, and how much damage can be done to wagons in the mud."

"Naturally," said Dassin, and went silent. Then: "The youngster did get into a brawl."

"That might not have been of his making," da San-Germain pointed out.

Dassin bent his head and thought. Finally he said, "The fine can be paid in gold. We take no promissory notes on matters of fines. Ten louis d'or, and a fee for his detention of six louis d'or." It was an outrageous sum and both men knew it, but da San-Germain reached for his wallet without protest.

"And another two for his speedy release?" He began to count out the gold coins, all the while remembering Telemachus Batsho in those heady days when Heliogabalus ruled in Roma.

It was an effort for Dassin not to goggle, but he managed. "A very . . . reasonable . . . payment."

Da San-Germain started to drop the stack of coins onto Dassin's desk, but held back after the first five lay in front of the clerk. "I will wait here for the boy. I think that would be best, don't you?"

"Oh, yes," said Dassin, having trouble concentrating on anything other than the money in front of him.

"Then perhaps you'd better go and fetch him?" Da San-Germain said gently, moving his hand so that the remaining gold coins clinked.

Dassin picked up a glass bell from the far side of his desk and rang in; ten seconds later, a Guard came through the smaller door and asked, "What is it, Citizen?"

"The young man? The one who cheated at cards?" He made this blunt, as if issuing a challenge to da San-Germain.

"Yes?" The Guard made a point of not looking at da San-Germain.

"Go get that young fool. The one with the black eye and swollen knuckles." Dassin waved him away and looked back at da San-Germain. "Well, Ragoczy, are you going to give me what you offered or was that merely a ruse to see the young hooligan?"

"As soon as you sign an authorization for his release, I will give the rest to you." He offered a slight bow.

"Eh bien," said Dassin, and took a piece of paper from the drawer at the side of the desk. He then drew the inkwell toward him and reached for a trimmed goose-quill. "On your oath, he will be gone from Avignon before sunset tomorrow."

"You have my Word," said da San-Germain.

Dassin dipped the nib of the quill into the ink and began to write; he had a fine, sloping hand; it had been the primary reason he had been given the job he held, for all his documents were elegant and legible. "If you are not gone by tomorrow sunset," he said as he wrote, "the young man will be returned to his cell and you will be with him, for misrepresentation. You will stand trial as well as the young man."

"I understand," said da San-Germain, and watched the clerk write, reading the words upside-down. As Dassin affixed a seal to the bottom of the page, da San-Germain put the rest of the louis d'or on the desk and reached for the paper, which he folded and tucked away in his coat's inner breast-pocket. "I appreciate your exercise of good sense, Citizen."

"And I appreciate your generosity," said Dassin with open, gratified venality. Whatever he might have added was silenced as the Guard opened the door and shoved a bedraggled and bruised Enee into the room. "Well, there he is, Ragoczy. Take him away."

Enee looked up sharply, a look of loathing on his battered face. *"You!"* he burst out in disgust.

Paying no attention to Enee's contempt, da San-Germain said, "Your mother is expecting you. Feo has horses, so you needn't walk back to the Cheval d'Argent."

"Teton du Marie!" Enee swore as he pulled his arm out of the hold the Guard had on it. "Why won't she let me lead my own life?"

Da San-Germain took hold of Enee's other arm and although he did not grip tightly, Enee could not pull free of him, try as he would. "Remember where you are, Enee, if you can't behave."

Enee muttered, glowering, his blackened eye lending menace to his truculence.

"You're welcome to him, Ragoczy," Dassin called out as da San-Germain did his best to guide Enee through the room, out the door, and toward the stairs that would take them out of the Hotel de Ville and into the glow of lanterns and torches, and the on-going bustle at the Place de Ville, where Feo waited with their horses.

"Where is my horse?" Enee demanded as he saw the mouse-colored mare and the gray gelding.

"You will ride behind Feo," said da San-Germain.

"I won't!" Enee shouted. "I'm not a child! Or a girl!"

"You will," said da San-Germain, his hand tightening on Enee's arm. "You've done enough on your own for one day; now you'll do as your mother wishes."

"As you wish, you mean," said Enee and spat.

Da San-Germain swung Enee around to face him. "What you do concerns me only insofar as it bears upon your mother and her troupe. If you wish to make a fool of yourself, so be it, if nothing derogatory redounds to the Commedia della Morte. But once you involve the troupe in any way, you have trespassed on my interests, and your mother's. You have gone beyond the bounds now, and for that reason, you have placed all of us in a hazardous position. I have just paid an exorbitant amount for your freedom. I don't expect you to be grateful, but I do expect you to realize what your rashness might have done to your mother. Do you understand me?"

"Why should I?" he snapped. "When you're tired of using us, you'll leave us with nothing but our wagons and our platform."

It took a few seconds for da San-Germain to decide upon his reply. "Think of me what you want, but show Photine the respect and regard she deserves from you." He fixed his compelling gaze on Enee's eyes until he looked away; satisfied, he turned Enee back toward Feo. "Now, go mount up. You're needed at rehearsal." Remaining a step or two behind the young man, in case he should attempt to break away from them, da San-Germain followed him to where Feo waited with the horses.

Text of a letter from Henri Bellefleur, postmaster of Lyon, to Jean-Marie Collot d'Herbois in Paris, carried by postal courier and delivered three days after it was written.

> *To the most dedicated servant of the Revolution, the esteemed Jean-Marie Collot d'Herbois, the personal greetings from Henri Bellefleur, postmaster of Lyon, confidentially,*
>
> *Most accomplished Citizen,*
>
> *As I pledged to do when last we met, I take pen in hand to inform you of developments here in Lyon, and seek your guidance and wisdom in their regard:*
>
> *The Girondais are becoming ever more active and brazen in their opposition to the government in Paris. Every day there are meetings and demonstrations; the more extreme of their numbers are the ones who are advocating more executions to force unity upon the populace. We have seen more heads removed, but the*

unity has not yet emerged. Those who are not so radical in their notions are still unwilling to reach an accord with the goals of the National Convention, where you distinguished yourself so remarkably. There are a few here in Lyon who believe that we need to reestablish our links to the Convention and to Paris for the sake of the Revolution, for if we allow the country to fragment and become bickering regions, it will be only a matter of time before all the country is defeated from within as well as from without.

The temperament here is bloody, and that means that our people are becoming more volatile; there are demonstrations and other displays of discontent among the populace. The broadsheets and banners all show divisions spreading while it becomes more and more difficult for our Assembly, our Courts, and our Tribunal to function. The Revolution has brought us freedom, but it has also brought us every kind of partisanship that can be imagined, and the number of men aligning themselves with new groups proliferates.

As a man of the theatre as well as of the arts, and the people, surely you have some recommendation for what we might do to inspire all Lyon to stand together for the glory of France. Your fetes have done much for Paris: might they not also inspire Lyon to hold to the principles for which so many have died? I volunteer all my available time and what resources I have to promote such events as you have arranged for Paris for Lyon. We are hungry for the new arts that the Revolution will bring forth, and the genius of great men, of which you are most emphatically in the vanguard. It is my belief that bringing revolutionary arts to the people here will instill a unity in their actions and purpose in their understanding, so that we may emerge from these tempestuous times truly manifesting the principles that the Revolution embodies. You have shown what art can do to achieve that end. Creation is passionate, occasionally violent, and we need artists who share your courage to establish the new vision that the Revolution is bringing to the arts as it is bringing justice to government and law, and philosophy to the halls of learning.

I plead with you to help us, or, if you cannot, to recommend those who might illuminate our new world here as you have done in Paris and elsewhere; I eagerly await your answer, and your inspiration.

This by my own hand on the 10th of October, 1792.

Vive la France!

Vive la Revolution!

> *Henri Bellefleur*
> *Postmaster of Lyon*

5

Five days north of Avignon, Hariot and Aloys became ill with fever and flux; Photine ordered them into the smallest of the wagons and gave orders that no one was to approach them, for fear of spreading the contagion to others, orders which the rest of the troupe were more than willing to obey as they continued northward. Urbain and Michau having left the troupe at Bollene, Pascal agreed to take the reins on the smaller cart, while Roger had taken over the task of driving their sickbed wagon, and kept to a short distance behind the rest of the vehicles; the rapid pace of the troupe's travel did not slacken. Four days later, Aloys began to vomit, and there was blood in his flux, as Roger reported to da San-Germain while the rest of the troupe broke their fasts with bread, cheese, and hot wine; their camp, a short distance from the river, was wreathed in river-mist that made a smirch of the early morning sun.

"Fever and bloody flux. No sign of a rash? Are there eruptions on their skin?" Da San-Germain saw Roger shake his head. "What do you think has sickened them?" he asked in Imperial Latin as he sat down on the rear of the larger cart, thinking aloud. "Is it from contaminated food, or some other cause? When I visited them yesterday, they seemed only to be ill from bad food, yet the tincture I gave them hasn't brought about much improvement."

"Yesterday it seemed to be caused by food. Today it looks like the fevers we saw in Praha in Otakar's time, the ones caused by animacules in the water," said Roger in the same language.

"It could be that; the symptoms usually occur within four or five days of drinking the tainted water, and that's consistent with their illness. You'd think the others would have it," da San-Germain remarked, shaking his head. "Did they go to the same taverns for drink—a place the rest of the troupe didn't visit?"

"Not a tavern, no, but most of the others do not drink water from horse-troughs," said Roger without any inflection at all. "Aloys does often, and Hariot occasionally."

"Ah." Da San-Germain glanced out at the troupe, all gathered around their campfire, most wrapped in cloaks and blankets against the chill. "Horse-troughs." He considered for a bit. "We have some of the sovereign remedy in our supplies, do we not?"

"Yes. A dozen vials."

"Good. That should be sufficient. For now, give them both the garlic-and-milk-thistle infusion, a double dose for Aloys, since his case is more severe. At noon, administer to each of them a vial of the sovereign remedy, and a second one to each at the end of the day." He stood up. "I'll come to have a look at them before we move on."

"What will you tell Madame?" Roger asked.

"I'll explain as much as I can, when she's finished eating. I don't think she has much interest in medical theory, but she wants to know how serious their condition is, and how it might affect the troupe. She resented being refused lodging at Valence because those two had fallen ill."

"Do you think she will accept what you tell her?"

"She might; she has to be careful for her troupe. Illness is dreadful for actors, so she may decide to keep Aloys and Hariot isolated, or order you to stay farther behind the rest of the troupe." It was more of a guess than a certainty. "It depends on how frightened the actors are of sickness, and how quickly Aloys and Hariot improve."

"Are you certain they will?"

Da San-Germain stared into the middle distance. "Hariot is likely to, but I'm not convinced that Aloys will—he's older and sicker, and the disease may linger in him." He took a long breath. "I wish I had brought my microscope with me. I could be more sure if I could examine their sputum and the flux under its magnification."

"But you are proceeding as if this is the cause? What if it isn't?" Roger inquired, his voice steady.

"I think it is the most prudent approach. If they're suffering from some other condition, the sovereign remedy will be a useful treatment, and the illness should run its course in a few days; if it is animacules, then they will need longer to recover."

"Will it delay our arrival in Lyon?" Roger studied da San-Germain for a long moment, his face impassive.

"I trust not," da San-Germain replied, his tone steely. "The speed of our travel should make no difference to them—not even to Aloys, who is more stricken."

"He is that. And his face has turned pasty."

"Understandably, if this is animacule infestation, but not a good sign. With that and bloody flux, it means there is bleeding somewhere in his bowels, and that can be a danger in itself. He will need more attention than Hariot." Da San-Germain moved restlessly, his countenance unreadable but his dark eyes bright. "Along with the tincture, give him some clean water with honey in it. That should lend him some strength until the fever passes. Nothing solid to eat until the blood is gone from his flux."

"Water? Not wine?"

"In this case, no; it will disguise the presence of blood. Use the water they've boiled for tea. There's usually a fair amount left."

"As you wish, my master." Roger got up and brushed off the back of his long canvas coat with his hands. "Two more days to Lyon, then."

"I believe so, assuming I can explain the nature of the men's illness to Photine, and she understands there is no danger of contagion," said da San-Germain, this time in French. "If we don't have to stop because—" he gestured toward the wagon where Aloys and Hariot lay.

"And if we do, what then?"

"You and I must set out on our own, with the troupe coming behind." His voice dropped. "I won't allow Madelaine to be brought to trial, not in Lyon; I won't."

Roger had rarely seen such fixity of purpose in da San-Germain; he regarded him closely, seeing the first signs of anguish in his dark eyes. "You are not responsible for her peril."

"But I am—she is one of my blood, and I promised her I would keep her safe."

"You took her out of France once, at the start of the Revolution, and she decided to return, against your advice."

This time when da San-Germain spoke it was in the language of his long-vanished people. "You don't understand, old friend. For more than two thousand years, my soul ached for a woman who would know me for what I am and accept that wholeheartedly from the first. That was a hard-won desire, one that took centuries to burgeon, but once it had wakened in me, I endeavored to search for . . ." He made a gesture of futility as he struggled to express the emotions his memories aroused. "Through the centuries, I feared that such a woman might not exist, until Madelaine, who welcomed my true nature with delectation. She had no reservations, no disgust, no loathing. For her, I offered what she had sought all her young life, and, when it came, she welcomed her change to my undead life." He pressed his lips together as if to stop his words;

Roger waited, and da San-Germain went on, "Though we can no longer be lovers, I can't endure the possibility of her nonexistence, not so soon, not if I can prevent it. If she dies the True Death when I can forestall it, my despair will be—" He went silent, his face a mask. "I must try to get her out for my sake, as well as hers."

For several seconds Roger could summon no words to comfort him. Finally he said, in da San-Germain's native tongue, "Then I will do all that I can to assist you, and her."

"I'm grateful," said da San-Germain, with utter sincerity.

"You've done as much for me, in restoring me to life, all those centuries ago," Roger said, his manner reserved as ever.

"If we start comparing obligations, we'll be here all day, at the least," da San-Germain remarked, and looked about him. "We'll be moving in an hour."

"And you'll speak with Madame about—" He gestured toward the smallest wagon where the two sick men lay.

Da San-Germain put his small hand on Roger's shoulder, and nodded once. "I'll look in on Hariot and Aloys shortly."

"Yes, you told me you would," Roger agreed. "I'll get the tincture out of your case now, administer it, and come back for the sovereign remedy before we depart from camp." He stepped into the larger cart and opened a carved-wood case that was strapped atop a clothes chest, removed a glass jar filled with a yellow-green liquid, and slipped it into the outer pocket of his coat, then closed the case again, and returned it to its place atop the chest. As he got out of the cart, he said, "I'll attend to them now. In ten minutes or so, they should be ready for your examination."

"Very good. If their flux worsens, or fever increases, inform me at once." He watched Photine rise from her seat on the bench near the fire and go to Enee's side, only to be rebuffed by him. "He has learned nothing."

"He's young and he's frightened," said Roger.

"Neither is a sufficient reason for him to behave so; he's churlish to no purpose," said da San-Germain, pulling the covering down over the back of the cart. "Not that you or I can alter that. Go attend to the men."

"I will," said Roger, walking away as he spoke.

Da San-Germain stood still for nearly a minute, then went to the remuda line where the horses and mules were tied. He pulled open the back of the wagon next to them and pulled out armloads of hay, which he distributed among the animals, then closed the wagon once more. He was about to leave when he heard approaching footsteps.

"How are Aloys and Hariot? Still feverish?" Feo asked as he came around the end of the wagon, his face shiny from shaving, his long muffler hanging loosely around his neck, his coachman's cloak over his arm; he gave da San-Germain a nod, adding as an afterthought, "Good morning, Ragoczy."

"And to you, Feo," he responded; he studied the coachman for a brief moment. "Tell me, do you ever drink water from horse-troughs?"

Startled by the question, Feo stared at him, then said, "Not since I was very young. My father beat me when he caught me doing it—I must have been six or seven—and I haven't tasted any since then. Not that it's very tempting. Why?" He ambled over toward the larger cart and leaned against its body, one leg crossed over the other.

"Roger has seen both Hariot and Aloys do it."

"It is unwholesome," said Feo.

"Have you seen them do it?" da San-Germain asked.

"I saw them at Montalia, when I reprimanded them for drinking it. That doesn't mean they've stopped."

"No, it doesn't," da San-Germain agreed. "And that is likely the cause of their illness. Have you noticed any of the others drinking from horse-troughs?"

Feo shook his head. "I would have spoken to anyone who did. There's no telling what is in those troughs."

"That, at least, is hopeful news," said da San-Germain. "If you learn of anyone doing that, will you inform me?"

"Certainly, if you wish it," said Feo. "You still haven't said how—"

"—Aloys and Hariot go on? No, I haven't, for I haven't seen them this morning. Yesterday they both appeared a bit recovered, but from what Roger has said, that's changed." He looked toward the smallest wagon, frowning slightly. "And if what you and Roger have told me is true, and they are suffering from an infestation of animacules in the water of the horse-trough at the Cheval d'Argent, then the medicaments I have should treat their illness in a few days. If they are the only ones who drank that water, and if that is truly the source of their illness, then there is no chance the infection will spread."

Feo shrugged, more from discomfort with disease than any lack of concern from its two victims. "Unfortunate for Hariot and Aloys, lucky for the rest of us. How soon will you know if their condition is an infestation?"

"By noon; the treatment they'll receive will either improve them or they will remain ill, in which case I will know it is something other than an infestation of animacules. Since no one else has shown symptoms they have, I believe that the condition is confined to them, and whatever the cause of their illness, I will do my utmost to treat it, rather than leave them to the care of strangers." He read doubt in Feo's eyes. "Traveling should do them no harm; it hasn't done so yet, and there is good reason for the troupe to keep moving. By the noon halt, when I will be able to assess the state of their illness, we should be at least three leagues from this place— perhaps four." There was a tone to da San-Germain's voice that discouraged argument.

"We move out when breakfast is done?" He reached into the wagon and brought out a collection of pails. "I'll go down to the river and bring water—assuming you say it is safe?—and then start grooming and harnessing the horses."

"You'll need two trips with the pails; there should be no danger to the horses," da San-Germain added a warning. "And be careful; the bank is slippery."

"No doubt." He sauntered away, whistling scraps of a melody.

Da San-Germain watched him go, thinking as he did that Feo was a steadier fellow than he had first given him credit for being. He decided to go to examine Aloys and Hariot while the rest of the troupe finished breakfast. The smallest wagon stood a short distance from the cluster of wagons and carts, a yellow fever-flag pinned to the canvas covering; da San-Germain approached, calling out, "Roger," to announce his presence.

"What do you want?" came from the wagon; after a moment, da San-Germain realized that the hoarse sound was Hariot's voice.

"It's Ragoczy. I want to see how you are faring."

"We're sick. That's how we're faring." Hariot sounded not only ill, but rancorous.

"No doubt you would like to be better," said da San-Germain, lifting the canvas flap and looking into the wagon.

"Yes. I don't know if we will be if we have to drink more of that vile liquid your man just gave us." He was lying on one of the three beds in the wagon; Aloys was on the second, and the third was still tied up against the side of the wall.

Ducking his head and bending over, da San-Germain climbed into the wagon, his head almost brushing the canvas top, his dark-seeing eyes unhampered by the dim interior. He bent over Aloys, who was moaning softly, his eyes half-closed, the heat of him palpable; his breath smelled of rotten meat. "How long has he been this way?"

"I don't know," Hariot muttered. "I didn't notice until an hour or two ago."

"So three hours at the least. Did he drink the tincture Roger gave him?"

"Most of it." Hariot rolled onto his side. "What do you think? Is he going to die?"

"We're all going to die," said da San-Germain. "But possibly not just yet." He touched Aloys' neck, taking stock of his pulse. "Fast and thready."

"Not good," said Hariot.

"It could be better," da San-Germain said. "But not dire, either." He adjusted the blanket so that it was higher on Aloys' chest. "He needs to stay warm."

"Why? He's burning up as it is."

"I would like his fever to break." Da San-Germain turned to Hariot. "You, on the other hand, seem to be on the way to recovery."

"I hope," said Hariot recalcitrantly. "My guts feel as if I've been eating thistles, but what comes out is more liquid than solid."

"Not surprising," said da San-Germain. He dropped down on one knee next to Hariot. "Both chamber pots are empty."

"Your man did that when he brought us the stuff to drink." He hesitated. "I don't suppose you'll let me lower my blanket?"

"I wouldn't advise it. You have a fever, though not so great a one as Aloys." He studied Hariot a little longer. "When did you last eat solid food?"

"I think two days ago. It wouldn't stay down. Your man has given us broth and water, but that's the whole of it except for the concoctions you have provided." He sighed abruptly. "I'm not hungry."

"I should think not." Da San-Germain got to his feet. "You should be improving in a day or two. Aloys will take longer."

"And by then we'll be in Lyon," said Hariot. "Your man told us that."

"We should enter the city tomorrow afternoon. Then we'll have to seek out a place to perform the play, and an inn where we can lodge." He paused. "We may need to make separate arrangements for you and Aloys, at least until you are on the road to recovery."

"That's to be expected," Hariot growled. "Revolution or not, cities still want to keep the sick away."

"Do you blame them? Haven't the cities got trouble enough without disease running rampant?" A brief, intense recollection of Avignon during the Black Plague four hundred years earlier took hold of him; he shook it off, knowing that the illness that had claimed these two men was nowhere near as catastrophically deadly as the Plague had been.

Hariot's answer was an incoherent mumble, and a sour look.

"When we stop at noon, I will check on you again; before we leave this morning, Roger will provide you with another . . . concoction to drink, which should lessen your fever and help rid you of the infection you have taken." He moved back from Hariot's bed and was about to take a last look at Aloys when he felt hot fingers on his hand.

Hariot was staring at him. "Tell me honestly. Will I recover?"

"I expect so," said da San-Germain. "And from now on, I would not drink from horse-troughs, if I were you."

"It is sufficient for the horses," Hariot protested.

"You are not a horse. You don't eat hay, do you?"

On his narrow bunk, Aloys moaned and wrapped his arms across his abdomen, bending over as far as the narrow bunk would allow.

Hariot glanced in Aloys' direction, worry and fright in his eyes. "He's worse off than I am."

"Yes."

For more than a minute, there was silence in the wagon; then Hariot grumbled, "Bring on your potions, then."

Da San-Germain nodded. "I will return when we halt to eat." He gave a small nod, then, still bent over to accommodate the low top, backed out of the wagon and out into the brightening morning. He noticed Feo brushing down the horses, Roger working along beside him; he calculated how long it would take them to have the horses and mules harnessed to their vehicles, and decided they would need an hour yet, with just the two of the men working at the task. He decided to come back to lend a hand when he had talked with Photine.

Crepin and Valence were busy putting out the fire as da San-Germain walked up to the three long benches where the troupe sat. Tereson was packing up the remainder of the wheel of cheese, and Constance was gathering the cups, setting them in their places in the crockery case. Olympe had a broad broom and was using it to push any stray sparks and clinkers back toward the dying fire. Photine had the large pot in her hand, wiping it out with a rag. There was no sign of Enee. As she saw da San-Germain approaching, she raised the rag in greeting. "Ragoczy. I was wondering where you were."

"I have been attending to Aloys and Hariot," he answered.

"And how do you find them?" She did her best to keep the worry from her voice.

"Hariot is improving, little as he may believe it; Aloys is not yet through the crisis."

Photine's expression was eloquent with worry. "Should we keep clear of him?"

"There is no reason; the illness the two of them have is not passed from person to person." He took one of her hands as a gesture of reassurance. "They have drunk tainted water and have become infested with animacules. Only those drinking such tainted water will become ill, and so far, no one else shows signs of the sickness."

"How appalling, to be . . . infested," Photine exclaimed, as if the very word were a contamination. "How did they manage to do that?"

"By drinking from horse-troughs, from what I have learned," said da San-Germain in as calm a voice as he could. "They were reckless, but as far as I can determine, none of the others shared their folly."

"Reckless?" She pulled away from him. "They've put us all in danger."

"No," he said. "They haven't. The disease cannot spread from them to any of you." He indicated the bench. "Sit down, and I'll explain it to you."

She hung back. "Are you certain you aren't telling me this simply to get us to travel on to Lyon? Can I rely upon you to put our welfare on balance with your kinswoman?"

"You can," he promised her. "What benefit would it be to

Madelaine if she were to sicken and die as a result of our attempts at deliverance?" This was stretching the truth more than he liked to do: no vampire, being undead, could succumb to any disease, no matter how fatal.

"I suppose there is something in that," Photine conceded.

"Of course there is," he said, and wondered if he had overplayed his hand.

The last of the fire hissed out under the deluge from three large buckets of water poured on it; pale steam arose to blend with the morning mists.

"Are you willing to continue to treat Aloys and Hariot while we travel?"

"That is certainly my intention," da San-Germain told her.

"Do you think they will improve by the time we reach Lyon?" She studied his face, searching for any trace of mendacity.

"Hariot may be; Aloys is likely to take a little longer."

"Then what if we're refused entry to the city?" Photine asked, anxiety sharpening her tone.

"Then we'll have to make arrangements to house Hariot and Aloys outside the walls until they are recovered, and have them come to us then. We'll face that when, and if, we must." He kissed her hand, smiling wryly. "It's unfortunate that the Revolution has closed so many of the monasteries: the monks would have been willing to look after the two men for a donation; as it is, we may have to deal with an innkeeper or farm wife, which could mean less attentive care and a higher cost."

"Will you pay for their treatment if it comes to that?"

"Most certainly I will; you need have no doubt of it." He paused a few seconds, then went on in a gentler voice. "I will not desert your troupe, Photine, and I will not expose you to more difficulties than the ones that face us now. If I have to go on ahead, I will see that you have funds and provisions, as well as Feo, to bring you safely to Lyon."

She considered him through narrowed eyes. "You have kept to our bargain most diligently."

"And I will continue to do so," he said.

She gave an abrupt sigh. "I know you are reliable, but you're also eager to gain release for your kinswoman, and I would be reckless with my people if I forgot that." She suddenly swung around. "Constance! Have a care with how you store that chest!"

"Yes, Madame," said Constance with exaggerated courtesy as she pulled the leather belt around the crockery chest and shoved it in the back of the wagon.

"What do you want us to do?" Photine asked, turning her attention to da San-Germain again. "Do we travel or do we wait?"

"We travel," he said, trying not to make it too much of an order. "The sooner we reach Lyon, the safer your troupe will be." He offered her a hint of a smile. "And the sooner you will be able to perform again; I will secure you a performance license as soon as we have found lodgings."

"Ah, yes, the license—from the Revolutionary Court. If you present yourself on our behalf, the better your chances to wrest your kinswoman from the Revolutionary Court, for the Guards will not be on alert for you," Photine added knowingly. "You will have the opportunity you seek, and you will be able to do what you must without drawing unwanted attention to yourself."

"Yes, of course," he said.

"Then we'll be on our way within the hour," said Photine, her demeanor brusque. "We will enter Lyon tomorrow, if we travel quickly today—that is what you said, isn't it?"

"Yes. Fortunately the weather is going to be clear as soon as the fog disperses."

"It's lifting already," said Olympe, who had been listening to the two of them talk. "We'll have full sun and warmth for most of the day."

The sound of a scuffle erupted behind the largest wagon, and as all activity around the cooling fire ceased, the sounds of oaths and blows grew louder.

Photine suddenly raised her voice. "Whoever is fighting, stop it right now!" She motioned to Crepin. "Go find out who is—"

There was a sudden outraged howl, and before Crepin could take more than three steps, Theron emerged from the far side of the wagon, dragging Enee by the ear; each of them had the marks of blows on their faces that would shortly become emphatic bruises. "I caught him in the supply wagon, trying to open the money-chest," Theron announced as he all but flung Enee to the ground.

Photine rushed toward her son, vexation and indignation warring for dominance of her expression. "Is that right?" she demanded as Enee struggled to sit up, his nose bleeding freely.

"He's lying," Enee muttered.

"I am telling the truth," Theron insisted.

"Ask him what he was doing at the supply wagon," Enee countered.

"I was going to put away my blanket when I heard a thump in the wagon,' Theron said, as if this were the obvious response.

"Hah!" Enee scoffed while he cupped his hands to catch the blood from his nose. "He was following me."

"I was not!" Theron protested.

Photine motioned Theron to silence, then knelt down next to Enee. "I want you to tell me the truth," she said to him, quietly and calmly. "You are no longer a child, to be excused for tricks and pranks. If you were in the supply wagon, and you were . . . were trying to open the money-chest, tell me why."

Enee pursed his lips, his face truculent. "I have to pay Lothaire the money I lost to him."

Lothaire, who had been supervising the loading of the wagons, rounded on Enee. "You lost nothing to me. If you have gambled, it wasn't with me."

"Liar!" Enee accused, trying to scramble to his feet.

That was more than Lothaire was willing to endure; he came toward Enee, his fists clenched. "How dare you call me a liar!"

Before another fight could begin, da San-Germain stepped forward, and seemingly without effort held Lothaire and Enee apart.

"Enough. All three of you, stop this now." He nodded to Theron. "Go wash your face and have Roger put a salve on it." He hauled Enee upright. "You should sit down with your head between your knees until the bleeding stops. We'll sort out what did and did not happen when we stop at mid-day. And Enee, you will apologize to your mother and to the troupe."

Enee shook his head, and succeeded in splattering a trail of blood drops on both Lothaire and da San-Germain. "I've done nothing wrong. Why should I apologize?"

"Do it," da San-Germain commanded him, his voice no louder than usual, his demeanor unflustered.

For several seconds, Enee looked as if he were going to lash out at da San-Germain, but finally he grumbled, "I apologize."

Photine regarded her son silently as she stood up, then said, "We'll discuss this later. Go sit down, as Ragoczy told you." She studied him, turbulence in her splendid eyes; she watched Enee trudge off to do as she ordered, then turned back to da San-Germain. "Thank you, thank you. I don't know what would have happened if you hadn't stepped in."

"There would have been another fight, perhaps a greater one, which none of us can afford," he said levelly.

She gestured a kind of concession. "True enough, I fear," she said, and raised her voice. "Let's get packed and on our way. We have four leagues to cover today." With great purpose, she walked toward her home-wagon. "Lothaire, help Roger and Feo get the teams harnessed. Valence, you're in charge of the remuda."

As the troupe once again resumed their preparations for travel, da San-Germain returned to the larger cart to help harness the mules to it, thinking as he did that this journey was becoming more complicated by the hour, and hoping that there would be no more altercations before they reached Lyon.

Text of a memorandum from Vivien Zacharie Charlot, Deputy Secretary for Public Safety of Lyon, to Egide Loup, Warden of the

Anti-Revolutionary Prisoners, carried by official messenger of the Revolutionary Court and delivered the day it was written.

> *To the Warden of the Anti-Revolutionary Prisoners, Egide Loup, the greetings of Vivien Zacharie Charlot, Deputy Secretary for Public Safety of Lyon, on this, the 13th day of October, 1792.*
>
> *My dear Warden Loup,*
>
> *After conferring with the members of the Revolutionary Tribunal and the Committee for Public Safety, it is my duty to inform you that these two august bodies have agreed that the most recently arrived prisoners are to be housed in the former Saint-Gautier Monastery on the bank of the Saone until they can be brought to trial and sentence pronounced upon them.*
>
> *Once the prisoners are installed in the former monastery, I will begin the process of interviewing them in order to have complete files to present to the Revolutionary Court when the trials begin, and I ask you to prepare your staff to receive me and my two assistants when we call upon you to admit us. To this end, I request that you prepare two chambers that we may use for our interrogations, and assign armed guards to those chambers to ensure that none of the prisoners will be tempted to escape.*
>
> *Vive la Revolution!*
> *Vive la France!*
>
> *Vivien Zacharie Charlot*
Deputy Secretary for Public Safety
Lyon

6

The clustered spires of the Basilica Notre-Dame de Fourviere rose over the city, a constant, stately, and troubling reminder of Lyon's illustrious, sanctioned past; it shone in the morning light like a castle in a fairy tale, its large, stained-glass bowed window glowing with rainbow colors. Around the old city walls, like a muddy hem on a ball-gown, there were warrens of narrow streets with tall, acerose houses looming together over them, where scrawny children ran and furtive men waited in the shadows for ill-conceived opportunities.

"What on earth has happened here? These streets weren't so . . . so sinister eight years ago. The populace was happy. There were parades and bonfires. People were singing. How could the place change so quickly?" Photine asked as she looked about her, her eyes wide with misgiving as she raised the hood of her cloak; beside her on the driving-box of the larger cart, da San-Germain kept alert for any trouble.

"You ask that, after you and your troupe originally left France in part to ensure your safety? I would guess the Revolution has unsettled the city; we'll find out once we're inside the walls," he answered, laying his hand on the driving-whip as a rag-tag pack of young men came sidling toward them, the four in the front keeping their hands in their pockets. "Pass on, fellows," he recommended. "And at a good distance. Keep your knives where they are. I don't want the mules' tendons cut so you can loot the cart." For emphasis, he snaked the lash of the driving-whip over their heads.

A dark-haired youth who appeared to be the leader offered a snarl, but kept away from the cart; he spat in the general direction of the troupe as he led his comrades into an alley, swaggering as he went.

"What did they want from us?" Photine asked uneasily.

"The chance to brag to others of their feats as much as any spoils they might be seeking," da San-Germain ventured, his hand still on the whip. "They chose the carts because we're behind the wagons and might not be able to summon help."

"Would they have killed us?"

Da San-Germain hesitated for a moment, then said, "They might have tried," before he kiss-whistled to his team to urge them onward.

The road turned northwest and grew a bit steeper, accommodating the swell of the hill; the city walls rose up ahead, the southeast gate standing open, half a dozen Revolutionary Guards already talking to Feo on the driving-box of the lead wagon.

"Do you think they'll allow Aloys and Hariot to enter?" Photine shifted on her seat, braiding the fringe of her shawl.

In an effort to reassure her, da San-Germain responded, "If they ask about them at all; I cannot see that the Guards would have any reason to refuse. Neither of them is suffering from—"

She shivered. "Do you think Feo will tell them anything?"

"If he is asked, he will—otherwise, no."

"But if they *do* ask, what is he likely to tell them?"

"Much the same that I would if I were asked: that Hariot is much improved," said da San-Germain steadily. "And Aloys is no longer feverish. I doubt they will be turned away, were they alone. At this time of year, many travelers have minor ailments. If the Guards prevented them all from entering, the markets would suffer, and the ailments would not go away. When the weather changes from warm to cool, the blood cannot keep the body warm, and illness of every sort results, just as when the weather warms, many suffer from antipathies that bring sneezing and itches and other—"

She cut him short, unwilling to be distracted. "But the Guards might not believe that they are getting better. The Guards could order us to remain outside the walls, couldn't they? For fear that our men might bring contagion into the city."

"They could, but it's not likely that they will. Players should be welcome here, and we've proven our worth in Avignon; if they have any reservations, I can salve their consciences with gold. I don't believe the Guards would refuse a . . . sign of our appreciation." His tone was sardonic, but his eyes were sad. "One way or another, we will be admitted."

"Because you demand it be so," Photine remarked, her expression a careful mix of admiration and irritation.

"Because the Guards are poorly paid, if it comes to that," said da San-Germain at his most urbane.

"But—" She stopped herself saying more. Her face became inscrutable as they neared the open maw of the gate.

The lead wagon passed through unimpeded, and the rest followed behind, moving slowly as they entered unfamiliar, crowded streets. The Guards offered them ironic salutes, a few of them making suggestive remarks to Olympe, riding on the driving-box of the third wagon; she waved back at them, laughing and flirting.

As da San-Germain started through, one of the Guards signaled him to halt; Photine looked about her as if seeking the means of escape.

The Guard approached da San-Germain. "These carts, tied together. Why is that?"

"Two of our drivers left us at Avignon," said da San-Germain calmly. "We've had to make the best of it. It's easier to pony the second cart than a loaded wagon."

"Two drivers left?"

"Yes. Ask anyone in the troupe," said Photine majestically, her fear masked by the grandeur she so often used on stage.

"Why did they leave?" the Guard persisted.

"They wished to return home, or so they said," Photine said with even more hauteur. "I took them at their word."

The Guard considered this, then chuckled. "So you have all the mules to contend with?"

Da San-Germain shrugged. "I don't mind mules."

"You like mules? What man likes mules?" Stepping back, the Guard motioned them on. "Good luck to you."

When they were out of earshot, Photine turned to da San-Germain. "What do you think he meant by that?"

"I think he meant what he said," da San-Germain replied kindly, puzzled by her growing anxiety. "He was wishing us good luck."

"Are you sure? Was he giving us a warning instead?" She pulled her cloak more closely around her. "Why didn't he stop any of the others? Why you?"

So that was it, he thought. She is afraid that the Guards are looking for me, that they know what I intend to do. "Because of the mules, as he said. He has no idea who I am, nor would it matter if he did."

"Are you certain of that?" Her voice had risen three notes and grown sharper.

"Not absolutely, no, but sure enough not to worry about it. He's enjoying the little authority he has, and there is no reason to deny him that." He looked around, trying to recall what the city had been like a little more than seven hundred years ago, when he and Roger had passed part of a winter within the old walls, on their way south. The basic skeleton of the city was not much changed—and had not altered at the center since the Romans had been here—but the look of the city, its tendons and ligaments, were different: many ancient buildings had been replaced with newer ones, and the limits of the city had expanded to walls that were built before the arrival of the Black Plague, more than four hundred years ago, giving the city itself more than twenty additional acres inside its protective ramparts than it had had in the thirteenth century.

"Where do we look for lodging?" Photine asked. "I don't know where the markets are these days."

"Feo will manage for us," said da San-Germain. "He's made inquiries in Saint-Vallier and Vienne about the most advantageous places for us to consider, and how to find them. He knows where he is going."

"Do you trust him?"

"Don't you?" da San-Germain asked calmly.

Photine turned to him, umbrage stiffening her posture. "Why did he do that? I didn't give him the task of . . . of . . ."

"No; you had so many things claiming your attention that I suggested it to him. You have enough to deal with." He did not add that Roger had also used their time in the towns and cities to learn what he could about conditions in Lyon, but not for the reception of the players; Roger had asked about the political prisoners. "I have an obligation, as your patron, to see that your way is smoothed as much as is possible. Isn't that part of our agreement?"

She peered at him, measuring his candor against her pique; then she allowed her attention to be claimed by a procession of tradesmen holding aloft signs declaring their right to sit with the officials of the Revolutionary Assembly, and to cast votes at odds with their Guilds. "Look! Why do you suppose they're marching?"

"As a sign of disagreement with Guild policies, I would assume, since that is what their banners say," da San-Germain observed.

She turned to watch the marchers as the carts rolled on. "Why would they want to vote contrary to the wishes of their Guilds?"

"Would you like me to turn around so you can ask them?" His manner was wholly unruffled, and his offer genuine.

After taking a moment to think, Photine said, "No; we'd lose track of the rest, and that could be awkward. You don't know where we're going, do you?" There was a note of spite in her question as she settled back on her seat, but remained edgy, staring around her as if she expected to be confronted by angry townspeople at every turn.

Feo led the troupe around the swell of the hill toward the west, passing two streets of shops, some of which were open, some of which were boarded up with bits of smashed windows on the flagstones in front of them. He slowed down as he approached a square with a statue of two medieval knights fighting from the backs of warhorses, their swords at a perpetual clash, in front of an empty church bearing the marks of fire along its facade on the north side of the oblong; there were a pair of inns on the south, one a large pile three centuries old, the other a more elegant, smaller building from the time of the Sun King. The troupe went toward the pair of inns, halting in front of the older building. Feo drew in his wagon, set the brake, and jumped down from the box, making his way back toward the carts, giving instructions to the drivers as he went. When he reached the team of mules, he called out, "This is the Place des Chevaliers. The Revolutionary Tribunal allows performances here, or so the Guards told me. They recommend the Jongleur. The tumblers and clowns stay there at Carnival."

"Very good," said Photine. "If they will take us."

"Roger will make the arrangements for us," said da San-Germain. "As soon as we're installed here, I'll go get us a license for performances. Would you think five performances to start with will suffice?" da San-Germain asked as he got down from the driving-box and held up his arms to assist Photine to descend.

"Why do you bother to inquire of me?" she countered, a trace of petulance in her voice. "You have made up your mind already what will suit your purpose, and, as you remind me, you are our patron. Though I would prefer six."

Da San-Germain remained at ease. "Then six it shall be."

"If they won't interfere with your plans," she flung at him.

He realized that denying this would only lead to more rancor, so he said, "Yes, I have my own reasons for being here—you've known that since we left Padova—but that doesn't mean I want to put your troupe at a disadvantage. I would like to see you given the attention and praise you seek, because you are greatly gifted and your troupe is a fine one. You gained many admirers in Avignon; you will do the same here as well."

Photine looked away from him as she allowed him to lift her out of the driving-box and onto the paving-stones of the square. "The Deux Canards and the Jongleur," she said, looking at the two sign-boards hanging over the entries to the inns, taking the time to scrutinize their fronts. "I suppose it should be the Jongleur, though it's older than the Deux Canards; it has more rooms, and the stable looks larger."

"It also appears to be more hospitable to players and other entertainers," da San-Germain remarked, and saw Roger approaching, his driving-coat spattered with bits of mud.

Feo nodded to Roger. "You agree with the Guards, then? The Jongleur would seem to be preferable?"

"It would, especially since the Guard recommended it," said Photine quickly so that da San-Germain could say nothing that might seem to demean her. "We'll need space in the stable and enough rooms for us all."

"Of course," said Roger, and added in an undervoice, "Madame, if you can spare a moment for your son? He has been restive for the last hour and wants to go to a tavern before you have settled into your quarters."

"Oh, dear," Photine murmured. "I'll have a word with him," she said more loudly, and set off toward the wagon in which he rode, her cloak flapping around her like a thundercloud.

Roger watched her go. "She seems discomfited."

"Yes," da San-Germain agreed. "I wish I knew why."

"She's jealous," said Roger.

"Perhaps," da San-Germain allowed. "She says she fears that the Guards here may be looking for me, and that troubles her, but I don't think that's the whole of it, nor is jealousy." He was silent for a long moment, then said, "The Jongleur. Get ten rooms if they can spare them, and stalls for the animals."

Roger ducked his head and went off toward the older, larger inn.

"What do you want me to do?" Feo inquired.

Da San-Germain was a little surprised at the question; Feo was used to the routine of travel with the troupe. "Ready the wagons and carts to be stabled."

"Nothing else?" Feo studied da San-Germain's features, his face revealing nothing of his thoughts.

"Not just at present. Why do you ask?"

"I just thought . . . since you have your own intentions here in Lyon . . . that there might be something . . . more . . . that you would like me to do?" His hesitation was more from uncertainty than tact.

"There may be, but not quite yet. Our first task is to get rooms, then we will unload the wagons and carts, as always." Da San-Germain glanced over the actors as they came out of their wagons and began to move about to loosen their joints. "We need to be more settled before I go to the Revolutionary Tribunal."

"Beyond what your man is doing?" Feo asked. "By the time you reach the Tribunal, if you leave now, Roger will have arranged for everything."

Da San-Germain took a long breath. "If we seem too eager, that may cause suspicion on the part of the Revolutionary Tribunal, to say nothing of the Revolutionary Court and Assembly, which could lead to the kinds of scrutiny we would all like to avoid. I will apply for the performance license when we are fully registered in our rooms and our vehicles and animals are in the stable. That way there can be no question about our intentions, or that we are a known commedia company, not a rabble of rogues and vagabonds." He drew out a leather purse from under his driving-coat. "Roger knows how much we can pay to the innkeeper. We'll take the rooms for eight days. If we need to be here longer, then we'll pay the additional amount then. For now, I have more than enough for the license."

"You will pay the extension fee after the troupe has collected money from their audiences?" Feo suggested.

"It would be better for us all if it seemed that way," da San-Germain told him, his eyes dark caverns in his expressionless face.

Feo held up his hands. "Whatever suits you, Ragoczy."

Da San-Germain shook his head. "What suits me is that the troupe should be housed and fed, and the animals stalled, groomed, and fed. After that I can tend to other things."

"Those that are your true purpose for being here?" Feo asked with cherubic innocence.

"Once we have a license to perform, then, yes. Until then, I have a duty to the troupe, and I will attend to it." Da San-Germain offered Feo a slight bow.

"Of course," said Feo, and turned away. "I'll see to the wagons and the horses, then the carts and the mules."

It was over an hour later when Roger met da San-Germain at the front of the Jongleur; he had changed his coat to one more suitable to calling upon the Revolutionary Tribunal; da San-Germain had also put on more appropriate clothing—his black wool hammer-claw coat, a waistcoat of dull-red damask, and buff-colored unmentionables were fashionable enough to gain the attention of almost any civil servant—and donned a bicorn hat edged in tricoleur rosettes. He went to the front of the Jongleur, pulling on black Florentine gloves as he went. A few minutes later, Feo led up two saddled horses for them.

"Madame has ordered dinner in an hour—not that that means anything to you." He held the stirrup for da San-Germain as he mounted the handsome blue roan gelding. "Shall I tell her you will take your meal elsewhere?"

"If you would," said da San-Germain, gathering up the reins and waiting while Roger got up on his mouse-colored mare.

As they put their horses in motion, Roger said quietly to da San-Germain in Byzantine Greek, "Feo is becoming insolent."

"More cheeky than insolent, I think," da San-Germain remarked, and added, "He masks his worry with jests."

"That may be so," said Roger. He rode in contemplative silence beside da San-Germain; when they reached their destination, Roger took the blue roan's reins while da San-Germain sought out whomever was in charge of issuing licenses.

The offices of the Revolutionary Tribunal were located in what had been the church of Saint-Jean le Moin; the Department of Public Safety occupied half the six-hundred-year-old building; the Revolutionary Tribunal had the other half; the central aisle provided the two bureaucracies a neutral ground where citizens could move without hindrance. Three clerks stationed in the aisle directed newcomers to the proper destination. The sanctuary had been converted into a kind of waiting room, the old wooden choir had been taken down and cabinets and shelving put up in its place, and most of the nave was filled with desks for the men who worked there.

After waiting nearly an hour, da San-Germain spoke to one of the secretaries of the Revolutionary Tribunal, who drew up a provisional license for six performances. "One of our officers will have to attend a rehearsal to ensure that your play is not seditious in any way. I will inform you when the officer will visit."

"Sooner rather than later would be preferable," said da San-Germain. "We have come all the way from Avignon—the troupe is eager to play." He held out two gold coins. "We would appreciate any assistance you can supply."

"I understand," said the secretary, accepting the coins. "Tomorrow or the next day—is that soon enough?"

"Certainly. Will you require the full staging, or will a rehearsal in the stable-yard be sufficient for your officer?"

The secretary considered the question. "A full staging would be best."

"In that case, we will need two hours' notice to set up our stage and ready our costumes," said da San-Germain, with another cordial gesture; he thought back to the venality of the royal court half a century ago and decided that the only thing the Revolution had changed in that regard was the recipients of the bribes.

"I will inform our officer of that." He stamped the provisional license and indicated the half of the church given over to the Department of Public Safety. "Once you have your actual license, you will need to arrange for Guards to be present at your performances, to keep the crowds from untoward acts. They will make sure no cutpurses or other thieves take advantage of the gathered throng, and will serve to quell any riot that might disrupt your play."

Although da San-Germain found this disquieting he said with complete affability, "A wise precaution in these turbulent times. Will you tell me how much we will have to pay for the Guards' protection?" He folded the license carefully and slid it into the inside breast-pocket of his coat.

"That I don't know. The Department of Public Safety will make the determination; it is their area of concern. Once you have your license, the Committee for Public Safety will decide how many Guards will be needed, and for how long. One of the Deputies will inform you, and the Department, how much you will be charged." He gave a thin, meaningless smile and bade da San-Germain a good morning.

Riding back to the Jongleur, they heard trumpets sound the mid-day; almost at once, activity increased around them as the people hurried to complete their morning tasks before going in for their dinners. Da San-Germain held his gelding to a strict walk, letting those on foot eddy around them like flood-water; Roger trailed behind him to make it easier for those on foot to pass them in the narrow streets. By the time they reached the Place des Chevaliers, the square was largely empty; only a single groom came to claim their horses.

"Where do the players dine?" da San-Germain asked as he and Roger stepped in the main door.

The young man behind the desk pointed to the closed door on the right. "In there."

"Thank you," said da San-Germain, and turned to Roger, speaking in Hungarian. "I'll go inform Photine of the conditions of our license. If you wish to get yourself a shoat or a goose to eat, please do, and take it to whichever chamber has been assigned to us."

Roger gave a nod of compliance. "Is there anything you will require of me during the next hour?"

"I doubt it," said da San-Germain. "If I do, I'll find you in the room, will I not?"

"Yes," said Roger, and moved away toward the inn's kitchen.

Da San-Germain paused a moment, then opened the door and stepped into the smaller dining room. He bowed slightly to the troupe, then went to the far end of the table where Photine was sitting, removing the provisional license from his coat pocket and holding it out to her. "A provisional license for six performances. You'll have to do a full performance for an officer of the Department of Public Safety before it will be official, but that should be no problem."

Photine took the paper from him and read it, her eyes narrowing. "They mean to spy on us," she declared.

"Would you expect otherwise?" da San-Germain asked. "At least they will be readily identified, unlike in some other places."

"Do you think we should change the play?" She wiped her mouth with her serviette and raised her hand to signal Theron. "We will have to discuss the script as soon as we're finished dining."

"Not again," Theron exclaimed. "I can't work at it again, Madame. I simply cannot."

"Then we will have the actors make the changes," Photine announced.

"I forbid it!" Theron declared, getting to his feet and spilling some of the sauteed vegetables onto the table and floor.

"There will be an officer of the Department of Public Safety coming to watch us rehearse—full dress, with music. He will be here tomorrow or the day after, so we must be prepared for him by then."

Theron swore comprehensively, stamping his foot for emphasis as he called on God and His Saints to end this desecration. "If you insist on this madness, I suppose I must do what you require," he told her as soon as he had ended his outburst.

"I think we must modify one of the scenes to praise the justice of the Revolutionary Courts," Photine said, doing her utmost to summon up enthusiasm; the actors looked at one another in various states of dismay.

Olympe smiled her most fetching smile. "Theron, could you see your way to writing me a few more lines?"

This brought howls of protest and indignation from the rest; Photine raised her hand to stop it.

"Why not wait until the officer has seen it?" da San-Germain suggested. "He may be satisfied with it the way it is."

Photine gave a prickly laugh. "You know nothing of censors, do you?" She did not wait for an answer, but shook her head. "And you may be sure, whomever they send will be a censor no matter what title he bears."

"I have dealt with my share of censors, over the years," da San-Germain assured her. "That is why I recommend letting him see the work—so he may take credit for any changes you may make to the script. It will make him less likely to complain about the play."

Crepin slapped his palm down on the table. "You're a clever one, Ragoczy, no doubt about it." He swung around with a broad gesture and faced Photine. "I think that is an excellent plan."

Constance leaned forward, her elbows on the table. "We'll perform better if we stick to the script we know. I'm for Ragoczy's plan."

Sibelle sighed. "A few new lines would be nice, though."

Pascal stared at Photine. "What if we work out a couple new versions, and if there are objections to the play, we can show the officer our alternatives for his approval?"

"What if he expects us to act the variations?" Constance protested.

"Tell him that we haven't rehearsed the variations recently because Avignon preferred the version we—"

"Too complicated," da San-Germain warned. "Keep the matter simple. Too many choices could cause more problems than they solve. The censor will be more inclined to ratify the license if he participates in the . . . improvements."

Valence spoke up, his voice carrying the same dramatic weight it would have had if he had been delivering Horatius' speech to his men at the bridge from desCastre's play. "While I wouldn't mind more lines, I think Ragoczy's right about preparedness and giving the censor a hand in the matter. Besides, I'm tired, and I want to spend the night sleeping, not trying to memorize lines that I would probably stumble over."

Hariot, still looking worn, nodded to Valence. "I agree with him."

At that, Photine reminded them all, "I did not ask you for a vote, or to choose sides." She waited while the room grew quiet. "But Ragoczy does have a point. Shall we agree to meet again after supper and look through the play for places where more can be said that is favorable to the Revolution, and make note of them in case the censor tells us we must modify the text?"

Theron sat down again. "I suppose we could do that," he admitted as he reached to refill his wine-glass.

"Then we're in accord," Photine said. "Someone pass what's left of the chickens."

As quickly as excitement had taken hold of the actors it was gone. The meal was resumed, the conversation became desultory, and there was no more mention of changes to the script.

Da San-Germain bent down to speak softly to Photine. "Would you like me to join you for your discussion, or not?"

"I think not," she replied after a short moment. "I'll probably have to smooth our poet's ruffled feathers, and that will be more difficult if you're around."

"As you wish," da San-Germain said, standing upright once more. "Then I'll spend my time putting new strings on my cimbalom; we don't want any sour notes."

"No, we don't," she said, and helped herself to another chicken-leg and some of the pickled onions that served as a garnish. "We'll talk in the morning."

Da San-Germain nodded. "I look forward to it," he said before he left the troupe to their dinner; as he closed the door, he found himself wondering what Photine was planning for the evening beyond the script discussion, and if she would ever tell him.

Text of a report to Vivien Zacharie Charlot, Deputy Secretary for Public Safety in Lyon, from Emile Louis Orgues, License-Clerk in the Department of Public Safety in Lyon, delivered in person the afternoon it was written,

*To the Deputy Secretary for Public Safety, Vivien
Zacharie Charlot, the dutiful greetings of Emile Louis
Orgues, License-Clerk in the Department of Public
Safety, on this, the 16th day of October, 1792.*

My dear Deputy Secretary,
*I have this morning attended the rehearsal of a theatri-
cal troupe calling their play and themselves the Commedia della Morte at the Jongleur in the Place des
Chevaliers. This troupe is led by Madame Photine
d'Auville, and consists of eleven actors, a musician, and
two or three men-of-all-work. Their stage is formed by
putting two of their wagons together, lowering the on-
sides to rest on braces not unlike saw-horses. Then they
set up a framework for curtains and similar devices for
the presentation of their play. Their musician plays an
Hungarian kind of hammered zither, offering somber
airs of what I am informed are his own compositions.*

*The play itself is intended to amuse and shock, and
for the most part, it succeeds in these goals, which also
contain certain moral lessons that keep the work from
being gratuitously morbid. I made notes during their
rehearsal and present the gist of them to you here: the
scenes are unusual, some of them amusing in their own
right, some as contrast for what is to come, for all end
with the appearance of increasing numbers of Corpses,
in their winding-sheets, their faces covered by skull-
masks, a sight that is most disquieting. Each scene is in
the manner of a vignette, showing some aspect of life
from days before the Revolution, and how it ends in the
arrival of the Corpses. Each appearance of the Corpses
includes the players from the previous scene, identified
by some point of recognition: a nosegay, a hat, a multi-
tude of rings, and so forth. There is an epilogue in verse
that sums up the themes of the scenes. It is clever in its*

way, and although some may find it too upsetting to be regarded as true entertainment, I have been assured by the author of the work, a Theron Baptiste Heurer, that some minor modifications of the play can be accomplished by next Friday; the leader of the troupe has told me that they need only two days of rehearsal to work the changes into their performance. They will deliver a copy of the changes and insertions to me in three days and I will review them before issuing the endorsed license for six performances, with the option to extend the license for another three performances if the reception of the work warrants such an extension.

I recommend that five Guards be assigned to the performances of the troupe, one of whom should keep watch behind the scenes, to prevent any disruption of the play by those overcome by the drama. It would be helpful if we could also provide a nurse, in case some in the audience should find the play too appalling to endure without support. I am certain that such a precaution is called for. Madame d'Auville agrees, and has thanked me for my attentiveness. I will inform you when I have reviewed the changes and insertions we have agreed upon, and see that the script is placed in the files of the Department of Public Safety. Any questions you may have in regard to the play and the troupe will receive my prompt attention, and will include the opportunity for you to see the play in rehearsal as I did, with the ameliorations I have authorized included.

Submitted for your attention, with respect,

Emile Louis Orgues
License-Clerk, the Department of Public Safety
Lyon

Vive la France!
Vive la Revolution!

7

"It looks like the rain will start before the play, more's the pity; people won't want to get wet at a play," Roger remarked to da San-Germain as they busied themselves in the stable, attending to the horses and mules with brushes and combs; they were speaking in Russian, their voices just loud enough for each to hear the other. "Have you done anything to provide shel—"

"I have arranged to have an awning stretched over the wall of the inn-yard. The landlord has one that he usually sets up in summer, to protect animals from the sun. The ostlers should be installing it shortly. It will cover the wagons and about half the space where the audience can stand. Some will have umbrellas, I suppose." He paused in brushing one of the mules. "The awning should be fully in place within the hour."

"Does Madame know about this? The prospect of rain must be disappointing for her." Roger did not sound surprised, but his curiosity got the better of him. He was almost through grooming the pair of Noniuses, stalled together now, as they were hitched together on the largest wagon when the troupe was on the road. There was a second pair of the same breed in the adjoining stall; Roger was finished with their care.

"I offered to make the arrangement last night, when the clouds came in; she was . . . amenable to the plan once she knew it would not be a charge on her," said da San-Germain, and resumed brushing back along the flank, then paused to scratch the mule's withers until its ears flopped and it craned its neck with pleasure. "I'll need to bring some camphor balls here. The mules have fleas and other insects on their skin."

"What about your appointment? about Madelaine?" Roger

inquired as if he were speaking about the most ordinary thing in the world.

"After the performance, I am to meet with a Deputy Secretary Charlot of the Department of Public Safety at the foot of the Chevaliers; he will have a sprig of evergreen in his buttonhole, and an embossed leather portfolio in his hands," said da San-Germain in the same commonplace tone. "He has told me he will have information for me."

"For which you will pay him," said Roger.

"Certainly." He took a soft brush and went over the mule's face, then went back to its coat and the stiffer brush. "Anything else would be folly."

"A great deal of money?"

Da San-Germain patted the mule again. "And we still must attend to our creatures before the play begins."

This time Roger would not be turned from the subject. "Are you sure he will give you accurate intelligence, whatever the price? He may be seeking to enrich himself, and will offer a false report; you would have no means of regaining the money without acknowledging the bribe you paid, and that would make it far less likely that you could find out anything useful, and your offer of payment would make it unlikely that you could approach another official to get real information, let alone access."

"You mean like Decios?" Da San-Germain laughed once. "That thought did cross my mind, but our situation here is rather different than what we encountered on Cyprus—wouldn't you agree? For one thing, I doubt Charlot would try to kill me."

"He could denounce you, and that would mean the Guillotine and the True Death." Roger made no apology for his blunt language.

"It would also mean the end of Charlot receiving bribes and prosecution for doing so; I'm willing to take the risk. He strikes me as a man who is eager to make his fortune and has more to gain by helping me than from condemning me."

"I hope so," Roger said, not at all satisfied with the situation.

"You and I can assess what he tells me after I have met with him," said da San-Germain in a tone that told Roger he did not want to speculate on what he would learn from Charlot.

"The Noniuses are getting their winter coats, and will need more clipping if they're not to become too long-coated," Roger pointed out, aware that da San-Germain would say nothing more about Charlot. "And the rest of the horses are putting on weight against the cold. They'll need more regular brushing."

"All the more reason for camphor balls," said da San-Germain. "The stable will be alive with all manner of pests if we don't stop them now."

"You'd think Feo would have said something about the problem," Roger said, and took a pair of heavy scissors to cut a knot of hair out of one of the Hungarian Nonius' tails. "I haven't seen Feo this morning."

"Nor I." Da San-Germain set his brush aside and picked up a broad, heavy-toothed wooden comb. "He may be out looking for Enee; he didn't come back to the inn last night, and Photine is worried about him."

"That youngster is being impudent and foolhardy. He's determined to upset his mother."

"Which she tolerates—it only encourages him,"

"That's obvious: to everyone but Madame." Roger dropped the knot of mane into the grooming-box. "But why is he so . . . feckless? Doesn't he realize he is more likely to damage himself than Madame."

Da San-Germain considered his answer. "It may be something more than the wildness of youth: I believe that, for all his protests to the contrary, he is trying to remain a child as long as possible, so that he need not give up the luxury of having his mother attend to all his wants and responsibilities. She has done so all his life, making him the center of her world while doing it. There is a kind of fear in him, that he will not be able to command his mother's love if he becomes an adult; he wants to be accepted as a grown man without sacrificing the advantages he has enjoyed as a boy."

Roger shook his head, thinking about his own children, dead

now for almost seventeen centuries. "He is a difficult son to Madame, for all he is fifteen and considers himself fully grown."

Da San-Germain was about to add something but went silent as Feo came into the stable and waved a greeting. "They told me you were here."

"Which *they* is that?" da San-Germain asked in Italian.

"The ostlers, the ones working on the awning," said Feo. "Do you know if Madame is busy with the play?"

"She and the rest of the troupe are reviewing the changes the censor demanded," said Roger. "They're in the rear parlor."

Feo stared at da San-Germain. "You're not with them?"

"I have no reason to be. The changes in twenty lines don't alter the music. This is Heurer's problem, and Madame's. I have other tasks to attend to."

"Such as procuring the licenses for performances and caring for the animals?" Feo asked with an impish smile. "Doesn't that get boring?"

"Most of life can become boring, if you allow yourself to be bored," said da San-Germain; he gave Feo a thoughtful stare, aware that the coachman was uneasy. "What is it? You're worried."

"It's Enee," said Feo. "I've tried to find him, but without success. I was out last night until nearly three, and I've been up since dawn. I've tried all the places I've found him before, and looked where others recommended." He glanced at the ceiling. "He's been dicing with the Guards, though Aloys and I have warned him against it. I tried to find him at their haunts, but I was told he wasn't with them." He said nothing for several seconds, then admitted, "That's the extent of my information. I don't want to have to tell Madame that Enee is not to be found, not so near the beginning of their performance."

"Such news will distress her," da San-Germain concurred. "Yet it will not be more welcome if it is delayed."

"Yes. She expects him to appear in the play. If he isn't here—"

"If he isn't here, someone must take his place," said da San-Germain.

Feo caught a note in da San-Germain's voice that alarmed him. "Oh, no," he said. "I'm not going to wrap myself up in cerements and recite poetry."

"Then you'd best tell her quickly, so she can appoint someone else who will, just in case," da San-Germain recommended.

Feo pressed his hands together. "What about Roger, then? He tends to the curtains, but I can do that, and assist with the costumes."

Roger offered a mirthless smile. "I'd rather not."

"Well, I'd rather not, too." Feo rounded on da San-Germain again. "What am I going to do? Should I keep looking, or speak with Madame now?"

"You should probably warn Madame as soon as possible. The troupe will be dressing shortly, and if Enee doesn't return, there will be trouble."

"That wretched boy!" Feo muttered.

"Yes. It would be easier for the whole company if Enee would not be so irresponsible, which suits him top to toe; all he has to do is enjoy himself and he brings on a spasm of anguish in his mother." He paused thoughtfully, then continued with more sadness than condemnation. "And this is just such another example of his disregard: Madame has a play to put on; little as she may like it, she needs to know that Enee hasn't returned. This first performance has to go well, whether Enee is part of it or not. If the play goes poorly, her license may be revoked, which would benefit none of us." He finished combing the mule's mane and went to work on its tail.

"All right! All *right!*" Feo exclaimed. "But it may fall to Roger to take his place." With that warning, he stomped out of the stable and made his way toward the side-door of the inn.

"Do you think I'll have to perform?" Roger asked, his manner showing no sign of consternation.

"You may. If you want to volunteer, that should ease Photine's mind. If she has to ask, it will vex her." Da San-Germain set the comb aside. "But speaking of the performance, it's time I put on my costume and tuned the cimbalom. In weather like this, the strings won't hold their pitch very long." He let himself out of the stall and was about to leave the stable when Roger stopped him with a single question asked in Imperial Latin.

"My master, how long has it been since you've taken nourishment?"

After a slight hesitation, da San-Germain said, "Ten days."

"With Madame?"

"No."

"Are you planning to visit one of the troupe in her sleep?"

"No."

Roger did not quite sigh, but he let out a long, slow breath. "Is that wise?"

"No, it's not, if nourishment were my only concern." He stared into the middle distance. "But at this time, I need to be circumspect. For one thing, you know how hazardous it is to be abroad in this city at night, with the Guards everywhere, and the street-gangs. I would be a fool to draw attention to myself, wouldn't I? The Revolution may have discarded religion, but that doesn't mean that it embraces vampires."

"That sounds more like an excuse than a precaution to me; you have moved about cities at night for almost double the time I have known you," Roger said flatly. "You wouldn't have to roam the night, in any case, for you have opportunities nearer to hand. Olympe or Tereson or Sibelle would welcome such a dream as you could give them."

"No, old friend; it would be too great a gamble. You've heard them rhapsodize about their dreams."

"They sound much like many other women's dreams," Roger told him.

"It would depend upon what they recall of their dreams, and how they describe them."

Roger frowned. "You assume you would be recognized."

"I'm assuming that Photine would not be fooled; if Tereson or Sibelle should describe me as a vision, Photine would not be pleased."

"She takes her pleasure with the men of her company; there is no one who doubts it, and none deny it, not even the two men who pleasure each other," Roger observed. "Where would be the harm in you doing likewise with the women, since you're their patron?"

Da San-Germain answered indirectly. "Gossip is often embroidered in the telling, as we learned in Praha, so consider this—and it was Photine who warned me—that it is impossible to keep a secret in a theatrical company. The players have suspicions about me already; why should I provide fuel for their fires? It would benefit no one, and could compromise my chances of reaching Madelaine."

"And she is the heart of the matter."

"She is, and has been from the start." Da San-Germain nodded to Roger. "I appreciate your concerns for my welfare, but there are times that isn't—"

"—worth an English farthing," Roger finished for him as da San-Germain resumed his walk to the inn; he called after him, "I'll be in to speak to Madame in a few minutes, about Enee's role."

The morning was busy throughout the Jongleur: scullions were hurrying into the kitchen with baskets of fresh produce from the morning market, and chambermaids bustled about from room to room, sweeping and tidying. Two hawkers for local shops had arrived and were crying the wares of their employers, much to the annoyance of the staff of the Jongleur. Four of the ostlers were busy working on setting up the awning, two of them setting masts into brick-lined sockets in the ground, the other two unrolling the heavy canvas and hooking its thickly darned buttonholes over the curved two-prong claws set in the top of the fence. There was an urgency about their work, a tension beyond diligence, that revealed their anticipation. It was the same for the actors, who lingered in the rear parlor, poring over their changes in the script for their first performance, which would begin in an hour and a half. Stopping by their parlor, da San-Germain saw that Photine was pale and seemed distracted, while the rest of the troupe were whispering among themselves; Feo had clearly been and gone again. He was about to go on to his room when she caught sight of him and raised her hand, motioning to him to approach.

He went to her at once. "What is it, Photine?"

"You know what it is. Enee isn't here, and though Feo has gone to search for him again, I can hardly be sure he will find him in time." She could see the mix of dejection and irritation that had taken hold of the rest of the troupe, and so she added for their benefit as much as his, "You will have to ask Roger to take Enee's place. There are few lines, and by now he must know everything about the play."

"Did Feo recommend Roger?" da San-Germain asked, slightly amused.

"He reminded me that he is in better fettle than Aloys," said Photine, then went on in wheedling supplication. "Promise me you'll ask him."

"And if he says no? Would you not prefer that he—"

"I must have someone ready to take my son's part, in case he doesn't return in time to perform," Photine said, this time speaking with real authority. "Your manservant is the one who can do it with the least disruption to the play, so it shall be he who takes on Enee's role. He speaks well enough for the part. If you are unwilling to tell him, then I'll send Pascal to inform him that he should ready himself for the play."

"You needn't do that," said da San-Germain, his expression affectionate and gentle. "He intends to offer to do the part; he knows you're in a demanding situation, and he's willing to help. As soon as he has finished tending to the horses, he will come to you."

"And welcome," said Photine, suddenly breathless. "Of course, all of us must dress. We will not begin later than we've announced, not when it's raining. That would make us seem like amateurs, and later audiences would stay away."

"Then all the more reason to get ready to perform," da San-Germain said with an enthusiasm he did not feel.

"Oh, yes," said Photine, her face brightening. She got to her feet and clapped her hands for attention. "Let us all go prepare. Remember to make sure your costumes don't get wet, and to mention any fraying or tears to Constance so she can repair them for our next performance."

The actors heard her out, their edginess of anticipation suddenly much more apparent. All but Sibelle and Valence rose and began to gather up their corrected sides; they said little, preferring not to engage in berating Enee where his mother could hear.

"Can we ask the innkeeper to light a fire for us in this room, so when we're through, we needn't be shivering?" Sibelle inquired as she pulled her second-best shawl around her shoulders. "The rain is bad enough, but it's windy, too."

"And some mulled wine, nice and hot, would be welcome," Valence added.

"I'll arrange both if you like, Madame," said da San-Germain to Photine before any contention could arise among the players.

Photine faltered, a harried look crossing her features. "Perhaps," she said.

"It would be my honor to take care of the matter for you." He bowed to her, and was rewarded with a burst of applause from the rest of the troupe.

"Go ahead, Ragoczy," she conceded. "Hurry, all of you. We have much to do before the curtains part." Her French had an edge to it.

Sibelle and Valence were the last to depart, leaving da San-Germain with Photine; she shook her head at him, forbidding him to speak. "Tell Roger I'll be in my room."

"One question, Photine," said da San-Germain. "Why not ask Heurer? It is his play, after all."

"Oh, my dear Comte," she said, forgetting all her own strictures about using his title, "that is the very reason I do not ask him: it *is* his play, and he may be moved to improve upon it while we have an audience, which would leave the rest of us in disarray; it would be like him to edit his speeches to what he thinks is an improvement. Theron is a poet, not an actor, and he is in love with his words."

"But the role is a small one," he said. "There's little opportunity for ad libbing."

"All the more reason to have Roger do it—he will not seek to enlarge it." She made a shooing gesture. "There is much to do, and we must all make haste."

Da San-Germain bowed again. "I will be in my costume in half an hour, and I'll take my cimbalom down to the wagon-stage."

"Many thanks," she said in a distracted tone as she hastened toward the door he held open for her. "If Feo finds Enee—"

"He will notify you at once. If you're on stage, he will signal you from the wings. If he isn't back by the end of the performance, then I'll send Roger to inquire at the Guards' main station, and engage them to find him."

"I wish Enee didn't hate you so much." With a final, lingering sigh, she turned down the corridor and made for the stairs; da San-Germain went toward the front of the inn, searching for the inn-keeper. He found the man in the taproom, checking out the levels in the bottles and ordering more to be brought up from the cellar. As he caught sight of da San-Germain, he all but shoved the waiter aside.

"Citizen Ragoczy. What may I do for you?" He rested his large arms on the bar, offering a broad, meaningless smile.

Da San-Germain did not correct the innkeeper's use of the ti-tle *citizen*. "Madame is requesting that a fire be built up in the rear parlor in the next hour or so for her troupe; they will want to gather there after the performance. And if you will heat up a large punch-bowl and fill it with hot wine and spices, that will delight them all."

"You'll bear the cost, will you?" the innkeeper asked, being aware that da San-Germain handled the money for the troupe.

"Of course," said da San-Germain. "If you would like to be paid in advance, I can do so now."

"Later will do. Who knows how much wine they will consume, or how many logs will need to be laid on the fire. Best to be ready to supply their needs lavishly than inadequately." He studied da San-Germain closely. "You're a careful fellow for someone who keeps company with players."

"It is my duty to care for such things for the troupe," said da San-Germain. "And to provide the music for the play."

"One of the actors told me you're an exile from Hungary," the innkeeper persisted.

"I am." He knew that any equivocation would lead to more questions, and he did not want to rouse any more suspicions than he already had, for this question led him to surmise that someone had made inquiry about him, and that his answer would be passed on to another.

"Um. Must be unpleasant."

"Upon occasion, but it is preferable to execution."

"I should think so." The innkeeper made a note in his ledger. "I'll submit my bill to you this evening. Pay me then."

"I will," said da San-Germain, and left the taproom, his stride seeming unhurried for all he covered the distance to his room with remarkable speed. Once in his room, he pulled off his coat and set about donning his costume, preoccupied with anticipation of what he would learn from Charlot when the performance was over. Perhaps, he thought, it was Charlot who had wanted to know more about him.

Roger arrived some twenty minutes later, a shroud over his arm, a skull-mask dangling from his hand. "I will help you with the lower part of your face, and you can assist me with dressing," he said.

Da San-Germain, who had finished putting on the last of his motley except for the mask, looked up from tuning his cimbalom. "Thank you, old friend. You're doing Madame a great service."

"Yes, I am," said Roger with no sign of emotion. "If Enee should turn up in the next half-hour, I'll forget every unkind thing I have said about him."

"He would be nettled to learn that," said da San-Germain.

"I expect so; I'll keep it to myself, then. I wouldn't want to encourage him to greater insolence." Roger coughed experimentally. "What's to be done with that boy? We can't go through all this distraint at every performance."

"In the next few days, we'll make other arrangements for En-ee's role, so this will not occur again." His shroud-like cloak was unlike the rest: it had slits for his arms so that he could play his cimbalom. "Put your coat aside and I'll wrap you."

"Very good," said Roger, getting out of his coat quickly, and folding it carefully before standing for da San-Germain. "It's something like a toga, isn't it?"

"Not so long or so complicated, or so large, but similar," said da San-Germain, opening the triangular piece of fabric. "The narrow point goes under your right arm, with the rest of the fabric to the rear," he said as he set about the winding process. "When I've finished, you may set the two pins in place, or I'll do it for you."

"Yours doesn't require all this draping; it drops over your head," said Roger, holding his right arm stiffly in place to keep the fabric from sliding.

"It does," da San-Germain agreed. "But I'm usually in the shadows, so I needn't be so careful in the costume as those of you who appear on stage. What I have on looks enough like the cerements the Corpses have on. So long as I wear the half-mask and let my costume hang like the other winding-sheets, Photine will be pleased."

"So Constance explained to me," said Roger. "She said that I'll have to be careful of the hem, so that it doesn't drag and trip me."

"Bow your left elbow. You'll need some room to move inside this swath," said da San-Germain as he continued to work. "This will pass under your right arm again, so you'll have only one length of cloth holding your arm, but two keeping the shroud in place. That way it won't slip when you move, so long as you don't raise your arm above the elbow. It's awkward, but you've seen how to do it."

Roger nodded once. "I've assisted Tereson to put on her shroud so many times, you'd think I'd know what's required. But all I do is hold the cloth in place for her, while she turns and wriggles. I should have paid more attention."

"You have no reason to chastise yourself, old friend," said da

San-Germain. "If you'll bend forward a little, so I can get this to fold properly on your shoulder?"

Roger complied. "I have three lines. I know them well, I've heard them countless times already, but I keep fearing that I'll forget them when I am on stage."

"Not an uncommon worry among players, I gather." He moved behind Roger again, and worked the broad end of the triangular cotton into folds on his shoulder, then dropped the rest of the shroud over his chest. "We're almost done. You can straighten up for the last of the wrapping."

"I feel bound up."

"Hardly surprising, since you are," said da San-Germain as he reached for the small pot of greasy white face-paint, which he handed to Roger. "My jaw, as usual; you will want to use it on your own face when you've finished with me."

Roger took the pot and pried up its lid. "How inconvenient is it for you, not to have a reflection?" he asked as he scooped out the paint with his fingers.

"At moments like this, it's damned inconvenient," said da San-Germain, sitting down on a three-legged stool near the bed. "When I first came to this life, I paid almost no attention to matters of reflection, and those centuries in the oubliette gave me no reason to look for a reflection. When I first arrived in Egypt, it bothered me, and I was often worried that one of the priests of Imhotep would notice my lack, and would denounce me as something unnatural— which I am."

"If you would be quiet while I even the paint," said Roger; da San-Germain went silent, holding himself in place while Roger smoothed the paint over his jaw and blended it down onto his neck with his fingers. When Roger was satisfied with the result, he said, "You're ready."

Da San-Germain got up and stepped aside, allowing Roger to take the stool. "Try not to scratch your face once I've done—the paint can get itchy, but if you touch it . . ."

Roger said, "I'll remember. I'll scratch when it's over."

The audience gathered under the awning was not very large; a few of the actors tried to conceal their disappointment, though Photine strove to encourage them all to do their best. "This is just the beginning. If we do well in spite of the rain and all the rest, we will command a larger audience next time, and the time after that."

"You hope," said Constance.

Photine turned to her, her eyes sharp and her voice cutting. "I know that if we do not do well today, we cannot hope to do better at another time, for no one will come to watch us."

From his position to the side of the stage, da San-Germain listened attentively. He could sense the players' states of mind, and he was alert to the problems confronting them with the rain, but he knew that they would rise to the occasion and engage the audience as best they could. He tapped the cimbalom strings softly, frowning at the slippage in pitch; he worked to correct it and waited for the signal to begin.

Halfway through the play, the audience had grown from twenty to more than thirty-five, which was encouraging. In spite of the weather, there were people watching the Commedia della Morte, captivated by the play's shocks and satire, their attention on the players, not on the persistent drizzle. When the play ended, there was genuine applause; even the Guards assigned to watch the crowd joined in, and as the hats were passed, more than silver dropped into them.

Behind the curtains, Sibelle was giddy; she bounced as she pulled off her mask and loosened her shroud. "Did you see them at the end? They were all but holding their breaths."

Crepin agreed, grinning. "They will come back, some of them, and they will bring their friends. Some of them will tell their comrades, and they may come. We'll do well here."

"Especially if the rain stops," said Constance.

Da San-Germain put his cimbalom in its leather case and left the stage for the inn, going directly to his room and getting out of his costume as quickly as he could. He took a rag and wiped off his face, hoping he had got all the paint; then he put on his hammer-tail coat, his black wool cloak, and his bicorn hat; as a last precaution, he tucked a charged pistol into his pocket and made sure his purse was securely fastened inside his waistcoat. As he left the room, he heard the troupe in the corridor bound for the rear parlor, the built-up fire and a punch-bowl filled with hot, spiced wine. For an instant he was sorry that he would not share in their celebration, but then he thought of Madelaine, and that lent purpose to his mission, and he left the inn, going through the last of the mizzle to the statue of the two knights, where a man in his late thirties was standing, a leather portfolio under his arm, and a sprig of pine in his buttonhole.

"Ragoczy?" the man ventured as da San-Germain approached. "Is this the way to address you?"

"Charlot?" he countered while he took stock of the man: there was little remarkable about him except his exceptional ordinariness. He was of medium height and medium build, but with a softness about him, like over-ripe fruit. His features were regular but without distinction. His thinning hair was a medium-brown, as were his eyes. Yet there was about him a subtle sense of cruelty, or debauchery, something that was dark and wriggling in his soul, and that awakened da San-Germain's misgiving. "Yes, among the Hungarians the family name precedes the personal name. You are the Deputy Secretary for Public Safety?"

"I have that honor," said Charlot with what was supposed to be a self-effacing smile.

"Thank you for meeting with me," said da San-Germain.

"It's not the sort of thing I usually do, but as you're a blood relative of the lady in question, I made an exception for you." He glanced around the nearly empty square. "I see your Guards are gone now that the play is finished."

"That they are." Da San-Germain wondered how much the price would be raised before Charlot would vouchsafe him the information he had promised. "I am deeply appreciative of your understanding; we have been most uneasy for her welfare. I am charged with discovering where she is being held and in what circumstances."

Charlot pretended to muse. "You intend to visit her?"

"Yes; I thought I made that clear."

"The people you represent are noble, are they not?" Charlot asked.

"For the most part," said da San-Germain, and volunteered no more.

"I understand you have a Hungarian title," Charlot said, cagily scrutinizing him.

"If an exile has a title, that's true," said da San-Germain. "I lost my estates and title a very long time ago." It was nearly four thousand years since his father's forces had been vanquished and he himself was taken prisoner, but he mentioned none of this.

"How unfortunate," said Charlot with spurious sympathy. "To be well-born but reduced to traveling with a company of players."

"You said you had information about Madelaine de Montalia?" da San-Germain reminded him.

"I had to pay six louis d'or to get specifics," Charlot said, and let this hang between them.

Then da San-Germain took eight golden coins from his purse. "This should cover the sum, and your trouble."

Charlot snatched them away. "Most kind of you, Ragoczy." He held up the portfolio. "You'll find there is a letter of introduction to the warden of the prison where she is being held. You must use it in the next five days, for on the sixth day, she goes to trial unless there is another postponement, and it will be beyond the warden's power to help you." He took a long moment to gather his thoughts. "If you should be asked, you did not get this from me."

"Of course," said da San-Germain, taking the portfolio and opening it. Sheltering the paper from the last of the rain with his hunched shoulders, he assured himself it said what Charlot had claimed, then folded it and tucked it into his inner breast-pocket before handing the portfolio back to Charlot.

"Are you satisfied that this gives value for money?"

"If she is truly being held at the old monastery, then yes, I am," said da San-Germain, taking a step back from the Deputy Secretary for Public Safety. "I will send word to our . . . relatives that I will see her shortly."

"You don't want to say who they are?" Charlot could not keep himself from asking.

"No," da San-Germain replied with as gracious a manner as he could muster.

"I imagine an exile would have to be cautious if he wants to survive," Charlot said with a smile that was more snide than courteous. He half-turned, then added, "If I can serve you in any other way, you may rely on my discretion."

Da San-Germain held up his hand as if suddenly recollecting a matter; recalling what Oddysio Lisson had advised him, he said, "Do you happen to know where I might find Gabrielle Donat?"

"Why do you want to know?" Charlot asked in a lazy way that revealed that he was listening with keen attention.

"A colleague of mine has done business with him in the past and desired me to deliver a message to him," da San-Germain answered.

"In what regard?"

"My colleague wishes to arrange with Donat for the shipping of certain goods."

"What sort of goods?" Charlot's eyes narrowed.

"Upholstery fabric and silverware," said da San-Germain. "Oh, and silver candlesticks."

Charlot studied him before he replied. "I regret to have to tell you that you will have to inform your colleague that Gabrielle Donat is no longer in Lyon. He will have to make other arrangements to get his upholstery fabric, silverware, and candlesticks." He was about to walk away, but added as an afterthought, "Rumor has it that Donat has gone to England, or perhaps to Canada."

"Ah. My colleague will be disappointed. Thank you," said da San-Germain, trying to keep the irony from his voice.

Charlot inclined his head, then trod off over the slippery paving-stones, taking care not to look back.

* * *

Text of a note from the warden of Saint-Gautier Prison for the Anti-Revolutionary Accused to Ragoczy Ferenz at the Jongleur, Place des Chevaliers, Lyon, carried by Revolutionary Tribunal courier and delivered the day after it was written.

To the Hungarian foreigner, Ragoczy Ferenz, currently resident at the Jongleur, Place des Chevaliers, the greetings of Egide Loup, Warden of the Saint-Gautier-en-Saone Prison for the Anti-Revolutionary Accused, on the 17th day of October, 1792,

 Citizen Ragoczy,

For so I understand from the Deputy Secretary of Public Safety that it is the custom among the Hungarians, you are to be addressed thus. I received your request yesterday morning along with the bona fides copy of the letter identifying the basis for your request to visit the prisoner Madelaine de Montalia. She is among those in my charge, and for a reasonable consideration, I will gladly undertake to grant you an hour with her tomorrow between six and seven in the morning. This will be the only time I can guarantee that you will be able to see her, for officers of the Revolutionary Tribunal and the Department of Public Safety will arrive shortly after seven to continue the interrogation of the prisoners, and Madelaine de Montalia will be among those who is to answer questions.

 Come to the southern gate at ten minutes to the hour and bring the letter of introduction, the original, with you, and such sums as you deem appropriate for the advantage you are being accorded.

 Vive la France!

Egide Loup
Warden of Anti-Revolutionary Prisoners
Saint-Gautier-en-Saone

8

Saint-Gautier-en-Saone was an ancient stone pile more than eight hundred years old, with thick, crumbling walls riddled with rotten mortar, encrustations of moss, and uneven surfaces, the main building having dilapidated chimneys, the refectory settled at a precarious angle, and the chapel missing half its roof; it had been neglected for more than two centuries. The waning moon, tumbling through thickening clouds in the western sky, limned the old monastery with an eerie, nacreous shine when it broke out of them. Approaching the southern gate in the darkness of night's end, da San-Germain felt a rush of consternation mixed with anger. That Madelaine should be kept in such a place! It did not matter to him that he had spent centuries in places worse than this: he loathed the thought of Madelaine having to endure such an ordeal. He could feel his horse tense under him, aware of his distress; he made himself contain his indignation as he dismounted and led the gray up to the warder-gatehouse next to the tall gate of iron-bound timbers. After a brief examination of the place, he found the bell-rope and pulled it, hearing a distant clang as he did.

It was almost ten minutes later when the warder-gate opened and a man in a rumpled Revolutionary Guard uniform peered into the night, an old-fashioned lanthorn throwing a narrow beam of yellow light. "Ragoczy?"

"I am he," said da San-Germain, deliberately thickening his usually faint accent.

"Come in, then. Warden Loup is waiting for you." He pushed open the gate with the look of one ill-used by fate, and stared at da San-Germain. "You will have to leave within the hour."

"I know," was the response.

"The warden has given orders that you are to be watched at all times."

"Understandably," said da San-Germain, unperturbed.

"If you have weapons with you, you must surrender them to me," the Guard said.

"I have a pistol in my boot; any night-traveler does. There are robbers about," said da San-Germain, bending down to remove the elegant weapon; he handed it to the Guard. "Have a care: it is charged."

"No robbers venture here." The Guard took the weapon gingerly and stepped back into the warder-gatehouse. "I have it here, and will return it if Warden Loup allows it, when you leave." He moved back so that da San-Germain could enter. "I'll watch your horse for you, in case there is trouble."

"Thank you," said da San-Germain; he realized that this meant he would not be allowed to bring his horse inside the monastery walls—probably a precaution against attempted escapes. He secured the reins to the largest cleat on the outside of the main gate, then returned to the warder-gate and went through.

"You'd better go to the warden. He is expecting you." This reiteration came with a lugubrious sigh.

"Where will I find him?" da San-Germain asked.

"Go through the cloister all the way to the main door on the ambulatory—the one with the brass hinges. It leads to his quarters." He sat down on a small round stool as if his efforts had exhausted him.

"Through the cloister to the door with brass hinges," da San-Germain repeated, and saw the Guard nod. "Very good."

The cloister was empty but for a pair of Guards standing in front of a flight of stairs that at one time had led up to the monks' cells; now the prisoners were kept there. Neither Guard did more than glance at the stranger, preferring instead to smoke their long-stemmed pipes while drawing their coats closely around them. The brass-hinged door was at right angles to the stairway. Lengthening his stride, da San-Germain headed toward it. He knocked twice on the door and waited to be summoned inside.

"Good morning, Citizen Ragoczy," said the man behind the imposing desk, his face illuminated to an uneven and sinister gold in the light from six brass lamps, two of which had untrimmed wicks and therefore sputtered and spat, darkening their glass chimneys with oily smoke. "You have come in good time."

"Good morning, Warden Loup," he responded with a slight bow. "I thank you for giving me this opportunity to visit my relative."

"You've expressed your thanks generously already," Loup said, and, as an afterthought, rose and offered his hand. Although clean-shaven, he was remarkably hirsute, with thick dark hair sprouting on the backs of his fingers and palms, and poking out from his ears; his eyebrows were thick as caterpillars, and a shadow of stubble on his jaw. He was dressed to keep out the chill in a heavy woolen knee-length coat of dark-blue over a long waistcoat of double-thick fustian and a shirt of super-fine wool; the fire in the hearth was smoky but not very warm, what little heat it provided extending no more than an arm's-length into the room.

Taking Loup's hand in his own, da San-Germain offered him two louis d'or. "I believe you have some questions to ask me," he said, wanting to make the most of his limited time.

"I do," said Loup, indicating an old-fashioned X-shaped chair, which da San-Germain refused. "You're in a hurry to see your relative, aren't you. Then I'll be brief."

"Thank you," said da San-Germain, resisting the urge to pace.

"You are most welcome," Warden Loup deftly slipped the gold coins into his waistcoat pocket as he sat down once more. "You are here to see Madelaine de Montalia, I recall."

"Yes. She and I are related by blood, as you have remarked; it was in the material I provided you." He kept his tone mannerly, but his purpose was clear: he would get what he had paid for.

"Um. Your request was most instructive." He considered da San-Germain with curiosity. "Yet, according to your missive, you are Hungarian and she is French." Loup's statement rose at the end, more like a question.

Da San-Germain shrugged. "Among the old nobility, such alliances have been common enough."

"That is true," said Loup, folding his hands atop a stack of papers; he looked up. "Do you have a title?"

There it was again, the issue of title. "Technically, you might see it that way," he answered smoothly, "in that I am the son of a . . . a prince"—this was the closest he could come to approximating the title his long-dead father had claimed, more than three thousand eight hundred years ago, when he fell in battle, and what seemed princely then now appeared more to be a regional warlord—"and I, for want of a clearer word, might be called a comte, were I not an exile."

"Oh, yes, an exile: you mentioned that." He pursed his lips as if caught up in cogitation. "Yet from the request you sent me, I must surmise that your other noble relatives still have their titles and holdings?"

"Some do, others are not so fortunate." This stretched the truth a little, but that did not trouble him.

"And you travel with a troupe of players."

"An exile must do something to . . . live."

"But a troupe of actors? Isn't that a come-down from what you had before?"

"It is preferable to being an impoverished pensioner to some other noble. I have my liberty with the players." The nod that Loup gave told da San-Germain that he had guessed correctly in providing his explanation.

Loup sat back and scrutinized da San-Germain, then said, "You are what?—forty-five?"

"Somewhat older," he said, reckoning that time in millennia.

"A wife? Children?"

Thinking back to Xenya and the Court of Ivan Grosny, he said, "I am a widower. We had no children."

"That's unfortunate. Still, given how things have turned out, it might be for the better." He rang a bell that stood on the corner of his desk. "Have you brought anything for her?—your relative?"

"I have a short cloak, if that is permissible?" He patted the side of his cloak.

"It is cold, and the cells are damp. We've already lost three prisoners to the chill, and another is failing." He weighed the matter as the door opened again. "I suppose it is to be expected. You may give it to her." He sighed and gestured acquiescence. "Montaube will guide you to her cell and escort you from it."

"He will listen?"

"Yes. He knows some Italian and a little German, so don't think to confuse him; I should probably tell you that there is a peep-hole in the door, as well, and he may use it if he thinks it necessary," Loup warned as an angular man of perhaps twenty-five in a broad-skirted, threadbare coat answered the summons of the bell. "I doubt I will see you before you leave, Ragoczy, so I will wish you bon chance now."

"Most appreciated," said da San-Germain before he turned to Montaube. "Citizen?"

"Come this way," said Montaube, turning the color of mulberries as he pointed to the door. Once out of the room, they passed between the two Guards with no more acknowledgment than a half-hearted salute. The steps up to what had been the monks' cells were lit by old lanthorns, making them appear more steep and narrow than they actually were, and had a trip-stair two steps from the stop. Montaube pointed it out silently. "The fourth on the left. I'll open the door for you."

"Thank you," said da San-Germain, his composure masking turmoil and anticipation. He nodded to Montaube as he watched the young man take out a ring of heavy keys from his coat-tail pocket. It was tempting to urge him to hasten, but that would arouse suspicions, so he stood silently while the wards in the lock grated.

Montaube took hold of the lock, worked the hasp, pushed the door open a short way. "I'll be here. You have forty minutes."

Da San-Germain handed him a golden Bohemian Emperor as

he went past him into the cell, then stood just inside the door, his whole attention on the figure sitting on the side of the narrow bed, a worn shawl around her shoulders, in a scuffed dress of damask silk. The bed, covered by a single blanket, showed no sign of being slept-in, but there was a slight indentation in the pillow at the far end. Pausing for a moment to permit Montaube to close the door, da San-Germain remained transfixed by Madelaine's presence: in this small, dank stone chamber with a single clerestory window, she was exotic as a jeweled bracelet in a coal-scuttle.

Lit by a solitary candle, it was hard to read her features as she turned toward da San-Germain, rising slowly to her feet. "Saint-Germain. You have come."

The sound of her voice stirred him to action; he took three uneven steps toward her and drew her into his arms, taking in the shape and texture and character of her, holding her more tightly than he realized, as if to leave the impression of her imprinted upon him. "Madelaine. My heart."

She returned his embrace, her hands shaking, and not from cold. "Oh, why can't I cry? It would feel so good to cry," she murmured to his shoulder.

He let her go enough to be able to look into her face. "You know the answer."

"We lose our tears when we lose our lives," she said as if reciting an unwelcome lesson. With a faint sigh, she moved a step back from him, unable to hide the sadness this admission brought. "How long have you been here in Lyon?"

"A few days; I wanted to come as soon as we arrived, but I had to get permission to come here, and that took time." He assumed she knew this, but that Montaube would expect to hear such an explanation.

"And money, no doubt." She lowered her voice. "Along with liberty, equality, and brotherhood, they ought to have added profit to their Revolutionary battle-cry."

"There are things more valuable than money," he said with a warning glance toward the door.

"I know they listen; they listen to everything." She sighed. "And they look. They don't see much, but they still look."

Closing the distance between them, he took her hand in his. "I bring you the greeting and concerns of our blood, and their hope that you might soon be free."

"How good of you, and of them," she said for Montaube's benefit.

"They encourage you to keep up your hope. They will want to hear that you haven't lost heart in gaining your freedom."

She was aware of what was expected of her. "Thank them for me, and tell them I do hope to be exonerated of the charges laid against me."

He reached under his cloak and pulled out a flat package, which he handed to her. "This is from your uncle at Lecco. He believes it will help keep you warm." He hoped this sounded much the same as other visitors to these cells, for its hidden message would be dangerous if discovered.

She felt the package, giving him a dejected smile. "Not a book, I take it? I've been longing for something to read."

"I doubt it would be allowed," he said, sympathy softening his words.

"You're probably right." She examined the package. "At least this may help keep out the damp." She, like the rest of his blood, was not very sensitive to changes in temperature, but humidity was another matter.

"That, I believe, was his intent."

"You must tell him how grateful I am," she said, her violet eyes fixed on his. She pulled the string and paper off the soft-violet garment, and smiled. "Very nice."

"When I return to Lecco, I will let him know you welcomed it; he will be most pleased," he said, relieved that she understood what he had told her—that she would be taken to Lecco when they left France.

She removed the shawl and donned the cloak he had given her. "It's much warmer than the shawl."

Aware that he must not forget that Montaube was listening, he went on to another topic. "Everyone has asked: have you got an advocate to plead your case? Your cousin in Cadiz has offered to cover the expenses if you require one."

She almost smiled at this oblique reference to Roger, who had been born in Cadiz when it was still a Roman port called Gades. "No. We're told there is one appointed for all of us, but that may change if the rumors we hear are true." She gave a little shake of her head.

Da San-Germain had heard many of the same rumors—that there would soon be a law that would make accusation commensurate with guilt. "But surely that won't happen before spring, and you are supposed to appear in—what?—five, six days is it now?"

"I've lost count, there have been so many postponements," she said. "Who knows? it may be spring by the time we're taken to the Revolutionary Court, when defense will be moot."

"Until the law is passed, if it is passed, you will have to have an advocate," he said.

"If you can discover who it is, I would be grateful."

"I can certainly make the effort." He bent and kissed her hand, its chill matching his own hand's. "Or would you prefer I seek out other counsel for you?"

"No. That would distinguish me too much, and that could lead to certain assumptions that might go against my interests. But tell my Cadiz cousin that I thank him for his generosity." She stared into his dark eyes. "I have missed you, Saint-Germain. I should have taken your advice, and remained in Italy, but . . ."

He finished her trailing thought for her. "But the advice of an exile is not always suitable."

"Oh, no," she protested, then saw him gesture to her; she collected her thoughts. "Not in the way you mean. I was certain that the Revolution would bring the justice it promised, and that those of us who have been responsible to our people would be able to lose only our titles, not our heads." She went back to his side. "But you've been through this kind of upheaval before, and your warnings were prudent."

"This is what the soldier should hear; it is what Warden Loup is expecting," he said in Turkish, a language she had recently learned in anticipation of a journey there. "You're doing well. I am sorry we cannot talk without anyone listening." He allowed himself a moment to touch her coffee-colored hair, so lightly that he might have been caressing the wings of butterflies.

"You know I can't speak Hungarian," she protested, a ghost of a smile on her lips at her deliberate misidentification.

"I apologize," he said in French. "It is the circumstances here—they remind me of what I endured, and I lapse." The oubliette had been long ago, when he had been regarded as a demon; there had been other prisons, in China, in Roma, in the New World, in Poland . . . He held her hand more tightly.

"Small wonder," she said, then added quietly, "Do you remember the old chapel, the one you showed me when I had been hunting?"

"Yes," he said, his mind going back to the dreadful pursuit of Saint Sebastien and his Circle that had brought her to an ancient chapel where he sheltered with her for the night, and the passion that brought her closer to becoming like him. "It was . . . some years ago, was it not?"

"A shame we can't return there," she said, her voice echoing the force of his memories, moving next to him. "Those elegant, vile men, trying to waylay me; were it not for you, I tremble to think what might have happened to me at their hands."

"Alas," was as much as he trusted himself to say.

She held up her hand, motioning him to silence. "Those days are gone."

"It is one of my dearest recollections of you," he told her gently.

"And mine of you," she said, leaning against his arm, then stepping back. "How long do you think you will be here?"

Da San-Germain felt her yearning as if it were the heat from a bonfire. "It depends upon the Commedia della Morte. I'm still with the troupe, you see. We were in Avignon not so many days ago, and decided to come north before winter set in." It was diffi-cult to keep talking of such commonplace things when he wanted to embrace her, but since that would be fruitless as well as dangerous, he made himself continue. "If the play is received well we could be here for two weeks or more; we have five more performances licensed, and may be granted more if there is a demand for them."

"Then you will remain with the players?" She stood beside him, both of them facing away from the door.

"Yes." He paused. "I wish you could see them."

"I would like to, but—"

"Of course: but."

She took a deep breath. "Well, I shall content myself with imagining you on the stage."

"I am not on the stage: I provide the music." He paused. "But I wear a costume, and a mask."

"Very gallant," she said, laying her hand on his.

He bowed slightly. "I am content to remain in the shadows." His tone was playful but his expression was not.

"Do any others share those shadows with you?"

He wanted to enfold her in his arms again, to feel her presence and her emotion with all of his being, but he restrained his impulse. "No; I hope that will change before long. It would enhance the play to have more music than what I can provide on the cimbalom; a flute-player, perhaps." He saw her start, and very nearly smile: she had learned to play the flute when she was alive, and had not entirely lost the touch of the instrument.

"I wish you good luck in finding such a person," she said, squeezing his fingers in acknowledgment of his message. Seeking some less precarious subject, she asked, "How was Theron when you left him?"

"Closeted with Madame d'Auville when I last saw him," said da San-Germain. "That was last evening, immediately after supper."

"Madame d'Auville?"

"The leader of the troupe," he said, wondering if this were unwelcome news. "She is an actress of broad experience. I saw her do *Phaedre,* not so many months ago."

Madelaine was only half-listening. "You mean he's here?"

"Oh, yes. He wrote the play the troupe is performing."

"I thought he'd have more sense than I did, and remain in Italy," she said, and caught her lower lip in her teeth.

"He insisted on coming with us, and Madame d'Auville could not refuse him."

"And how is he?"

Da San-Germain thought about his answer. "For the most part, he is well. He misses you."

"I wish I could see him," she said, her face showing the esurience that had become keen during her imprisonment. "Will you tell him I asked about him?"

"If that is to your liking; I expect he'll have many questions when I return to the Jongleur, the inn where we are presently staying."

She faltered, trying to summon up what she wanted Theron to know and Montaube to hear. Finally she said, "Tell him I wish I could see his play, and thank him for the service he has done me."

"I will," he promised just as there was a rap on the door.

"Five more minutes," said Montaube.

"Five minutes it will be," da San-Germain said, raising his voice enough to be heard.

"So we'll have to say good-bye. So soon." She stared at him, her eyes echoing the loneliness in his.

"Lamentably," he agreed, again reaching for her hands.

This time she gave them to him freely. "Do you think you'll be allowed to come back?"

"That's in the hands of others," he told her, and bent to kiss her palms.

"But you'll make—"

"—every effort: yes, of course."

She nodded, trying to summon up something to say. At last, she asked, "Will you write to our relatives about this meeting?"

"That is my intention," he said, drawing her to him by putting her hands on his shoulders. "As soon as I am permitted to return, I will." He touched his lips to her brow. "Remember that you are dear to . . . to all of us."

"Most kind," she murmured, holding him as if to draw strength from him, all the while knowing that what both of them sought and needed, neither could provide. She cleared her throat. "Your visit has been . . . has been"—she wanted to say *wonderful* but settled for the much safer "most welcome. I'm sorry it could not be longer." Then, gathering her courage, she pushed back from him. "Go now, so they will let you come back."

"My heart," he said with a slight, elegant bow.

"Tell Theron that I'm grateful for what he has done."

"I will," he said as he heard the door behind him pulled open; he swung around to face Montaube. "The time is up. I know."

"If you will come with me?" Montaube said automatically. He locked the door with care, then pointed to the corridor.

"I thank you for tending to my visit," said da San-Germain, and handed the young man two silver coins.

Without a single change in expression, Montaube said, "I hope you will come again," and clinked the coins to make his point as he made his way out of the dark prison into the murky dawn.

Text of a letter from Geoffrey George Eustace Wattle on tour in France to his uncle, Eustace Charles St. Ives Bradleigh, Fellow at King's College, Cambridge, in England, carried by university postal courier and delivered nineteen days after it was written.

> *To my esteemed Uncle E. C. St.I. Bradleigh, the affectionate greetings of his nephew G. G. E. Wattle, on the road to Lyon on this, the 18th day of October, 1792.*
>
> *My dear Uncle,*
> *I trust this finds you in your customary good health after your holiday in Northumberland, and that you will pass on to your sister (my devoted Mater) such news of me as will be welcome to her and my brothers.*

I further trust you had my letter from Amsterdam, where most of the Dutch still greet us as comrades, although some are less cordial than they have been of late, fearing we may withdraw our support of them if this war with the French becomes more vigorous. Whatever alliances Pitt decides to honor, I fear the Dutch will not emerge unscathed from the war. I will give you a full report upon my return, which I may advance to February rather than April, if the weather will allow me to travel safely.

So without further rodomontade:

On your suggestion, I avoided Paris, but I have discovered that even outside of the Capital, the French are unusually volatile, and there is talk of the Parisian Jacobins demanding the submission of the Girondists, who are particularly strong in Lyon, whither I am presently bound. I have found the French in turmoil, which was to be expected, but which has led to some instances that trouble me. I have had to pay more "fees," by which I mean bribes, than either you or I anticipated, and that may leave me with a lean purse by the end of the year.

Of course, most French are wary of all English, and that is still the case, and growing steadily more entrenched, though not without cause. I have several times been approached by persons claiming to represent various French persons who wish to leave the country as discreetly as possible, and are willing to pay some considerable sums to gain the means of travel that does not involve going through any of the official points of egress. I have let it be known that I cannot do anything myself, but have recommended contacting the captains of English merchant ships, who are not as particular as many about their passengers, and are often inclined to overlook a lack of official permits for a purse full of gold. That may be the case with French merchants as well, but since there are rewards offered to those denouncing those seeking to escape, I have given it as my opinion that foreign merchants are safer than French ones. I happened upon a captain from the other side of the Atlantic; I do not know for certain if he were American, or of some other nation, but he told me that he had given up carrying slaves and was earning his living by carrying the French who could meet his price to the New World. He said that his hold had been converted from cargo holds to cabins, and that although these passengers demanded better food, there were fewer of them, and they were better-behaved than the slaves he bought in African markets.

From what I have been hearing, it is not unlikely that if Lyon does not capitulate and join with the National Convention on its policies, they may be subject to military action. Fine way to express their Revolutionary unity! You would think that with the war in Holland, they would not seek to turn their soldiers on their own cities. When first I heard of this, I thought it was impossible, but I am no longer convinced of that, which has resulted in many qualms. I am sorry now that only Humphries elected to accompany me (which he has informed me he now regrets doing), for as two foreigners alone in a place where the mob is ever more in charge, and the Government itching to bring it to heel, we are exposed to greater risks than either Humphries or I anticipated, and I believe even you did not perceive for the dangers they have proven to be. Poor Humphries has declared that we must leave soon, despite all the assurances he gave Mr. Priestley and the members of the Lunar Society. Whatever flattery he found in their request that he report events here to them has withered away, and small wonder.

*The executions which have been generally decried
are still being carried out, and in some places in increasing numbers. I understand that situations in various of the larger towns have reached such a state that
ordinary folk are no longer safe from accusations, and
that, should Robespierre have his way, accusation and
condemnation will become the law of the land, if it is
not already accepted by the National Convention. To
add to the grotesquerie, there have been grand festivi-
ties in Paris, staged to celebrate the death and lawless-
ness that they say has taken over that city, and is
becoming the order of the day in the towns. In Paris, it
is the dramatist Jean-Marie Collot d'Herbois who has
charge of the merry-making, and it seems that there
will be more of that kind of thing, macabre as it appears. Many towns have already announced their
intentions to emulate Paris and d'Herbois, which can
only mean more trouble for the people, and for foreigners as well. Of all the troublesome signs coming out of
this Revolution, these (dare I call them?) ghoulish rev-
els are the most disturbing to me. The praise of carnage
for its own sake does not augur well for the outcome of
this Revolution: it is not like the American Revolution,
when there was no opportunity for the rebels to strike
down the monarchy or redress the wrongs of centuries.
This is quite another upheaval, and it promotes destruction and mayhem, not independence and identity.*

*If any of this may be useful to any of your associ-
ates in the Government, and those in the Lunar Society,
you may make use of it in any way you see fit.*

*Until I see England and you again, I commend my-
self to you, and to our family.*

*Your most Ob't nephew,
G. G. E. Wattle*

PART III

Madelaine Roxanne Bertrande de Montalia

Text of a letter from Jules Topinard, physician of Lyon, to the Department of Public Safety in Lyon, carried by the physician's servant and delivered the day it was written.

To the members of the Department of Public Safety, the greetings from Jules Topinard, physician, and resident of the city, on this, the 18th day of October, 1792,

Citizens and officers of the Department,

I have just come from my mandated duty at the prison of Saint-Gautier-en-Saone, where I accompanied your officers for the purpose of attending to the health of the prisoners. As I told your colleagues, I would most stringently recommend that the prisoners be removed from that place and housed in more salubrious facilities, for the current site of their detention is contributing significantly to the general decline in the prisoners' health. Of those I have examined, only half can be said to be in reasonable health; not that they are hale and hearty, but they are at least not showing signs of illness or starvation.

Of those that have apparent illness, six of the prisoners have marked fever, brought about by the cold and damp of their housing, and among them, four show indications of putrid lungs. Among the rest, there are a few alarming symptoms: the young prisoner de Montalia has what I must call the reverse of a fever, her body being dangerously cold and her pulse barely perceptible, signs of advanced enervation, no doubt due to the conditions under which she is presently being incarcerated.

The monks abandoned the place for a reason, which had a direct bearing on its location and the resultant damp; it would be prudent if you were to consider transferring the remaining detainees while you still have some to bring to trial. I fear that even the most obdurate member of the Revolutionary Court would be disinclined to condemn a man to the Guillotine when it was apparent that he was already condemned to perish from disease, and as the stated goal of the Revolutionary Court is to redress wrongs, I do not see how this approach to meting out justice can produce public approbation.

If you are willing to consider my thoughts on this matter, I recommend moving the prisoners to the old Customs House near the south gate: it is not much used, and the merchants presently occupying the ground floor can be compensated for having to move. The Guards could be installed on that floor, the shops converted to barracks and dining hall. The offices above, while small, are drier and the building warmer than Saint-Gautier, and they may readily be fitted with iron doors, or simple heavy braces put on the doors presently in place, making cells that are every bit as guardable as the cells of Saint-Gautier. There is another advantage to such a move: it will be possible to maintain watch on them more easily inside the city walls than outside, for escape within the town is less likely than it is from a remote building like Saint-Gautier, a league beyond the city walls.

Whatever your decision, I have to say that in my opinion, another two, and possibly three, of the prisoners will be dead in five days if they are not moved, and quickly. They will require nursing care at once in any case. *This is not a matter to be debated at length; this problem must be addressed hastily, or there will not be much left to address.*

This is what comes of taking in more prisoners than we can put up, and may turn out to be a more certain death for the prisoners than the blade can provide. Surely the ideals of the Revolution would compel you to show mercy to these wretches, little though they or their families may have shown it to you.

Tomorrow morning I will present myself to you at nine of the clock, and will answer any questions you may have for me regarding the prisoners; I pray you will be prepared to make a thorough inquiry and to arrive at your conclusion by evening. I know some of you will think it unwise to bring illness into the city, and there is an argument on that point, but prison is prison, and it is not likely that those among the prisoners who are most stricken will have the opportunity to move among the populace to spread the contagion. Nurses assigned to the prisoners may be housed in the same building, so that any exposure they have to disease will be kept within the walls of the prison, and given no opportunity to spread amid the people.

Do not let dread rob you of your compassion. I tell you again that the time for action is short if you are to save those who are not yet displaying symptoms: something must be done or you will lose more of them than those presently near death. In the name of the Revolution and its purpose, I ask you to show mercy to these unfortunates, who presently suffer the same agonies as any person struck with such diseases.

Vive la France!
Vive la Revolution!

Jules Topinard, physician
#27, Rue des Bergers

1

"Are you going to try to see her again?" Photine asked as she rolled into da San-Germain's arms; her linen sheet slid off her shoulder, exposing her breast almost by accident. She gazed into his face with a look that bordered on adoration. She had been with him for the better part of an hour, and most of that time had been taken up with rapturous love-making that had left her deeply pleasured, yet oddly unsated, though she was gratified for all he had done for her; her disappointment was that he still had not used her as all other men had, and this bothered her, keeping her from achieving the maximal satisfaction she yearned for; it seemed to her that she had been cheated of applause.

"Yes," he replied, and laid his hand on the rise of her hip; her skin was silky and warm in the chilly room. "If I am permitted."

"If you have enough money to pay the clerks and the warden, you will be, never fear," Photine assured him.

He thought for an instant of his athanor, waiting in Padova in his laboratory, where he made gold and jewels; he would be glad of having it with him, but that, he reminded himself, would require another, heavier wagon and that would mean questions he was not eager to answer, and more problems than he already faced. It was not that he lacked money, but his reserve was shrinking. He still had a store of jewels in the hidden safe in the larger cart, but he was reluctant to use any of them. "I believe I can afford another round of bribes," he said, feeling her continuing desire flare.

"Will you take the poet with you?" She tweaked the collar of his nightshirt. "He tells me he wants to see her."

"I think not, nor should I encourage him to go to see her alone," da San-Germain said, a sardonic curl to his mouth. "Theron is becoming too well-known in this city, and his presence at the prison would draw attention to our mission, which could defeat the whole reason for visiting her."

"Yes, it would cause notice; as you say, he has garnered a following, and is not afraid to make the most of that, which is good for the play, but not for anything private," Photine agreed, and hugged him emphatically, clinging to him as voluptuously as she could in the narrow confines of her bed. She was able to sound only mildly interested when she asked, "I suppose I'll have to give you up to her when she is free?"

"Not as you think, not in any way that would rob you of our enjoyment," he answered, his hand wandering down from her hip to the sea-scented cleft between her legs, moving in ways that made her gasp with delectation. "She is of my blood."

She wriggled to accommodate his hand, making little, purring sighs as he touched the soft folds. "And that stops you?" If only, she thought, he would remove his nightshirt, but he had told her he would not, and she was not going to seek an explanation now.

"It does," he said, and bent to kiss her mouth, responding to the passion that had wakened in her, trying to find the source of her inmost ardor as his esurience increased, reacting to her reawakened carnality.

She broke their kiss. "But why would that—"

"Vampires do not—"

"I wish you wouldn't use that word," she complained, but with a softened look that took the sharpness of her protest away. "It sounds so dire, like harpies or devils."

"Nevertheless, it is what I am," he murmured, stroking the rise of her thigh. "Those of my blood have no life to give one another and it is life we must seek. Living blood is not only life, it is unique to every living person who has it, and it is that distinction that makes those of my kind seek out those who are still breathing, to be revivified by that uniqueness that is found in intimacy, in knowing another person completely, and making that knowledge part of ourselves."

"Do you have such knowledge of me?" Photine asked, a defensive edge to her tone. "What do you know?"

"I know you to the limit you will allow me to know you, as is the case with all those who accept me with understanding," he answered and went on, "Madelaine and I may have love for each other, but not in any way that we can express as the living do. Lying with her would benefit neither of us," he told her gently.

"But you did at one time, didn't you? At least six times, if what you've told me is right." There was an implacable note in her observation.

"That was some time ago." His manner warned her that this was not a matter to pursue.

Photine took a few seconds to frame her reaction in such a way that it would not seem a challenge to him. Finally she said, "So, supposing that your warnings are well-founded, if I lie with you two more times—or is it one more time?—and become like you when I die, as you've said I would, you and I could not be lovers again?" She put her hand to his mouth to stop anything he might answer; she shivered artfully. "That's a dreadful thought."

"You will have to decide what you wish to do," he said calmly. He had been asked such questions many times and had grown more used to explaining. "I will answer anything you would like to know, but the decision you make must be your own; anything else would be folly. If you cannot live by touching the lives of others through this kind of exchange"—he recalled how distressed Demetrice had been when the full realization of the needs of her vampire life struck her, and how she had given herself the True Death shortly after—"then do not risk coming to this undead life."

"Is there no other way?"

He gazed into the middle distance. "There is strong emotion in terror, if you would prefer to become a hunter, but I wouldn't advise it: terror provides little nutriment, and raises the chance of being hunted yourself."

"Would I live as long as you have?" There was a plaintive note in the question.

"I have no idea: I have lived a very long time. Those of my blood who do not court risks or attract the notice of those who dread our kind can have many centuries to walk the earth. That which destroys our bodies can kill us, of course; we're proof against most dangers, but not all of them: we can die the True Death if our spine is broken—or if our heads are struck off, as the Guillotine does so neatly—if we are burned, or if we are stripped of all our flesh, but we cannot starve or become ill or succumb to poisons or die of injuries, even severe ones that cause debilitation and pain. We cannot drown, but water immobilizes us unless we are protected by our native earth, so it is possible to lie in the ocean or in a lake or river, fully conscious, until some creature devours us." He saw her shudder. "Some of my blood have lived for many centuries"— Olivia, he reminded himself, had lived for more than sixteen hundred years before she met her True Death in a collapsing building, more than a century ago—"and others far more briefly." He was startled that his comments had spurred her passion; she was breathing more rapidly now.

"To live so long a time: what must that be like?" She intended to provoke him into revealing himself, and waited for what he would tell her.

"If you live a long, long time, you lose . . ." He steadied himself and spoke with remote tranquillity. "You will lose all your family: your brothers and sisters and cousins, uncles, aunts, parents, grand-parents, children, all of them, their children, their children's children, until no one remains who regards you as anything but a legend. You will lose your people, your nation, your language, your religion, your—"

She kissed him suddenly to silence him, then said, "Do you forget, or are you lonely?"

"I don't know if I forget, or how much, from the first half of my life, though I admit there isn't much that pleases me in what I can recall. No one else remains to tell me if my memories of those breathing days are correct; I think that they are . . . incomplete until I came to Egypt, but I have no way to be certain. Roger has been with me half my life and I rely upon him to lessen the disruption of my memories from those days until now, as I do for him."

"Why did you bring him to your life?"

"I didn't," he said, and saw surprise in her face. "I restored him to life through alchemy, techniques I learned long ago in Egypt." He decided not to mention how many centuries had gone by since then. "He isn't a vampire: he is a ghoul, and has been with me since Vespasianus ruled in Roma."

"So long? Really?" It was impossible to tell if she believed him.

"Yes." He took her free hand and kissed it.

"And the loneliness?"

His face was haunted. "That is unavoidable."

For more than a minute she thought about his loneliness, and finally she realized what he was saying to her. "Would I need to take many lovers?" There was a shine to her eyes, and a quick smile.

"If you become a vampire, yes."

"Would you be jealous?" Her voice was filled with mischief.

"I am not jealous of Theron, nor any of those Madelaine has loved since she came to my life; with the others of my blood it has been much the same. Jealousy is for the breathing, not for us. We may have sorrow that our intimacy ends, but jealousy? no." That was not entirely true: on Cyprus he had experienced jealousy and it had almost led him to the True Death, and it had lost him Jinou completely through his suspicions and demands; he could still feel chagrin when he thought back to that time. He had known qualms that were seen as jealousy by others, but that was not the same thing, and did not leave the same self-distaste behind. "I think that the loneliness burns jealousy away. And it is our nature, to seek out those living who will nourish us, and to whom we can offer some succor they cannot find among the living. Most of those who accept us are those who cannot have what they want among the living; we give a closeness that eludes them otherwise. When such closeness is not possible, we can deepen a sleeper's stupor and visit them as dreams; it is rare that we can find knowing lovers. The knowing is better, provided the connection is genuine," he said, with a sudden image of Rozsa of Borsod in his mind; he pulled the sheet higher up Photine's arm, then moved his hand back down her body to continue his arousal, suiting his rhythm to hers, for he had felt her excitement increase as he described his life to her.

"I have some sense of that, I think—that closeness—when the audience is with me," she said, unaware of the perplexity in his eyes. "If we must use the word: has anyone become a vampire by you and then changed her mind about it?"

"Yes, a few have. Some planned in advance not to continue in this undead life for very long, or to prevent the change from happening," he said, flinching at the memories of Melidulci and Heugenet. "And there was one who ignored all I told her about how to live so that there is no trouble with the living; she rejected me and all I tried to teach her, made a tribe of her own kind, and brought ruin upon them all. She paid a terrible price for her choices, and so did those who came to her life." Csimenae filled his thoughts again, and he wondered if she were still in Spain, or had suffered the True Death: with the Blood Bond between them broken, he could not tell anything about her.

"You're reigniting my desire," she warned him, recalling him from his unwelcome recollections; she smiled in anticipation, moving with the rhythm of his hand.

"Your fulfillment is unfinished," he said, seeing a flush of color in her face and neck, and becoming aware of her strong ardor.

"But you've made what we've had tonight so . . . so wonderful, that—oh! that's just right!—right there!" For a long moment she luxuriated in the increasing sensations that had taken hold of her. "Not yet, I want more time to savor your skills," she murmured, and stopped moving so that culmination would not overtake her again before she could give herself over to her ecstatic release. She licked her lips and made herself speak. "If you go much further, we'll have one less time to lie together."

"If you'd rather not . . ." he whispered, his fingers doing wonderful things to the little bud at the top of her inner lips. "I will take nothing more from you."

She shook her head emphatically. "You will not deny yourself. I would not be pleased to have you give me my culmination and have none yourself."

It was this unusual openness that had drawn him to her, and he responded to it now, in spite of his reservations. "Since it is what you want." He devoted the next several minutes to discovering the full range of her excitation, evoking blissful sensations from her toes to the top of her head, always returning to the sweet depths at the top of her thighs.

"Oh. Oh." Her body was shaking with her gathering passion, from the limits of her flesh to the portals of her soul, she reveled in the anticipation of her approaching rapture. "Don't stop." She tried to keep from panting, but could only slow down her breaths a little. The transports were almost upon her, when she would lose and find herself in the same infinite instant. Her thoughts scattered, overwhelmed by the tide of pleasure sweeping through her in a culmination of desire that engulfed her as with a storm of exaltation that approached apotheosis. She made no attempt to stop her delirious spasms, clasping his hair in her hands and bringing his mouth to her neck, all but weeping with the glory of her release. Gradually the elation faded, although little tremors ran through her, codas to her climax, and gradually she loosened her hold on him, sighing with satisfaction and a touch of regret. "*Now* I am replete. Now I am Helen and Cleopatra and Venus herself." In a grand demonstration, she flung one arm up and let it fall beautifully between them.

He regarded her with a fine mixture of shared gratification and dubiety; as intimate as they were, he still could not determine how much of what she offered him was genuine and how much was expert performance. "You are Photine," he said softly, fingering the damp tendrils of her hair that lay on her cheek. "That is what I love in you."

"Strange," she said. "Most who think they love me love what

they imagine me to be." After lying contemplatively for a few minutes, Photine half-sat up and reached for her satin robe-de-chambre, and pulled it around her, then snuggled back against da San-Germain. "It's getting cold in here," she said with a giggle.

"Would you like me to build up the fire?" he offered, watching her struggles with the robe.

"I would like you to warm me up through your own efforts, but that isn't what you do, is it?"

"No, at least not with my body," he admitted, and swung out of the bed, going to the hearth and reaching for a log to put on the embers winking in the fireplace.

She pulled a pillow nearer and leaned on it. "You are very good to me, you know, and I am shrewish not to treasure you as you deserve. Most men would take their pleasure and that would be the end of it."

"And you have been good to me," he said, watching the log beginning to smoke. When he was certain that it would burn, he went back to her bed and got under the sheet and blanket. "The room will be warmer shortly."

"Yes," she said. "Will you promise to tell me one day how you learned to do all the things you know how to do?"

"I will tell you some of it, if you would like to know." He stretched out beside her, leaning toward her and changing the subject. "What do you plan to do tomorrow?"

"We need to rehearse; Crepin and Olympe are getting lax in their lines," she said, turning her attention willingly to her plans for the coming day. "We need to be more alert to the audience, as well. And Theron has an idea he wants to discuss with the troupe. I don't think many of them will agree with him, but he has every right to ask."

"Would you tell me what this idea is, or would you rather not until the matter is decided?"

She considered him, then said, "Since you are our patron, I suppose he couldn't object to my telling you." Grabbing a second pillow and shoving it under her shoulder, she said in a musing tone,

"He thinks that the Corpses should march through the town at the end of the play; I think the beginning would be better if we must do it at all."

"Why is that?"

"If we march at the end, our audience could leave without paying anything for the entertainment. If we march at the beginning, we may bring a larger audience to see us," she said with happy conviction. "But the troupe might not like taking on something so unpredictable. Out in the streets, in such costumes, there could be trouble, and everyone would have to change their costumes for the play."

"What if half the Corpses went out, leaving those in the first three scenes to get ready for the play? That way, you could open the curtain as soon as the troupe was back, and that would hold many of those who might follow us." She beamed. "It gives us a willing audience."

"Your plan makes better sense, if the parade is to happen at all," said da San-Germain. "Theron's would rob you of your bows as well as your money, and might earn all of you scorn from those who do not like the play."

Her laughter was brief but rang utterly true. "You know us so well: players do like applause." After a pause, she added, "And money."

He chuckled wryly. "Merci du compliment."

"Will we need another license for the parade?"

"Probably. I will find out for you, and secure one if it's necessary," he said.

"You are always so helpful, Ragoczy. It's quite remarkable of you."

"My motives aren't entirely altruistic," he told her. "I would like to find out when they are bringing the prisoners into the city."

"It would be less obvious to ask while you obtained a license for a parade—yes, I see that." She shifted on her pillow again, watching him, gauging how much more to say. "While we have a little more time together, I'd like to thank you for putting Feo to be companion to Enee. I no longer know what to do with my son, and he worries me."

"It would help none of us if Enee should earn the condemnation of the Revolutionary Court." Da San-Germain sat up across the bed from her. "If there is trouble, at least we'll have timely warning of it."

"You trust Feo," she said, a little doubt easing the statement toward being an inquiry.

"I have found him to be reliable," he said, preparing to rise. "The company will be up in another hour."

"With such heavy clouds, how can you be sure sunrise is near?"

"I am not lying on my native earth, and my feet are bare: seen or unseen, I can feel the presence of the sun. All of my blood can do that." He touched her face. "I should return to my room now, don't you think."

"Oh, I suppose so, though most of the players know that you passed most of the night with me. It is to be expected." She held out her hands to him. "Actors understand these arrangements. Constance thinks it odd that I don't spend all my nights with you."

He rose to offer her a profound leg. "And how do you answer her impertinence?"

"I have said to her that I have my first loyalty to the company: patrons may come and go, but the dependability of troupers is essential to our success." She got out of the bed, adjusted her robe, and tugged at the bedding, making an effort to restore a little order to the marvelous disarray. "You're right, though," she conceded as she plumped a pillow. "You should go back to your room, much as I delight in having you here."

"Keep in mind that it will only be safe to lie with me one more time without facing the change to my nature upon your death."

"Yes, yes. I do remember that much," she said, and as he went toward the door, "How long do you think the rain will last? We're supposed to perform in two days, but if it's still raining, we may have to cancel, or find an indoor place to perform."

"I don't have the same sense of weather as I do of the movements of the sun, but the innkeeper said that unless there are high winds, the rain will last for two days. In December, it will last for three."

"Will we be here in December?" Photine asked.

"I think not," said da San-Germain.

She nodded, pausing in her bed-making, to blow him a kiss. "You're almost a perfect lover, and almost a perfect patron, Ragoczy. When this is over, I will miss you."

He bowed again, in the fashion of three hundred years before. "I am honored to be of service while I may," and before she could speak again, he was out in the hall. He moved quickly and with only the slightest sound along the corridor to his room, where he tapped twice before opening the door.

Roger was sitting before the small fireplace, a plate in his hands with the remains of a raw duck upon it. "My master," he said, starting to rise.

"There's no reason to get up, old friend. Finish your meal, by all means," da San-Germain said, then went to pinch out a guttering candle that stood with four companions on the night-stand next to the bed.

"How is Madame?" Roger asked as he resumed his seat.

"She seems well, or so I think she must be," said da San-Germain, staring at the mirror on the armoire door, where there was no sign of his reflection; many centuries ago, the lack of an image would have distressed him, now he felt only caution and the desire not to have anyone discover his missing reflection.

Long experience of da San-Germain made Roger ask, "Seems? Not is? Is it Enee who causes the problem?"

"In part, I think. He is constantly goading his mother, provoking her to have to choose between him and me, and occasionally I wonder if she encourages that in him." He shrugged and opened the mirrored door so that it no longer faced the room. "She puzzles me."

"I am aware of that," said Roger, cutting another slice of duck thigh.

"There are times I feel that she has revealed herself to me, but then, something in her shifts and I find myself wondering if she was providing another convincing performance, and that the performance satisfies her as much as anything I may do for her."

"Do you think she is dependable?" Roger asked as if discussing the weather.

"To a point. I am persuaded that she values her own welfare more than she may possess any loyalty to me beyond what is pragmatic, but I trust that is enough. I would rather not be caught up in a contest between mother and son." He rubbed his chin. "I need a shave."

"You do; it's been five days since your last, and your beard is beginning to show. I'll get the basin when I'm done," Roger said. "And I should trim your hair; it's gotten a little wild at the back."

Da San-Germain ran his fingers through it. "Indeed it has. We might as well do both at the same time."

"I can ask the innkeeper to send up a tub and hot water, if you would like a bath as well."

"I probably need one," he agreed. "I'll go get the seat-pad out of the cart. We can slide it under the tub." The seat-pad was filled with his native earth and would counteract the enervating effects of the water.

"Hadn't you better dress first? A nightshirt is—"

"—inappropriate; I agree. I'll put on something more acceptable," he said, looking into the open armoire. "The driving-britches and the coachman's canvas cloak should do it. I'll tuck in the nightshirt."

"It's early enough that no one will pay much attention," said Roger, continuing to eat slices of duck.

"This shouldn't take long," said da San-Germain, pulling the garments from their pegs and tossing them onto the bed. "I'm not going to bother with underclothes."

"No reason to," Roger agreed.

"So let me . . ." He did not finish his thought as he pulled on the driving-britches, adjusting the waist after he tucked in his nightshirt. "Is this suitable?"

Roger studied him. "Yes, I think so," he said. "With the cloak, you'll do."

"Thank you," said da San-Germain before he tugged on his boots. "Shall I order the bath on my way out?"

"I don't think so," Roger said. "That would give rise to talk; you may be sure some of the servants know where you spent the night. They make a point of sharing what they know, as well. I'll attend to it in a few minutes, when I take these bones down to the kitchen."

"As you like. I shouldn't take long," he said, and let himself out of the room, going toward the backstairs since at this hour no one would be at the front door to bolt it behind him. In the kitchen, a sleepy scullion let him out of the building; da San-Germain crossed the yard to the stable and went in through the tack-room door. His dark-seeing eyes had little trouble with the lack of illumination, but he used flint-and-steel to light a small lantern that hung on a hook on the main pillar in the stable before he stepped into the wide central aisle of the structure, where the wagons and carts were stored at the end opposite the stalls. A few of the horses gave whickers of recognition, and one of the mules made a sound like a pan dragged over pebbles, but otherwise his presence went unnoticed.

The larger cart was between the rear wall and one of the smaller wagons, with just enough room to let him slip along the wall. Here the lantern cast more shadow than light, which was a minor inconvenience. As he reached the driving-box of the cart, he felt for the small latch that held the seat in place, and began to work it; the latch was stiff but loosened under his persistent fingers. The strengthening effect of his native earth made it easier for him to work his way around the front of the cart to the other side, where he started on the second latch. He was distantly aware of the sound of an opening door, followed by the half-neigh of a pair of the horses, and assumed that the grooms had arrived to begin their morning chores; the mizzling dawn was nearly upon them, and the inn was showing the first signs of the new day. He continued to worry the latch, somewhat hampered by the nearness of the wagon, which left him having to reach at an awkward angle, yet in a few minutes he was able to swing the seat up, and, holding it overhead, ease his way out from in between the cart and the wagon.

The first knife-thrust felt more like a blow than a cut; da San-Germain staggered back half a step, the seat slipping from his hands as he strove to keep himself upright; it briefly served as a shield from the next three thrusts, then dropped down at his feet. He blinked, but there was blood in his eyes from a slash across his forehead; he realized that he was being stabbed just as the next lunge sent the blade ripping the heavy canvas, down through his shoulder into his chest. Had he been a living man, that one wound would have been fatal. As it was, he fell across the seat, and drew himself into a ball while another eleven knife blows pierced his arms, hip, and back. He made an attempt to kick his assailant, and earned himself four more stabs before he heard the stable door open and a shout of horror; hasty steps drew near, and a scuffle began, marked by angry voices and the approach of more hurried footsteps; da San-Germain lapsed into stupor, an unfamiliar cold eating into him as his thoughts blurred and faded.

Text of a letter from Vivien Zacharie Charlot, Deputy Secretary of Public Safety in Lyon, to Egide Loup, Warden of Anti-Revolutionary Prisoners at Saint-Gautier-en-Saone, carried by a courier of the Revolutionary Tribunal of Lyon, delivered the day it was written.

> *To the Warden of Anti-Revolutionary Prisoners at Saint-Gautier-en-Saone, Egide Loup, the greetings of Vivien Zacharie Charlot, Deputy Secretary of Public Safety in Lyon, on this, the 20th day of October, 1792.*
>
> *My dear Warden Loup,*
>
> *I have in hand your note of this morning, and I must agree that it would not be wise to move the prisoners in this rain; we will postpone the event until the 24th, when I have been assured by Citizen Grostete, who is regarded as expert in matters of weather, that it will*

be dry enough to move the prisoners. Too many of them, already ill, would be chilled and soaked, which would ensure their quick demise without the decision of the Revolutionary Court. I believe you are wise in postponing the move, little as the physician Topinard may approve. I cannot countenance such an obvious transfer, for it could easily result in a public outcry, should any of the prisoners die as a result of being moved.

I applaud your care, which shows your good sense and your good judgment, and will report my opinions to the Secretary of Public Safety before I leave this afternoon to deliver my daily report to the Revolutionary Tribunal. You may be certain of my support of your actions as well as my determination to see that the prisoners answer for their crimes before the Revolutionary Court instead of eluding justice by dying of cold and neglect.

You have my permission to make a proper stew for the prisoners this evening, and to serve it with cheese and bread. Do not allow them to waste away. Those who are unwell, allow them a little wine to fortify them even more. There is no benefit in sending emaciated aristos to the Guillotine any more than there is in executing sick ones. With our combined efforts we should yet come through this cleansing of anti-Revolutionaries with our contributions known and praiseworthy, and our reputations made.

Vive la France!
Vive la Revolution!

Vivien Zacharie Charlot
Deputy Secretary of Public Safety
Lyon

2

Obscenities and oaths were the first things that da San-Germain noticed as his consciousness returned; the next was an all-encompassing hurt that no movement could lessen. He moaned, and saw a foot near his head move back, accompanied by a startled yelp. He struggled to open his eyes and found that blood from the cut on his forehead had made the lids stick together; he managed to wave his arm, grateful for the annealing presence of his native earth in the seat that he lay atop, which kept him from being incapacitated by pain.

"God Almighty! He's alive!"

"No! He can't be!" This was from his attacker, a shrill howl of disbelief.

"He is," came the answer with ferocious glee. "You failed, boy." There was a moment's pause. "For God's sake, someone take the knife and put it in a safe place."

Da San-Germain recognized Feo's voice, and, almost at once, felt the coachman kneel next to him. "I'm hurt." He was amazed when he heard himself, for the words were barely more than a whisper.

"I know. Madame's worthless son set upon you with a knife. Lie still. Crepin will bring Roger out shortly; he's gone to fetch him." He cleared his throat with difficulty and resumed talking. "Enee attacked you. We have him. The grooms and Pascal are holding him. He won't get away with this, Ragoczy."

"I've lost . . . blood," da San-Germain muttered, attempting to wipe the drying gore from his face without much success; he had only a sliver of vision. Yet he could see part of the broad skirts of his driving-cloak, and noticed that the heavy fabric was saturated with blood, which he decided in a remote way had to be his, for although there was a great deal of it, none of it pumped from cut vessels, and he, lacking a pulse, was the only one in the stable who could bleed so much without gouts spurting from deep wounds. He almost laughed, thinking that what he had had from Photine so recently would not suffice to sustain him now.

"Lie still. Help is coming. Roger will attend to you shortly, and you'll be better," said Feo with desperate conviction; all of da San-Germain's clothes were red-soaked, and the leather-covered seat was slick with it. "And the Guards will come."

There was another abrupt struggle, a flurry of slaps and grunts, then Enee shouted, "Die! You should be dead! I want you dead!"

If he had been able to respond, da San-Germain might have said that he was dead already, but that required more effort than he could muster, so he only shook his head.

"I'll kill you, Comte. If not now, another time."

"Enough! What you've done is bad for all of us, so keep silent!" Pascal commanded in a voice that rang like a clarion; it was accompanied by another series of blows and more outraged exclamations; the horses fretted and milled at the disruption going on. "Keep him away from the horses. We don't need them trying to—"

"I'll take care of it." Feo went to close the various stall doors and the main stable door as well, glancing back at da San-Germain as he did.

"The blood . . . bothers them," da San-Germain muttered. "The smell . . ."

"That should keep them all in their places. We can turn them out later." Feo jiggled a closed latch to demonstrate that the stalls were secure.

"Good," Pascal declared as Feo finished setting the latch on the main door; he did not lock it so that Crepin and Roger would not have to knock to enter.

Enee continued to curse and blaspheme under his breath, more growling than speech; one of the grooms gave him a hard slap. "Quiet, you."

"Lock him in the tack-room and summon the Guards. He must

be taken into custody, and soon, before this place becomes busy." Feo came back to da San-Germain's side. "I'll get a cloth and some water. Where is Crepin, and Roger?"

Pascal bristled. "Why should we follow your orders? This is a matter for the troupe to handle. We can restrain him here, where we can watch him."

"And he might escape. He has to be confined." Feo looked down at da San-Germain. "Just do it: lock him up. There's going to be enough gossip as it is. One of the grooms can stay with him, to make sure he doesn't escape. Don't let any of the company in with him. Madame wouldn't want her son beaten, and he will be if the rest of the troupe gets here before the Guards arrive." Feo moved off toward the water-trough.

"Andre has already gone to the barracks," said one of the grooms; he had secured Enee's hands behind his back with a lead-rope, and now had him by the elbow, preparing to shove him into the tack-room.

Da San-Germain had worked the blood off one of his eyelids, permitting him to see enough to make out Enee and Pascal and the groom. He managed to sit up, though his head rang and he felt dizzy; he had a brief, intense recollection of coming to out at the edge of the swamp at Sankt Piterburkh, not quite ninety years ago. Who had assaulted him then he had never discovered; in this instance, he had no doubts. "I . . ." The exertion it took to breathe in order to speak was staggering.

"Don't talk," Pascal advised him, holding Enee's collar in a firm hand. "Renaud, you can stay with him. Just you. Don't let anyone but the Guards in. We don't need any more confusion than we already have."

"They won't hold me," Enee boasted. "My mother will deal with them. You'll see. The troupe will defend me." He glared at da San-Germain. "You're a piece of shit, using my mother for your own ends."

The groom paid no attention to this outburst; he nodded to Pascal. "I can do that."

"They'll thank me for trying to get rid of you," Enee announced loudly and was slapped for his temerity.

"Keep him secure. The state he's in, he may try something drastic," said Pascal to the groom.

Da San-Germain did his best to follow all this, willing himself not to faint. He attempted to raise his voice enough to be heard. "Why . . . did he . . ."

Feo returned with a small pail and a length of cloth. "I'll get the blood off your face, Ragoczy," he said as he knelt down next to da San-Germain.

Pascal pushed Enee's back and Renaud jerked at his elbow; gradually Enee was propelled toward the tack-room even while he twisted and wrenched in an attempt to break free of his captors as they jostled him along.

The cloth was rough and smelled of horses, but da San-Germain was relieved to have his eyes finally wiped clear of blood, and smiled as he opened them. "Thank you, Feo."

"You're fortunate that the knife didn't cut a main vessel. You couldn't have survived that." He sounded a bit mystified as he said it. "That cut into your shoulder . . . I thought it was deep, but I guess your clothing . . ."

"It may not . . . be deep . . . but it is painful; the . . . knife could have . . . cut my lung"—which he knew it had—"but the canvas . . . is so . . . thick, it stopped . . . the blade," said da San-Germain, claiming the strip of cloth and gingerly wiping his hands and neck with it. He was about to thrust his hands into the pail to wash them and the cloth when the stable door was flung open and Crepin came in with Roger, both of them moving rapidly. "Ah."

"My master," Roger cried out as he came up to da San-Germain and saw the blood. "How badly are you—"

"—hurt?" he asked.

"Enee used a knife on him," Feo explained. "There are a lot of strikes, if the clothes are any reckoning, and there's the blood."

"So Crepin told me, and half the inn's staff," Roger said, no sign of distress visible in his face, but with tension in his voice.

"We have him in the tack-room, and we'll keep him there." Feo added, "Andre has gone for the Guards."

"A wise precaution," Roger approved.

Da San-Germain did his unsuccessful best to smile. "I trust you have . . . ordered the bath."

"I did, ten minutes ago," he said, baffled by the remark, but with his demeanor unflustered. "They will be filling it now."

"Good." He blinked twice, trying to rid himself of the last of the tacky blood around his eyes. "I need it . . . We can . . . count the . . . number of cuts . . . that wretched young . . . man inflicted and . . . clean them at the . . . same time . . . we wash away . . . the blood." He struggled to get up, and was grateful to Roger, who reached out and helped him to rise. "We'll need . . . the seat, too."

Roger picked it up. "So we will," he said. "Crepin, add to your goodness and help Ragoczy get to his room. I'll be right behind you."

"Certainly," said Crepin, taking the seat from him, holding it away from his clothes so that there would be no blood on his own garments.

Pascal emerged from the tack-room, saying to no one in particular, "We've tied him to the harness-pegs. Renaud will stay with him until the Guards come." He paused. "I must say, the boy's in a vile mood."

Although he already knew this, Roger said, "Very good. Then we may safely take my master back to his room." He helped da San-Germain to steady himself on his feet, then draped the injured man's arm across his shoulder and took hold of his waist. "Tell Madame what we've done," he said to Feo and Pascal.

Some of Pascal's calm was deserting him, though he tried to maintain it. "Of course. When the Guards have come. I'll stay here until then. With Feo. In case we're needed in the tack-room." Pascal was looking a bit harried, but did not try to dispute with Roger. "We can give a report to the Guards. Then go to Madame."

"That you can, though she'll hear of it before you tell her, unless you gag the entire staff," said Roger, and carefully edged away from the carts and wagons toward the door, holding da San-Germain so that he remained upright. All the way across the stable-yard, he could feel da San-Germain's consciousness drift in and out, so he began to speak, giving his master something to focus on beyond moving. "This time, that impetuous young man will have to bear the consequences of his acts, unpleasant as they may be. He's gone too far for mere wildness. It's one thing to try to cheat while gambling, but another to attack someone with the intent of killing him with witnesses about."

"He thinks he's . . . protecting . . . his mother," said da San-Germain in Visigothic Spanish. "He has . . . wanted me . . . out of her life . . . since they arrived . . . in Padova."

"He's in error. She will take no harm from you, but Enee is another matter," said Roger in the same language; he glimpsed Crepin moving a little closer to them, listening.

"That he is," said da San-Germain, pressing his lips together as Roger eased him over the threshold into the kitchen, which was now filled with activity.

Roger raised his voice to the main scullery maid. "Is the bath ready? My master must have his wounds cleaned. I'll need a sheet, torn into strips, to bandage him." He knew that the staff was curious about da San-Germain, thanks to Crepin's rush through the kitchen to summon him to the stable.

The scullery maid stared at da San-Germain with unabashed horror and curiosity, then answered Roger's question. "The bath has just been poured. I'll have a torn sheet ready in half an hour, if that will suit you?"

"Fine; fine," said Roger, and kept going, entering the corridor three strides from the rear stairs. He saw Crepin coming after them, and motioned him to go ahead up the stairs. "This may take a while: there's a deep wound in his hip and climbing won't be easy. Put the seat in the room; we'll be up in a while."

Crepin paled but said with the assumption of aplomb, "If you need my help, you have only to call me. I'm at your disposal." With that, he went up the stairs with unusual haste, the seat held ahead of him.

"Best not . . . to ask for . . . his help," said da San-Germain, no condemnation in his observation. "He's upset . . . already."

"That he is," Roger agreed.

Da San-Germain took a long, unsteady breath. "Shall we try . . . the stairs?"

"This will be difficult, my master," Roger warned as they reached the bottom of the flight. "Tell me if this is too painful."

"Better to . . . have it over with," said da San-Germain, steeling himself for the ascent, clamping his teeth closed so that he would make no sound.

"There are eight treads, a landing, then six more treads," Roger said as he moved onto the first stair. "Use your left leg; it should be less painful—the wound is in your right hip." He contrived to maneuver da San-Germain into a position that would allow him to pull himself up the banister with his free hand. "Are you ready?"

"I hope so," was his response.

It took an adjustment in how da San-Germain kept hold of Roger before the two of them were prepared to continue. Roger shifted his weight, half-lifting da San-Germain with him.

"Do you remember . . . getting me down . . . from the cross in . . . Mexico?" da San-Germain asked, trying to distract himself and Roger from their current situation.

"That was difficult," Roger concurred, going to the second step.

"I wasn't much . . . help then . . . either."

"Can you lift your leg a little more?"

Da San-Germain complied and was a bit surprised to realize he had done what was needed. Then he reminded himself that there were still thirteen stairs and a landing to go. He stifled a groan and prepared to try for the next step.

It took a bit more than twenty minutes to climb to the upper corridor and another five minutes to make it to the room; they encountered no one on the stairs, and Roger assumed the innkeeper had warned the staff away from the rear stairs. When they finally got to the room Crepin was already there, standing next to the driving-seat, which he had leaned against the side of the armoire; he was doing his best to appear composed, but he was pale and his hands were shaking. The middle of the room was taken up by the enameled iron bathtub, standing on four lion's-paw feet; it was two-thirds full of water that steamed in the wan morning.

"I can help you get him undressed," Crepin volunteered.

"Yes. Thanks," said Roger, easing da San-Germain down on the edge of the bed. "Start with his boots."

Crepin knelt to remove the boots, and said as he did, "They're ruined. There's slashes on both of them, and so much blood . . ."

"Everything he's wearing is ruined," said Roger, working to ease da San-Germain's right arm out of the cloak's half-sleeve; there were three wide rents in the canvas, all of them rimed in dark-red.

Da San-Germain shuddered. "Pardon me . . . I'm . . . exhausted." He slumped where he sat, his head drooping, the pain eating at him like a mob of starving rats.

Roger continued on his work while Crepin finished pulling the first boot off. "Set it aside. I'll take care of it later."

"You should probably save the clothes for the Department of Public Safety and the Revolutionary Court. In case there are questions about the extent of his injuries. My uncle is an advocate, and he's always keeping exhibits for the Court." Crepin brushed his hands together fastidiously. "If you have a sack where I can put them?"

"I'll take care of it once Ragoczy is safely bathed and in bed," Roger said patiently. "You're right about the sack."

Crepin stared at da San-Germain, taking stock of his condition and his livid pallor. "Do you think he's going to . . . recover?"

"In time," said Roger, thinking of the many things da San-Germain had survived over their seventeen hundred years together. "Those of his blood have great . . . stamina."

"I can . . . hear you," da San-Germain reminded them. "And I . . . will . . . recover."

"I'll tell the troupe," Crepin said, tugging on the other boot. "They'll want to know."

"You can tell the staff of the inn, as well," Roger suggested, freeing da San-Germain's left arm; da San-Germain straightened up a little to make it easier to remove the cloak. "Thank you, my master; this will be more comfortable coming off now."

Crepin set the second boot aside. "The britches?"

"I'll attend to them." He snapped his fingers. "I have it: why don't you go get a bottle of wine and take it out to Pascal and Feo?"

"Are you sure you want them to drink while they guard Enee?" Crepin asked with some surprise.

"If they're as distressed as you and I are, I should think it would help them. You may drink with them, if you like. You will find it steadies your nerves." Roger now had the cloak free except for the portion of it that da San-Germain was sitting on.

"Oh. All right," he said, getting up and wandering toward the door. "What do I tell the barkeeper?"

"Tell him that Ragoczy will pay for it."

"But he might worry. Undoubtedly he knows what's happened," Crepin said, hovering near the door. "He might fear—" He broke off, unwilling to say what he was afraid might happen.

"You may be right," said Roger with a sigh. "I have some coins you may use." He reached into one of his capacious pockets and brought out a small purse. "There's silver and gold in here. There should be enough for a bottle each for the whole troupe and the grooms besides. Use it wisely." He tossed the purse to Crepin, and heard it clink as Crepin fumbled his catch. "Go on, with my thanks and my master's."

Crepin bent to pick up the purse. "You're very generous. I'll make sure we drink to Ragoczy's health."

Da San-Germain lifted his head. "And justice . . . Drink to . . . justice."

"Yes," said Crepin, "to justice," and bolted from the room, slamming the door behind him with unusual force.

When it was clear that Crepin would not return, Roger shoved the driving-box seat under the bathtub, turning it so that it gave the most exposure to the bathtub; when he was satisfied with his efforts, he said, "I thought you'd prefer that I take off your night-shirt after he left, rather than while he was here."

"You did . . . well, old friend," said da San-Germain. He did not battle for air as he had while Crepin was with them, and for a short while as Roger went to get scissors, he stopped breathing altogether while the pain eased a little.

Roger brought the scissors and proceeded to cut the nightshirt off da San-Germain, taking care to keep the pieces of the garment together. He handed da San-Germain a pillow, aware of how much the vampire disliked being seen naked: the massive scar tissue that covered his abdomen from the base of his ribs to his pubis was worrisome to him. "I'll bring you a drying sheet in a moment." He paused to look at the wound in the top of his shoulder; it was no longer bleeding, but the blood had not yet clotted completely. "It appears to go straight down."

"Yes. That's why it . . . hurts . . . to breathe."

Roger nodded. "You have more wounds than I supposed you had, and worse ones."

"Enee . . . was very angry." Da San-Germain strove to stand up but fell back with a soft cry of frustration. "If you . . . will lend me . . . your arm?"

"As soon as I bring you a drying sheet," said Roger, taking the scissors and the nightshirt away to the armoire, returning at once with the large square of Turkish cotton. Even without the stairs to slow them, it took nearly five minutes to get da San-Germain from the bed to the bathtub and into it, and left Roger with damp cuffs and sleeves. "There. Rest a while, my master. I'm going to get the bandages from the girl in the kitchen, and I'll use your healing tincture when I return. You have ten wounds that I can see, and there may be more. The sooner they are cleaned and dressed, the more comfortable you will be."

"At least . . . my throat wasn't . . . cut." That had happened twelve centuries ago, and it had been several months before he had been able to speak properly.

"Then there's something to be grateful for," said Roger.

Da San-Germain waved him away, leaning back in the steaming water, watching it turn from clear to pink to dull-red; though the room was cool, the bath was almost too hot for comfort. He closed his eyes and let his thoughts drift, turning from Enee to Madelaine and the first time he met her, at the ball in 1743, and all that came after. He had no desire to occupy his mind with cataloguing his injuries; he would do that when Roger returned. The ache that the many thrusts Enee's knife had inflicted began to lose their intensity; he welcomed the languor that small relief provided, as soothing as the unguent of blue lotus would be for the living.

A sharp knock on the door brought him out of his daze; before he could take in sufficient air to speak, the door opened and Photine surged into the room, her face wet with tears, her robe-de-chambre thrown over her corsage and petticoat, and an air of disarray about her that made da San-Germain sit up and reach for the drying sheet, pulling it across the top of the tub so that only his head, shoulders, and right arm were visible.

"Oh, Jesus, Mary, and Joseph! How could it come to this?" Photine cried, seeing da San-Germain, and noting the purple gouge on his shoulder. "Then it is true!" She crossed herself and wiped at her streaming eyes with a sodden handkerchief.

"What is true?" he asked her, trying to collect himself.

"You've been hurt! Someone has attacked you!" She hurried to the bathtub and knelt beside it, artlessly offering a glimpse of her magnificent bosom. "I can see cuts on your arm and shoulder. How dreadful! That you should be set upon!"

Da San-Germain tried to think of something to say that would not add to her distraught state. "Photine . . ." he began.

"Crepin told me that Enee did it, but he couldn't have. He's incapable of such behavior. He doesn't like you very much, but he's a boy—he wouldn't do anything so . . . so grievous. I know he wouldn't." There was despair in every aspect of her demeanor; she trembled as if about to collapse. "Crepin must be mistaken. It wasn't Enee, was it?"

"I regret to . . . to tell you . . . that it was your . . . son who . . . did this," he said as kindly as he could, and read consternation in the look she shot at him.

"But it couldn't be," she insisted. "You must be confused. He wouldn't do anything so . . . so reckless. He promised me that he would never bring dishonor upon the troupe, or on me. He's impulsive, yes, but not deranged."

"He certainly . . . seemed that . . . way when he . . . came at me," da San-Germain said, and saw her face crumple as she began to cry in earnest. "It is nothing . . . against you, Photine . . . It was his . . . act, not yours. You . . . are a devoted mother, . . . but you're not . . . responsible for what he does."

"But it can't be, it can't be that he would do such a thing to you," she wailed, lifting her head to look at him. "Don't you understand? Enee is no criminal, he's just not very wise yet. He gave in to the abandon of youth."

"I fear the Revo . . . lutionary Court . . . will . . . see it differently."

Her eyes flashed, tears lending more shine to them. "Why? Because he is not an aristocrat with rich friends to act for him?" She shook her head emphatically. "Why should your relation be saved and Enee abandoned? You can afford to rescue both, can't you?"

Fatigue and lassitude were growing within him; he would soon slip into the stupor that among his kind passed for sleep, which he abjectly needed. "Photine . . . can't we . . . talk later?"

"Why later? Don't you know how urgent this state of affairs is? Would you say the same if it were your precious Madelaine who was in danger, and not my son?" she demanded, all supplication gone, her tears vanishing to be replaced by indignation. "The Guards are coming, and my son will be taken to prison. Prison!" she repeated, stamping her foot for emphasis.

"That would . . . happen whether I . . . speak to them . . . or not, or . . . how many . . . bribes I . . . pay." He could feel a small trail of blood run down his lung, and he coughed, spraying fine red droplets on the drying sheet.

"Only if you tell them he did it! Without that, he cannot be held." She rose to her feet, a vision of purpose and righteousness. "We are here to remove your relation from prison, yet you will allow my son to be taken there."

The accusation stung him, but he said quietly, "My relation . . . has not . . . stabbed me . . . repeatedly."

"Are you mocking me?"

"No . . . myself."

She folded her arms. "Then you will make a complaint?"

"I need . . . not. Feo will . . . and Pascal."

"You will permit them to turn on my boy? You will encourage them?" She shook her head in splendid defiance. "You could pay them to keep quiet, and explain to the Guards that there was a misunderstanding. Couldn't you? You could promise that we will be gone from Lyon within the week, and that we will confine Enee until we are ten leagues from the city."

"Did you . . . just now . . . think of this?" He was panting now, every word an agonizing effort.

Photine paused, then lowered her eyes. "Crepin came to me before he sought out your manservant, as he should do. I have been trying to decide how to see to Enee's freedom ever since." She paced down the room, as restless as a caged tiger. "I didn't think you would refuse to help me."

Watching her, da San-Germain could not determine how much of her behavior was genuine emotion and how much was performance, as he had so many times. He was convinced that she was genuinely upset, but the mercurial shifts and dramatic delivery could be the product of a scenario, gauged to persuade him to withdraw any complaint that might be given against her son. "He . . . has broken the . . . law, in front of . . . witnesses. I cannot . . . keep the . . . Court from . . . charging him and . . . trying him."

She rounded on him, as grand as anything in Racine. "If you

paid a large enough bribe, you could. You have already bribed the Warden of Anti-Revolutionary Prisoners in order to see your noble relation. You could bribe the clerks of the Revolutionary Court to rescind the complaint. I know you could." She came back to the bathtub, an eloquent remorse in her face. "You have done so much for us. Can't you do this as well? Is it so different than paying bribes for the troupe to perform?"

He was trying to decide how to answer her so that they could delay this confrontation when the door to the room opened and Roger came in, a basket filled with long strips of linen in one hand and a branch of lit candles in the other. Da San-Germain gestured to Roger to shut the door. "What news?" he asked breathlessly.

"The Guards have just arrived. They're talking with Feo and Pascal. The groom apparently summarized the problem as he brought them back here," he replied, looking toward Photine with a wary shine in his faded-blue eyes. "I believe they will interview Enee when they have finished with the witnesses. Then, if my master can receive them, they will ask him what transpired, or so their sergeant informs me."

"Tell them that you were mistaken!" Photine exclaimed. "Roger, go get them. Tell them that your master wishes to modify his complaint."

Roger regarded her steadily for several seconds, then said without any outward show of emotion. "I am sorry, Madame, but I cannot do that."

"But if you don't, Enee will face trial," she all but shrieked.

"That is for the Department of Public Safety to decide," said Roger. "They will advise the Revolutionary Court if a trial is warranted."

"Did the . . . sergeant tell you . . . that, too?" da San-Germain inquired muzzily; his attention was slipping, and warm as the water was, he was beginning to feel something he rarely felt: cold.

Photine gave a frenzied scream and rushed out of the room, calling for Constance and Olympe, for Sibelle and Tereson, proclaiming that they had been betrayed.

Roger went and closed the door. "Don't fret, my master. The Department of Public Safety will explain the matter to her. She won't intrude on you until you are better."

"Do you . . . think so?" da San-Germain asked, and stared at the closed door. "I wonder."

Text of a report to the Department of Public Safety of Lyon from their advisory physician, Jules Topinard, carried by Topinard's footman the morning after the report was written.

> *To the Department of Public Safety, the greetings of Jules Topinard, physician, and the report on the condition of the foreigner, Ragoczy Ferenz, Hungarian exile, with the troupe known as Commedia della Morte, on this, the night of the 21ˢᵗ of October, 1792.*
>
> *To the Secretary of Public Safety,*
>
> *As you have required of me, I called at the Jongleur, the inn where the Commedia della Morte is presently residing, in response to your order that I should examine Ragoczy Ferenz to determine the extent of injuries inflicted upon him yesterday, October 20ᵗʰ, 1792, at the hands of Enee d'Auville, son of the leader of the Commedia della Morte, currently held in detention in the cells of the Revolutionary Guard barrack at #52, Place et Porte en Sur.*
>
> *I arrived at the Jongleur at seven of the clock in the evening and was directed to Ragoczy's room at the rear of the first floor of guest-rooms. Ragoczy's manservant admitted me, and described the measures he had taken to care for his employer's injuries, most of which were prudent and appropriate to Ragoczy's state.*
>
> *Ragoczy himself lay in bed, dozing. He showed no signs of fever: he was, in fact, quite chilly, so while I do*

not believe he will suffer any putrescence of his wounds, he may be reacting to the severity of the attack upon him, which can be dangerous in its own way. There were sixteen severe stabs to his body, another twenty-three assorted cuts and slices, and two abrasions that appear to have been caused when he fell to the ground.

That his assailant intended to inflict serious or even deadly injuries there can be no doubt: the number of wounds indicates that the injuries were deliberate. The reports from the witnesses all confirm: that Enee d'Auville was doing his utmost to deliver fatal blows to the said Ragoczy is beyond cavil; his detention is a sensible precaution, given the extent to which he tried to incapacitate Ragoczy. It required four men to pull the youth off of Ragoczy and to hold him, so I believe it is fair to assume that Enee d'Auville poses a real danger to Ragoczy Ferenz, and for all we can guess, perhaps to others as well.

Let me recommend an extension of the performance license for the Commedia della Morte, for between the rain and this unfortunate incident, it would be unreasonable to expect the troupe to be able to present their play with two of the company unable to participate, and they have paid for the right to perform. It would appear to be that the city has extorted fees from them without providing the opportunity the license is intended to authorize. I have been told that Theron Heurer, the dramatist of the work, is presently revising the script to allow for the loss of one of the actors and the musician.

Since Ragoczy will not be able to travel for some weeks I would recommend adding performances to their license so that they will be able to maintain themselves at the Jongleur until the Revolutionary Court has come to a decision in regard to Enee d'Auville, and

Ragoczy Ferenz has improved to a point that he can safely take to the roads again.

It being close on midnight, this will be put in your hands by nine of the clock tomorrow morning. If you have any additional questions in regard to this case, I will be honored to answer them.

Vive la France!

Vive Lyon

Vive la Revolution

Jules Topinard, physician
#27, Rue des Bergers

3

"The prisoners will be moved within the city walls in four days, which is a performing day for our commedia; the next will be tomorrow," Roger informed da San-Germain three days after the attack upon him; it was mid-morning and the troupe was already setting up the stage on the two wagons in the inn's yard in anticipation of the next day's performance, and the sounds of their labors drifted up to their room. "Their run has been extended by two more performances. The Revolutionary Tribunal approves of it, and thus far there has been no scandal about Enee's attack, or his accusations. Heurer has changed the script so that they won't need Enee."

"How set is that—the day they will move the prisoners? This makes the sixth change so far; is it likely the day will be changed again?"

"It may, but probably not. The weather isn't going to stay clear for much longer, and they don't want to move them in a downpour, or worse."

"And the horses? Have you purchased the number we agreed upon?"

"Yes. They're being kept at a stable on the Saone Road, half a league from the city gates."

Da San-Germain sat a little straighter. "Were they bought outside the city?"

"Of course. And I made sure there was no connection with any member of the troupe. The agent I employed was informed that the horses were needed for a courier service." He did not smile, but a look of satisfaction came over his features.

"How does Photine feel about the run being extended again?" da San-Germain asked abruptly, glancing toward the window and the sound of the players' preparation. For once the sky was nearly clear, and the hazy sunshine brought a brilliance to the world that it had lacked for the greater part of a week.

"She says little to me: only tells me that she expects you to provide the music. Other than that, she isn't forthcoming; Pascal says she's embarrassed by what happened," said Roger. "I believe that embarrassment is a factor for her, but not the only one."

"Does she mean Enee's attempt to kill me when she says 'what happened'?" The question was sharper than he intended, and he cleared his throat and added, "I understand why she might want to express it that way."

Roger nodded. "It's her hope to put the incident in the past; she is giving all her attention to the play and her troupe. That's why they're rehearsing again today, and why she's said she has to have the music for the parade tomorrow, and in four days, since the license for it has come through. Heurer agrees."

"So nothing more about Enee."

"He remains in jail, or so Constance tells me," said Roger.

"I gather he will not be brought to trial soon." For all his voice revealed, they might have been discussing the stenciled decoration above the windows. "By the way, of what crimes has he accused me?"

"Seduction, lewdness, fraud, coercion, endangering Photine's welfare. There may be more, but these are what I've heard."

"Being his mother's lover and forcing her to come to France, in other words," said da San-Germain as if he were talking about something from his distant past. "I suppose he'll bring those things up at his trial."

"It's likely."

"Do you think we'll be here when he does?" He sounded even more detached.

In his long experience with da San-Germain, Roger knew it was folly to challenge him on his apparent indifference. "No; there is too much of a back-log for political cases—he will have to wait his turn, and by then we should be well away from France."

Da San-Germain took a long, slow breath. "Which means that Photine will want to remain here until he's been before the Revolutionary Court."

Roger nodded his agreement. "So she has declared."

"What does the rest of the troupe say?"

"Nothing that they will discuss with me." He shook his head slowly. "No, that's not quite accurate. Valence told me that they weren't all in agreement with her."

"That's hardly surprising," da San-Germain said as he fiddled with the bandage on his thigh. "I doubt they'd discuss it with me, either."

"Probably not, though you are their patron. Pascal is encouraging the rest of the troupe to take no more money from you, and pay their way from the money their play brings in."

"Do the others concur?"

"Some do." Roger faltered, then went on. "The rest do not. They argue about it often. There is growing rancor in the troupe because of this debate."

"All the more reason to keep their opinions to themselves." He stretched awkwardly. "Well, I imagine it would be best for me to make an appearance before them, since there is a performance tomorrow, and with a parade. I'll need something less fitted than most of my clothes."

Roger pulled a black wool swallow-tail coat from the armoire. "Will this do?"

"I trust so; and one of the looser shirts." Da San-Germain, sitting on a chest of his native earth, had recovered a little from Enee's assault, though he still had moments of incapacitating pain; beneath his dressing-robe he was swathed in bandages, and both his eyes were black from the cut on his forehead. "Concerning the prisoners: do we know what time of day they'll be moved?" He considered the possibilities. "It could be a ploy, to continue to announce changes and move them at an entirely different time."

"That's possible," said Roger. "But in this instance, I think there may be some truth to what I've learned."

"Why?"

He considered his response carefully. "It is how I came to learn of it: I had it from one of the Revolutionary Court clerks, who is making arrangements for the transfer and setting up the escort. He was at the Cinq Etoiles—you know, the tavern near the Revolutionary Court's building?—complaining to his fellows about the complications they were encountering in arranging for Guards along the route they were going to use; I happened to overhear him." He studied da San-Germain with concern.

"Happened, old friend?" da San-Germain inquired, a sardonic lift to his brows. "It was an opportunity you came upon by accident?"

"A fortunate chance," Roger said, refusing to be needled.

"Fortunate indeed, if it is accurate. Were the clerks good enough to mention the time of this endeavor?"

Roger had observed this remote, sardonic mood before, and knew that it masked profound misgivings. "Not one of the clerks: a Guard was in the Cinq Etoiles, and he was upset that the plan was for the afternoon, during the riposino. He disapproved of the time: he doesn't want to give up his nap."

"The performance is supposed to be immediately after the riposino rather than before," said da San-Germain, doubts making him critical. "Will the parade permission be upheld, or will the Department of Public Safety withdraw the license?"

"There has been no notice of withdrawal," said Roger. "But

that doesn't mean that the Revolutionary Tribunal or the Revolutionary Court couldn't change its mind."

For a short while, da San-Germain said nothing while he pondered the likelihood of a change; when he looked up at last, he said, "I doubt they will withdraw it: it could give public attention to the transferring of prisoners, assuming that takes place according to plan, and the Department of Public Safety will try to keep everyone distracted while they move their prisoners. The parade will make that possible. It's likely that they chose the time of the parade as a diversion."

"That is likely," said Roger emotionlessly.

"Or I want to believe it enough to decide it must be so," said da San-Germain with a mirthless smile.

"You know my opinion on that," said Roger.

"Yes; and ordinarily I would share it, but just at present, I can't," said da San-Germain, rising from his earth-filled chest. "And for our plan to succeed, I will have to keep the troupe aligned with my purpose, and that will not happen unless they see that I am ready to carry out my part. So I will have to attend at least some of the rehearsal today and join the performance tomorrow, and the parade."

"And what if they decide not to support your plan? That could happen."

Da San-Germain sighed as he straightened up, assuming some of his usual manner. "Ah, you are too acute, old friend. I need to take stock of them, as much as they need to see that I am recovering, to find the answer to your question."

"Are you certain they will tell you their thoughts? Matters here in Lyon are more volatile than they were in Avignon. There are apt to be rifts among the players, as there are rifts in the Revolutionary Court here. The Girondais are holding to their position, let the Assembly in Paris say what it will." Roger glanced toward the door as if he expected to be interrupted. "And there's still the matter of Enee to deal with."

"When we have Madelaine safe, I'll give Photine money

enough to buy his release. That should inspire her to continue with our connivances."

Roger stared at him, unable to conceal his disbelief. "Do you truly want that boy released?"

"Not as a gesture of altruism, I admit: to be certain of Photine's good-will, and to make sure she honors our agreement," said da San-Germain slowly.

"He won't be grateful," Roger warned.

"No, he won't." He untied the sash of his dressing-robe. "He will resent anything I do, or fail to do, so I must put emphasis on Photine, not her son."

"He may try to kill you again."

Da San-Germain shrugged. "If he wants to keep his mother's good opinion that would be unwise." He reached for the shirt Roger held out to him. "He can be bribed out of a cell once, but not twice."

"Do you think that would stop him? He is as likely to defy her as not."

"Very probably," said da San-Germain, taking the shirt as he turned away and took off the dressing-robe in order to don the shirt.

Roger watched him dress, noting the care he took with his movements, the way he guarded his left side where most of the wounds had been inflicted; there was an air of fragility to da San-Germain that Roger rarely detected in him, and it worried him to think that his master was preparing to undertake something as hazardous as removing Madelaine from the Department of Public Safety in just four days. He was aware that da San-Germain would persevere in his plans whether or not he was hurt, and that mentioning his reservations would do no good. Without a word, he gave da San-Germain his black wool unmentionables and watched while he pulled them on. "Do you want help with the coat?" He knew as soon as the words were out that he should not have made the offer.

"I think I'm strong enough to put on a coat," he said, and did his best to demonstrate, taking more time than he would have before the attack, but not bungling the attempt. "There. You see?" He felt the garment, satisfied with what his fingers revealed. "The sleeves aren't twisted and the collar is lying correctly."

"And playing the cimbalom—will you be able to do that?"

"Not terribly well, but enough to satisfy the needs of the play; I'll ask for a stool to sit on at rehearsal. That should help," da San-Germain said as he turned around to face Roger. "You can tell me if the buttons are—"

"Your appearance is quite satisfactory," Roger conceded. "Not quite as elegant as usual, but not disheveled, either."

"The bandages aren't obvious." He felt the front of his coat.

"No. Your eyes are black, but there's nothing beyond that that would suggest you survived a murder attempt three days ago. I'd recommend that you don't overplay your recovery; take the time to show some sign of discomfort, at least."

"It would be nothing less than the truth," said da San-Germain ruefully.

"Good," Roger told him. "They must see the pain of all those stab wounds, or they will begin to wonder."

"Such is my intention," said da San-Germain with genuine satisfaction.

Yet Roger persisted. "And sustenance? have you made any arrangements for that? You won't get over your weakness until you get living blood into you." This blunt a statement was unusual for him, and he emphasized his apprehension with a hard stare. "If you're going to help Madelaine, you need to take nourishment before then."

"I know," da San-Germain admitted. "I think I can find one or two women to visit as a dream, and that will provide enough for now."

"Not Photine?"

"No; she's caught up in performing and would find me disquieting." He said nothing more as he reached for a neck-cloth and began to tie it around his neck.

"She's a risk to your contrivance to gain Madelaine's freedom, my master." He did not add that he thought she was not as reliable as she had been before Enee's assault on da San-Germain.

"Not just at present, I think. She's too concerned about Enee."

"I'm not so sanguine. It seems to be quite a gamble to trust her now, if you ask me—although you didn't." Roger did not raise his voice, or make any sign of distress at da San-Germain's position, but added, "As you say, she is concerned about Enee: who knows what she might use to bargain for his release."

"You mean she might inform on me?"

"Directly or indirectly, yes. She might even believe that she was doing you a service."

"Why would you say that?"

"Because she wants her son out of prison, and I'm not convinced that she would hesitate to use you to bring that about."

Da San-Germain took a minute to ruminate on Roger's worry. When he looked up, he said, "Revealing the intention to remove a prisoner from the Revolutionary Court would not be sufficiently remarkable to warrant any favors beyond something very minor; everyone knows that such attempts are possible, and revealing such a plot—it would not be sufficient to get Enee out of jail no matter how persuasive Photine may be. The spies report constantly on such rumors, and nothing comes of them. To have such a account from a player would likely be regarded as more common gossip."

"But she does know what you plan to do," Roger reminded him. "That could lead to the kind of investigation that—"

"Actually, no; she does not know what I plan to do. Neither she nor Theron knows that: they know what I've told them, which is not my actual plan. Other than you, only Feo knows what I intend, and he won't mention it to anyone." He looked toward the armoire and the chest that stood next to it. "My walking shoes—where are they?"

"I have them in the closet. I refilled the soles and heels yesterday." He went to get them, a little surprised that da San-Germain had not asked for his boots.

As if aware of this, da San-Germain said, "The cut on my calf is too tender for boots. The shoes will be more comfortable."

"They will," Roger agreed, bringing the shoes and stockings to him. "The stockings aren't high enough to bind on the cut."

"Fortunately, they aren't." Da San-Germain went to the upholstered chair at the end of the bed and sat down to allow Roger to put on his stockings and shoes. "When the bandages are off, I can do this well enough, but right now, I can't bend my waist very much, and won't be able to for another month or two."

"Not as bad as Sankt Piterburkh, or Mexico," Roger remarked.

"Or Delhi, or Moscow, or Gorwiecz, or Cyprus, or Lo-Yang, or Fiorenza, or Tunis." He sighed. "Or, or, or."

"It's a long list." Roger put the stockings on with care, and then slid the shoes on. "Try standing."

Da San-Germain complied. "They'll do. I may need to go down the stairs one at a time, but otherwise I can manage."

"Would you like to have a cane?" Roger suggested, anticipating the answer.

"No, old friend. That would give rise to comments from the troupe that could be troublesome." He crossed the room with only a slight limp to show how badly he had been injured.

"You conceal your pain very well, my master," said Roger drily.

"Not well enough if you can see it," was da San-Germain's rejoinder.

"But I know what to look for," Roger said.

"Point conceded," da San-Germain told him with a slight bow. "You have the advantage over the others, old friend, and for that I am relieved."

Roger gave him an austere smile. "Then be willing to take my advice: do not walk far today. There is no reason for you to do more than play for the rehearsal; you need not join the parade before tomorrow's performance."

"Photine wants music, or at least noise, to attract attention. I will need to provide that for her, though she won't expect me to carry the cimbalom and march with the rest." He paused. "Besides, Corpse costumes aside, I want it established that I am part of the parade, so that I will be able to account for my time if I'm asked to do so."

"So you can be elsewhere," Roger said in Byzantine Greek. "You have two drums in your chest that haven't been used, and there is that Turkish trumpet; they can provide noise."

"That's why I brought them," da San-Germain said. "I thought we might have use for them."

"Would you like me to take them out of their trunk?"

"If you would, and bring them down to the inn-yard in an hour or so," said da San-Germain. He started to the door, then stopped. "The physician's report that the Guard demanded: do you know if he has completed it yet?"

"He has. It's with the Department of Public Safety," said Roger.

"Do you know what it says?"

Roger was nonplussed by the question. "I haven't seen it. Does it matter?"

Da San-Germain avoided the question by asking another. "Did the physician tell you anything?"

"Only that you were lucky to be alive, and that your pulse was so faint he wasn't sure you would survive."

"I see. Then, I will have to let my weakness be visible, for if you have learned so much from the physician, then I must assume that Photine has found out much the same information." He stood still, thinking. "I suppose I should use the cane for now, since the physician said my case is severe."

Roger nodded. "A wise decision, my master," he said as he rose.

"You're being most accommodating," said da San-Germain, a speculative flicker in his dark eyes.

"I want to see you and Madelaine safely out of Lyon," said Roger. "If that requires the troupe to achieve that, then I want them to come with us."

"And I want to be done with our tasks here and be on our way out of France as soon as we have Madelaine free from Warden Loup and the Guards, before the city can be shut and the buildings searched. That's going to be more difficult than we originally thought, what with the Commedia della Morte having become so popular." Da San-Germain patted the chest next to the armoire. "Some of the troupe will have to follow us in hired wagons, if they decide to return to Padova; they might not be allowed to cross the border at all."

"That may not be possible no matter when they depart; if we leave riding, the wagons will go more slowly than we do; the troupe won't be willing to go ahead of their wagons and carts, and so will have to stick to the main roads." He frowned as the extent of the problem was borne in on him. "You can hardly blame them: all the things they need to perform are in the wagons and carts."

"You have the right of it. Photine has been very set on that point," da San-Germain concurred.

"Mounted we can use the minor roads, which the wagons cannot traverse. With a little care, we could put ten leagues between us and any pursuit." Roger paused. "If your injuries won't stop you from such a ride."

"Indeed; I will have to manage it. We have several days' journey to reach the border on horseback—longer with the troupe and the vehicles," said da San-Germain. "I've been considering our options for the last day or so. If we were departing from Montalia, we might have been across the frontier in two or three days, and the troupe with us; that was the end of summer, not the end of autumn, and there were few Guards at the crossing we used. Now the roads are muddy and we have perhaps seven days of hard riding on back roads to reach the nearest crossing, where there are few Guards and we are not likely to be detained. If the weather worsens, then it will take longer to leave the country." He pondered their predicament, then said, "I believe we should consult Feo for his advice."

"Do you think he will be able to guide us?" Roger asked, giving da San-Germain his cane; it was of a fashionable height and topped with a jade ferrule.

"I trust he will; I'll have a word with him after rehearsal," said da San-Germain, taking the cane and testing his moving with it. "This will do well enough."

"Very good," said Roger, and went to open the door for him.

It was difficult for da San-Germain to make his way down the main stairs of the Jongleur, but he accomplished his descent in little more than five minutes, with only one uncertain moment when his grip on the banister nearly failed, and when he reached the ground floor, he exchanged greetings with the innkeeper before going out into the yard where the wagons were now set up for the troupe's rehearsal. He stood for a short while at a dozen paces from the troupe, watching them place their set props for the second scene.

Tereson was the first to notice him; she had been sitting on the edge of the stage, but was now on her feet, gesticulating and calling out, "Ragoczy! Ragoczy! You're up!" She swung around toward the stage. "Look, everybody! Ragoczy's here!"

The troupe turned to stare in his direction, and there was a moment of surprised silence. Then Photine got down from the stage and bustled over to him. She had a thick woolen shawl around her shoulders, for once concealing the swell of her bosom, but she curtsied to da San-Germain, and made sure he noticed her sumptuous figure. "I am glad to see you, Ragoczy. I was afraid you would have to remain abed for several more days."

"I'm weaker than I would like to be," he said in a neutral tone.

"But you're much improved," she enthused. "You have some of your color back, and you need only that cane to walk."

Before da San-Germain could speak, Pascal hurried up to him. "Oh, thank God. You seem to be over the worst."

"So I hope," said da San-Germain as Valence and Constance got down from the stage and came toward him. "How good of you to greet me so—"

"Are you going to rehearse with us?" Crepin asked, offering a practiced smile.

"That is my intention," said da San-Germain at his most genial. "I hope that I have stamina enough to complete the whole play with you, but I may have to stop before the end; if I do, you have my apology." He inclined his head a little, in a manner that made him seem somehow taller than he was. "So if I may ask one of you to bring me a stool, we can find out if I am truly improving."

Photine signaled to Pascal, who was still standing next to the joined wagons. "A stool, a tall one, and the cimbalom. It's still in the larger cart. Put them on the stage left side." She took his hand, patting it affectionately. "I hope you will tell me what you think of the new version of the text."

"I will," he pledged. "And to add to your parade, Roger will bring you some drums and pipes and trumpets for all of you to carry. You needn't play them well, just use them for noise. I think there may be cymbals, as well." Da San-Germain gave a slight smile that found a faint reflection in Photine's face. "You'll attract attention, most assuredly."

"Oh, very good. It will give us the opportunity to demonstrate our popularity. Theron, if you would?" She raised her arm and gestured to the poet to approach; Theron complied at once, jumping down from the stage and rushing to her side.

"What is it, Photine?" he asked, watching her with possessive zeal mixed with pride.

This time her smile beamed. "Our problems may be solved. We won't have to bother with chanting or shouting. Ragoczy will provide simple instruments for us." She opened her arms to encompass all her players. "You will all choose your instruments shortly, and you will play them when the Corpses parade through the streets." She started back toward the stage. "We'll talk later, Ragoczy. When the rehearsal is over, there are matters we must discuss."

"As you wish," said da San-Germain, and glanced at Theron. "Have you any time to spare just now?"

Theron nodded to da San-Germain. "Ten minutes. A pleasure to see you out of bed and on your feet, Com—" He stopped himself before he finished the title.

"It is good to be out of bed," da San-Germain said smoothly, then lowered his voice. "I gather there have been some changes in our plans."

Color mounted in Theron's face. "Yes. Yes, there have."

"Can you tell me what these changes comprise?"

"Not now. We should discuss them later."

"After rehearsal?" da San-Germain suggested.

"If you aren't too tired," Theron said.

"We'll have to see." He motioned toward the stage as if content to wait to talk over the changes. "Are you satisfied with your revisions?"

"Not entirely, no," Theron admitted. "But, given the circumstance, I think they'll do well enough. We can make adjustments later." He smiled self-consciously, and hurried on, "The play is gaining quite a reputation. We may have to find a larger stage for the performance after next."

"You must be pleased," said da San-Germain, thinking that Theron was no longer planning to leave the company when Madelaine was free.

"We're doing better here than we did in Avignon. The whole troupe is pleased." He moved a little closer to the stage. "Frankly, I'm glad we don't have to put up with Enee's antics any longer."

"You have found him difficult?" da San-Germain asked at his most urbane.

"Not as difficult as you have, but yes, a problem."

"Heurer!" Photine called from the edge of the stage.

"Coming!" he answered, turned back toward da San-Germain, and shrugged. "She needs me. May we meet later?"

"Later will be fine," was da San-Germain's answer addressed to Theron's back. He stood for a short while, staring into the distance, his thoughts buzzing like saws as he set about how to deliver Madelaine from danger without the help or specific knowledge of Theron Heurer. When he had satisfied himself that he had the skeleton of a plan, he went to tune the cimbalom which was set up at the edge of the stage, sat on the stool, and got out his tuning key.

* * *

Text of a letter from Jean-Marie Collot d'Herbois in Paris to Theron
Baptiste Heurer in Lyon, carried by Revolutionary Assembly courier and delivered three days after it was written.

> *To the most celebrated playwright in all of Lyon,*
> *Theron Baptiste Heurer, Jean-Marie Collot d'Herbois*
> *sends his most profound greetings on this, the 22ⁿᵈ day*
> *of October, 1792.*
>
>   *Esteemed Heurer,*
>
>   *I have had many reports of your remarkable play,*
> Commedia della Morte, *which have reached me in*
> *Paris, and roused my admiration for your talent and*
> *invention, and I have decided that we may be of ser-*
> *vice to one another. All commentary regarding your*
> *play has been fulsome in its praise of your cleverness,*
> *expounding on your wit and philosophy with enthusi-*
> *asm that is not often encountered in these times. There*
> *have been those who claim they were shocked at the*
> *subject matter, but in such an age as this one, who has*
> *not seen much the same in everyday life? Please convey*
> *my congratulations to the troupe performing your*
> *work, for it is generally agreed that they have brought*
> *your scenario to vivid life.*
>
>   *I have recently been informed that I am to be sent*
> *to Lyon shortly to deal with the Girondais there, and*
> *to show them, who are so recalcitrant regarding the*
> *necessity of Louis XVI's execution, which you must*
> *know I have called for a month since, that they are*
> *committing a grave error in seeking to establish a con-*
> *stitutional monarchy and a judicially responsible*
> *Church. Dare I hope that you would be willing to lend*
> *your pen and great gifs to my cause? There would be*
> *opportunities not only for you, but for the troupe with*
> *whom you work. Such decisions cannot be taken with-*

out reflection, so I will not expect your response before the end of this month. Let me assure you that those who do not support or endorse my policies will be permitted to leave Lyon without let or hindrance, if there are members of the troupe who are not in sympathy with the goals I have stated for the progress of the Revolution.

I envision two new scenarios, the texts of which you will pen, showing the future we will have once we are free of the chains wrought by the aristocracy, the clergy, and royalty. When those shackles are at last broken, when the last tool of our subjugation is dead, when our enemies are gone from the earth, France will emerge as a shining example for all the nations of the world to be guided by and emulate. Tyranny must end, and those who embrace tyranny must perish with it. Unlike America, where no one ever had to endure the burdens imposed by high-born despots and the minions of a corrupt clergy, we have an obligation to sweep away those elements of oppression and awaken the spirits of our people. Our collaboration will make it possible for everyone to see what we may achieve once those despicable nobles and clerics are no longer our masters.

I ask you in the name of the glorious Revolution to help me complete the work that has at last begun, to raze the edifice of monocracy from the land we both love, to banish all trace of the land-holders and aristocracy from within our borders through the device Doctor Guillotine has provided for that purpose, and to usher in the new age of Liberty, Fraternity, and Equality.

Vive la France!

Vive le Revolution!

Jean-Marie Collot d'Herbois

4

"Are you sure of this?" da San-Germain asked Feo in a near-whisper; they were in the stable grooming the horses and mules while the troupe gathered in the large parlor to confer on the offer that had arrived from Jean-Marie Collot d'Herbois yesterday; most of the actors were eager to accept the offer, but Crepin and Constance were leery of the dangers of being caught up in politics, and Valence worried about how they would be paid; Photine's excitement for the project ranged from forcefully logical to grandiloquent. So far they had spent two hours in discussion, and it seemed likely that they would continue for another two hours, giving da San-Germain and Feo ample time to tend to the horses and mules; as the afternoon was waning, a thin fog was moving in off the river, bringing a penetrating chill to the city. "They've changed plans again?" He cursed himself for the time he had spent lying atop his native earth instead of seeking to free Madelaine from prison. "I dislike having to improvise."

"Yes, the plans are changed: I'm certain of it because I heard it from two officers," Feo said in Italian while using the stiff brush on the muddy legs of a liver sorrel gelding; he was crouched down behind the half-wall that separated the stalls. "The Guard in the tavern by the north gate was complaining about yet another change just as you are. He's unhappy with the old Saone River Road. He thinks his superiors are being too clever, trying to outwit an opponent who doesn't exist. He dislikes night duty: he says it's too easy for enemies to attack late at night, and to make good their escape."

"He may be right," said da San-Germain with grim humor. "Who was your second source?"

"A groom at the Guards' stable. He told me that they were going to have to house another fifteen horses at two in the morning. He wasn't very happy about it."

"Why did he tell you this?"

"He knows I'm a coachman, and we occasionally talk about what our work demands of us. I see him at the horse-market, where I go to buy the feed you require. Since his family is from Torino, he regards me almost as a cousin, being frank with me and expressing himself openly when we talk." Feo sensed some reservation from da San-Germain, so he added, "He and I discuss the horses for sale, and we usually agree about them, so we've become a bit friendly."

"How much have you told him about your own work?"

Feo grinned roguishly as he stood up, returning the brush to the box of grooming tools set on the top of the half-wall. "I tell him what it's like to drive for a troupe of performers, with just enough gossip to give him a thrill. He's occasionally said he'd like doing my job for a change—drive around the country, staying here a while and there a while. He used to be a coachman, before he overturned one of those heavy Hessian coaches and broke three bones from the crash. He misses driving." As if in sympathy with the groom, Feo found a rag and used it on the bridle hanging on a hook outside the door, giving it a cursory cleaning.

"Do you think he's reliable?"

"He gains nothing by lying."

Da San-Germain gave himself a little time to cogitate, and finally asked, "Do you have any reason to suspect he might be misinformed?"

"Deliberately, you mean? I doubt it. What would be the benefit?" Feo shook his head. "Most Guards still seem to think that it will be during the day, and on the new road."

"No benefit to the groom, but the same thing you and I are doing now—doing our best to keep a secret secret." He was growing tired, but did not stop his chore. "Photine was right about theatrical companies—keeping secrets is impossible—and I imagine that it's much the same for others who must live and work closely together."

"The groom isn't privy to most of the rumors the Guards share among themselves. He has his own sources," Feo said.

"And what are they?"

"The Guards' servants, of course." Feo chuckled. "Servants know everything."

"But why tell him the truth?"

"They need his help; same with the Guard. There are occasional clandestine missions the Guards undertake that require his services. He told me about this in confidence."

"As you've been told other information in confidence." Da San-Germain shook his head. "If this is the plan they will use, we will have much to do in the next few hours." He wished he were stronger, more recovered from Enee's attack, for he would need every atom of strength he possessed to get through what lay ahead. At least, he reminded himself, the transfer would be at night when he would have more energy than he would in daylight, and he could use the time to rest on his native earth.

"That means that we must take her tonight. She'll be in the new jail by morning, and then the thing becomes insurmountable." Feo put the bridle back on the hook, then took a heavy comb to work on the liver sorrel's flaxen mane. "The plan for tomorrow is for show, but with no real prisoners, so it may have another purpose. They want to bring out the supporters—"

"—of those who oppose wholesale executions, and the Girondais." Da San-Germain nodded his understanding.

"All those who don't like the idea of killing King Louis." He stopped combing the mane on the large gelding. "It's a trap, Conte, the announced transfer. They want the Girondais to make an attempt to save the prisoners, so that they can be detained."

"It may well be," da San-Germain said, unperturbed. "It's what others have done before them." He recalled a similar feint used by Gaius Julius Caesar during his campaign in Gaul, and the deceptions practiced on the pilgrims bound for Ethiopia.

"What will that do to the troupe? If there is a disruption that isn't of their making, will they be held responsible?"

"As a scapegoat, you mean? I think it likely that the Department of Public Safety is inclined to see the parade and performance as the work of pawns in their chess game, to be moved and sacrificed as needed. So long as we serve their purpose, the troupe is safe enough." He took a jar of ointment and spread some of the odorous contents on a small cut on the mule's rump. "Looks like a buckle-rub from the crupper," he remarked to the mule.

"Then you don't expect any trouble coming to the troupe on account of our rescue of your kinswoman?" For the first time Feo seemed worried.

"Why should there be?" He was less certain of this than he sounded, but kept his reservations to himself.

"The Guards and the Department of Public Safety know about you. You've been to see her. There's a record of your visit. If she's gone, the Guards will want to question you."

"Then she mustn't be the only prisoner freed, so that she and I are not singled out," said da San-Germain, casting back over all the possibilities that had occupied his thoughts while he struggled to overcome the pain of his wounds. "We must take as many of the prisoners as we can, and set them moving away from Lyon by as many roads as possible, so that the Guards will have to spend days trying to hunt them all down. Madelaine will stay with us—not here, but near enough—through the coming performance, but then she, and you and I and Roger, must be on the road away from here. We can't risk her recapture; the troupe would suffer for it."

"So!" Feo exclaimed.

"And if we disable the carriages with the prisoners outside the city walls, the officials are more likely to suppose the troupe had nothing to do with it."

"But, Conte, they might think that you did."

"Why would they suspect that? I am known to be recovering from stab wounds and am only just out of bed. I haven't been asking for information about the prisoners except when and how I might present a plea on Madelaine's behalf before the Revolutionary Court." Da San-Germain wiped his hands free of the last bit of ointment. "The only schedule for the prisoners I know is the one given to the troupe yesterday, the one that coordinates our parade with their transfer. Anything they might be expecting me to do would have to be based on what the troupe knows, since I've had no other notification." Da San-Germain patted the mule's neck.

"Are you certain that the troupe will stand by you?" Feo asked. "Madame is already saying the troupe may decide to remain here when we leave."

"I will be more certain once you and I have prepared for to-night. Since we must improvise, let us keep our plans to ourselves. Only Roger should know of them." It was not an answer and he knew it; he could not admit the doubts that had been burgeoning in him since Enee was taken to jail; Photine had been busy trying to get him released, and would let nothing interfere with her mission, no matter who might be damaged by her efforts. "It's inconvenient to be so pressed, but that's out of our hands." He stepped back from the mule, turning his attention to the jenny on the other side of the stall.

"Are you planning to use any of these horses for our delivering tonight?"

"No," da San-Germain replied. "Their absence would be noticed."

"But you can't go out and buy a dozen horses in the next two hours and expect no one will see the—"

"The horses are taken care of already."

"You've had a ruse in mind all along."

"Not all along, perhaps, but I have developed one in my mind during the last two days. I hope it will suffice." Da San-Germain tapped the stiff brush against the side of the stall to be rid of the flakes of mud on it. "One that may work more effectively at night, provided the new schedule for the transfer holds. Roger has already set it in motion."

"What does that do for the parade?" Feo asked a short while later as he finished picking out the hooves of the red-spotted mare who shared the stall with the liver sorrel.

"I don't know, and that troubles me." Da San-Germain's wounds were aching; he moved away from the jenny he had started brushing in order to stretch, easing his muscles. "The Department of Public Safety may postpone it, or they may want it as a distraction, as we've supposed from the start."

"So what do we do?"

The question hovered like a mote in the air; da San-Germain took more than a minute to form his response. "You and I and Roger will have to take Madelaine tonight; if we can discover it, we'll want to know which coach she's in—they're still planning to use coaches, aren't they?—and what route they will take. The route is more important than the coach."

"The three of us? Not the poet?"

"No," said da San-Germain, picking up the shears to clip the mule's mane. "He has other things on his mind."

Feo did his best not to laugh. "Just as well; he talks too much for safety," he said, and took the soft face-brush to use on the mare's head. "Are you still going to bring your kinswoman to the troupe to conceal her?"

"No. I had thought it might be feasible, but clearly it's not. It would be too dangerous for all of us." After a brief silence, he looked over at Feo. "What time are they planning to start the move?"

"The Guard said they'd leave the old monastery around eleven. That would bring them into the city before two of the clock."

"Then we'll need to be gone from here by nine." He flexed his hands and felt a sharpening ache in his shoulder. "What more have you learned?"

"Three reinforced coaches with three armed coachmen and postilions, twenty-two prisoners, and an escort of ten riders: three in front, three behind, and two between the coaches. The Guard thought they should have more." Feo looked up from his grooming. "Three of us against ten riders and three postilions. Not very good odds."

Da San-Germain was pleased to know the escort was minimal. "Better ten than fifteen riders and six postilions. I want you to go to the Guards' headquarters. Do not be obvious. Have an excuse for your presence—perhaps say you have a nephew who wants to join and needs to know how to apply, or that you would like to find out the condition of the road between here and Nevers, or that you're looking for a dependable harness-maker. Those are questions any-one might ask the Guards."

Feo nodded with excitement. "I will do it. I will be back before nine tonight, if that will lend you enough time to complete your plans."

"There is work to do yet, but we should be able to accomplish it handily. Roger has found the place where we can waylay the coaches, and will take us there." He hoped he would not be worn down by pain before they had Madelaine safe. "I trust they will go on the Saone Road as far as the Saone River Gate."

"I reckon that's their plan. The other roads would require at least an hour more to traverse, and none of the Guards wants to be outside the city at night." Feo took flint-and-steel from his waist-coat pocket and went to light the lantern hanging from a nail on the nearest pillar.

Da San-Germain stopped him. "Leave it dark. The grooms will have finished their supper and we should be gone from here before they return."

"Why? Don't you want them to be able to say we were here?"

"They know that; they saw us come out to tend to the horses while they were crossing the stable-yard from the stage," said da San-Germain. "Let them assume what they will."

"If you insist," said Feo, returning the flint-and-steel to his pocket. "We've finished the grooming. The ostlers will see that."

"Then let's return to the inn. The troupe should have com-pleted their meeting and will be sitting down to supper shortly." He stretched again, wincing a little at the pain this caused. "If you'll tell them I've gone up to bed, I would be grateful."

"Should I tell them I'll be at the Guards' tavern?" Feo ventured.

"If that seems sensible, yes; otherwise tell them nothing." Da

San-Germain let himself out of the mules' stall, and shot the brace, taking care to set the latch so that the mules could not reach it; he picked up his cane and started toward the door.

Feo came out of the horses' stall, and shoved the brace into position, flipping the latch to hold it in place. "I'll be back a little before nine. Where should I meet you?" He fell in beside da San-Germain.

"Roger and I will be at the side-gate, the one facing the alley. We'll have to go on foot to the old Saone Road Gate, and we don't want to be noticed, or stopped. I'll bring a cloak for you, one that none of the troupe has seen."

"But if they don't see us go, why—?"

"Because if our descriptions are given, our garments mustn't be familiar; that would excite more suspicions than if the stopping of the coaches appears to be the work of mercenaries," said da San-Germain, and held the stable-door open for Feo. "It would have been easier had we been able to keep to the plan with the troupe."

Feo scowled. "The actors agreed to the risks at the beginning."

"When we believed that the farthest we would have to go was Avignon. We have mountains to cross and bad weather coming. Circumstances have changed."

"They knew that was a possibility, and they consented," Feo said, stamping one foot for emphasis. "They must be ready to keep to our purpose."

"Not if they aren't reliable, or if it puts them in greater danger than they already are." Da San-Germain worked to swing his leg without any sign of discomfort.

"You're walking better," Feo observed as they set the brace on the door and went across the stable-yard.

"Not well enough to be rid of this cane," da San-Germain said, his face set in lines of dissatisfaction.

A scullion was busy scrubbing a large pot outside the kitchen door; he looked up as da San-Germain and Feo went past him and through the servants' door.

"Will he be a problem?" Feo asked, cocking his head in the direction of the scullion.

"I doubt it," said da San-Germain, steadying himself for the climb up the narrow, steep stairs. "Learn what you can and be ready to go at nine."

"I will," said Feo, remaining at the foot of the stairs. "Rest well, Ragoczy."

"Thank you; it is my intention." He offered Feo a hint of a bow, then continued up to his room as quickly as his aching hip would allow, where he found that Roger had laid out garments for their night escapade, with an English four-caped driving-cloak atop the garments, concealing them from curious eyes. The Russian tunic and wide pantaloons made interesting lumps under the cloak, but could not easily be recognized by the odd shapes they presented. Smiling, da San-Germain saw the small table by the window set with a plate, a knife, and a fork; Roger would return shortly with his supper. Sighing, da San-Germain removed his paddock boots and lay down on the thin mattress spread out on one of his chests; this one contained not clothes, but his native earth. He settled himself, his arms at his sides, his legs together, letting the annealing presence of his native earth work to restore him while he sank into the stupor that was his version of sleep.

The room was dark when he awoke, with only a single candle to relieve the gloom. He sat up slowly, feeling renewed strength in his body, though the wounds still hurt.

"It is eight of the clock, my master," said Roger in Byzantine Greek from the far side of the room.

"Time to be up. We have just under an hour," da San-Germain said in the same language as he got down from the chest, then turned to roll up the mattress, securing it with two lengths of rope when he was done.

"I'll put that away for you," said Roger, coming to take it from him.

"Then take what I'm wearing, would you? The shirt is in need of washing, don't you think?" da San-Germain asked as he unfastened the buttons of his coat and let it drop to the floor. "The coat wants brushing."

"As well as the unmentionables and the waistcoat," Roger agreed, picking up the coat and holding out his hand for the rest of the clothes.

Before he put on the Russian apparel, da San-Germain checked his nine bandages, and found them to be securely in place. "When we come back tonight, I'd like to bathe. It will be very late, and that may cause difficulties."

Roger understood his meaning. "Some of the servants will know of it, and that could be reported if there are questions asked here."

"Can you arrange now for a bath to be brought up at dawn?" da San-Germain asked. "You can say that is so my wounds can be properly cleaned and treated, which is near the truth." He pulled the cincture at the waist, then slipped two franciscas into place at the small of his back; the little throwing-knives lay comfortably there.

"It would be better if I went down when the cook begins his day, so I can say you didn't sleep well," said Roger as he watched da San-Germain tie the dark-red pantaloons' drawstring before he donned the black tunic with the standing collar and embroidered cuffs. "The boots are in the armoire."

"Excellent." Low light did not interfere with his sight; da San-Germain gave Roger a quick scrutiny. "Dull-gray. A good color for going about at night."

"So I thought," said Roger. He wore a workman's smock over old-fashioned trews; he was shod with Polish shearling boots.

"Do you have somewhere in the chest a cloak that would do for Feo? Everyone in the troupe can describe his coachman's cloak."

"There's a Bohemian sleeved cape that should fit him; you know the one? It's dull-green," said Roger after a brief reflection.

"And hats?"

"I'll put on the Polish hat once we're beyond the walls; I'll have yours as well: the Russian one with the ermine crown. I can find something for Feo."

"The horses are ready?"

"They will be; the posting inn has been informed of our coming: I attended to that during the afternoon," said Roger, dismissing the gesture of thanks da San-Germain offered with a turn of his hand. "It should take half an hour to reach the posting inn. The old road is narrow, but lightly traveled, and those both suit our purpose."

"Very good." He found the boots, with leggings rolled up in them; sitting on the edge of the bed, he pulled them on. "Is the troupe up?"

"They're in the rear parlor."

"Still discussing whether to remain here or not?" da San-Germain inquired, his fine brows raised incredulously.

"No. Heurer has written some new lines that Photine is eager to try out." He tossed da San-Germain his cloak.

"More changes for the performance, I suppose?"

"No; this is something new, for Collot d'Herbois."

"Ah," said da San-Germain. "Then the troupe is planning to remain here." He realized his hold on them was over and that he could not depend upon them any longer.

"Heurer is, and so long as Enee is in jail, Photine is as well; I don't know about the rest."

"Those who have reservations may want to follow us back to Padova," said da San-Germain, and returned to more pressing matters. "We can go out the kitchen door. The scullions should be at their supper."

"The cook is in the taproom, cutting slabs off the roasted pig, so we're not likely to be noticed." Roger nodded.

"Or so we trust," said da San-Germain, a faint, mordant smile curving his lips.

"How long will it take you to get down the stairs?"

This was a crucial problem, and da San-Germain weighed his reply carefully. "If I don't use the cane, perhaps three minutes: with the cane, two."

"Then we should start down in ten minutes."

"I concur," said da San-Germain.

"What of Feo?" Roger asked a few minutes later.

"He'll be at the side-gate. Is it open, do you know?"

Roger patted his pocket. "I have the key, and I oiled the hinges while you were asleep, after I'd been to the posting inn."

"Provident as always," da San-Germain said. "Is there anything else you have anticipated that I have not?"

"I have sacking to wrap our boots if we need to be silent," said Roger, his faded-blue eyes revealing little of the satisfaction he felt. "And I have lengths of cord, to tie up the Guards."

"My apologies, old friend," said da San-Germain. "I have been inexcusably lax. You have thought of everything."

"As you would have done, had you not been injured. I will neaten the room," he declared, and went to gather up the bones from the rabbit that had served as his supper and piled them neatly on the tray that the serving girl had brought up while da San-Germain had been resting. He said nothing more until da San-Germain glanced at the clock on the mantel.

"Time to be gone," he said, getting to his feet and setting his cane aside.

Roger picked up a small bag that bulged. "You will bring your English cloak?"

"Certainly." He took it from the end of the bed and hung it over his arm. "I assume you have the pistols in there?"

"Yes; they're charged and ready. There's also a duck's-foot. It's old-fashioned but it serves its purpose. The six barrels are all ready."

"Very good," da San-Germain approved as they went out into the hall; he looked in both directions and was glad that he saw no one. "Let us go down." He began to ease himself down the stairs. "Remember to speak with a German accent when we stop the coaches. The Guards will take note of it when they make their report."

"Of course," said Roger. "What of Feo?"

"His accent is enough as it is," da San-Germain said, and went down another step.

There was a good deal of noise from the taproom that covered the sound of their descent. As they reached the lower hall, Roger went ahead of da San-Germain, making a swift surveillance of the kitchen, then, satisfied that the room was empty, motioning to da San-Germain to follow. They went through the kitchen rapidly, without incident, and into the kitchen-yard, where they kept to the shadows to avoid attracting any attention while they took stock of their situation. The stable-yard appeared to be vast as the Piazza San Pietro in Roma, and as exposed; they stopped again to determine how best to cross it.

"There're two ostlers by the main gate," da San-Germain whispered. "We'll have to go along the wall. It will take a little longer, but it will be safe."

Roger peered into the darkness, and was able to make out the two ostlers who kept their post by the main gate, smoking their pipes and engaging in a desultory conversation. "Should we put on our cloaks?"

"I think so," said da San-Germain, and pulled his around his shoulders; the deep-brown wool served to conceal him where he stood in the shadows.

When Roger had donned his cloak, he raised the collar so that only the upper half of his head was visible above it. "Hats?"

"Not yet. They're distinctive enough to be identified later, if it comes to that. Keep them under your cloak until we're outside the city." Da San-Germain eased his way along the wall, not moving quickly, but steadily, toward the side-gate, having recourse to his cane only once; he reminded himself that he had endured much worse at the hands of Timur-i and Srau's cousins, memories that kept him moving. Ten paces from the side-gate, he stopped at the sound of two cats challenging each other to battle on the wall above them.

The ostlers looked toward the sound; one of them picked up a pebble and shied it at the animals, cursing good-naturedly. Only when they had resumed their meandering conversation did da San-Germain and Roger move again.

At the side-gate, Roger took out the key and carefully turned it, cringing at the faint sound of moving wards that ended in a snick. "It's open."

Da San-Germain went through ahead of Roger, making a swift scrutiny of the alley. To his relief, he saw Feo in the shelter of the door opposite the side-gate, lounging against the iron-work grille. He hurried across the narrow pave-stones to where Feo waited. "You're here in good time."

"Fortunate, isn't it?" Feo's irreverent smile glinted.

"For you as well as us," da San-Germain responded without amusement. "We may jest when we've done."

Roger opened his bag and brought out the green Bohemian sleeved cape, handing it to Feo as he said, "You'd best put this on after we pass through the city gate. I'll dispose of it before we get back to the Jongleur."

Feo took the Bohemian cape and folded it with the lining out. "Part of our disguises?"

"Yes," said da San-Germain. "Tell me what you've found out."

"The transfer will go according to plan, but some of the prisoners will be held back and moved tomorrow as announced; from what I heard, they're shifting the riskier ones tonight. The Guards think the notion is foolish, but they know that orders are orders, and there is extra pay for night escort. The prisoners being moved tonight are the ones deemed to be most dangerous, which probably means rich. I couldn't find out who they were, but it's likely your kinswoman is among them."

"How likely?" da San-Germain demanded in a whisper.

"If she's rich and she isn't ill, she'll be in one of the coaches, probably the one in the middle." Feo lifted his chin. "So, do we go or not?"

"We go," said da San-Germain, with a side-long glance at Roger. Quelling his doubts, he moved to the end of the alley and gazed out at the street, trying to take in as much as possible without exposing himself to notice: there was a small, rowdy group in front of the tavern at the corner, where gambling was allowed, and occasional cock-fights were held; beyond them a pair of street-sweepers were pushing their well-laden barrow toward the riverbank; four merchants on horseback with a train of pack-mules loaded with casks and crates were approaching from the south; and three thin women shivered with cold as they strutted toward the men in front of the tavern, seeking customers among them.

"We can fall in behind the merchants," Feo suggested. "That will get us across the place and into another street."

"If we make it seem we are part of their company, we aren't likely to attract much attention," da San-Germain agreed. "Be ready to slip in after the mules pass." He could feel his hip tightening and willed it to relax; he could not let himself limp now.

"Ready?" Feo asked as he moved, adopting the same plodding pace of the half-dozen attendants leading the mules.

Roger and da San-Germain followed after him, taking him as their example, and paying no heed to the stares of the attendants.

Approaching the nearest attendant, Feo murmured, "Footpads tried to rob us; we need cover," and nodded his thanks at the glimmer of understanding in the man's eyes.

Nothing more was asked or said as they went on across the place, where they left the merchants' train behind for the long, twisting, dark street that led to the old Saone River Gate.

Text of a letter from Oddysio Lisson in Venezia to Cataline Utoc in Marseilles, written in French, carried on the Eclipse Trading Company ship *West Wind,* and delivered twelve days after it was written.

> *To the distinguished merchant Cataline Utoc of Utoc &*
> *Fils in the port of Marseilles, greetings from Oddysio*
> *Lisson of Eclipse Trading Company in Venezia on this,*
> *the 19th day of October, 1792,*
> > *My dear Utoc,*
> > *I have in hand your letter of September 22nd, and I*

*thank you for the efforts you have made on behalf of
my employer, Ferenz Ragoczy, Conte da San-Germain:
I know it cannot have been easy to gather such intelligence. While your people did not discover where he is,
they did find out where he isn't, and that, in its way, is
most useful. If you should learn anything of him, I ask
you to send me word as quickly as possible. From what
I have been able to learn, there have been many changes
in France in the last few months, and reports received
here are causing a great deal of alarm. If half of what
we're being told is true, how very sad for France.*

*Would you advise me on what would be best to do?
I implore you to be candid with me, for I am in such a
dither that I can hardly clear my thoughts enough to
consider the problem sensibly. I am considering sending a few of my men to France to make inquiries regarding il Conte. He has, as you know, been traveling
with a theatrical troupe, but that may have changed,
and since we have had no word from him or about him,
I believe it is part of my duties as his factor to do what
I can to locate him and discover if any mischance has
befallen him. Yet with all the dreadful accounts coming
from France, I think it may be possible to increase his
danger if there should be inquiries made regarding
him. Were you in my position, what would you advise?
What little information your agents were able to glean
is sufficient to convince me that seeking il Conte out
could have exactly the opposite result than what I am
hoping for: it could attract notice that would be detri-
mental to him, and to his trading company.*

*If there is someone you know who could be of use
in sorting out this conundrum, I ask you to send me his
name and where he may be found, for I am presently of
the opinion that having a Frenchman rather than a
Venezian pursue this matter would be prudent at this*

time, but that may be a misapprehension on my part. As you can see from what I have written, I am of two minds in regard to this state of affairs, and I am certain that nothing I can do or say at this point will answer the problem that confronts me.

You can understand why I am eager to proceed, but in what way do I go? And to what end? How can I gain the information I seek without jeopardizing my inquirer and his object of inquiry? Yet I must do something, and soon. There are ships in need of refitting, and ships that are ready to set out, but without il Conte's approval, their captains are reluctant to set to sea. Il Conte gave me letters of authorization, but for those captains not based in Venezia, they are dubious about accepting my orders without the certainty that they are il Conte's as well. In order to keep trading, I must know what has become of il Conte, and the sooner I know, the better.

Whatever guidance you can provide me, I will welcome, and thank you from the depths of my heart for it. Truly, I haven't any plan that would seem workable at this time, yet it is apparent to me that I must do something, which is why I importune you in this way to lend your wisdom to my predicament.

With a humble heart, I commend myself to your good offices, and thank you for your service on my behalf. May you find rich rewards for your kindness here on earth as well as in Heaven.

> *Oddysio Lisson*
> *Factor, the Eclipse Trading Company*
> *Venezia*

5

In the taproom below, the clock was striking ten, its unmelodic clang penetrating the clamor of the patrons; in her room, Photine sat in front of her mirror, putting the finishing touches on her make-up. She moved the candles a little closer to the shiny surface, then leaned forward and painted the lip rouge on her mouth, taking care to keep the color even. When she was done, she put the small pot of reddened woolfat-and-wax aside, sat back, and subjected herself to critical scrutiny. "This is for Enee," she whispered over and over to herself, making a litany of the words. "You know how to handle men, my girl," she told her reflection. "This man is little more than a clerk; Enee needs his good-will. I will secure it for him, if it's in my power." Since she had received the invitation from Deputy Secretary Charlot to call at his house to discuss Enee's case, she had been of two minds. Was he actually willing to accept a bribe to set her son free, or was this a ploy to get her alone with him for other reasons? That was the one possibility that bothered her, and deprived her any trace of a thrill she might have had from such an undertaking; she had seen enough of men to know that they often sought to take advantage of women through their greatest vulnerability—their children. "If it's my body he wants, so be it, so long as Enee is released," she said with the firm commitment that she used when she played Antigone, even while trying to decide if she were presenting the appearance Charlot hoped for. Was this what Deputy Secretary for Public Safety Vivien Zacharie Charlot desired? She had tried for a careful mix of matronly and courtesanish. Would he find her pleas convincing? Would he be willing to spare her son? She was still a little perplexed by his agreeing to speak with her about Enee—she had been told by several Guards that the Deputy Secretary did not grant interviews to anyone with a relative in custody, and so had not expected the invitation that had arrived the day before, asking her to call at his house at ten-thirty this evening. "Remember, he's a man; he will welcome flattery as his due; you know how to do that," she advised herself.

A ragged chorus of *En Avaunt* rose from the taproom, and the stomping of feet for the verse. It grew steadily louder, then quieted when the innkeeper bellowed something at the singers.

Photine let the stirring melody spur her to action. "It would not do to be late," she said. Then she frowned at her face in the mirror, once again trying to decide what his purpose might be. "This is for Enee," she told herself again, resuming her inspection. If only she knew more about his tastes, she could shape her appearance to suit his fancy, but as it was, she would have to find a way to make the most of the evening or leave Enee to the capricious mercy of the Revolutionary Tribunal and the Revolutionary Courts—a thought that left her queasy. Deciding at last that she had done what she could to make herself compelling, she blew out her dressing-table candle and got to her feet, her taffeta petticoats rustling as she moved. Her corsage was simple—white silk embroidered with pale flowers, with a small ruff around the Italian neckline—and complemented the light-green sash that set off her figure admirably, and made the silken skirt flare over the very moderate bolster-roll beneath. She took her evening cloak—a fashionable garment of super-fine wool lined in pale-blue satin—and drew it over her elegant attire, picked up her muff by thrusting her left hand into it, and after a last glance in the mirror, let herself out of her room, moving as quietly as she could along the corridor. It would be difficult to explain to her troupe what she was doing, going out so late at night—she reminded herself that her departure had to be clandestine, "For Enee's sake."

At da San-Germain's room she paused, debating if she ought to inform him of what she was about to do, knowing that she could rely on his confidence. But as quickly as the notion occurred, she realized he would caution her against her plan, and perhaps go so far as to spell out the risks she was taking, or insist on accompanying her, which would discourage her at the time she needed encouragement. With a short, regretful sigh, she moved on, deciding she would explain herself the following morning, when she would know if she had succeeded in gaining Enee's liberty, and could rely on him for praise or sympathy. In the morning she would speak to him, she promised herself, when the evening with Charlot was over.

She had forgotten how dark the streets could be on a cloudy night, how cavernous the narrow streets with lanterns only at the corners were; leaving the torch-lit inn-yard, she struck off in the direction of Rue Thomas Paine—which not so long ago had been the Rue Saint-Hilaire—and the house of Deputy Secretary Charlot. She had memorized the directions that were included with the invitation, but now she had trouble remembering them as she made her way toward the Rue Tilleul; the darkness made the distances hard to judge, and the landmarks unfamiliar. To her surprise, she was shivering, and not only from the evening chill. Chiding herself for lack of purpose, she nevertheless made a point of avoiding the Guards Patrols making their way through the city streets; there were stories about what they did to women found out alone after dark, and it did not suit her purposes to be thrust into a prostitutes' cell to wait for morning and the indignity of appearing in court. Briefly she wondered if she should have told one of the troupe where she was going, but quickly decided that would have been folly, and not because all the actors would know within an hour of her errand; that might mean that da San-Germain would hear of her actions before she returned, and she could not believe that he would not attempt to intervene. She shook her head and hurried on, wanting to get off the street as soon as she could. The sooner she reached Charlot, the sooner Enee would be safe.

The house, when she found it, gave her a feeling of disquiet: it was about a century old, narrow, three storeys topped by a mansard roof, set between two larger buildings, both of which looked to her to be unoccupied, and having only three windows facing the street. Since it was placed back a little way from the pavement, it gave the appearance of something concealed. A single lantern over the door provided the light up the short walk to the front door. Photine looked down, suppressing a shudder, for the movement of her skirts cast shadows eerie as slithering serpents. Reaching the door, Photine had a sudden urge to turn back, but she staunchly over-ruled her trepidations, telling herself that she had handled more difficult men than Charlot in her time. She pulled her right hand from her muff, and sounded the knocker, making herself breathe slowly and steadily while she waited for the door to open; while she listened for the approach of a servant, she prompted herself of her coming interview of her intent—"This is for Enee, for my son"—and that she had sufficient experience of men to be able to handle this one bureaucrat, no matter what powers he wielded.

"You arrive promptly; it lacks two minutes of ten-thirty," said Charlot as he opened the door. "Do come in, Madame d'Auville." He stepped back, giving her room to pass into the small foyer; he was dressed in an amber-colored dressing-robe over woolen unmentionables and Ottoman slippers. His shirt was open at the throat and she was fairly certain that he wore no waistcoat. Stubble darkened his jaw, and his medium-brown hair was caught at the back of his neck with a narrow ribband. "I am delighted to see you."

"And I you," she said as she had rehearsed it. "And to be asked to your house is an honor, for which I am most grateful."

"I suppose you were . . . discreet?"

Photine managed not to bristle. "I would not want to compromise either of us. Only one of my troupe knows I'm gone from the inn."

"That is wise of you. If it were known that I occasionally hear petitioners here, in private, I would be besieged. I trust you will keep my confidence regarding this evening." His chuckle was without warmth. "Enter. Please."

Photine gave a slight curtsy before she entered the small room, half-expecting a servant to relieve her of her cloak and muff, but none came. Making the best of an awkward situation, she divested herself of her cloak and held it out to him. "Where shall you hang this, Deputy Secretary? Or tell me where and I will attend to it." Her smile was deliberately tantalizing, showing that she did not mind that they seemed to be alone.

Charlot confirmed this, saying, "My housekeeper is with her brother's family tonight, and my cook retired an hour since. We will not be disturbed," as he took her cloak and dropped it over a broad peg behind the front door. "If you will give me your muff?"

She relinquished it to him, noticing that he dropped it on a narrow bench under the high window that would provide the only daylight to the room; it seemed an odd place to put it. Perhaps, she thought, he had no cloak closet at all—many of these old houses did not. "I am aware that you are a busy man, Deputy Secretary."

"The burden of my office, Madame," he said with a kind of automatic courtesy that reminded her that she would have to be succinct. "You wish to discuss your son's incarceration with me."

The bluntness of his statement brought her up short; she struggled to keep from launching into disclaimers, and instead nodded, matching candor with candor. "Yes, that is my intention, if you will give me the opportunity to do so."

"Of course, Madame." He very nearly smiled.

"You are the official who has the authority to decide what will become of my son—"

"Yes, yes; I understand your reason for accepting my invitation."

She felt a grue slide up her spine; she covered this with a winsome glance. "Then I appreciate you taking time to hear me out, Deputy Secretary. I would not like to think I am on a fool's errand."

"And I am disinclined to waste time, as well." He touched her shoulder, hardly more than a brush of his fingers, but he had Photine's full attention. "The trouble is that your son murderously attacked one of your company, and that cannot be entirely set aside.

Now, if there are extenuating circumstances to his act, there may be a means to resolve the case without the necessity of a trial." He paused, pursing his lips thoughtfully. "You must know that I'm eager to discuss this legal predicament with you, Madame," he said; Photine wondered if she had heard a note of derision in his words; she questioned herself inwardly if this might be because he was used to listening to the pleas of distraught mothers, fathers, sisters, brothers, and children on behalf of those the Department of Public Safety had detained. "If you will go through the door on your left?"

"Thank you, Deputy Secretary," she said, and opened the door into a small but surprisingly elegant salon, with a fire burning and two branches of candles lit. The walls were covered with watered silk the color of pomegranates, and there were two small, scroll-armed sophas upholstered in wine-colored brocade flanking a low, claw-footed table with a brass top, where a bottle filled with an opalescent liquid stood, with two small glasses and a bowl of sugar beside it. "What a charming room," she said, and went to warm her hands at the hearth; she could feel his gaze following her, and for the first time since she entered the house, she began to relax, certain she would be able to persuade him to release Enee to her if only she mixed her appeal to him with a little flirtation and hid the desperation that possessed her.

"It is one of my few indulgences, this room," he said with pride that bordered on smugness. "It has taken me four years to bring it to this state."

"You have done a splendid job, Deputy Secretary."

"You're most kind, Madame. I confess I take pride in what I have accomplished here." He closed the door and moved to the center of the room, next to the table, where the light was brightest. "So few have enjoyed it that your praise means a great deal to me, for you must have seen many elegant rooms in the course of your work."

She made the most of the cue he offered her, ignoring the snide undertone in his remark. "Then I am doubly pleased—first, that you have agreed to talk to me, and second, that you do so in this lovely room. Thank you again for receiving me. I hadn't dared to hope until I received your invitation."

He made a sound that might have meant agreement. "Then complete your gesture of courtesy: if you will sit down, and allow me to pour you a little liqueur of wormwood"—he used the German word for *wormwood*—"we can get down to discussion." Seeing her hesitate. "Take whichever sopha suits you best," he urged.

Photine chose the sopha nearer the door, reclining against the rolled arm with a languor she did not feel. "You're most gracious, Deputy Secretary."

"Your company makes it easy for me to be so," he responded with a gallantry that astonished her; so this very ordinary man fancied himself a chevalier, she realized, and determined to use that understanding to her advantage.

"Then we should be able to manage our business without difficulty," she said, wanting to keep him on point.

"I think that's possible," he said, strolling to the table, picking up the bottle, and pouring a small amount of the liqueur into each of the glasses. "This is remarkable stuff. Are you familiar with it?"

"Liqueur of wormwood? I don't believe so," she said,

"You will find it most unusual," he said, a bit remotely. "I know I do."

Photine stared at the glass handed to her. She took it from him, saying, "Then I thank you in advance."

"To you, Madame," Charlot said, lifting his glass before touching the rim to his lips. "And your mission of mercy."

The taste, Photine thought as she sipped the liqueur, was not entirely pleasant, but she took a second nip. "It's . . . interesting."

"Some poets say it provides them visions," Charlot informed her. "You, as an actress, may find it does the same for you."

"Then I should probably wait until our business is finished. It would be unhelpful for me to become lost in a vision when we should be talking sensibly." She spoke in a level voice as she put the little glass down, still half-full, but the alarm she had felt as she made her way from the Jongleur to this house returned.

"You had best finish the glass—it goes off rapidly once poured, not the usual thing for a liqueur, but there it is," said Charlot. "I dislike seeing anything so rare go to waste."

Now Photine was torn: did she refuse Charlot's hospitality and lose what good opinion he had of her, or did she risk drinking the liqueur of wormwood and hope that she kept her wits about her? After a silence of a dozen seconds or so, she reached for the glass and took another, very small sip. The taste was almost musty, with underlying bitterness that made her wonder if she should put some sugar into the glass with the drink. The vapors wound their way into her skull and slunk into her keyed-up nerves. She realized she had to treat the liqueur with a great deal of respect. "Most unusual, Deputy Secretary."

"Thank you, Madame. For an instant it seemed that you did not trust me," he said, putting his own glass on the mantel, where he rested his arm, his ordinary features changing in the flickering light from the fire, lending him a certain air of danger that she found disconcerting. "Tell me about your son—he *is* your son, I presume? Not a nephew or the by-blow of one of your company?"

"Oh, yes, he is mine," she said, not letting his insinuation stop her from answering his first question. "He's fifteen. He was born in Beauvais, the son of my first patron, who provided for him—for his education and his livelihood—until he was thirteen, then settled a trust upon him that ended last year when his property was seized by the Revolutionary Tribunal there. He cannot continue to support him." She looked up at Charlot. "Enee's father has left the country, or so I've been told."

"He has actually left the country? Are you certain?" Charlot asked with minimal interest.

"I have been told that he has," she repeated, imbuing her words with certainty. "His banker sent word to Enee that there would be no more money for him unless he came to Jamaica, where there is a family estate, and where he would be provided for. So far, Enee has had no interest in joining his father—assuming that's where he has gone—but now, who knows? He might be more than willing to live there." It was difficult to gauge how much to tell this bureau-crat, for his expression revealed nothing of his thoughts. "It an-gered Enee to be so cruelly cut off. He didn't grasp the gravity of his father's situation, but I believe in time he will."

"A harsh reality for your son," Charlot mused aloud, then brightened. "So tell me what his childhood was like—did your son know his father at all?"

"Until he was nine, my son spent time with him fairly fre-quently, a week in his company four times a year, and a month in the winter. Enee always enjoyed himself, for his father shamelessly indulged him. After he turned nine, his father's wife finally gave him a son instead of daughters, and so he lessened the amount of time they—"

Rather absent-mindedly, Charlot topped off Photine's glass of wormwood liqueur. "It must have distressed Enee."

"He came to travel with me in that year, and that eased his suf-fering." She shifted on the sopha so that she could lean toward Charlot. "I was thrilled to have his company, and the actors in the troupe appointed themselves his family, as troupes do." This was not quite true, but she solaced herself with the certainty that the company would agree with her claim if they were ever questioned in that regard.

"Had he traveled with you before?"

"No; I traveled little while Enee was growing up. Why are you asking me so many questions? Shouldn't we be talking about my son?"

Charlot stared at her, nothing amicable in his eyes. "If you want to see your son released, you will answer any question I put to you." He waited until she nodded. "How much did your son travel with you?"

Stilling her increasing qualms, Photine took a deep breath. "My patron kept the troupe as his own and was most generous with us. We were housed and fed at his major country estate, with three houses for our own use, and a small theater for us to rehearse in, and present occasional farces for my patron's guests." Most of those scenarios had been bawdy and satiric, and nothing whatever like what she liked most to do. "For the most part, we mounted three or four full productions a year for him, and occasionally took a play to Paris; once we played at Versailles. That was some years ago, of course. I was an ingenue then." Without thinking, she drank a little more of the liqueur of wormwood, finding its effect on her soothing. "He had a taste for the classics, did Jean-Raoul, and encouraged us to produce those plays often, especially the Greek tragedies."

"Then I take it you're classically trained—an unusual thing in a commedia leader, I'd have thought." He seemed slightly surprised.

"Yes, it is unusual; the aunt who raised me was a renowned actress and taught me the craft." She wondered why he asked, and if she ought to have dissembled in her response. "I didn't learn Commedia del'Arte until I was twenty-five."

"Um. So your present troupe is new to you?"

"No; these are members of my company. Just now we are doing our Commedia della Morte because there are few theaters in France where the classics are played, and we must eat." She tried for a whimsical note, and very nearly succeeded.

"You have a patron now, or are you without support?"

"I have a patron." Before she could stop herself, she added, "He is traveling with us now: Ragoczy Ferenz. He's an Hungarian in exile."

"A nobleman."

"In exile," she reiterated. "He has a house in Padova."

"This is the man your son stabbed," Charlot inquired as if he knew the answer.

"It is most unfortunate, but yes."

Charlot said nothing for almost half a minute. "You have no family to whom you can turn on your boy's behalf?" He paused, adding, "Someone who might provide for him?"

"I have a brother and a half-sister. Both are married. One lives . . . lived in Nancy, the other in Rouen. They have families, and are not in any position to take Enee into their households, or as an apprentice. My half-sister's husband is a mercer, and my brother was a printer." I'm telling him too much, she thought, and tried not to panic; she realized the liqueur had loosened her tongue more than she had supposed. Color mounted in her face and only her long training gave her the poise she needed to continue without revealing her agitation. "I'm afraid I don't know where my brother and his family have gone."

"A pity. Should either of them be able to offer him a position, perhaps the Revolutionary Tribunal would be willing to release your son to his aunt or uncle. But . . ." He went to the sopha opposite Photine and sprawled upon it, untying the sash on his robe so that the front of the garment fell open. "We will find another way."

This display bothered her, but not enough to keep her from pursuing her mission; she almost offered to remember him in her prayers, but stopped herself in time: the Revolution had put an end to the rites and rituals of religion. "That is most kind of you, Deputy Secretary. I have to tell you that I have been nearly at my wits' end, worrying about Enee. I know he has done a great wrong, but it is my duty, as his mother, to protect him from all dangers, including those he creates himself."

"It is good to know you remain firm in your conviction," he said, his eyes lingering on the slope of her breasts longer than was seemly. "I hope you will continue to keep that duty in mind."

Photine sat up straighter, trying to pull her scattering thoughts to order. "Deputy Secretary," she said with all the dignity she could summon, "it would be better if you were to sit up."

"Oh, very good," Charlot said through his predatory laughter. "You might try indignation next. Protest that you do not do such things, or tell me you'll complain to the Revolutionary Court. No doubt you could make an admirable scene. It would cost you your son, of course, but it would be a glorious performance."

"Monsieur!"

"Citizen," he corrected her, so condescendingly that she longed to slap his face.

"Deputy Secretary," she said punctiliously, "if you have no

intention of helping Enee, then I must thank you for giving me your time, and leave you to your own thoughts."

He got up from the sopha, his movement deliberate as he approached her: he unbuttoned the front of his unmentionables. "Don't pretend you are a chaste miss, Madame, that you don't know how this game is played. Your son proves you know the ways of men well enough."

Photine turned her dread to outrage, forcing herself to face him. "You have insulted me profoundly, Deputy Secretary. You have been derogatory regarding my profession and the nature of my connection to my son's father. You have treated me like the lowest harlot, and offended me deeply." She felt a first hint of courage flicker within her. "I will leave now and say nothing about any of this."

"No, woman, you will not," Charlot said, taking hold of her hair.

"Release me!" She used the voice that could stop crowds and bend them to her will, but all Charlot did was grin.

"When I am done with you," he said in a silky voice. "But I have not yet begun."

She could feel a knot form in her vitals, and she cursed herself for a gullible dupe, thinking that this man would ever extend himself on behalf of another without requiring recompense for it. "I can give you money."

"I have money—more than anyone knows," he told her before bestowing a ferocious kiss on her mouth, one that pressed his teeth into her lips, forcing them apart for the invasion of his tongue. "I want other compensation from you."

She resisted the impulse to wipe her mouth with the back of her hand. "You disgrace your office, Deputy Secretary."

He laughed again, though it came out more like a growl. "Power is to be used, Madame. That's what it's for."

The fear she had held at bay flared within her, and she started to rise. "I'm going to leave. You cannot keep me here."

"Stay where you are. Unless you want Enee to be answerable for your petulance with his head." He countered her turmoil with an increasing tranquillity. "I am giving you a chance to keep your son alive. I will abide by my word if you'll obey me."

Distressed and confused, Photine took a hasty step toward the door, half-stumbled, and swore.

From his place on the sopha, Charlot laughed, holding up a key. "The door's locked, Madame." He put the key back in a pocket in his dressing-robe, then reached to the opening in his unmentionables, wriggling as he worked to lower his underdrawers. "Come back and sit down while I explain matters to you." He tugged his penis free from his undergarment and fondled it, smiling as it began to rise. "Like a sail filling with wind," he murmured.

"You are insulting, Deputy Secretary," said Photine, matching his coldness with her own; she could see the red, blister-like sores on his organ and on his lower abdomen where some of his hair had fallen away from the pustules. "Cupid's Measles," she said with as much fear as contempt.

"Yes, I have them," he agreed with a lupine smile. "But doubtless you will know how best to manage me. Actresses are adaptable, aren't they?"

"Cochon!"

"What a fine representation of revulsion," he approved, amused by her distress. "You're beginning to sense what I like." He pulled at his foreskin, then rolled it back, exposing the broad red head of his penis. "You've noticed the sores, of course, and you know what it means."

"You seek to pass your disease to me," she said.

"A small price to pay for the life of your son," he countered, motioning her to approach him. "You are going to do what I ask you, everything I ask you, until I order you to leave, or your son will go to the Guillotine by the end of this month, as he should. Or didn't you mean it when you wrote to me that you would do anything to secure his freedom?" Charlot's voice was sharp, like the blade of the Guillotine itself. "Drink the liqueur—it will make this easier for you, and you won't remember most of it—and then come and suck my organ. I'll tell you what to do while you satisfy me."

"You're obscene," she said, but moved toward him, her mind reciting *For Enee, for Enee,* as she went.

"The liqueur, Madame," he said, pointing to the glass of liqueur of wormwood on the table next to her. "You will find it easier to accommodate me with its effects to soothe you." His penis was standing out from his body now, its tip dark-red and marked by developing pustules. "And don't think you will bite me and subdue me. If you try such a sluttish trick, your son loses his head in three days."

"You cannot order me to—"

"I can order you to do whatever I like. For now, I would like you to suck my member dry. Later I have more questions for you, and then perhaps I will have you do other things as well." His gaze flicked lazily over her, as if assessing possibilities for later. "Open your corsage, Madame. I want to see your breasts as you service me."

Photine drank the liqueur as if it were poison, letting the muzziness it imparted claim her. She reached to unfasten her sash, dropping it before she loosened the lacing of her corsage, exposing her breasts. "Since you order," she said with icy contempt. She knelt in the narrow space between the sopha and the table, and leaned forward, disgusted with herself and nauseated by the odor coming from Charlot's body—the man had not washed in several days and his disease imparted a sweetish aroma of rotting meat to the sweat. As she took his penis into her mouth, she felt his hand in her hair again.

"You will swallow what I give you, then beg me for more," he said through clenched teeth.

She could not speak and would not have known what to say if she had made the attempt. For an instant, she thought of da San-Germain and his way with her when they lay together, but banished the memories as quickly as she thought of it: this was going to be a long night, and she had Enee to think about, not the man who had brought her into danger for no purpose but to save his beloved blood relative; she could hope for nothing from him tonight. Nor could she convince herself that Theron Heurer would seek her out, for he, too, was looking to aid that unknown noblewoman who was the cause of all that had transpired. As she began her efforts, she heard a clock somewhere in the house begin to sound eleven; the night was stretching out ahead of her like a road into hell.

Charlot was right about the liqueur of wormwood—it provided a dream-like state that allowed her to view all that would be required of her for the next four hours as a kind of nightmare, one that would end in forgetfulness, and reward her with her son's freedom.

Text of an order issued by the Department of Public Safety presented to the Warden of the Revolutionary Court Prison of Lyon.

> *On this, the 24th day of October, 1792, the Warden and officers of the prison maintained by the Revolutionary Court in Lyon are ordered by the Department of Public Safety to send the prisoner Enee d'Auville under guard in a prison van directly to Calais, and to place him as a prisoner aboard the first military ship bound for any French port in Africa, where he is to be put into the hands of the military commander for dispatch to the most remote outpost under French command, there to serve the country for the rest of his life. He is not to be allowed any correspondence for a period of five years, at which time, he may be allowed to write letters but not to receive any until he has served a decade at the outpost, at which time he may be permitted a one-week leave in the nearest city or town boasting more than ten thousand residents. All records of his transport are to be made in the name Josef Menuisier. All records of his name are to be destroyed, including this order.*

Vive la France!
Vive la Revolution!

Luc Theophille Avoine
Secretary, Department of Public Safety
Lyon

Witness: Vivien Zacharie Charlot
Deputy Secretary, Department of Public Safety
Lyon

6

Da San-Germain, Roger, and Feo were not far from the old Saone River Gate, going north toward the posting inn and the horses that waited for them; the outline of the walls, and the spires of the city's churches, might have been visible behind them but for the fog, which muffled everything in its frigid embrace. Not far away, the murmur of the Saone was loud in the silence of the night. Then, the uneven sounding of eleven that tolled from various of Lyon's bells seemed to come from farther away than the half-league they were, and from more directions than from the city to the south. It was disorienting; the three paused until the clamor died away.

"The Virgin's Tits!" Feo exclaimed. "Are we lost? We could be, in this infernal murk."

"If we keep to the road, we'll be at the inn shortly," said Roger.

"How much farther to the posting inn?" da San-Germain asked, keeping his voice low; the ache in his hip was worse, but he kept on, limping as little as possible.

"Not far," said Roger. "We should reach it in ten to fifteen minutes."

"Assuming we can find it at all. I can't see two paces ahead," said Feo, rounding on da San-Germain. "How you manage to keep on the road without a lantern—"

"Those of my blood see better in the dark than most," said da San-Germain in a tone that blighted further inquiry.

"There's a dip in the road ahead, and a bend to the left; we're almost there now," Roger said. "The posting inn is about fifty paces beyond, on the right side of the road. The turning is broad and easily seen, in spite of the fog." He pulled his hat down farther on his brow, putting his face in added shadow. "The horses will be saddled and ready; three for us, and the rest on leads. The women will have to ride astride."

"Will we have enough horses? There are twenty-two prisoners, a few of them women," Feo reminded them.

"If some of the prisoners take the Guards' horses, the ones we bring will suffice, and if saddles are a problem, it is a small one compared to losing one's head." Da San-Germain recalled a night in the forest outside Paris, when Saint Sebastien and his Satanists had chased Madelaine for hours; she had ridden astride then, and would not protest doing so now. "Side-saddles would raise suspicions."

"So I thought," said Roger, picking his way through a tangle of fallen branches. "This will slow down the wagons carrying the prisoners."

"Then let us hope for more of it." Da San-Germain could feel the pull of his exertions working on the two deepest stab wounds, and he knew they might open if he demanded too much of himself. With a frown, he shortened his stride—this was not the time to risk a fall on the muddy ruts of the old road.

The three kept on grimly, each of them listening intently to the night around them as they went forward. The dip was more slippery than most of the road, and as they reached its lowest point, there was the sound of something moving in the brush next to the road, but nothing came toward them or fled them. A few steps farther along, a large water-bird erupted out of the undergrowth, giving a mournful *hoon* as it went. The men waited until the bird was gone before they moved on.

"We must be mad to be out in this," Feo muttered. "How are we going to see the Guards and the coaches? I can barely make out the road as it is."

"We did not choose the time or the place, so we must make the best we can; it's likely the Guards won't be expecting us in this weather," da San-Germain said quietly, testing the ground underfoot, then stepping onto the narrow verge.

"Or anyone else," Feo added.

"We can avoid the ruts if we walk this way," da San-Germain said, moving forward.

The other two fell in behind him, and as they climbed up the short rise, they were glad for the matting of decaying plants that kept them from slipping. Roger moved to the head of the line, saying, "Let me find my way."

"Gladly," said da San-Germain.

They trudged on for a short distance; then Roger stopped and pointed. "There. This is the turning into the inn-yard. The gate will be open; I've paid them for that, and promised a bonus for their help."

"You continue to amaze me, old friend," said da San-Germain, assuming a German accent. "Your choice of this posting inn was inspired."

The three of them went through the gate, accompanied by the barking of dogs from their kennel. Ahead was the door to the stable, and in the lantern-lit main aisle were three strings of saddled horses. A bearded ostler came up to Roger and bowed. "We have what you asked for, Citizen."

"I will need a few minutes to inspect the horses and tack, as we agreed," said Roger, seizing the man's elbow and propelling him toward the stable.

Feo watched them go. "Should we join them?"

"No," said da San-Germain. "They will become more leery of us than they are already. Roger is one man dealing with one man, which makes the ostler sure he's safe."

"If you say so." Feo moved back into the shadows, adjusting his hat as he went.

"Be ready to ride," da San-Germain told him.

Feo nodded, and bent over to be certain that his pistol was safely tucked in the top of his boot. "Do you think we'll have to kill anyone?"

"I hope not," said da San-Germain, and turned toward the stable as Roger emerged, mounted on a dark dun and leading a string of five horses.

"I've checked them all. The horses are sound enough, and the tack is adequate; they've all been fed and watered," he said as he came up to them; he patted his pocket, and there was the unmistakable clink of coins. "As soon as you're mounted and we're at the gate, I'll pay the rest of the money—we won't have another Gonder here."

"Prudent as always," said da San-Germain, having a swift memory of the troubles they had had with the pilgrims in Ethiopia, over five hundred years before; he shook off the disturbing recollection and headed for the stable where the bearded ostler was holding two more strings of horses. "You take the larger horse; I'll take the smaller."

"Good," said Feo, and swung up into the saddle of a square-built dapple-gray gelding. He settled into the saddle, then moved to adjust the length of the stirrup-leathers. "Seems hearty enough."

"I should hope so," said da San-Germain; he had mounted a neat mouse-colored Spanish mare, and was also adjusting stirrup-leathers.

"Careful with her," the ostler advised da San-Germain, "she's touchy. Don't job the bit."

"I'll bear that in mind, thank you." He reached for the leads, and started the mare moving, and as soon as he was out of the stable, heard Feo come after him.

At the gate, Roger handed the ostler a small purse. "As agreed, and a bonus."

"My thanks, Citizen." The ostler ducked his head in the old-fashioned way, then made a sign for luck as he moved aside so that the three men and their horses could leave the posting inn, and return to the old Saone River Road. As soon as they had cleared the gate, the ostler closed it behind them with a thud.

Making the turn onto the old Saone River Road, da San-Germain brought his string up next to Roger's. "What did you tell him?"

"The ostler? About why we needed the horses? That we are here to escort a group of Protestants to Holland, and with the war we have to—"

"—guide them at night. A clever ruse. Do you think he believes it?" Da San-Germain drew rein as he spoke, for the road was beginning to descend again; his back twinged as he shifted in the saddle.

"I doubt he cares," Feo observed. "He's been paid well enough not to."

Da San-Germain held up his hand, signaling a halt. "Listen," he said. The night was quiet but for the sound of the horses they were leading; after a minute or two, he motioned them on, his mouth pressed to a grim line.

Roger saw da San-Germain's apprehension, and said, "There's another dip up ahead, with a bridge over a stream."

"This is the place you mentioned?"

"It is. The coaches should be along within the hour. We ought to move the horses away from the road as soon as we can."

"That seems wise," said da San-Germain. "How deep is the stream and how wide is the bridge? I assume you discovered that, too."

Now it was Roger's turn to frown. "The stream is running fairly high now; up to your chest at its deepest point. The current is not very fast, but fast enough to be risky to anyone caught in it. The bridge is old, and narrow. The flanking Guards will have to move between the coaches to cross it, and that will provide the greatest opportunity for us to act."

Da San-Germain summoned up the ghost of a smile. "I'd just as soon not wait in the water. Is there room enough on the edge of the road to conceal ourselves?"

"What do we do with the horses? Surely you don't mean to keep them with us?" Feo had pulled his string up so close to the horse he rode that the gelding kicked out at the closest one on the string.

"There's a little meadow not far off the road just before we reach the stream." Roger pointed off to the right.

"You did a good job of scouting," Feo approved, regarding Roger with a mix of curiosity and deference he had not shown before.

"He knows how to observe without being noticed," da San-Germain said.

"I've had some experience," said Roger levelly. "There's a goat-track the other side of that stand of willows; it leads to a clearing. We can tie them there." He tugged on the lead and pulled his string of horses off the river road onto the narrow pathway; da San-Germain fell in behind the last horse in Roger's string, and could hear Feo prepare to leave the road as well.

A few minutes later they reached the small meadow. They dismounted and put up a remuda-line, then secured all the horses but their mounts to it.

"Will it be safe to leave them here?" Feo asked.

"In this fog?" da San-Germain responded. "Had Roger not found this place, I would never have suspected it was here."

They remounted and went back toward the road and the bridge over the stream. When they found a place behind a boulder near the bridge, they took up their station behind it.

"Pistols," said Roger, handing a second one to Feo, and one to da San-Germain. "Do you want the duck's-foot, or shall I keep it?"

"Give me the long-barreled Tower and Crown flintlock, and six cords; you take the duck's-foot," he said, reaching out for the weapon and the restraints. "I want the escort to see what they're facing."

Roger gave the pistol to him, then the cords. "Do you intend to stop the coaches from the front?"

"If Feo will take the flank, and you take the rear, then I'll put myself ahead of them, as soon as the first coach is on the bridge.

The front escort won't have got all the way across, which will block it. That sharp turn will force the coaches to slow to a walk, and once on the bridge, they won't be able to retreat." He tapped his mount with his heels, moving back toward the road. "I expect the coaches will be along shortly. We'll need to be in position before then."

"Should we stay mounted?" Feo asked.

Da San-Germain nodded. "Yes; you don't want to scramble into the saddle and try to block the escorts all at once."

"But if these horses should whinny, they could give us away." Feo had raised his voice to be heard, and could barely make out the gesture da San-Germain gave to quiet him.

"Speak softly. Our voices are more of a danger than a whinny," da San-Germain said in an undervoice. "There are other horses along the road, and the Guards will pay no attention to any sound our horses make."

Concealing his annoyance, Feo whispered, "I'll get on the other side of the road, near the turn."

"I'll cross the bridge and move back into the brush. Remember to pull your hat down, so they won't see your features." Da San-Germain watched Feo move off, then gave a quick sign to Roger, indicating that he was ready for what was to come. For nearly half an hour they waited in silence, the dank cold seeping into them, their horses fretting occasionally; da San-Germain's thoughts wandered back to another bridge, in the Audiencia de Peru, and Acana Tupac, a memory he turned away from in favor of an afternoon, not quite fifty years before, when he and Madelaine had talked on a bridge, when she had learned more of his true nature. He let this hold his attention until there were the first sounds of the approaching coaches and their escorts. At once he shifted his mind to his present task: he moved in the saddle, readying his mare to bound out in front of the Guards riding in the lead; he drew his English pistol and pulled his hat lower on his brow.

The lead horses were moving at a walk—anything faster would not be safe on such a poor road in the fog; the rest of the Guards were holding to the same pace, the postilions concentrating on the road while the Guards worked to maintain their formation. The center lead Guard held a lantern, which cast a soft, unsteady glow on the deep ruts and rendered the night darker by comparison, and all three coaches had lanterns on either sides of their vehicles. The first coach was two horse-lengths behind the three Guards, the postilion on the on-side lead struggling to stay in the saddle as the coachman pulled the four mincing horses in for the slope and the turn; the off-side wheeler sank above the pastern in mud, and the coachman tugged on the reins to keep the horse from falling.

"There's more mud. The road's softer!" the postilion for the front coach called out to the coachman on the box behind him.

The coachman cursed by the Devil and his imps. "Be careful, Houle," he ordered the postilion. "All we need now is a broken wheel, or a crippled horse."

Da San-Germain could see Feo move a little closer, pistol in hand, reins in his teeth. He watched him as closely as he watched the escort and coaches, fearing that Feo might do something impetuous. He sensed Madelaine's nearness, and her fear.

The first three riders were on the bridge, paying more attention to the coach behind them trying to negotiate the turn onto the bridge than they were to their own progress. This was what da San-Germain had been waiting for: he clapped his heels to the mare's sides, pulled in her head, and felt her jump onto the road, coming to a jarring halt, his pistol directed at the lead Guard. "Hands up!" he ordered in a strong German accent. "At once!"

The lead Guard stared at him, then flung the lantern at da San-Germain; it fell short of him and went out just as Roger and Feo emerged from their cover.

"What do you want?" the lead Guard asked, the slight tremor in his voice revealing his fear.

"Your prisoners. All of them." Da San-Germain swung around in his saddle and fired at the lead postilion, who had just drawn a pistol; the man cried out, dropped his weapon, and clung to the neck of the horse he was riding. "Toss down your weapons. I don't want to have to shoot more of you, but if you insist . . ." He let the words fade so that the Guards could consider their situation. "Pistols, guns, knives, the lot. Throw them down now."

Most of the Guards complied, some more reluctantly than others. Feo noticed one of the Guards riding between the first and second coaches had only pretended to drop his weapon. "You, too, Guard," he ordered, preparing to fire.

The Guard swore, but flung his pistol away from him. "There."

Roger, at the rear of the group, rode up behind the three Guards at the back, and, pulling several lengths of heavy cording from his pommel D-ring, soon tied the hands of the Guards before ordering them to dismount. As soon as they were on the road, Roger took their horses in charge, then went to open the door of the rear coach. "If you want to live, get out," he said.

Just as the eight men began to descend from the rear coach, the lead Guard charged da San-Germain, yelling and waving his arms to frighten the mouse-colored mare; remembering the ostler's warning, da San-Germain used his lower legs to hold the mare in place while he drew one of the two franciscas from under his cincture and flicked it in the direction of the lead Guard. The little knife caught him on the side of the face, slicing into his cheek and removing his earlobe.

The Guard bellowed, trying to turn his horse around in the confines of the bridge; his horse reared, and the Guard fell backward into the stream. The two Guards riding with him backed their horses away from where he had fallen. There were shouts coming from inside the first coach, demands to know what was going on.

"Gui, are you all right?" one of the two mounted Guards called down over the bridge-rail.

Da San-Germain caught the lead Guard's horse as the animal attempted to bolt, and held him in, calming him.

A sputtering cry came from the stream, and was met by a hesitant cheer from the prisoners who were now out of the rear coach, and more exclamations from the first coach, where the coachman on the first coach started to climb down from his box, shouting, "We'll get you out, Gui!"

"Stay where you are," da San-Germain ordered him.

"He'll freeze if we don't get him out," the coachman said, stopping as soon as he reached the surface of the bridge.

"Secure the hands of these two first," said da San-Germain. "Then you may go alone to pull him out of the stream, if he's unable to manage that for himself." The thrashing from the water, accompanied by coughs and obscenities, grew more purposeful. "Here are some cords," he said, holding out a few.

The coachman took them, and went to tie the Guards' hands. "What about the postilion?" he asked.

"When the coach is empty, put him inside and bind his hands."

"He's losing blood," the coachman observed.

"The head bleeds heavily, but it will clot," said da San-Germain; he saw that Roger had tied the hands of the third coachman and was about to do the same to the two mounted Guards between the second and third coaches. "You can help him down, if you want. He'll do better on the ground. Then you may attend to . . . Gui, is it?"

"I have to help Gui first," said the coachman, still showing no outward signs of distress. "I'll attend to Sancoeur when Gui is out of the water. I'll bring Gui onto the bank, but may need help getting him up to the road." He went to the end of the bridge and looked down into the stream, listening intently. "He's sliding toward the river: he can't swim, you see." With a nod to da San-Germain, he let himself down the bridge-footing, and was quickly lost in the fog.

Roger had got the two mounted Guards out of their saddles and onto the rutted road; he called to the eight men who had huddled together at the side of the third coach. "You. Five of you take the Guards' horses and ride out from here at once. Don't go home. Don't take main roads. Don't stay together; you'll attract too much attention. Get as far away from here as you can. If you make for the coast, avoid Calais." Then he ordered the coachman to come down from his box. The coachman reached to secure the reins and grabbed his whip, letting the lash uncurl. Before he could swing it, the duck's-foot barked, and the coachman fell onto the road, a messy tear in his shoulder; the prisoners hurried to catch the horses and mount up. "You three," Roger shouted to the remaining men, "tie the postilion's hands and get him on the ground."

Feo was busy securing the hands of the two Guards between the first and second coaches, keeping a wary eye on the driver of the second coach. "Dismount," he said, helping the two Guards to get down. "We have two more horses free."

"Good," said Roger. "You men, take them."

"May God bless you, good men, though you're Germans," said one of the freed prisoners as he reached for the reins of one of the horses. He glanced around at the others, then said, "What are we waiting for? Mount up." In the next breath, he had vaulted into the saddle and gathered the reins and was headed back the way they had come at a rapid trot, bravery mixed with panic in his flight.

One of the younger men called out, "Oui, Monsieur le Marquis," and stepped away from the coach. "God be with you!"

"Mind the ruts," Roger warned them all. "Hold to a trot until the road improves; a broken leg or strained tendons will not help you escape." He held his duck's-foot up and made sure those around him saw it. "You Guards. Step aside."

The hesitation that had kept the rest milling by the coach faded. The six men who had horses to ride scrambled into the saddles and, while Feo struggled to open the double latch on the door of the second coach, followed the first of their number back along the muddy road, into the thickening fog.

"Don't stay together!" Roger shouted after them as they vanished, and then motioned to the one remaining man. "See if the coachman is still alive," he said. "We'll have a horse for you shortly, and you can be off."

"But where should I go?" he asked in bewilderment.

Roger looked down at him. "Away from here. Try for the coast, and look for an American ship. You might be able to work off your passage."

"*Misericordia, Domini,*" the man mumbled, crossing himself.

Feo came up beside the driving-box of the second coach and pointed his pistol at the coachman. "You saw what happened to your comrade. Secure the reins and get down. Tie the hands of the postilion, then step to the side of the road."

The coachman glared at him. "You're freeing monsters."

"I may be," said Feo. "Better than helping to murder the innocent."

"Innocent?" The coachman laughed angrily. "Them? Little you know." He folded his arms, his chin up defiantly.

"Get down, or I will knock you down," Feo warned him.

The coachman took a moment to decide, then set the reins and swung down from the box. As he reached the road, he stumbled on the ruts and leaned against Feo's horse, holding Feo's leg, seeming to steady himself.

"Back!" Feo ordered, kicking out at the coachman. He immediately realized his mistake as he felt a knife-blade slide along his thigh, digging deeply into the inner muscles; a welling of wet heat told him the wound was serious. Without thinking, he shot the coachman in the face and pulled in his horse as the dead coachman plicated into a heap underneath the coach's step. Staring down at his leg, Feo saw darkness spreading down toward his boot, steaming.

Roger called out to him. "Are you—?"

"He got me. With a knife." Feo answered, ending in a shout as the pain sank into him.

"Can you manage the second coach?" da San-Germain asked loudly; he was assisting two of the prisoners from the first coach to get out of it.

"If I can get a bandage around my leg, I can," Feo told him, then came up to the postilion, gesturing with his pistol. "Get down. Move the body off the road. Open the door of the coach, then stand back." He felt hot and cold at once, and he knew that he was badly hurt. "Move. Now."

The postilion did as he was ordered, torn between ire and fear.

"I'll help," said one of the men from the first coach. "We need to be gone from here, and soon."

"That you do. Help move the body, and tie the hands of the postilion," da San-Germain said, and pressed his mare forward toward the second coach, already worried for Feo. "How deep is the wound?"

"Deep enough," said Feo through clenched teeth; he was becoming more aware of the cold, and realized this was a troubling sign.

"Then as soon as we get a bandage around your thigh, lead the released men to the meadow and put them on horses. Get them on their way as quickly as you can. Then bring the rest of the horses here for the women." He signaled to Roger. "Do you have a good length of cotton with you?"

"But—" Feo protested.

One of the Guards lurched to his feet and attempted to run. He fell almost immediately, and in an instant, the prisoner from the first coach was on him, pummeling him, and tearing at his shirt. Roger made a move in an attempt to get between them, but without success.

Da San-Germain reached down and pulled the door on the second coach open, releasing its occupants so precipitously that the first woman out nearly fell onto the body of the coachman.

From beneath the bridge there was a sudden flailing, and a loud gasp. "I couldn't find him!" the first coachman shouted. "The current's taken him! Gui's gone!"

"Climb back up and lend a hand!" da San-Germain ordered, helping the two older women to get out of the coach. The third woman took his proffered hand, and said quietly, "Thank you," as she alighted on the road.

"You are most welcome," he said to Madelaine de Montalia, his voice more mellifluous than it had been.

The prisoner on top of the Guard yelled in triumph and offered Feo a strip of the Guard's shirt. "Bind your wound with this."

Feo took a little time to wrap the length of cotton around the top of his leg and knot it tightly, determined to stay alert, for as much as he was enjoying himself, the wound was a bad one. "You men, come with me," he called out while the coachman from the first coach clambered up the bank and back onto the end of the bridge. "It's not far. You'll be away before half an hour passes."

The men began to straggle around him, some pausing to look at the three coaches, others refusing to do so.

A fourth woman descended from the second coach, and then two men, both of whom were old and moved with difficulty.

The coachman came up to da San-Germain. "He'll drown because of you."

"That's unfortunate," da San-Germain said, making his German accent particularly strong. "But such things happen." There was no way for the coachman to see the compassion in da San-Germain's dark eyes.

"You'll lose your head for this," the coachman promised.

"Only if we're caught," said da San-Germain, testing the knot on Feo's bandage. "Good enough. Take the men to the horses. You have time, so don't rush, and don't exert yourself." He paused. "All but these two will go with you now; bring horses for them. Six horses," he added, indicating the old men and the women. He then looked at the drenched coachman. "Get a blanket and wrap up in it. Then you may attend to your foolish postilion."

In the distance, the bells of midnight rang.

"The Guards?" Roger asked after a single glance in the direction of the bells.

"Put them in the coaches, along with the postilions and coachmen, and set the latches on the doors." Da San-Germain could feel Madelaine's eyes on him, and it was all he could do to keep from dismounting and folding her in his arms; he gave his attention to the prisoners gathering around Feo. "There is a floating bridge over the river about three leagues north of here, if you want to go west, or south. If you go east, stay away from the major roads—there will be warrants for you at all the major crossings. Find some simple clothes to wear, not too dirty, and get rid of the Guards' saddle-pads; grain sacks will suffice. If you can, choose lesser roads, or, if the weather permits, go across country, and find small villages near the borders, and cross out of France from there. Or find a covered boat and a fisherman's coat and float down to the sea if riding does not appeal to you."

A few of the men nodded, but most of them seemed dazed; they followed Feo with dogged determination as much to have something to do as to get away from the coaches. In little more than two minutes, they topped the slope and disappeared from view.

"Old friend," he said to Roger, "would you tie the coachman's hands once he's done with the postilion? They can be put in the first coach."

The coachman, who was pulling a threadbare blanket around his shoulders, glowered at da San-Germain. "Your masters in Germany will answer for this."

"Do you think so?" Da San-Germain gave a slight, ironic bow before taking up a position that allowed him to watch the road in both directions. "I shall warn them of that possibility."

While the coachman tended to the postilion, Roger began to move the Guards into the empty coaches, paying little heed to the curses hurled upon him. Those who were injured he treated more gently than their sturdier fellows. He paused to help move San-coeur, the postilion from the first coach, into it, then tied the coachman's hands behind him and helped him mount the step into the coach.

"We can kick the door open; we'll be out as soon as you're gone," the coachman said, looking past Roger to da San-Germain.

"If you think it would be useful, you may try," said da San-Germain. "The doors have a double-latch and they're iron-banded, as you will recall."

The coachman spat as Roger shoved a Guard in to join them, saying to da San-Germain, "That's four."

"Very good. We'll load the third coach now, and leave the middle for last." He motioned to the four women. "If you would like to move back from the road, you will not get so muddy."

"What about . . . him?" the tallest of the women asked, pointing to the body of the coachman.

"We will load it into the boot," da San-Germain said, dismounting and going to pull the corpse of the coachman to the rear of the vehicle. Ordinarily this would not have been difficult, but the wounds in his shoulder and hip were aching badly, and it took him some little time to drag him.

Roger, who had seen da San-Germain scrambling over the ruts, got all but the last two Guards into the third coach, then came to help. "You're tired, my master."

"In a good cause," said da San-Germain as he bent to grab the coachman's shoulders while Roger took his feet. They slung the body into the boot and buckled it in place with leather straps. "We should be away from here shortly. There's still much to do."

"And we'll need to be back at the inn before dawn," Roger said, pulling his horse after him. "Are you going to leave the coaches here, or—"

"Leave them here, I think. They won't be found before morning, and by then most of the prisoners will be some distance from here."

"And traveling alone," Roger added.

"If they're sensible," da San-Germain added. He was about to say something more, but stopped as Madelaine approached them. He bowed in the German manner. "What may I have the honor of doing for you?"

"I wanted to thank you for doing this for . . . us." She indicated the remaining three women and two men. "We were all certain we would die."

"There is still that risk," da San-Germain said somberly. "But this way, you have a chance."

The smile she gave him, while secret, conveyed the depth of her emotion.

"Do you think the coach horses will get restive once we leave?" Roger asked, deliberately intruding on Madelaine and da San-Germain's quiet preoccupation.

"We'll ask Maffeo as soon as he returns," said da San-Germain quietly, using Feo's full name to guard against any accidental identification later.

The three of them moved apart and returned to the former prisoners waiting for horses. There was an edginess in the air now, and a growing anxiety that was as restively oppressive as the fog. One of the two male prisoners looked up at them. "I want to find a boat. I can be many leagues downstream by dawn. I'm too old for hard rides."

"That you can," da San-Germain said. "There should be a few boats tied up along the bank above and below this stream. If you want a lantern so you can explore?"

"Yes," he declared without hesitation. "Josef-Pierre," he said to one of his companions. "Would you like to come with me?"

"I would, Geoffroi," said the other of the remaining male prisoners. "Where is the lantern?"

From some little distance away there came the sound of trotting horses; all those near the coaches stopped still, listening, preparing to run, then visibly relaxed as the hoofbeats receded.

Da San-Germain reached up and took one of the coach's lanterns from its hook on the front of the coach. "Here." He handed the lantern to Josef-Pierre. "Bon chance, gentlemen, and don't come to the shore for at least a day."

"Thank you," the two said, and made their way gingerly down the steep slope to the stream, their footsteps fading as they went toward the river.

"Have you found a place?" Madelaine whispered to da San-Germain in Arabic.

"For you—yes. You'll need to stay hidden until tomorrow afternoon," he answered in the same language.

She nodded, and glanced at the other women, wondering how much curiosity she had awakened in them; she moved away from da San-Germain, giving him a demi-curtsy as she went.

A few minutes later there came the sound of approaching horses; the three women hurried to conceal themselves at the side of the road. Roger aimed his duck's-foot, ready to fire, but then lowered it. "The horses are here."

"Very good," said da San-Germain, and turned to the women. "I fear you'll all have to ride astride, but it is far safer that way."

The most timid of the women looked dismayed, but stood as straight as she could. "If I must, I must."

The lead horse reached the coaches and stopped, as did the string behind. There was a fidgety stillness; then da San-Germain stepped toward Feo's horse, distressed certainty growing in him. He reached the horse and caught it by the reins below the bit, his dark-seeing eyes revealing to him what he had hoped not to see: Feo was lying forward on the horse's neck, the lead for the string secured to the saddle. His hat had been lost somewhere between the road and the meadow; blood dripped slowly from the wound in his thigh, and his sightless eyes were fixed on the far distance, a look of puzzlement etched forever on his dead face.

Text of a bill of sale from Roger Gadouin to Marc de Brisac, innkeeper at the Batteau Jaune, four leagues west of Lyon on the Chouans Road.

> *Sold to Marc de Brisac by Roger Gadouin on this, the 26th of October, 1792, 3:40 a.m., at the inn, the Batteau Jaune, two horses with tack included, for the sum of 20 louis d'or.*
>
> *Vive la France!*
> *Vive la Revolution!*
>
>
>
> *Roger Gadouin*
> *major domo to*
> *il Conte da San-Germain*
>
>

7

It was past four of the clock and starting to rain by the time da San-Germain entered the kitchen door at the Jongleur and made his way—so quietly that a shadow might make more noise—through the kitchen and painfully up the servants' stairs to his room, where he put aside his Hungarian clothes in favor of a long dressing-robe in dark-red velvet. He gave himself a little time to review all that had happened that night—the death of Feo and the improvised funeral he and Roger had given him in an old cemetery among the broken tombs, the dispatching of Roger to sell the extra horses, and the place he had found for Madelaine: he had left her in the un-used chapel on the outside of the old city walls twenty minutes before, and was satisfied that she would be safe there until the coming evening, when she would depart with him. Looking around the room, he was relieved that Roger had done such a thorough job of packing without making it appear that they would be gone in twelve hours. He was about to climb onto the mattress on top of the chest filled with his native earth, when he heard a sharp knock on his door. He gave the clock on the mantel a quick glance: four-thirty. Chiding himself for being noticed on his return, he went to the door and asked, "Who is it?"

"Photine," was the answer, followed at once by sobs.

He opened the door at once. The fear that she had been waiting for him vanished as soon as he saw her, her beautiful cloak clutched around her, her hair in disarray, her make-up raddled, her lips swollen, her face bruised, a bit of torn ruff poking out of the cloak's collar, and a strap of her left shoe broken. "Photine," he exclaimed softly as he drew her into the room, closing the door quietly behind her. "What on earth—?"

"I've done something . . . dreadful," she said, attempting to stifle her weeping.

"What happened?" He reached to take her cloak, but she held it closed, shaking her head repeatedly.

"I can't . . ." She pushed away from him, and he saw what looked like a small burn on the back of her hand, which she pulled back under the folds of her cloak.

"Photine," he said, kindly and persuasively, "tell me."

"I can't," she said again, waving her hand as if to ward off any questions. "Not yet."

Puzzled, he offered her his arm for support, but she cringed. He felt alarm awaken in him. "Can you tell me what sort of trouble—"

"I've . . . I've . . ." She stumbled toward the bed and dropped onto it, and began to cry in earnest.

He wondered if she and Heurer had had a spat, but decided that was unlikely; for all their volatile dealings, they had never come to blows, let alone any exchange that was as vicious as her appearance indicated. She would never be as distraught as she was now about anything her playwright had done. Going to her side, he repeated, "What happened?"

"I . . ." She steadied herself and tried again, this time at the beginning. "I received an invitation."

"What manner of invitation?" he asked when she did not go on.

Photine coughed, took a deep, uneven breath. "From an official. One of the men at the Department of Public Safety. He said . . ." Once again she wept. "He said that he could help Enee."

Da San-Germain spoke very gently. "And could he?"

"He said he could; he's in the right position to do it. He had intimated that he would. He has the authority, and offered . . . to spare him. For . . . a price." She doubled over, her arms folded across her torso, and rocked, giving abrupt little sobs.

For an instant he considered that she might be performing, expressing turmoil on an enhanced scale rather than experiencing it deep within herself; one look into her eyes convinced him that her anguish was genuine. With a consoling murmur, he put his hand on her shoulder only to have her shrug it away. "What did he do to you?" he asked calmly, speaking in the same tone he would use to quiet a frightened horse.

Her mouth turned down and her lips trembled. "He's disgusting!" She turned to him. "He demanded I . . . I serve him . . . *service* him." Suddenly she gagged; he handed her a towel as she vomited. When she was done, he took the towel from her and carried it to the ewer-and-basin sitting atop the discreet commode.

"If you'd rather not continue," he offered.

"I'm *sorry,* I didn't think I was so upset," she apologized, her face reddening. "He was loathsome." She trembled, revulsion gripping her again. "He has . . ."—she searched for a proper description—"Soldiers' Pox. There were little sores and blisters all around his member."

"And you . . . did more than touch him?"

"Yes," she said with a sudden trembling. "Will I take it? Has he passed it to me?" Her anxiety was visible.

Rather than answer directly, da San-Germain rose and went to his old chest where he kept his medicaments. He opened the front panel and removed four vials of an opalescent liquid and brought them to her. "Drink one of these now, and the rest over the next three days, first thing in the morning."

She eyed the vials suspiciously. "He gave me something to drink. It looked like that, only darker. That isn't of wormwood, is it?"

He smiled faintly. "No. It begins as bread," he said, and did not add that the bread he used was moldy, and went through a process to purify its substance. "This is my sovereign remedy. If you take it as I instruct, you should not take the Soldiers' Pox."

Staring at the vials with some suspicion, she asked him, "Are you certain?" She took hold of her cloak once more as if to retreat behind it.

"As certain as I am of any medicament," he said, smiling encouragement. "Take it, Photine. Please."

She handled the vials as if she feared they might suddenly explode. "Made from bread, you say?"

"From bread," he pledged. "It has served its purpose a thousand times over. It doesn't taste very pleasant, but it does relieve fever and infection. And it stops certain diseases, like Soldiers' Pox, completely."

With a sigh of capitulation, she took the vials. "If it will stop the Soldiers' Pox, then it may taste bitter as gall for all I care." She removed the stopper in one of the vials and tipped the contents down her throat. "You're right: it tastes foul," she said, and wiped her mouth with the edge of her cloak.

"The same again tomorrow, and for two days after," he told her.

She pulled back her cloak and put the vials into the concealed pocket, then closed the front again. "If I don't sicken before nightfall, I'll do it." She turned away from him. "Don't let the others know."

"I won't," he assured her, and waited to hear more.

"It was . . . hideous. Now it is over, and Enee will be free." She said it as if to convince herself. "If he is free, it will be worth enduring that man."

"You have doubts that Enee will be released?" Da San-Germain shared her dubiety, but kept this to himself.

"He promised, but promises are easily broken," she said, avoiding his eyes. "He may have been . . . pretending . . ." She let the words fade.

"What will you do then, if he fails to honor his promise?"

"I don't know. If I had any way to force him to answer for his actions—" She stopped, changing her demeanor and tone with the ease of a magician. "But who am I, to denounce him? What proof is there of what I say? He is a Deputy Secretary of Public Safety, and I am an actress. Which of us would be believed?"

"You have injuries," da San-Germain pointed out; he had seen the purple welts on her neck and shoulders, and the disheveled state of her clothing. "If a physician examined you and gave his report to the Revolutionary Tribunal, the officials would have to hear you out." He drew up the single straight-backed chair from its position by the fireplace and set it so he could face her without pressing too close to her. "You've been badly used," he said.

"He would claim that someone else did that, and could then accuse me of malice toward him, an attempt to discredit him for imprisoning my son."

"There would be a scandal, and if he had ever done such things before, he could be disgraced." Da San-Germain watched her more closely than she realized.

She ducked her head. "He said if I didn't do whatever he wanted, Enee would die, because of what he did to you, and he would make no effort to prevent it." She sighed. "I thought he was like so many men—seeing what they want to see in me, and perhaps he did. I can accommodate such imaginings, and have, often and often, but not with this man."

He chose his next words carefully. "And what did he want from you, in exchange for your son?"

"He wanted my acquiescence in all he demanded—I wanted to save my son," she said with such simplicity that he was astonished. "He wanted to . . . debauch me." When he said nothing in response, she went on. "I know it was foolish to go, but what choice did I have? I thought if it would deliver Enee from harm, I had to see Charlot"—she spoke his name as if it were vitriol—"to beg him to spare my child. He said he would. He said Enee would live. What could I do?"

Although he agreed that she had been reckless to go to Charlot, he understood how Photine might believe she would be able to control the situation, to handle the man as she would handle any audience. "I'm sorry he used you so shamefully in the name of your son," he said, hoping to draw her out.

"It will achieve what I sought, if he is true to his word." For Photine, this was an unusually stolid response.

"But it was a cruel price," said da San-Germain.

"I had to do all that he asked, cruel or sweet," she whispered. "If I balked, he struck me with a thin cane, one with a ferrule on the head. He used that . . . in distasteful ways." She smoothed one hand over her petticoat.

"How long were you with him?" He extended his hand to her, but did not touch her, for there was a shine to her eyes that told him she was barely able to hold her panic at bay. "I assume you went alone."

"I got there at half-past-ten of the clock, and he let me go shortly after three in the morning. Not truly let me go—he threw me out onto the street, calling me a bawd, and spitting on me." She spoke as if she were reciting by rote words in a foreign language. "It took me some time to get back here. I . . . I didn't want to be seen."

"Did you get here without incident?" he asked, seeing a concealed wince in her last remark.

"You mean, was I accosted? I was, by a drunken Guard. He was easily dealt with: I kicked his shin, stamped on his foot, and ran." There was a brief flash of satisfaction in her eyes, and then the appalled sheen returned.

The silence between them stretched out, threatening to become impenetrable; finally da San-Germain moved his chair back. "I am sorry you had to—"

"It wasn't just the demands he made of my body, he asked me questions. Many questions. Not just about Enee. It wasn't all coupling and accommodating, he wanted to know things." Her face revealed a defiance that da San-Germain knew boded ill. "He did ask me about Enee, and the troupe, about Heurer. And you. He wanted to know why Enee stabbed you."

"And what did you tell him?"

She sighed. "That I didn't know why. He didn't press me about that." There was a suggestion of more.

Da San-Germain went very still. "What other things did he ask?"

"How long I had been an actress. Who my patrons had been. Where I had performed. How long had I known you. Where had we met. What your connection was to the troupe. When did you decide to sponsor us. Were you in love with me. How you arranged our travel. Why you should pay us to bring our Commedia della Morte to France. That was the worst, explaining the purpose of the tour." She turned a pleading glance on him. "I tried not to tell him, but he didn't believe you were doing a service for your family. He said it had to be more than that, that no nobleman, not even an exiled one, would come into France as a favor."

"And what did you say?" he asked without a hint of emotion.

"I said that you wanted to free one of your relations from prison." Having admitted that, she began once more to cry, this time in a dejected, listless way.

"Did you tell him who that relation is?"

She nodded several times. "He heated up a poker and said he'd put it into me if I lied." She put her hand to her mouth, as if she might throw up again. "So I told him. I . . . I was afraid to lie, don't you see? I knew he would do it; I think he hoped I would equivocate, so he would have an excuse to do it." Her eyes were jumpy and she looked at everything but him. "I said you planned to hide her as one of the troupe and to take her with us when we left France." Her expression changed again, taking on an apologetic servility that da San-Germain was fairly sure was a performance, for there was an undercurrent to her mannerisms that had been lacking before, a slyness that was new. "But we may not leave France now in any case, not if Collot d'Herbois will sponsor us here, for that would be a triumph. In such a place, Charlot would have reason to fear me." She flung this last at him as if to stop any argument he might raise with her over what she had done. "It is a great opportunity for us."

"It is," he said, trying to discern what lay behind her mercurial shift.

"If Collot d'Herbois sponsors us, we can go far. We might have our own theater. I long to have my own theater again." She stared at him as if trying to anticipate his protest. "This may be my last chance to have it. I answered all that he asked of me."

Da San-Germain refused to be baited into a dispute with her

about this possibility, asking her with the utmost urbanity, "Did you tell Charlot when the attempt to save Madame de Montalia would occur?"

Photine hesitated before she answered, baffled by his formidable reserve. "I had to. He said he would beat me again if I refused, and would cut my face. I explained about the parade tomorrow . . . today, really. How we are going to disrupt the transfer of the prisoners, create an incident, and slip her away in one of our shrouds." She reached out for his hand, her face eloquent of remorse. "I'm sorry, Comte, I'm sorry. I'm so sorry. I had to tell him, don't you see? I didn't have any choice, not with what he wanted to do." A little of her dramatic flare had returned, and she threw open her cloak to show the ruin of her clothes and the visible extent of her injuries. "Charlot is a monster. He would have done worse than this to me if I hadn't told him what he wanted to know. Not just cut my face, but break my legs. That would destroy me as an actress, to be scarred and lame."

"Yes. I understand," he said, with a growing relief that Photine had not learned of his work this night, that she still assumed the rescue would take place in the coming afternoon. He also realized that he would have to get Madelaine out of her hiding-place between the inner and outer walls of the city sooner than he had planned, and start for the frontier before noon, during the day and in rain, both enervating for those of their blood; they would be gone before the Commedia della Morte's parade began. They would have to travel clandestinely and in disguise, for no doubt, Charlot would have Guards after them before the next sunset.

"Don't be angry with me, Comte. I couldn't bear it if you were angry," she appealed to him, her eyes filling with tears but not to the point of overflowing.

"I'm not angry with you, Photine, I'm angry at Charlot, that he should abuse his power and you so insolently."

This time she wept with gratitude. "Oh, Comte, you are so good, so generous. I am so grateful to you." She gathered her cloak around her again. "If I could apologize for all this . . . I know I've betrayed your confidence, which is a despicable thing, but if I hadn't, my son would be executed. I'm his mother. I had to—"

"Yes," he said, cutting her effusions short. "Never mind that now. We haven't time to sort this out. Morning is coming, and there is much you have to do before your performance. You will need to clean yourself up as much as you can, and choose how to conceal your injuries before you perform today. We can discuss this later, perhaps this afternoon, perhaps when we're in Padova again."

"But the troupe is staying here, to work with Collot d'Herbois; we may not return to Padova for months, or years, and who knows what will become of us before such a meeting?" she reminded him; she got to her feet. There was an air of purpose about her now, a kind of familiar anticipation that restored her self-confidence. "After today's performance—we'll talk then, not just about . . . what happened tonight, but all the rest. You deserve to know the whole of it. But you're right. Just at present, there are so many arrangements to be made that neither of us can—" She laid her burned hand on his arm, giving him a melting smile. "You won't be trying to rescue your kinswoman now, will you? We won't have to disrupt the transfer of prisoners, will we? You would be caught if you made the attempt now."

"You're right—I won't do that," he said, opening the door for her. "Remember to take the remedy in the vials."

"Oh, yes. I will. And I thank you for your remedy. I would not want to have the Soldiers' Pox." She did a skittish half-curtsy, then went along almost on tip-toe to the door to her chamber; she turned to give him a last smile, then let herself in, closing the door silently.

Da San-Germain listened intently, but the Jongleur was quiet. No servants were about yet, which he hoped meant that their meeting had been unobserved. He stepped back into the chamber and closed the door, then sat down to revise his plans yet again. If only he had more time, he thought as he mentally reviewed the problem.

It was almost six of the clock when Roger returned, remarking as he came in, "The scullions are up in the kitchen and will bring the tub up for your bath shortly." He pulled off his long-coat and rubbed his chin. "I'll get the basin. We both need a shave."

"The basin is presently unusable," said da San-Germain, and explained about Photine's desecrated evening with Charlot. "There has to be bath-water we can use, before I bathe."

Roger studied da San-Germain. "You've worked another plan, haven't you, my master?"

"Circumstances require it," da San-Germain replied in Byzantine Greek. "I don't like it, but it should suffice."

"Tell me," said Roger in the same language, no sign of doubts or distress in his faded-blue eyes.

"It will require that you and I travel apart," da San-Germain said. "I have tried to come up with a better way than this, but I haven't been able to."

"We've done so before," said Roger, more resigned than annoyed.

"Yes, but I would rather not." Memories of Spain, of Cyprus, of Leosan Fortress, of the Pilgrim's Road in Abyssinia all flickered through his mind.

Roger absent-mindedly picked up the Hungarian clothing da San-Germain had draped over the end of the bed. "Will you be needing these, or shall I pack them?"

"Pack them, in one of the false-bottomed trunks, in case the Guards from the escort give descriptions of what we were wearing," he said, adding, "If you can, dispose of them when you reach Valence."

"So I am to go south along the river," said Roger. "You will take another road, with Madelaine?"

"I believe we must." He paused contemplatively. "The first leg of the journey is the riskiest—we'll make for Grenoble, and then take the country roads through the mountains and on to Torino." He said it easily enough, but he knew the roads would be muddy or covered in snow or slick with ice, and they might be pursued. "I believe if we take the mules, we can manage four leagues in a day."

"Provided the weather doesn't stop you," Roger pointed out. "If you take the mules, do you plan to drive the larger cart?"

"No," da San-Germain said. "We will ride. We can make better time that way, and can use the game trails and shepherds' tracks through the mountains. You will take the larger cart, and four of the horses, and—"

"—go south to what? Montelimar? Bollene? And from there east into Italy?" Roger guessed aloud.

"Montelimar would be the better choice, I think," said da San-Germain, and turned his head at a scratch on the door. "Who is it?" he called out in French.

"Your bathtub, Citizen," called the porter from the hall. "May we bring it in?'

Roger went to open the door, and directed the two men to the open area in front of the fireplace. "There. When will the water be hot?"

"A quarter hour," said the older porter. "Perhaps a little longer; they're just building up the fires in the kitchen."

"Very good," said Roger, handing each of the men a silver coin. "For your trouble," he said and let the men out of the room.

"At least we can get clean," said da San-Germain, once more speaking Byzantine Greek.

"And shaved," said Roger. "So I should cross the frontier on the Pinerolo Road."

"If it is clear enough. It's not an easy road, but it isn't much patrolled or guarded, either. Best to stay away from the ports: there are too many spies there, looking for escaping Frenchmen." He went to put a log on the embers in the grate. "I would advise you to leave before the performance begins, and complain to the ostlers that I am an unreasonable man, requiring you to run foolish errands."

"What foolish errands?" Roger asked.

"Think of something, something that you would find in Marseilles, or perhaps Avignon, but not here. Try not to sound angry, for that might lead those who hear you to suspect you've done something illegal, and once they learn that I'm gone from Lyon, they may conclude you are responsible. World-weariness, old friend, not resentment." Da San-Germain thought again. "I'll want four mules, with a pack-saddle on one, so that I can carry my native earth with me, and the cask we have of the earth from Madelaine's estate. The fourth we'll use as a remount."

"Will you take weapons?"

"A sword and the duck's-foot, with powder and ammunition. You keep the pistols with you."

"Do you intend to bring Madelaine to Padova with you?" It was the one thing that bothered Roger, for although da San-Germain and Madelaine could no longer be lovers, if she lived in his house, it could give rise to speculation and attention that would be dangerous for them both.

"Lecco would be the better place for Madelaine; it is a beautiful setting, and with the large number of strangers who frequent the lake, she will have many opportunities to find nourishment without rousing unwanted misgivings among those she visits in sleep." He looked toward the fire where the log was beginning to smolder.

"And you will return to Padova?"

"Oh, yes; and remain there for another year at least," said da San-Germain, his face unreadable.

Roger reflected upon this, and said, "If I leave just before or during the performance, what will you do?"

There was a wry amusement in da San-Germain's dark eyes as he answered, "I will set up for the performance, and when the troupe gets ready for their parade, I'll go to the stable for the mules—I trust you'll ready them for me?" He had a sharp pang of grief, recalling how this would have been work for Feo.

"Of course," said Roger.

"Little as I want to do it, I'll leave my cimbalom. I want it to appear that my departure was precipitate, as if there might be pressing reasons for me to leave. That assumption would be reinforced by your sudden departure."

"World-weary and resigned," Roger interjected.

Da San-Germain nodded, then fell silent, speaking suddenly more than a minute later. "I'll contrive a disguise not only for me, but for Madelaine."

"Traders, perhaps?" Roger suggested.

"That would probably be your disguise. No, I believe I must come up with another explanation." He looked down into the fire as the log popped and a spark flew out onto the floor; he stepped on it, and kicked the cinder away. "If Madelaine is willing to braid her hair like a boy, I might be able to convince the Guards at the borders that I'm his tutor and he is on an educational tour."

"Feeble," said Roger.

"No doubt, but she and I will have time to modify the story and make it more convincing. No innkeeper would refuse us a room we could share if we can make that story convincing." He put his hands together, studying the steeple of his fingers. "We will need to dress quickly when we're through with the bath."

Roger looked up at the ceiling, trying to find ways to express his qualms about this most recent plan. "If you and Madelaine were to come with me, and we were to go along the roads we traveled to get here, we might be able to make a more persuasive tale for Guards and other officials," he said slowly. "There are few people crossing along those roads in winter. If we're careful, and have a good enough story, we might be in Italy without problems."

"Possibly," said da San-Germain in a tone that Roger knew meant no. "If you'll get out three changes of clothes for me and for Madelaine and pack them in the soft leather bags? They can be tied to the cantles of our saddles. We'll need cloaks as well, the fur-lined ones. And half-blankets for the mules."

"I'll attend to it after shaving and bathing, you and then me." Roger went to fetch the leather bags and was almost out of the room when da San-Germain stopped him.

"Thank you, old friend. You may dislike this latest extemporization, but it does make our successful escape more probable." There was a trace of irony in his smile. "If we're pursued, the Guards will expect us to be together, so separating increases our chances."

Roger started to speak, but a knock on the door announced the arrival of the first large cauldron of hot water; he put his uncertainties aside and went to get the shaving gear while da San-Germain admitted the first pair of several servants bearing the cauldron to the room.

Text of a letter from Theron Baptiste Heurer to Madelaine de Montalia, entrusted to da San-Germain and delivered into her hands at one of the clock the same day.

> *To my most dear, my most adored Madelaine, my heart-felt greetings, Your deliverance from the executioner's hands has filled me with delight; I am grateful to da San-Germain and his two comrades for all they did to bring you safely out of imprisonment and the threat of death. Be sure I will thank all three of them most heart-ily when our performance today is complete and our wagons are sheltered from the rain.*
>
> *No doubt you have been told that the Commedia della Morte troupe has been performing my play by the same name, and you will not be surprised to learn that, due to the great success we have enjoyed, we are em-barked upon a second project. Even now I am writing the second act of the new drama, and we are rehears-ing the first act in the morning. We have every reason to hope that this will lead to further opportunities, and the attention of truly great men. I know you will be thrilled for me, though this will mean that we will not have the opportunity to be reunited for some consider-able time. For this, I beg your understanding. You have been a staunch supporter of my work before your mis-fortunes and I have the hope that your enthusiasm has not waned during your unfortunate time in prison.*
>
> *I have taken the liberty of dedicating my new play*

to you, although with initials only, since there could be difficulty with the officials if they learned that the work is in tribute to an aristocratic fugitive from justice. You, I know, will understand my reluctance to put you in danger, however indirectly, by revealing a connection that could lead to your discovery and arrest. Would that we lived in more accepting times, but, the demands of the Revolution require the people of France to restore the balance of society, and if in doing so, some are penalized who should not be, for the sake of the country, we must acquiesce in the process. It is my most fervent desire that some day, you will be able to attend a performance of The Triumph of Liberty, which is based upon a narrative poem by Jean-Marie Collot d'Herbois, who did me the honor of encouraging me to undertake the work. I will send you a copy of the manuscript as soon as I can afford to hire a copyist, so that you may see how much my work has improved.

Photine d'Auville, the leader of the Commedia della Morte, has been kind enough to take an interest in my future and has asked me to deliberate upon forming an official partnership, one that would give us both the advantages of continued association. She is a fine actress, a most remarkable artist. Ask da San-Germain, who has been her patron, to describe her talents. The range of her gifts and the strength of her abilities inspire awe in all who see her. You must surely grasp the advantage of such an alliance, as well as the benefits that would accrue to the Commedia della Morte as well as to me. Already she and I are discussing what other works we might essay, a prospect which will keep me busy for some time.

Yet I miss the pleasure of your company, the passion we have shared, and your generosity. One day it may be possible for us to resume our intimacy, but I *fear for now, that will not be prudent for either of us, for all the reasons I have put forth already. You and I have been star-crossed in every sense of the word, but I find I must bow to Fate, and to release you from the love and expectations you have had of me. It is with a heavy heart that I must bid you farewell, and hold my precious memories of our treasured time together in lieu of you yourself. I have come to realize that you are beyond my highest aspirations, and that all that you offered me is beyond the scope of my understanding; reluctantly I will have to accept what has happened. That in no way diminishes my ardor or my esteem, but it has shown me that until I have attained the reputation for my work that I seek, I will not be worthy to pursue you; I can only promise my enduring idolatry, as well as my thankfulness for the inspiration you have provided, little as I deserve it. Your greatness of mind and your sweetness of heart must always be an example to me as I continue my aesthetic crusade.*

May you find safety where you are going, and may you one day return to France to resume your title and estates, free from the threat of arrest and trial. Until that day, know that I will long for you, lovely and desirable as you are, and will remember you with exaltation.

With amorous devotion,
Theron Baptiste Heurer

8

Madelaine stared down at the single crossed sheet of paper, her face darkening as she read; when she finished it, she wadded it into a ball. "Of all the inane drivel!" she exclaimed, not as loudly as she would have liked, and threw it across the small, musty room at the back of the abandoned chapel near the north wall of the city where she had been hiding since dawn. "And to think I was attracted to him!"

Da San-Germain bent and picked up the bunched letter, opening it and smoothing it, its crackle mixing with the steady patter of rain on the old roof. "Best not to leave it here. If it's found, it could bring trouble."

"To us, or to the troupe?" Madelaine asked, her voice sharp.

"Either, or both, more likely." He thrust it into the pocket of his caped Russian greatcoat. "We can dispose of it later, once we're away from here."

"Which we must be shortly," said Madelaine, still glaring at the letter he held.

"Yes. We will have to get as far beyond Lyon as we can in the next three hours, for after that, they will know we are missing. If you still want to dispose of it by the time we halt to rest, we can burn it with all due ceremony." He thought for an instant of Sarai, of Aachen, of Delhi, of Fiorenza, of Amsterdam, of Cuzco, of—with an effort he thrust those memories away as useless. "They'll send out couriers, or Guards."

Some of the ire faded from her violet eyes. "No doubt you're right, Saint-Germain. But all that self-serving twaddle—*remember me with exaltation!* If he believes that this is an example of his improvement on his earlier work—well!" She lifted her chin.

"He is eager to exhibit—" da San-Germain began only to be interrupted.

"Don't defend him to me—not you," she said, bending down to finish pulling on her boots; arrayed in boy's clothes, she still had an air of femininity about her that da San-Germain found compelling. "You know as well as I that he doesn't deserve it."

"I wasn't defending; he asked that I explain his circumstances to you, which I have done. He declares himself your sworn cavalier." He was glad to see that her indignation was already fading.

"Oh, spare me," she pleaded, laughing.

"As you wish." He made a leg, giving her an ironic half-smile. "My duty is discharged, at least so far as Theron Heurer is concerned."

"Enough of Theron," Madelaine said, shaking her head and regarding da San-Germain with apprehension; after a brief moment of hesitation, she asked the question that had been bothering her since he had awakened her half an hour before, proffering a valise of boy's clothes and delivering Theron's letter. "I'm happy you're with me, but why are you here at mid-day? It's not simply because of that miserable letter, is it? You told me you'd come at sundown."

He held up his gloved hand. "Sadly, we have yet another change of plans."

"Oh? Again? How many times does this make?" No matter how much she wanted to know more, she held her tongue; when he remained silent, she asked, "What happened? Do you think the three coaches have been found yet?"

"I would imagine so, but that is not what's caused our predicament." He met her eyes with his own.

She regarded him steadily. "What, then?"

"Something neither you nor I could have anticipated: an official in the Department of Public Safety was . . . informed of our contrivance." This oblique statement did not succeed as he thought it would.

"One of the players talked?" Madelaine pressed her lips together to keep from saying anything more.

Da San-Germain shrugged. "Does it matter? The mischief is done." He shook his head and went on, "Luckily I discovered that the official had been told in time to alter our hour of departure, or we would have been trapped here, and that would bring us both to the True Death within days, and put others in danger because of it. With all you have been through, that would be intolerable to me." His gaze was tender. "Had you gone through no misery, it would still be intolerable to me; losing you." He took a step back. "We need to be gone soon, my heart, so that we have a fair lead on whomever they send after us. And they *will* send someone after us; they cannot afford not to. What I told you wasn't supposition; the officials here must try to recapture any fugitives from their jurisdiction, or risk interference from Paris."

She gave an exasperate sigh. "Of course they will hunt us. They cannot afford to let us go without an attempt to reassert themselves through our capture. It would be folly to remain here." She waved her hand in the direction of the ceiling, indicating the rain. "No matter what the weather, and the state of the roads."

"The mules will manage it better than horses," he said, pulling another greatcoat from the bag of clothes he had brought her. "You'll need this, and I have a tricorn for you."

"A good choice," she said, then offered him an indirect apology. "I didn't mean to be so tactless, Saint-Germain. You didn't write that wretched letter."

"Then just as well that he didn't bring it in person," said da San-Germain, wanting to ease her aggravation.

"Might he have done so?" she asked in disbelief.

"He thought you would want to see him," said da San-Germain, handing her the three-cornered hat.

"God save us," she exclaimed, and surprised them both by chuckling. "I hadn't realized he had such a high opinion of himself."

"I believe he thinks you have the high opinion of him, not he."

Her laughter increased; then she made an effort to quiet her mirth. "He is so very young."

"He assumes the same of you," da San-Germain reminded her.

"I've told him my age, but you're right, he thought I was . . . fabricating a tale."

"Well, he *is* a poet; would you expect anything less?" He turned his attention to their immediate situation. "The mules are in the narthex. Four of them: two for riding, one to carry, and a spare in case one of the others falls by the wayside. We have grain enough for them to last a week. Then we must find more. I have money and jewels, but it might not be enough."

"I'm going to take my dress." She raised her hand to silence him. "I won't put it in the valise, and once we're out of France I'll dispose of it. It's hardly fit to wear, but if we should be detained, I would like to have it."

He waited a moment to answer. "If you think you may need it, then bring it with you."

"Good. If we are snowbound, I won't be able to pass for a boy for very long, and this way— We won't be out of France in a week, will we?" She knew the answer, but could not keep from asking.

"It would take longer than that on main roads in summer with no troubles at the borders," he said. "You and I are going on lesser roads, with winter coming on." His enigmatic eyes remain fixed on her. "Fifteen days will be as rapid a passage as we can hope for, if we face nothing more than poor roads and bad weather, let alone pursuit. Beyond leaving the country, we will also have to get out of the mountains after we're over the border."

"Do you think we could be pursued into Switzerland, or Italy?" That prospect troubled her, but she would not allow her fear to overcome her.

"I don't know," he admitted. "It would be wise to be on the alert for some kind of chase."

She considered this. "I dislike agreeing with you, but I do. This Revolution is becoming vindictive; they may want to set an example by tracking me and some of the others you released. They'd gain a lot of power by showing that no one escapes."

"Which makes the next few hours so crucial." He gave her a pair of boy's gloves. "Keep these on; your hands are too . . . too well-kept."

"They might take me for a Ganymede, you mean," she said.

"That would be a risk we can easily avoid," he responded. "Put on the gloves. They'll help you stay dry."

"And conceal my sex," she added.

"Yes. You don't have boy's hands." He took a deep breath, changing the subject. "I have a route we can follow, one that takes us out of the country in about fifteen to twenty days, if we don't have to hide ourselves, or travel over the mountains without roads, and making allowances for rain and snow."

"That seems likely, though, doesn't it?" she asked. "That we may have to hide."

"It may be necessary: I hope it won't be."

"Is that why you're sending Roger another way, down the river? So they will chase the wrong man?" She did not wait for an answer. "When you told me we'd be traveling alone, I assumed you intended him to lead the soldiers astray, to buy us more time. That's the sort of thing I'd expect Roger to do."

"That is part of it, yes. It also spares the troupe being suspect in my leaving so abruptly. Roger has a story he will tell to Photine, to account for his unexpected departure, as well as mine, and she will inform the Department of Public Safety." He looked about, hearing an odd sound from the side of the building; he dropped his voice. "We should hurry."

"What was that?" Madelaine asked, barely louder than a whisper.

"I don't know, and that troubles me."

"And it troubles me," she said. "Next I'll be flinching at shadows."

He permitted himself a wan smile. "That would show good sense, given where we are and what's ahead. Shadows will be the least of it."

She kept her voice low. "You needn't try to cheer me, Saint-Germain. I know the risks we are running."

"I don't doubt it," he said. "I know you have good reason to be careful, yet I can't free myself from worry."

"We're both worried," she allowed, feeling a grue slide down her spine as a soft scritching noise came from the side of the broken altar. "The Guillotine is so utterly final."

"We need to be gone from here." He watched her don the greatcoat he had provided. "Remember, don't let them see your hands, and keep your coat closed, so they can't see how you're shaped."

"All right," she sighed, "since you're determined to turn me into a young gentleman."

"If we would not rouse suspicions in the Guards, you could wear petticoats and jewels if you wished, but as they will be looking for a young woman—"

"If only they knew," she murmured, pulling on the gloves.

Da San-Germain nodded. "So when we reach the northeast gate, say as little as possible, and be truculent if you can. Treat me like a servant if we are questioned. Blame me for making you ride a mule instead of a horse, complain of your accommodations and the lack of good company, anything that makes you seem the arrogant youth."

"You're my tutor, escorting me on some kind of Grand Tour, is that what you would like?"

"It would be useful to have the Guards think so; it might help if you spoke French with an English accent; a few English have come through Lyon in the last three months," he said, and impulsively stepped to her side to brush her cheek with his lips.

She touched his face, her expression wistful. "Will we do more than this, when we are alone?"

"It will depend upon the circumstances," he said after slightly too long a pause.

She glanced away from him. "Which means no."

"You know the problem, my heart," he said to her as gently as he could. "It is our true nature that keeps us from—"

"I know: vampires cannot love vampires because the undead have no life to give each other," she said, repeating an unwelcome lesson by rote. "We must seek our nourishment from the living."

"Yes." There was no regret in his admission, but there was a loneliness that stopped her own discontent abruptly.

"Oh, Saint-Germain, I'm sorry." She laid her hand on his arm. "It seems so unfair."

"Neither death nor life is fair," he said without emotion. "We are what we are: there is no question of fairness." He turned away from her. "Button your coat. You'll want it closed when the rain gets heavier. And be ready to act like a spoiled youngster on his Grand Tour. The Guards will remember all the wrong things if you can convince them."

"Yes, I will," she said, wishing she had some means to break his maddening reserve, and knew she could not.

"As soon as you are ready, we will go," he said.

"I'm ready now," she told him, picking up the valise he had given her. "There're only boy's clothes in here, aren't there?"

"Only boy's clothes," he confirmed as he held the door open for her and led her into the narthex where the four mules were tied, flakes of hay set out at their feet so that they could eat rather than make noise. "The spotted mule is yours. I'll take the gray one." He checked the girth on the spotted mule's saddle, then offered Madelaine a leg up.

"Best to let me get used to mounting," she said, refusing his assistance. "I haven't ridden astride in decades."

"Well enough," he said, and went to gather up the leads of the pack-mule and the spare before vaulting into the saddle on the gray. "Remember, English accent."

"What do I call you?" she asked, settling her feet in the stirrups. "And what will you call me?"

"A good question," he said. "Call me Sanders; it's near enough to what we're both used to, but English in sound. I will call you . . . Madison. Not quite as close a fit, but if you don't object?"

"I think it will do," she said, demonstrating her version of an Englishman speaking French.

"That should convince all but those who are knowledgeable," he approved, and started toward the open door of the chapel; a pair of rats ran out from behind the altar and skittered away into the room Madelaine had been using. "Ah. There's the source of the noises."

"Are you sure?" Madelaine asked, and received no answer. Within the minute she was following him and the two mules on leads out of the chapel, through an old cemetery and onto the old street that would take them to the northeast gate of the city. She had to remind herself to behave as if nothing were wrong, and when they reached the gate, she complained vociferously that her tutor was exceeding his authority in forcing her to ride a mule.

The Guards had cast a knowing eye on da San-Germain and saw nothing sinister in the harried academic he presented. It took no more than a few minutes for the Guards to wave them through, warning them that there were desperate men about, outlaws who might steal their mules and clothing if the tutor and his charge should be abroad after sundown.

"For they're bold foreigners. They let loose thirty prisoners last night, and killed six Guards. Five armed men. Don't let them catch you," the oldest Guard said as he raised the bar for them.

"Thank you; we'll be careful," said da San-Germain as he pulled his mules aside so that Madelaine could precede him out of the city. He fell in behind her, after giving a deferential shrug to the Guard, satisfied that he would not report them as persons the Department of Public Safety would find interesting. The light rain washed the color from the countryside, turning all to gray and sepia, like an aged charcoal sketch.

They traveled in silence east by north, rarely going faster than a walk due to the thickening mud, encountering as they went three detachments of Guards on the road, four shepherds with their flocks, and one long merchants' train coming from the east. At the fork in the road, they took the less-traveled route to the village of Meyzieu, and stopped at the posting inn there, the largest building in the place, to rest their mules and seek some relief from the increasing rain. While they sat at the fire, water beginning to steam from their coats hanging over the backs of their chairs, Madelaine asked da San-Germain, "Sanders, did the Guard say there were five armed men who released thirty prisoners?"

"That they did." Da San-Germain reached for the cup of hot brandy that he had ordered, and surreptitiously poured a little of it into the padded arm of the chair.

"Five men freed thirty. Enterprising, wouldn't you say?"

"One assumes they were desperate." He cocked his head in the direction of a man in a long black coat who slumped in the inglenook next to the fireplace. "Acting against the Revolution."

"Then they were most surely desperate." Madelaine nodded, aware of the warning, but persisted, "Killed what was it? six Guards?"

"I think that's what they said." He put the cup down again. "They do a good toddy here."

"Must truly be dangerous men." She studied the glass of wine in her hand. "Should we shift saddles when we go on?"

"It would be a good idea," he said.

An hour later they moved on, carrying a bull's-eye lantern to mark their way in the night. In five more days, they had crossed La Chartreuse to La Batie, where they stayed for three days while a violent snow-storm buffeted the mountains. They emerged to find drifts as high as the tops of houses, which meant that they would not be able to see the tall stakes that marked the roadway. They went with the village men to help clear the way by dragging the trunk of a large tree behind a team of gray draught horses, a service which earned them the thanks of the villagers and got them a league and a half beyond La Batie, to a farm-house where they paid four English sovereigns for food for their mules and a place to sleep. The brilliantly clear skies of the day had faded, and now a veil of high clouds hid all but the brightest stars.

"I'm becoming hungry," said Madelaine in a whisper as they reclined fully clothed on the bed allotted to them by the farmer.

"That isn't surprising." Da San-Germain stared up at the wood-blackened ceiling.

"You must be hungry, too," she prompted.

"I would be glad of some sustenance," he admitted. "But I've known far worse."

"Did you see the dogs the farmer released in the yard?"

"I did," he said, his voice barely audible. "They are the reason I won't go looking for a woman I can provide with a pleasant dream in return for what little I need."

"You think they would give the alarm if we—"

"—moved about? It's not something I would want to put to the test." He folded his arms. "When we reach Le Monetier-les-Bains we'll both be able to find nutriment."

"That's a long way," she murmured.

"With the spas there, strangers will not be observed as we would be in villages and the remnants of monasteries. We will be able to move more freely, seek out those who welcome the dreams we provide."

She shivered, but not from cold. "Do you think we'd have to make do with the blood of sheep, or geese, or . . . rats?"

"There are worse things to eat," he said, speaking gently but with purpose. "For now, we should rest."

"Did you purchase grain from our host?" she asked.

"I did, for an outrageous price. We'll have to expect that the nearer we get to the border."

She sighed, saying disheartenedly, "It will be more than twenty days gone when we reach Italy, I fear."

"It may," he agreed, and took her hand in his before sinking into the stupefaction that served all of his kind as sleep.

Madelaine lay awake past midnight, her mind occupied with fears and plans; when she surrendered to fatigue, she had set three plans in place—one of them would get them out of France, she was certain of it, and she would have a few days to refine them before she had to persuade da San-Germain of their effectiveness.

They set off from the farm-house under cloudy skies, and made their way toward the distant border. They skirted Le Monetier-les-Bains when they discovered it was full of soldiers who had come to root out fugitives, and to claim the contents of the extensive wine-cellars as their reward for their diligence; their carousing had reached the depraved stage, and the soldiers were now fighting among themselves as well as abusing their prisoners.

"We take no nourishment here," da San-Germain said as he and Madelaine watched the town from the safety of a burned-out Carthusian hostel.

"Then we make for Briancon, and the border-crossing on the Torino Road?" Madelaine considered this. "If there is no more snow, we could reach Briancon in what—four days?"

"It is possible."

"But not likely," she said. "So five more days at least."

"I should think so," he said.

In Le Monetier-les-Bains, a fire was spreading, accompanied by the sounds of collapsing houses. "Do you think it will get worse?" Madelaine asked as she watched another building succumb to the flames.

"Oh, yes," he said.

"Like the Revolution? You were right about that." She watched the flames. "I should not have come back. I thought Montalia could provide a haven until sense returned."

"This fire will only burn itself out; the Revolution will have to destroy half its founders before it ends." He turned away. "The mules can supply us a little blood tonight. There are deer and boar in the woods, as well, but hunting would be dangerous."

"In the morning, do we press on toward Briancon?" She was sure he would say yes, for what other choice did they have?

"We should leave before dawn." He laid his hand on her shoulder, his voice still and musical. "We will win free, my heart."

"I know," she said without any hint of confidence.

"We will."

She leaned against him to kiss his cheek. "I know," she repeated, this time with more certainty; she turned her back on the burning town and returned to the wreck of the hostel; after a short while, he followed her.

Snow held off for three days, and they made good progress along narrow mountain roads marginally cleared of snow by the short journeys of the farmers and crofters and herders living in the high villages and hamlets. On the fourth day as they neared Briancon, they noticed a build-up of soldiers and Guards around the town; farm-houses and inns were filled with uniformed men, and the people were reticent and cautious in all their activities.

"Not very promising," said Madelaine. "The border isn't far beyond."

"No, it's not, but it will be hard getting there." Da San-Germain looked up at the darkening sky. "There will be more snow by morning."

"Then we'll have to find shelter beyond the town."

"Not too far from the Torino Road, if we want to cross there." He paused. "They may be looking for us by now."

"Why do you say that?" She masked her alarm with a gesture of impatience.

"Because it is impossible to keep a secret in a theatrical company. Someone will know something of our plans, and will have made a report." He pointed out the company of Guards patrolling along the limits of the town. "I've seen two couriers arrive."

"Not necessarily from Lyon," Madelaine interjected.

"No, not necessarily from there, but if there have been two today, how many others have arrived since we left?" He shaded his eyes from the shine off the snow. "We may have to turn north, to one of the lesser crossings."

She rounded on him. "We'll cross here, and get out of this dreadful country. We're too close to turn away."

"And that is how fugitives are caught."

They both said nothing for almost a minute; then Madelaine

took her courage in her hands. "I have an idea—a plan, or so I hope. If you consent to it, I think it will get us across, but it will require much of you."

He saw the determination in her eyes. "Tell me your plan."

So it was that two mornings later the Guard at the border on the Briancon–Torino Road saw a young woman in a ragged dress beneath a man's greatcoat approach the crossing station, riding a mule, and leading three others, two of them laden with chests and cases. The light snowfall had stopped almost all travelers, and the Guard on duty regarded her with curiosity.

"How are the fires in Briancon?" the Guard asked as he came out of his small cabin to confront her.

"Bad enough that I spent the night outside the town, in a barn," said Madelaine, making a point of looking tired.

"Sensible little chicken, you are," the Guard said with an appreciative grin.

"It's that or get killed one way or another." She reached for the wallet slung bandolier-style from her shoulder. "How much?"

"Ten louis d'or for you, five for each of the mules, two for each chest, one for each case, including the valise at the back of your saddle. Unless you'd like to bargain?" He licked his lips, just to make himself clear as to the kind of bargain he had in mind.

"I have the money," she said brusquely.

"I'll have to inspect the chests and cases," he said, no longer smiling. "There may be extra charges for them."

Madelaine stared at him but revealed no emotion beyond resignation. "I have one diamond necklace left. I keep it with my money."

"And how do you come to have a diamond necklace?" The lascivious light was back in his eyes.

"From my patron," she said without apology. "He provided well for me, and when he was arrested, he gave me my jewels, a purse of coins, and the mules in his stable. His manservant got the horses. I was allowed to take only the clothes on my back, and a nightrail; the soldiers took everything else. He told me to go to his uncle in

Grenoble, who would arrange for me to go into Switzerland, but his uncle had fled before I arrived, so now I'm trying to find his sister. She's married to an Italian."

"And you think she'll take in her brother's whore?" The Guard laughed furiously. "If you're so naive as that!"

"I'm bringing her things her brother wanted her to have. They aren't much, but it's all she'll get from him now that the Revolutionary Courts have taken his lands and houses."

"Entrusting a fallen woman with family treasure. What sort of fool do you take me for?" He strode to the first pack-mule and unfastened the broad leather straps that held two large cases, one on each side of the animal.

"They both have earth in them. My patron wanted her to have a remembrance of her birthplace. The Court wouldn't let him provide anything more."

"Really?" The Guard lifted the lid on the on-side chest and was sprinkled with reddish earth for his pains.

"If you empty it out on the ground, I'll have to shovel it back in," Madelaine said slowly. "I've already had to do that twice, and lost some of the earth each time."

"It would be a clever place to hide gems and other valuables." The Guard pondered if he, too, should turn the chest over.

"Had there been anything beyond the earth in the chests, it is long gone," Madelaine told him, a sad indifference in her words.

The Guard was torn between greedy curiosity and a desire to get in out of the cold. Finally he reached up and spilled the contents of the chest onto the road. "I guess you'll have to shovel this back in. I'll watch."

Madelaine dismounted, went to the second pack-mule, and untied the shovel from where it lay atop three cases. "If you have a sieve, you may want to fetch it," she said sardonically.

"And give you the chance to conceal what you carry? I'm not such a fool, me." He reached for his pipe and lit it, content to lean on the side of his cabin and watch her slowly shovel the earth back into the chest, taking satisfaction in Madelaine's discomfirture.

When Madelaine was almost done, a merchant with a train of nine mules and an escort of six men came up behind her; reluctantly the Guard ambled out to see them. When he came back, he spoke sharply to her. "Get the rest of that dirt stowed, pay me your fee, and be on your way."

"The merchant paid you better than I can?" she asked as she added another shovel of earth to the chest.

"Do it, or expect to lose your necklace," the Guard threatened, glowering at her.

Madelaine did as she was told, then scrambled awkwardly into the saddle, pulled her greatcoat tightly around her, and went through the gate with her mules and her baggage after paying her forty-three louis d'or. The road was icy, and the snowfall continued lightly but persistently, so that she dared not try to rush; the mules kept on their steady walk, never straying from the road until late afternoon when she took the turning that led to a posting inn, where she had to pay a handsome bribe to be allowed, as a single woman without a maid or a nurse, to stay in one of the guest-rooms for the night.

"I am to meet a relative here. It was he who secured my passage out of France," she said as she handed the innkeeper forty louis d'or beyond the price of her room and the care of her mules.

"No one has come here asking for a woman from France," said the innkeeper.

"I will wait in my room until he arrives; he will need a room of his own," she said. "You need have no worry about my presence." She hesitated. "I've asked your ostlers to bring my two large chests to the room, along with my valise."

"So long as you pay for them, I have no objection," said the innkeeper piously, bowing her toward the stairs to the upper floors.

It was over an hour until the ostlers struggled up the stairs with the two chests and her valise; they set them unceremoniously in the middle of the room and collected their silver.

"Feels like you've got rocks in those chests," one of the ostlers grumbled.

Madelaine managed a rueful chuckle. "It does seem so," she said as she shut the ostlers out of the room, then went to the darker of the two chests to unbuckle the straps. Moments later, she stepped back as da San-Germain, wrapped in a sheet like a shroud, unfolded himself and climbed out of the chest that now contained only a small amount of his native earth.

"Thank all the forgotten gods, we don't need to breathe but to speak," he said as he worked his way out of the sheet. He took her hands and kissed them. "I am greatly obliged to you, my heart."

"I was afraid the Guard at the border would make me open the second chest," she confessed, her face pale, her violet eyes appearing huge in her face.

"So was I. That merchant was fortuitous." He was surprised at the force of her embrace.

"I was so frightened, I thought I wouldn't be able to fool the Guard."

"He is used to frightened people. You did very well." He wondered briefly if Photine could have faced such an audience as the border Guard with such composure, and supposed that she could.

After holding him for a long minute, Madelaine stepped back. "There's a drop to the stable-yard from the window. The innkeeper knows you are coming."

"Provident again," he said, going to look out the window; night was closing in, and he would have to announce his arrival shortly or risk being locked out.

Madelaine stopped him. "There is a widow on the floor above. She's in the company of her son, who is in the taproom. Tonight she might be glad of a dream."

"And you?" he asked, testing the hinges on the window before opening it.

"There is a man in a private parlor. He is a banker, according to the registry. He, too, may welcome a dream," she said.

He looked down to make sure they were unnoticed. "I'll return directly, and then we shall decide how to proceed." With a hint of a bow, he climbed out of the window, dropped silently to

the stable-yard, then went around to the front of the inn to officially welcome Madelaine de Montalia to Italy.

Text of a letter from Photine d'Auville in Lyon, to Ragoczy Ferenz,
Conte da San-Germain, in Padova, sent by letter carrier, and delivered eighteen days after it was written.

> *To Ragoczy Ferenz, Conte da San-Germain, the affec-*
> *tionate greetings of Photine d'Auville, in Lyon, on this*
> *the 13th day of March, 1793.*
>
> *My dear Conte,*
>
> *They are trying to impose new dates on us, but I can-*
> *not give up the calendar I know in favor of the new, but*
> *in time, I suppose I will become accustomed to the new.*
>
> *I hope you are well and safely back in Padova. I am*
> *sending this to you there, trusting that it will be deliv-*
> *ered to you eventually. I was sorry that we had no*
> *chance to make our farewells, but I understand the*
> *circumstances, and I can only be grateful to the letter*
> *you provided, along with the very generous sum you*
> *provided for the troupe. Because of that gift, we are*
> *now about to open a proper theater here in Lyon, with*
> *the approval of Collot d'Herbois, who has taken an in-*
> *terest in us, and in Heurer.*
>
> *You will want to know that Tereson has left us for a*
> *time. The baby is due in May, and since Feo has not*
> *returned, despite his promise, Tereson has gone back to*
> *her family. She will give the baby to her cousin to raise*
> *and will rejoin us. If you encounter Feo, I ask that you*
> *inform him of these events.*
>
> *Theron Heurer has gained much more fame, and*
> *has provided us with two more plays. We are beginning*
> *to look for more actors to play the roles Heurer has*
> *written. I begin to see that we might become the center*

of the arts in this city, to which end Theron is wholly committed.

I am deeply minded of your kindness and your patronage that brought us to this place. Without all you have done for us, I would never again have performed in France, let alone been able to have my own theater. Let me thank you now, from the fullness of my heart. For one who is not of the theater, you have shown much greater understanding of our art than most patrons could ever have done.

This last winter we had a great deal of rain, and it is still continuing, which has reduced the number of performances we have been able to give. For that reason alone your contribution to us upon your departure has been most helpful, and will continue to help us as we move into our new theater. As a tribute to all you have done, our first production will be Phaedre, and we will dedicate it to you.

I've not had word from Enee yet, though the records of the Courts show that he was released, but beyond that, I can find nothing more, though I have sent letters to his father in the hope that he may have taken him in. I know he has realized the error of his actions in attacking you, and will doubtless one day make you an apology. For now, I offer one in his stead. You should never have been stabbed. You should not have endured such injuries as you received from him. I will be happy on the day he learns from you that he is forgiven.

I must now join the troupe for our supper. This is the last night we will be at the Jongleur, and we will toast you as we take our leave of this place and all it has provided us. I know this will find you happy and successful as ever you were.

Devotedly,
Photine d'Auville

EPILOGUE

Text of a letter from Madelaine de Montalia from Lecco on Lake Como, to Ferenz Ragoczy, Comte de Saint-Germain, at Padova, carried by Eclipse Trading Company courier and delivered three days after it was written.

> *To my most-dear Saint-Germain,*
>
> *Before you take ship for Greece, I want to tell you how much I have enjoyed my time here at Lecco; only your presence could have made it better, and you needn't remind me that it would be difficult for us both to remain near to each other with nothing but yearning to express our love. Still, I miss you; I always miss you, and I suppose I always will. You are the joy of my life, the haven of my soul. There is no reason to dwell on such matters as the risks of proximity, for that would lead to resentment, which would do neither of us any good; it would blight what we have, have had since you brought me to your life, and will have until the True Death. The Blood Bond does sustain us, so that whether or not we are able to lie together, we are always able to sense each other, and the love that is in our blood as surely as it pervades all the rest of the undeath we share.*
>
> *Much as I despair of France and the endless blood-shed there, I cannot give way to hopelessness, for that*

*would be to surrender to the forces that are the instiga-
tors of the destruction. Yet I am saddened to hear that
Theron Heurer has been executed for writing works
against the Revolution and the people. What nonsense
that is, to think that Theron wanted anything more
than fame. So long as the Revolution brought him
praise, he was its champion. Do you suppose Collot
d'Herbois might have become jealous of Theron's success? I am glad that none of the players were accused
when he was, for it is unfortunate enough to have one
artist die in such a firestorm as the one in France now,
but to sacrifice more than one is a tragedy that belongs
in Greek tragedies, not in the streets of Lyon.*

*By the time you return, I will have moved from
here to Firenze, to see the art accumulated there. It will
be my first visit in thirty years, and I intend to make
the most of it. I am resolved to remain in that city until
the end of November; I will let you know where I plan
to go next when I have decided. For now, I have leased
a house on the Via Fiesolana, very much in the center
of the city; I will see if it suits me, and for how long.*

*Thank you for sending Roger to me for April. He
has been a prize among major domos: he has organized
my books in the room you set aside for them, and has
set up my study to admiration. I wonder that you can
manage without him. Do not remind me that our recent travels were without his presence, for no doubt we
would have fared more easily having him with us. He
has said that his leaving France was less perilous than
our own, and that he had only one awkward moment,
in Valence, when an official demanded proof that he
was no thief. He had the inventory you had prepared
with him, and you fixed it with your seal, so all he had
to do was pay an extra tax, and he was permitted to
resume his journey.*

Should there be trouble in Athens while you are there, do me the favor of leaving before it becomes overwhelming. I was foolish enough to enter a country in revolution and very nearly paid for it with my undead life. Give me your Word that you will not be so reckless as I was. And accept my vow, if at all possible, that I will not do so again.

Evermore yours,
Madelaine
this at Lecco, 22nd June, 1793